YP

P9-CML-847

35674059905399

RECEIVED MAY - X 2022

CH

THE KINDRED

Books by Alechia Dow
available from Inkyard Press

The Kindred
The Sound of Stars

ALECHIA DOW

THE KINDRED

inkyard
PRESS

ISBN-13: 978-1-335-41861-6

The Kindred

Copyright © 2022 by Alechia Dow

Recycling programs
for this product may
not exist in your area

This edition published by arrangement with Harlequin Books S.A.

For questions and comments about the quality of this book, please contact us at
CustomerService@Harlequin.com.

Inkyard Press
22 Adelaide St. West, 41st Floor
Toronto, Ontario M5H 4E3, Canada
www.InkyardPress.com

Printed in U.S.A.

To Liv.
I'm proud of you always. I'll love you always.

The Inkara Royal Palace of Maru

For Immediate Release

PRINCESS LATANYA QADIN AND HER KINDRED, JOHANN KAO, TO WED

Her Royal Highness, Princess LaTanya, and her Kindred, Johann Kao, from Beyla-Monchuri, are officially set to wed in the coming week.

King Jevor, the Duke of Estrella, and the Queen Mother are delighted with the news.

Before their impending nuptials, the royal family will tour the Monchuri system to celebrate with their subjects and to schedule interviews with each planetary leader to discuss what this news will bring for the future of the Qadin Kingdom.

Thank you for welcoming Johann to our family.

PART I
THE CRASH

CHAPTER 1
FELIX

Looking this pretty takes time.

The clothes must be expensive but not gaudy, complex but not as if I put in all my effort. My hair must look styled but like I've walked through a gentle, aimless breeze, and I cannot be sweaty, which, on a planet known for having three suns, is rather difficult.

Parties that start early are the worst anyway. Everyone should be thanking me, not giving me the stink-eye, which they are. For some reason, they expect me to actually show up on time.

"Look who decided to join us," the drummer from The Monchoos mutters as I step into the dimly lit hallway. We're from the same planet, Maru-Monchuri, but there's no comradery between us. Who could be friends with a pompous, spoiled duke like me, right? I could be better, could be the person I'm expected to be, but why waste the effort?

I give him a quick wink as I look around. This coveted, hard-to-get gig's on Outpost 32: a man-made station between XiGra and Hali-Monchuri—Joy's homeworld. XiGra's a rich planet that's not a part of the Qadin Kingdom (yet), and Hali *is* a part of the Qadin Kingdom, but also extremely poor. Thankfully, this outpost is the perfect mash-up of the two: international enough to be popular among wealthy travelers, cool and gritty enough to reflect the rock 'n' roll aesthetic.

The black stone walls are plastered with band posters, grime, and beneath it all, the touch of musicians that would either make it or break it onstage. I wonder which one we'll be tonight.

Joy *humphs* in my brain, but doesn't elaborate.

She said she wouldn't watch me choke, couldn't be a part of another concert experience that sets off her anxiety. And yet, she can't stay out of my head.

Of course, I'd be paired with the most judgmental Kindred in the system.

A coordinator peeks out from the curtain, a detached comm-ball hovering around their blue tentacled head. Dosani. They're music geniuses, and probably the friendliest species in the universe. They speak Dosan into the comm, and then it flies over to us, translating.

"You're late. Get onstage." The voice doesn't sound all that friendly. Weird.

My bandmates stalk behind the curtain, leaving me there in the deserted hallway for just a second. My nerves begin to spiral in the pit of my stomach, and I reach out to her, because she's there, she's always there—well, usually there—and she knows what I need.

Joy, I say through our connection. We've been together since birth. I'm exactly three minutes older than her, and I had to wait for our chips to sync for those three minutes. Not that I can remember. Still, that's the longest I've been without her in my life.

The Kindred Program was created decades ago, after The Second Chaos, aka "The Revolution." Apparently, the poor rose up, feeling like their voices weren't heard by the rich, powerful rulers, and so the lower classes threatened a reckoning. Maru's top scientists offered a solution: the citizens of the Monchuri system could be paired, one from the upper class, one from the lower. Establishing this would allow everyone to have a voice that could be heard, blah-blah-blah, and no more revolution. How could anyone ignore a mind pairing?

Given that I'm a duke and cousin to the Qadin royals, I was supposed to be paired with someone a little closer in economic class, because not just anyone should have a voice with the royals. Yet, I got paired with Joy.

Joy, who is dreadfully poor, living on the most impoverished planet in our system. Joy, who is my best friend, my moral compass, my judge, jury, and sometimes executioner. She's not always my biggest fan, but she supports me in whatever I choose to do. Which isn't much. I like traveling, adventuring to new worlds as long as my amenities are acceptable, and playing in a band. We both love music. She loves listening in as I practice, hearing new melodies outside of her Halin hymns. She thinks music has the power to transform you and make you feel anything and everything. She believes in it, just like she believes in me.

Which is why I need her right now.

Because as much as I love music—and I do, with all of my small black heart—my stage fright keeps me from making it. Already, the nausea creeps up my throat and my breaths come too fast to let oxygen into my lungs.

Joy, I say again with some urgency.

Yes, Felix…? Her question whispers through our connection. She's there inside my mind like a perfectly clear radio channel, the only one on my brain's frequency. She can read my thoughts, converse with me, feel my emotions. She can see what I see. She's the one consistency in my world, and I can't live without her. Even if our worlds seem hell-bent on keeping us apart… Nah, I don't need to be thinking about *that* now.

Tell me I can do it. I run a hand through my hair and blow air out between my teeth. My feet bounce on the dirty tiles. *Tell me it's not a big deal. Easy.*

You're the most talented person I know. You can do this. And I swear, if you make me sick again, Felix, I will murder you.

I chuckle. *It's not my fault you get sympathy pains.*

The stronger we accept the bond in our minds, the stronger the feelings, including negative ones. Pain, illness, anxiety, sadness, anger… It can be so intense in such bonds that if one Kindred were to die, the other might follow shortly after. It occurs in maybe one in a thousand pairings, but it happens. Until recently, I would have thought Joy and I would be one of those pairs. But she's been pulling away more and more.

Go get onstage! They've been waiting hours for you and your beautiful voice. She laughs, shifting her body on the couch in her apartment, nearly toppling her sketch pad off her lap. *Get up there*, she commands again, and then she's gone. She's turned the volume down to a whisper and tuned me out.

I hate when she does that. I also don't know *how* she does that. Why can't we just always stay connected? Who needs space? Not me.

With that thought, I take another deep breath and strut down the hall. I tug on the velvet red curtain and step through onto the sticky levitating stage. We lift a few feet off the ground, but thankfully, unlike in most of the more modern venues, the floor doesn't spin. Thank the Gods.

My bandmates stare at me, wide-eyed as the crowd goes wild. The excitement in the room is palpable, like a glittery haze that coats my limbs and makes me want to sing and dance and be alive. My chest rises and falls in sync with their cheers and stomps.

I both love it and hate it up here.

The band's set up and the microphone's hot. The lights are low, the room's packed, and I'm going to sing, even if my stomach churns and threatens to upchuck my dinner of steamed hopfal leaves packed with gooey black rice.

I swagger up to that mic, my legs wobbling like jelly. "Hello. I'm—"

"I love you, Felix!" someone in the audience shouts, though who it is, I can't see. They're all shadows and faceless bodies from up here. Just the way I like them.

The light beats down on me, and sweat prickles at the edge of my scalp.

"I love you, too." I laugh into the mic, which earns a few grumbles from my bandmates. "Now I want to…" I trail off as a shadowed body comes into view. Their eyes bore into mine. The face is one I'd know anywhere. A face that shouldn't be here.

My throat dries up as he stalks through the crowd, waiting for me to finish. I step back, almost stumbling over my own feet. With a fleeting glance at my bandmates, I trip offstage and toward him.

The crowd boos. My brain's short-circuiting. He's not supposed to be in this part of my life. He's part of the Duke's life, the one I shrug off and leave at home whenever the opportunity arises. His being here can only be bad for me. It can only mean trouble.

My feet are on autopilot as he nods his head over to a private booth reserved just for us. I can feel my bandmates' glares, but they begin strumming on their guitars as if I was never really a part of their group anyway—which I wasn't. The drums pick up and the audience forgets all about me and my promises of a good time as they dance.

My visitor wears a long black tunic embroidered with crimson thread and matching pants. His golden hair's slicked back and his vibrant golden eyes flash as I slide into the booth first. He takes the seat opposite me, flips on the privacy switch in the center of the table, and then folds his hands on the table as a translucent wall falls around the perimeter of the booth.

We sit in silence for only a moment but it feels like a lifetime as my heart hammers unsteadily in my chest.

"Do you know why I'm here, Duke Hamdi?" he asks finally, his head tilting to the side.

I suck my teeth. "My parents think I'm at some interplanetary summit for the children of dignitaries on Kippilu and they found out I was lying?"

"I don't work for your parents." Arren huffs, leaning back. "I work for the Qadins. You may remember them as the royals that pay for the pricey state-of-the-art ships you use to jump planets and slum in music halls—" he waves his arm at the room "—your flashy clothes and instruments that you seemingly never play onstage, and the countless opportunities that have been provided to you over the course of your short life." There's a bitter edge to his words that has me sitting taller. "You are a disappointment to their name."

Arren's a royal advisor—*the* royal advisor, and he has done enough over the years to earn my fear and respect. But there has to come a time when I crack.

Tonight, I was going to finally get over my stage fright and make a name for myself that had nothing to do with my actual name. All of my hard work, practicing until late at night, and pushing myself to new limits both artistically and mentally would have paid off. Instead, I'm here, missing my chance, being scolded for chasing my dreams by the royal advisor that threatened my Kindred's life.

I will not forget, and I will not forgive.

"Do you think by doing all the Qadins' dirty work, it'll make you one of them? Do you think they consider you their equal?" I try to twist my lips at the corners, even if dread sinks into the bottom of my stomach. "What'll happen if I go into politics like they so desire and come for your job?" I'm balancing on the tip of a sword, and at any second, I'll get cut.

"You're a fool." Arren chuckles, though there's no humor in it. "I do not wish to be a Qadin. I am not their equal. And you…" He trails off suddenly to look at the carefree dancers and the band that went on without me. "You have responsibilities that come with your title."

"There are other dukes, other cousins." My nostrils flare as I watch him. "Why do they hold me to such high standards when the others are free to do what they want?"

"Because you are meant to be much more than you are. Soon, you'll need to step in and step up." He holds my gaze now, and in it, I see a flicker of something that's not frustration. It's a thoughtful, plotting look. Arren's got plans, and he wants me to follow them. "Soon your Kindred will marry and move on with her life. But where will *you* be? Failing on the stages of dingy bars—because at some point the good ones will stop booking you no matter your title—and burning through your trust fund? Do you know how many people would kill for the opportunities you have?"

Something about that question furthers my unease. Who would kill for opportunities? The Kindred Program makes sure that people are heard and happy. Murder doesn't happen anymore. Citizens are content with their roles in life.

"Don't you have other things to do, like I don't know, figure out the Ilori conflict or something? Aren't they trying to colonize us? The Qadins should be putting their energy into that, not whatever this is. What could they possibly want with me? I have no power or ambitions in politics."

"The Qadins didn't send me, so I don't rightly know." He stands, running his hands down his spotless tunic as I digest that news. If they didn't send him, why is he here? "*I* came because I am looking out for *your* best interests. King Qadin would have no issue ignoring your existence, but I know you have a great destiny. One day, you may have power, and you could create change. Stop this music nonsense and join me, join my side. Together, we can pave our own paths in this kingdom. You could find your voice, since you can't seem to find it onstage, and finally reach your potential. I believe in you—can you say that about anyone else?"

I barely keep the anger from my voice as I shuffle my legs beneath the table. "Is that why you threatened my Kindred?" I remember the way he had guards surround her without her noticing, pointing their weapons at her as he made me promise to never see her. Never allow her into my heart. "Was that your way of believing in me?"

"I was following orders. I work for the Qadins, but I am not one of them, and with Princess LaTanya's impending nuptials with her Kindred, Johann Kao, I never will be." He shakes his head, as if he didn't mean to say that. Admittedly, it was a weird thing to say, but then I do know from the tabloids that he's enamored with LaTanya… Still, that thought flees my mind as he continues, "They were right to make sure you keep your distance from your Kindred. There is only one person you can rely on, Duke Hamdi, and I believe, in time, you'll come to see that. Someday soon, you will need my help. And I won't hesitate to give it." He slips a card onto the table and with that, he strides off, disappearing into the dancing fray.

My fingers edge the tip of the card. It's solid black. It's an upload, something I'd need to stick into a holo-frame monitor to access. It probably has Arren's private info encrypted for me, so that I can learn to live up to my potential and what— overthrow the Qadins and stage a coup with him? Why would I do that? What makes him think I want any responsibility that big? Despite what he says, I learned early that my name gets me in doors, gets me a seat at the table, but that's it. I don't matter. No one cares about my opinions or thoughts, so why should I have them anymore?

I shove it deep in my pocket and punch the button in the center of the table for service.

He chose this night, this moment, on purpose. He probably even had Outpost 32 book this gig for me just so he could ruin it. So I would be miserable and malleable to whatever he's plotting. But he underestimated my indifference.

At least I'm here where I can get drunk enough to drown my sorrow as the crowd dances and the music thrums through them, and me.

At least his newest power move will keep me from thinking about Joy.

CHAPTER 2
JOY

*"YOU LIVED IN MY MIND, BABY, ALL THE TIME, AND
NEVER ONCE COULD YOU READ IT."*
—DEJA REESE, "THE SAME SONG AND DANCE"

My fingers twitch, wanting desperately to reach for the fork
beside the beautiful slice of starberry vanilla cake. There's a
rumble in my stomach as my nose fills with the scent of spicy
stardust that's sprinkled all over the ornate gilded plate. A
special-occasion plate, the only one we have.

"Happy birthday, sweet girl." The eyes of my mother—
Adora Jaqui Abara—sparkle in the morning sun filtering
through the windows.

I gaze through the thick glass separating us from the city
outside. We're up so high, yet we can't see the world below
through the smog. Still, dawn on my home planet of Hali-
Monchuri is said to be the most beautiful in the entire system, and it certainly is gorgeous. But I've never left Hali,

never left the capital city of Darben, so how can I compare it to anywhere else?

I turn back to her, back to the cake. My fingers ache to grasp the fork, but they don't. "Thanks, Mum."

Her head tilts to the side, her dark brown skin glistening as if it, too, has been sprinkled with stardust. The yellow of her waitress uniform almost glows neon in the light. "Aren't you going to eat it?"

"Umm…" Before I can answer, a groan reverberates in my mind, along with a prompt to accept a visual call. My mind requires the prompt to allow the visual since the injections, since the override, but Felix's doesn't. His connection is normal because the brunt of the pain is mine to endure. Not that he knows. I close my eyes and think, *Yes.*

Your stomach is disrupting my sleep, Joy.

One second, I'm staring at Mum, the next, my thoughts are in a massively disheveled room in Estrella, the capital of planet Maru-Monchuri. Capital of the Monchuri system. Home of the royals, home to the distant suns of Gola that can only be seen from this one planet, and home to Felix. My Kindred.

Everyone in the Monchuri system is linked with another person since birth, as long as they're born around the same time. We learned about our separate worlds together, we took our first steps together. He was my first playmate, my best friend. What he sees, I see. What he knows, I know. Through our minds, we can laugh, cry, hope together.

I see him where he is, see his immediate surroundings as he can, like I'm just on the other side of the room from him, close but I can't touch. I can't touch him. It's like looking through a window and seeing someone else, somewhere else.

It wasn't supposed to happen.

Felix punches his feather pillow in an attempt to make it more like a cloud to rest his precious head. He's hungover and exhausted. I purse my lips. *How much did you drink this time?*

He tosses his head to the side and glares at me through heavy-lidded violet eyes. *More than I should have.* His accent's all posh and proper. His hair's a tangle of greasy black waves. His brown skin looks pale, as if he never goes out into the suns, of which there are three, so he really has no excuse.

He squints and growls as he wiggles on his maroon sheets. *Eat the damn cake.*

He sure does have it nice, and I'm reminded again that our connection was a mistake; royals and peasants aren't meant to be connected. Probably because it makes the lower class one far more bitter than we should be.

I…can't. I'm on a diet. Maxon told me I look a bit rounder than usual.

Felix's voice is half groan, half aggravation. *Maxon's a douchenozzle.*

You're so judgmental. I roll my eyes and tap my fingers against the table beside my cake. I mean, Felix isn't wrong. Yet, Maxon's my mom's choice for a suitor. He's loaded, whereas we definitely aren't. The only reason he's marrying me is because my Kindred is the beloved Duke Hamdi. Apparently, he can forgive my poverty and round body if it means he's a step closer to celebrity. *It's our seventeenth birthday, Felix,* is all I can add. He knows how significant that age is on my planet, Hali-Monchuri. He knows that, in my culture, it means I have one year to secure a partner or else my prospects slim significantly. Normally, that could mean my Kindred, but Felix is off-limits. *You know the position I'm in. Keep it up and you can deal with your drunken stupor alone.*

Don't go. He reaches an arm out to me like he could pull me closer, even if I'm worlds away. *You are absolute perfection, every bit and piece and curve of you.*

I huff as my gaze flicks up to the black band posters hanging askew all over the walls. The books toppling off every surface. The movie and concert stubs, and someone's bra that dangles from his closet door. *You have to say that. You're my Kindred.*

His response comes quick as he stretches in his luxurious bed. *As if I'd ever say what I thought you wanted to hear.*

True. I laugh before changing the subject. *Did you fill out that application, by the way? The Grand Academy's music program is competitive and you know those spaces fill up quickly. I mean, I get you're a duke and all, but surely you still have to apply?*

He moans. *You can't tell me about my responsibilities early in the morning—it ruins my entire day.*

I glance at my wrist. Nine in the morning here, plus the three-hour time difference. *It's past noon in Maru, Felix.* I chuckle, though my heart's not in it. He's free. He can do anything. He doesn't have to find an advantageous match and marry by his eighteenth birthday. He has every opportunity, and still he doesn't see it. A bitterness rises up my throat and I swallow it down. Sometimes I think I hate him.

You're getting mad at me again. He sits up.

I don't want to argue. Not today, not on our birthday. *I gotta go.*

He shakes his head. *You're always so…busy.*

You mean working. I play with the fork beside my plate. *You rich people don't like to work.* Felix has never worked a day in his life, and the way it is now, I doubt he ever will. He's nobility, whereas I'm a commoner. Nobles should only get paired with other nobles.

He cackles and finally opens his eyes fully to gaze at me. *That's true.*

You're spoiled.

He kisses his fingers, blows a kiss, and then sings in his beautiful voice, *Happy birthday, baby.*

A smile finds my lips despite myself. *Happy birthday.*

His next words warm my heart as he sinks back into his bed. *I adore you, Joy.*

We never say the *L* word; that's reserved for our significant others, and we aren't allowed to love each other. Felix will be matched to someone more "suitable"—meaning rich, similar in class, someone of whom his parents approve. While I'm matched with Maxon.

Besides, we don't love each other like that.

I adore you, too. And for Gods' sake, take a shower.

And with that, I turn off the visual connection, and I'm back to looking at my own mum on my own world. I can turn off the visual component as it's an entirely optional mental switch, but I still hear him and his soft snores. It's like having a radio on in my brain. The override allows me to turn it off with effort and pain, but sometimes I can just lower the volume.

Mum's staring at me. She cocks an eyebrow my way. "I suppose Felix wished you a happy birthday?"

"Yup," I respond, taking the fork finally. "He's hungover."

She cackles. "That boy believes he's a rock star, huh?"

"He would be if he got over his stage fright." I shake my

head. Felix is a master on the guitar, and his voice is angelic. Unfortunately, every time he gets onstage, he hurls. And after, he goes on a bender like last night. Because of him—well, because of my sympathy pains, I feel a bit bloated and have a slight prickling of a headache coming on. Thanks, Felix.

"Danio also says happy birthday." Mum stands up. She pushes the table a little as she crosses to the windows and pulls the curtains shut. The heat is bearable in the morning on Hali, but soon it'll be sweltering.

"How is she?" Mum's Kindred is a divorced perfume-making mother of three in the garden district on Kippilu-Monchuri, the lush green planet known for the best produce and variations of flowers. She and Mum barely go minutes without talking to each other. They sometimes argue, like when Mum married Dad, whom Danio didn't believe was good enough for her, or when Dad left and Mum refused to move to Kippilu. Any day now, I suspect Mum will finally agree and move there near Danio, finally give in to the love they share. Mum would never admit it—it's not just platonic; it's romantic, and she deserves it.

She'll no doubt leave after I'm married off. Hali is just a planet of bad memories for her.

"She's good." Mum moves the rest of the cake to the counter behind us. Our apartment is small. A kitchenette, one bedroom where Mum sleeps, one couch where I sleep. One prayer corner where we ask Indigo, the God of Creation, to grant us love, acceptance, protection, kindness, and to keep Ozvios, the God of Destruction, out of our lives, and one dining table between the couch and kitchen, where we eat, do our work, talk about our day.

Dad took Mum's savings and prized possessions and ran off before I was born. Danio was right; he wasn't good enough for her.

"She's sad. All of her children are out of the house. And her ex won't leave her alone. Blames me for their divorce."

I roll my eyes at the drama of that. "I thought she was gonna date someone new?"

Mum shakes her head. "Her heart's not interested."

"Her heart's interested in you." I take the smallest bite of cake, savoring the flavors sliding across my tongue. Cake will always be my downfall. I can already feel the inches adding to my waist, but how can I care when it tastes this good?

Mum slaps the counter, ruining my cake-high. "Danio is my Kindred. Everyone lives in my heart temporarily, but you two reside there permanently. You must understand."

"Uh." My eyebrows melt into my forehead as I turn toward her. "I'm pretty sure I do?"

"There is no love comparable to that of your Kindred." Her voice softens. "I know it's not fair that you got paired with someone whom you can never be with, not like me and Danio… That's why you must use Felix's love to survive, and Maxon's money to provide you with a life. It's for the better that you and Felix can never be more than what you are."

"Ew, Mum." I cringe for the millionth time. I think I saw on a holo that 83 percent of people marry their Kindred, and 99 percent live with them…but that doesn't apply to us. I love Felix with my entire heart, I do…but he's a brat, with questionable taste in ambitions, and even more questionable taste in alcohol. Not to mention, he is constantly hooking up with bad boys, girls, genderfluid, and nonbinary folks who leave their undergarments around his room as if to stake a claim. He's indiscriminate in his quest for passion. He even hooked up with a Bargle from the Iftra system, and those have a ton of tentacles that can kill you, which Felix said was a delightful challenge.

I try to avoid those moments in our connection. Whenever Felix tries to talk to me about it, I tell him to stop. That's not my business, and I don't want to know. And though I loathe Arren for it, the override is especially useful for blocking out the things I don't want.

Kindreds can withdraw, take their space when needed, but the connection's there, always on in the background. Arren made it possible for me to temporarily disconnect. It's painful; the headaches I get make it nearly unbearable, but the Duke deserves his privacy and it's my job to give it to him.

On our birthday, Felix usually does his annual checkup at a royal medical spa that keeps him in optimum health while he plugs into a simulator that temporarily takes our connection offline. At the same time, Arren made it that I receive an annual injection that keeps the override in place. It's not fair, but at least I still have my Kindred. At least he's still mine.

I clear my head of those thoughts. "I'll marry Maxon. I know I need the money and stability. We can't live like this for much longer." My gaze whips around our humble abode to the counter stacked with bills that are far past due, and lands on my mum's pinched face. "Don't worry, I'm doing—and will do—everything I can to make him happy. Promise." Which is why I push the cake away and I stand up. "I have to get to work."

Mum nods as she begins to clean the dishes. "See you to-night?"

"I'll be home late. There's an event at the bookstore that'll run till midnight." I shrug, looking down at my outfit for the day. Tan sandals, a basic pale blue dress that's a bit tight in the arms. But then everything I own is a bit tight in my arms. They are the bane of my existence. I smooth a kinky curl behind my ear. The rest of them are toppled high on my head behind a floral headscarf I made myself.

"You look good. I hope you don't sweat through it on your way there. They're saying it's a scorcher." Mum smiles as I grab my purse, storing two books, some fruit for lunch and dinner (this diet is going to kill me), and a standard government stunner Mum was assigned back when crime was running rampant in the capital and folks complained. Crime's low now, but it's good to have protection in case anyone gets the bright idea to jump me. Most never get close enough, though. I walk like a tank and my lips curl into a snarl whenever a stranger looks my way. Mum taught me well. "Oh, and don't forget to stop by the clinic for your injection. They called to remind me yesterday, as if we needed the reminder. You know we need the money—"

"I know, I know. I'll stop by during my lunch break. See ya." I check my pockets, making sure my key's in one of them. I've been locked out too many times, and waking Mum from the dreams she shares with Danio is damn near impossible.

Sometimes I wish I could still share dreams with Felix, but I can't anymore. Not with the override. Ugh, just the thought of a needle makes me cringe.

Another birthday, another injection to keep us both together and apart. Arren and his doctors pay me for the inconvenience—which is what they call it. That payment helps buy groceries for a month and keeps the air-con running on the especially hot days.

It's not enough for what I'm giving up, though. The connection is my lifeline to worlds outside my own. Having Felix in my mind makes me feel less lonely, less destined to live on this hot planet, marrying a man who judges me for my every single flaw.

No, I won't think more about Maxon. Or the injection. It's my birthday. I get to enjoy this, too. Even if for a few hours working at the bookstore.

After a quick wiggle to shake off all my misgivings, I tread down the stained carpeted hallway, past dark green doors of equally small spaces. The smells send my stomach rumbling. All sorts of cultural delicacies are being prepared for the day.

With the tip of my finger, I press the elevator button and turn to see Ms. Kore exiting her apartment. Her frizzled white hair is pulled back in a loose bun and, bent over a walker, she's at least a head shorter than me.

"Hold that, won't you?" The elevator hasn't arrived, but we both know it'll take her a while to get there.

"No problem," I shout. She's also hard of hearing. When it pings open, I stick my foot in the elevator door, waiting. She continues mumbling to herself. I'm assuming she's having a nonsensical conversation with her Kindred. I've seen it before. The older you get, the more words are no longer needed between connected minds. It's both beautiful and alarming.

I wonder if Felix and I will get to that phase. I wonder what he'll be like when he's old… If he'll be covered in warped tattoos, still wear ripped jeans and keep his hair just a bit too long. If his violet eyes will lose a little shine and if he'll slow down and smell the roses sometimes instead of jet-setting somewhere new and exciting for a night.

And then I think about him getting married one day in the distant future, settling down with someone, raising an heir to the dukedom. Which leads me to think about my upcoming engagement to Maxon because apparently my brain won't let me rest and it hates me.

Maxon, who wears button-down shirts that his maid irons every morning. Maxon, who only eats to sustain his body, who has told me several times that he doesn't actually enjoy food—as if that's normal. Maxon, who likes old movies pilfered from Maru files (which are seriously the most boring), and listens to orchestral music when he's solving an especially difficult mathematical problem. He's going to be a university mathematician, if his other plan doesn't work out. His dream is to become a consultant for holo-vision, showing his pretty face all over the system and becoming a celebrity.

Maxon, who says I'm fat and foolish for having my head in fictitious stories when I could be broadening my knowledge with sacred texts from our religion, so I can be a very traditional wife.

Maxon who, if I'm honest, I kinda despise and is definitely a douchenozzle.

Suddenly, I'm sad and hungry for that cake I pushed away.

My future is not my choice, because of our past.

Hali-Monchuri law dictates all eligible women must marry by eighteen in order to maintain (and breed) our religion, our culture, and our traditions. It is our great duty since most of our world was destroyed and our population decimated.

The Second Chaos was led by Hali—which was then the technological center of Monchuri. Our planet was the oldest, most valuable, most profitable in all of the system. Our elders and leaders, wise and fair, decided they were tired of the colonizing Qadins stealing our accomplishments and money, while being treated like low-class commoners. So my ancestors took to the streets and skies, demanding revolution. And they were persuasive, tapping into the growing distrust and unfairness of the classist system.

They established a following among other planets within Monchuri, and the Qadins became scared that they would lose their throne. Suddenly, the Kindred Program was introduced. The other planets cheered, thinking we won, while Hali thought it was just another way of appeasing the lower rungs of society without actually having to commit to anything besides sharing our minds with others.

As citizens across Monchuri joyfully inserted the chips into their brains, Hali decided to stand defiant. A decision that nearly destroyed us. Without the support of the other planets, the Qadins invaded.

Hali was devastated; our elders were murdered, our technological advancements broken, our riches stolen. Anyone in opposition was slaughtered. Those who survived joined the Kindred Program, swore fealty to the Qadins. In return, the Qadins, who now painted themselves as fair and kind, appointed a religious butt-kissing zealot and misogynist as our chancellor.

We were taught to eschew technology so we could never

have the opportunity to rise up again. We were told to focus on our dying culture, commit ourselves to making sure our way of life endured. We are the only hope Hali has of ever rebuilding.

But over a century later, we've barely recovered. Most of our great buildings are still in ruins, our population still small, even if they try to breed us by marrying us younger. We're surviving, but we aren't living. If I don't marry by eighteen, besides Mum and I being ostracized from society, all of our health and food benefits would be denied. We'd lose everything. Mum could go to Danio because she already procreated, but legally I'm not allowed. My anatomy is just too important for Hali to let me go.

So I'll do what's best for my world, and that means marrying well. Even if that's the death of my own dreams. Dreams that feel elusive even to me.

I wish I could've seen more of the universe and found my calling in life. Like maybe I could've been a creator, an author and illustrator of adventure stories for children. Maybe I'd paint gorgeous pictures to accompany my words... *Maybe, maybe, maybe.*

"Dear, would you push the button?"

I snap out of it, shaking my head. Ms. Kore smiles at me, her back skimming the edge of the railing. "Sorry," I mutter. I hit the button for the ground floor and try to collect my thoughts.

"You're much too young to have so much on your mind." Ms. Kore winks at me, her wrinkles etching into her cheeks as she smiles. The lift creakily plummets the hundred and three stories only bumping along a few times.

I return the smile. "It's my seventeenth birthday. Seems like my life is already over."

"No," she says, her brows melting into the lines of her forehead. "It's just beginning."

The door opens, and I'm saved from having to reply to that. "Goodbye, Ms. Kore."

"Bye-bye, baby Joy." She moves her walker closer to me as I keep the door open. "Happy birthday. Wish for something good."

My mind whirs with the possible wishes I could make, like new shoes or maybe a night of frivolous dancing at Hali Cloud—a popular nightclub hovering above Darben that I sometimes go to with my dwindling group of unmarried friends. Instead, the moment I step outside into the sweltering sunlight, the only thing I can hope for is to make it to the bookstore before I melt.

I grab a book from my purse and hold it over my forehead to keep my face from burning. My *round* body maneuvers easily through the market crowd, and I smile at strangers and acquaintances alike, though no one seems to notice. My fellow Darbenians mostly have their heads down, staring at their holo-handys—the only tech allowed on Hali. People murmur, hands held over their mouths. Probably some royal news like Princess LaTanya's wedding plans with her Kindred, Johann Kao. Sure, his dark brown skin is reviled in noble society, much like my own, but goodness knows people love a royal wedding. I pay them no mind. Royals are just pretty distractions from the democracy the Monchuri system desperately deserves.

The scent of cake, maybe cacaoberry with a vanilla drizzle, wafts by me from the bakery down the street, the one where the prices don't match my wallet, and I quicken my pace to get away from it. This diet will actually kill me.

I'm rounding the corner to the store when a couple bolts by, knocking a small child to the stone ground. Before I think better of it, I scream a curse at the couple, but they don't stop, only waving me off as they continue on their way.

The child wails, and I shuffle over in the sweltering sunshine to them. I crouch down, my bare knees hitting the hot stone.

"Where does it hurt, *mignya*?" The word for precious one, usually only used on children, slips from my lips.

She points to her knee, and I unwrap my hair, letting the curls fall down my back, and I slide the scarf around her leg tightly. A smattering of blood seeps through, but the pressure dulls the pain. She looks up at me with wide eyes and I smile.

"You're very brave. Like a great warrior in battle, or a sorceress who saves the world with her magic."

"I want to be the warrior," she says dreamily.

I smile down at her. "Now you'll carry the mark of one. You can tell—"

"I will attend the child, *mignya*." I'm gently batted aside by an elder, and I dip my head. The old woman smiles, the action flashing in her beautiful orange eyes. She has stopped by the store many times, searching for traditional Halin fairy tales. But these stories have been stolen from us and rebranded as Marun, and she refuses those, waiting instead for a new Halin author to reclaim them.

I bow once more, tossing a smile at the now-calm child, who stays perfectly still in the elder's hands, and head on my way. As I walk into the bookstore, my boss darts past me through the door, sending my hair flipping around my shoulders.

Argu Maurti's bookshop has been in his family for centuries. The first son's duty is to keep it profitable, keep it running, and sire an heir to run it when he's gone. He does his job well enough, but most times it seems more like a burden to him than a privilege. He flicks me a look, his eyes wide, lips twisted.

"The Qadins are here! In Hali! Can you believe it?"

"Huh?" I call after him, but he's already outside. I shrug, sauntering over to the cart full of new picture books. Stories from all over Monchuri... The ones from Maru have holo pop-ups that send sparks of glitter in the air with each turn of the page. My fingers trace the illustrations of green trees—things I've only seen because of Felix. The leaves drip from the deep brown bark like strands of green pearls, another thing I've only seen because of Felix.

I think...if I had a choice in my future, this is possibly what I want to do. I want to tell stories like this, draw like this, have children all over the system read my books and feel something come alive in the pits of their stomachs. I want them to feel like children.

Despite my mother's efforts, she couldn't keep the horrors of the world from me—not when we barely had food or clean clothes. The only time I could escape was when I played with Felix. Maybe I could help children escape, too, through fanciful, indulgent, colorful stories.

I imagine myself in a studio overlooking water—*Gods*, how I'd love that, with the newest art tech like a holo-easel, paintless brushes that come in every color in the universe, and space...space to walk, and dream, string words together, and sleep... Space I could call my own.

That dream—which is all it can be—has me walking on clouds as I rearrange shelves to accommodate new and old books. When the early-morning sunshine begins to falter outside, my brows furrow and I peek out the window. Has so much time slipped away? Did I miss lunch and my injection appointment?

Instead, though, a massive silver ship hovers far above. I gasp, my heart racing, as I take in a sight I've never seen before in person. Not like this. The ship is so smooth and glossy and state-of-the-art with the light blue jets on its underbelly emitting nontoxic gas into our atmosphere. It doesn't move; it just sits there blocking out the sun.

It's royal. A Qadin ship.

That's when I realize not a single customer has come in today, not in the while I've been here. Normally, we'd have a line by now…with limited tech on Hali, books are our number one entertainment. Which, honestly, makes me love our home planet a little.

But that's when I also realize that Argu, who usually stays in his office in the back, hasn't returned after muttering that nonsense…about the Qadins.

Something is wrong.

★ ★ ★

Seventeen Years Ago

MONCHURI MORNING NEWS NOW!

Transcript featuring L'avi Jonu and Nyla Harkibi of *Good Morning Monchuri*, filmed in front of a live studio audience in Maru-Monchuri

LJ: Royal cousin Marivia Hamdi and her husband, Jesa, welcome their first child, Felix Hinada Hamdi. Look at those pictures! What a stunning baby! And those cheeks!

NH: *(takes sip from mug)* Ohhh, that's exciting news.

Duchess Hamdi has had *such* a difficult time with fertility over the years.

LJ: But it's curious, isn't it? *(audience chatter)* Close acquaintances question whether she was pregnant. In fact, if we study the pictures, you'll hardly notice a bump… And at her age…

NH: Not to mention the…skin color. So what are we thinking? Surrogacy? Adoption?

LJ: I think, given the press, she'll confirm one or another soon. Better for her to be ahead of the news than concealing a noble secret…which brings us to something even bigger. Baby Felix or Lord Felix, future Duke Hamdi, as he will be called, was successfully paired with a little girl *(audience coos)*. Always the best news when a pairing's made, right?

NH: Awww, how cute! I love a good pairing and especially a good love story, as you know.

LJ: I do know! *(laughs)* But not so fast on this one. The girl, Joy Mirari Abara, is a commoner from Hali-Monchuri, the poorest planet in our system. We don't have pictures, as per her family's privacy, but I will say, given what I know, she's not the right *fit* for a royal baby *(audience chatter)*.

NH: *(gasps)* How did that happen? The Hamdis are royal cousins, and the royals generally don't get paired with anyone outside of nobility or at the very least— to appease commoners—with someone closer in class.

LJ: I know. The Hamdis could sue, but as you know, removing the connection is illegal.

NH: How are these connections even made?

LJ: Since The Second Chaos, all babies are inserted

with a microscopic chip upon birth that latches to their brain, and is activated within the first few minutes of their lives. All chips have a corresponding match, somewhere in our system. It's random, yet, for the royals and the royal adjacent, it's not supposed to be.

NH: Poor Lord Felix, stuck with a commoner Kindred.

LJ: What we do know, is that advisor and fix-it man, Arren Sai, will be in charge of handling the press, and the Kindred pair. When asked by reporters, he refused to comment. Not even to defend Princess LaTanya's prolonged absence after her latest heartbreak.

NH: Aww, heartache and heartbreak are the Princess's great burden to carry. Well, anyway, back to Duke Felix! One thing's for certain, this is bound to be a juicy scandal as he ages...and I, for one, can't wait to see what happens next.

LJ: You're right...but this could change our politics... It could change everything.

CHAPTER 3
FELIX

I roll over in bed and let out a long yawn as I stretch out my limbs. It's been a few hours since I saw Joy, and I already miss her and her judgment, her smile, her disapproving glare. Just the idea of her makes me want to get up and be a productive member of society. I turn over on the silk sheets and look at the clock.

The numbers hover, blurry. One in the afternoon. I'm waking up early for once. My parents might even be proud of me. With one big heave, I roll myself up. My body protests, the muscles pulling in my hamstrings as my feet splay on the shag-carpeted floor. I let my head fall back on my shoulders to stare up at the ceiling, painted like the Indigo constellation. My favorite. Though Monchurans believe and pray to many Gods or none at all, it's Indigo we talk about the most, it's Indigo we pray to if we choose to.

Indigo was the god of music and the creator of the Monchuri system and all its people. There wasn't an instrument they couldn't master, a note they couldn't play. Each song they created birthed a new planet in the galaxy. If the song was forlorn, so then was the planet: gray, neither cold nor warm…just unrelenting nothingness. If the song was lively and ecstatic, so then was the planet: the ground always shifting in the warmth of the sun, oceans full of beautiful beasts that swam with the tide. The people, too, were happy. Every person was a note, every species a part of Indigo's movement.

But as Indigo began playing newer songs, each more complex than the last, the first planets spawned from their music disappeared. Civilizations, stories, beauty, history, all lost. Indigo became inconsolable. For they no longer could remember the first songs, or the first people they had created. They vowed to never play again, lest more be destroyed.

This was marked by a period of turmoil. Black holes and gaps between the worlds opened and swallowed space. Monsters flung planets to the farthest reaches of the galaxy. In this time, Ozvios, God of Destruction, came to rule.

In our history books, we call this period The First Chaos.

Indigo, fearing for the safety of their creations, determined to restore order. They began composing a symphony, "A Song of the Universe." Every living being was already a note; now they would have to come together to be played. Indigo traveled between each world, teaching the people music, giving them instruments, bringing peace, togetherness, and hope. When Indigo returned to their overworld perch comprised of scales, they played the notes all together, one after another. The First Chaos and Ozvios were defeated. And now the people had music, too. Not music to create, but music to express…

Honestly, I haven't decided how I feel about the story, but I like the idea of music creating our worlds. I like the idea of Indigo. It all sounds a lot prettier than the reality of it— bacteria colliding with stardust and a conveniently located sun…

Still, I look at the constellation of Indigo. A god on a mountain of notes and scales, looking down upon the Monchuri system. My mother calls it rubbish. My father thinks it's romantic because he's a dreamer.

As if on cue, my father pounds on the door.

Before he met Mom, he used to be a skilled heavyweight fighter, probably one of the best in all of Monchuri. He was up on holo-screens across the galaxy, winking and wooing and winning. Now he's old, laughs at his own jokes, and while he still exercises to keep fit, I can't imagine him ever hurting someone else. Still, his thunderous knocks rattle the walls.

"Felix Hinada Hamdi! Are you awake yet? You've slept the morning away. Your mother is expecting you in twenty minutes, or did you forget?"

"I'm up!" I shout, rolling my shoulders. "I'm still a little drunk, give me a minute."

Most people wouldn't tell their parents that. I certainly wouldn't tell my mom, but my dad understands these things. He knows how much energy it takes to shine just enough for people to like you while there's a wave of loathing threatening to crash upon you any minute you make a mistake. That's the nature of celebrity.

His tone softens, and I think I hear a slight chuckle. "Idu

will bring you some sobering serum. Until then, get ready. You have meetings and the spa today! You know how your mother gets."

"I know," I mutter, pushing myself to standing. I beat my arms against my bare chest as I yawn again. My gaze catches on the gilded mirror at the far end of the room. Even from here, I see the dark rings around my eyes, the shaggy hair I really should have gotten trimmed last week. And my skin looks sickly pale, which, given my complexion, is abnormal. Both Mom and Dad are light brown, whereas I'm far darker. But on my sunny planet of Maru where everyone's sun-kissed, my ethnicity almost goes unnoticed. Almost.

I was adopted as a newborn—a scandal that went public only a few weeks after my birth, though no one seemed to care after a few months. I look enough like a Hamdi, or more like their slightly darker cousins, the Qadins, so I imagine there were more pressing issues.

Or the Qadins made it go away.

Something's off. Joy's voice pierces through my mind as I cross into the bathroom. *And I swear to the Gods, your mom is going to kill you if you're late to her afternoon tea again. You know she has big expectations for your political career.*

"Hello, darling," I say aloud, both to Joy and to voice-activate the bathroom facilities. The low lights flicker on, the stone floor heats to my desired temperature. Info pops up on the holo-mirror with advice on a proper skincare routine to have that fresh-and-awake look that's appreciated in Maru. The shower begins misting hot water in the middle of the room. *Why is today weird?*

There's a Qadin ship in the sky. People are acting weird. Her gaze flicks to the window and then back to me. She's in the bookstore, placing old costly tomes upon dusty shelves. Hali-Monchuri lacks technology. When The Second Chaos struck, it was the most affected; they lost everything. Now they prefer a simpler way of life. If Joy's bookstore were here on Maru, her job would be performed by an AI, and the government would pay her a living fee to pursue whatever she wanted to do in life. That's why most people in Maru-Monchuri live casually.

Though, not my mother. She lives to work.

It's probably just to do with Princess LaTanya's engagement tour. I wouldn't worry about it. With that, I strip naked, letting my pajama pants drift to the bottom of the floor where a clean-bot will collect them for laundering. As I step into the water, I focus on Joy. The worry creases in her forehead smooth over. She tends to worry about nothing often.

I do not want to look at your naked butt, Felix, Joy harshly whispers, her eyes averted.

I turn away from her, tsk-tsking. *You've seen me naked as much as you've seen yourself naked.*

She slides another book on the shelf, this one a guide to star-fishing. *I don't even like looking at myself naked!*

Soap sprays from a tube in the ceiling, and the water pressure rises to scrub my skin. I can see the bookstore in my mind, while my body's in the shower. It still confuses me, even though it's been like this forever. *Shame, I rather enjoy your nakedness.*

Her brown cheeks pinken and I find myself stifling a laugh. It's so easy to goad Joy.

Don't use your flirty prowess on me. I know your every secret. Re-

member that time with the professor's son in the museum bathroom?
She cocks an eyebrow.

I groan, water dripping into my mouth, which I promptly
spit out. *Don't bring that up.*

*I won't, just don't flirt with me like you do with all those suckers
who fall for your charms and let you into their pants.*

*Joy. I have so many responses to that. First of all, I never flirt
with you, I only ever speak the truth. Second, my charms work on
everyone, not just the suckers, thank you very much. And third—* I
close my eyes, letting the water drip down on my face, washing away last night's grime *—I don't want to get in your pants.
You're the only person I trust.*

She lets out a long breath. *Felix—*

Besides, I cut her off, *I've seen your only pair of pants. The
brown ones that look like you've been roaming the desert for a few
years? I'd rather have you without them.*

She chuckles loudly. *You're the worst.*

Or the best, depending how you look at it.

She huffs. *Hurry up and get to your lunch. I want to know what
your mom has planned. Things have been tense lately between you. I
get the impression that… I don't know, your mom's hiding something.*

I gaze at her, the water sliding down my cheeks. *You no-
ticed that, too?*

I notice everything. She juts her chin out, lips tilting into a
smirk. *Think she's going to ask you to give up music again and hun-
ker down, get involved with politics like her?*

I'm not sure. My feet tap the button on the floor, and the
water disappears, replaced by a soundless drying wind that's
warm and welcome on my skin. *Promise you'll be there.*

I'm always with you, she says with a sniff.

My heart flips unnecessarily, and my voice becomes a whisper. *Sometimes… I don't feel you.*

She stares at me as if I'm in front of her and not three planets over, facing different moons and suns. *I've been giving you space.*

I don't want space.

Felix. Her brows rise. *We're growing up. We're seventeen now. Next year I'll be married to Maxon, becoming a dutiful housewife, and you'll be doing the same song and dance with different partners. We're stuck in these roles. It's tedious and mundane and it's all we can do.*

I lean my forehead against hers. *Let's get unstuck.*

I— She twists around suddenly. The walls around her shake, screams echo outside, a massive *boom* resounds through our minds. *Felix.* Her eyes widen. She howls over the noise. *Something's happening.*

And then our connection's gone.

A panic rises in my throat and I try to swallow it before it swallows me. The drunkenness has dried up and left me sober and terrified.

I run through the bathroom, hopping into my blue embroidered pants and throwing the matching tunic over my head. My hair's a tangled, wet mess that slaps me in my face as I bolt down the halls toward my mother. She'll know what's going on. My mother is a hawk for the news, and has a finger on the pulse of our system. Dad says it's uncanny; I say information is her oxygen. If she knows what's happening on Hali—whatever must involve the Qadins—she'll have to let me take a transport.

My bare feet slide on the cool smooth marble as the connection comes through again. I can't see Joy. I can't talk to her. But I can feel her. My own heart's racing. Screams linger in my ears. The ground feels uneven beneath me.

That's when I run into my mother's security guard, whose arms wrap around me before I can slam into the dining table holding delicacies from all over Monchuri. Mother and her guest sit with their backs to the windows, hands on their tea-cups, laughter lines crinkling their faces after what I assume is a shared joke. The three golden suns of Gola reflect on every surface, blindingly bright behind them, creating halos around their heads.

Mother's eyes pierce mine. Her lips curl in distaste. "Felix, you're hardly presentable."

"Something's wrong with Joy. Something bad is happening in Hali. There's a Qadin ship there." The words leave my mouth in a rush. I can barely breathe. Joy's fear races my heart. Joy is never afraid. I'm the fearful one. She's brave. I'm a coward.

"Calm yourself." My mother's voice is authoritative, and I try desperately to do as she commands. "I'm sure there's nothing to worry about. Probably the royal wedding engagement tour…" Her gaze flicks to her security guard, Bilau. He's been with us for as long as I can remember. His dark brown skin sticks out against the golden walls. He pushes a button on the room panel, and the holo-news pops up over the tea platter.

A reporter's voice fills the room. "The ship *Majesty*, the royal family's luxury liner, has gone missing since early this morning—" The voice is cut off and replaced with a new one. "Breaking news. We've now been told that *Majesty*, the royal family's personal ship, has just been shot down over Beyla-Monchuri. All passengers are assumed dead."

My mother's teacup smashes on the floor. Her friend, a Beylan-Monchuran with vibrant orange skin and blue features, shrieks before jumping up and grabbing their purse, presumably to rush home. They dart out of the room, leaving me gasping. I know I'm supposed to digest that information, that I'm supposed to want to know if that means the royals are dead, but Joy comes first. Always.

"What about Hali-Monchuri?" I shake my head. "There was an explosion. What else would knock out our connection?"

"Oh, *Gods*…" Mother's head whips to the side, jaw dropped open, ignoring me.

"Mom." I try to get her attention. "There has to be more news."

She's just sitting there, blank. Shocked. I wave my wrist, changing to another breaking news development from another planet.

A Kippilu news channel fills the holo. The reporter wears the traditional green leaves across her forehead to symbolize the growth and prosperity of their forest planet, and the pin on her lapel with the Qadin crest to show loyalty. "We've just received news that another royal transport was shot down over Darben of Hali-Monchuri. The *Inkara*, the Queen Mother's personal convoy."

Oh, Gods.

"Mom. I need to get Joy."

"No, no, no. You can't leave." Mom's voice is unusually soft, uncertain almost.

I don't have time to grieve the royals or figure out what's freaking her out. "Joy's in danger. I have to get her."

"No." She smacks her hand on her leg, eyes suddenly locked on mine. As per usual, she makes me feel powerless, like my voice is a needless thing that only shows my age and lack of intelligence. That I've done nothing to prove my worth. She turns up the volume.

"The bodies of King Jevor Qadin and his husband have been found within their crashed craft on Beyla-Monchuri—" The reporter's voice cracks. "We still don't have details on Princess LaTanya's whereabouts…"

"Oh, no, no, no." My mother's hand hovers over her mouth. "No."

"Mom." The news slowly sinks into my mind. The Queen Mother, Eliane Qadin, is my mom's great-aunt. We met only a few times. She was overly interested in my studies, and disappointed I lacked the family ambition, and that's all I can remember. I know I'm supposed to feel something about this, but my mind's on Joy. I slow down the words, hoping they seep through her hysteria. "Joy's in trouble."

My mom's breath comes in short bursts like any moment now she's going to hyperventilate. "*You* are in trouble."

"You're not thinking clearly." Whatever she's going on about can wait. "The transport? Can I take it?"

She flicks the news off and rubs a hand over her smooth slicked-back hair. "With the Qadin family gone…you might… Well, it's very likely you are the heir to the Monchuri throne. We signed papers… It was a long time ago. We couldn't get pregnant. And the Qadins… LaTanya, she offered… Maybe there are others, I just don't know… Whoever struck them down may come after us, after you."

"What?" The air sails out of my lungs. I don't have time to unpack whatever she's saying. "None of that matters right now. I'm sure there's someone waiting around to be crowned—I don't care. I need the transport."

"Your *Kindred* will be fine. Do you think we don't have security in place to get her to safety should you be threatened? We are careful." My mother's tone is sharp. It's not that she doesn't care about Joy; she even believes Joy's a good influence on me… It's that Mom's not close to her own Kindred. She doesn't understand our bond. She's still angry we were paired. She would have much preferred another noble. One who'd teach me to be a better noble. "Two ships were just shot down. It's not the right time to be flying given your… position."

A commotion in the hallway cuts off my annoyed reply. Our butler shouts as thunderous steps stomp down the hall.

"Excuse me! You can't just go in there. There's protocol for this! Stop!"

Six guards, dressed in purple with the royal golden sun embroidery, march into the room. The Soleil, the royal army meant to protect the Qadins… Their forms block the windows and doorway. Their golden masks obscure their faces. Although they vary in height, that's the extent of their distinguishing traits. Their presence causes terror in the pit of my stomach. I've never seen them before, only heard rumors. They're elite.

They're killers.

There's a tense second where Bilau levels his stunner at a

royal guard, but it's over when my mom throws up a hand. She steps into the center of the room, the light from the three suns shining down on her. "What is the meaning of this?"

Just like that, the uncertainty from before is replaced by a posh accent and authority. My mom, even in the presence of the royal army, doesn't back down. She is a force to be reckoned with and I love her for that. I wish I had her confidence.

The royal guard steps closer to her, without bowing. That's a sign of disrespect. My mother's eyes flash. "This is untoward."

"Duchess Hamdi." The guard finally bows, though he does so reluctantly. "I am sorry to…barge into your home. It is of importance that your son comes with me."

My mom cranes her neck up to look into his golden mask. "Why?"

I cough, inserting myself into this weirdly tense conversation. The clock is ticking and Joy's not in my head. "Sorry, is this something we can figure out later? I really have to go… Mom, the transport?"

They both ignore me and I shift anxiously from foot to foot. For ferk's sake, this game of chicken could last forever, and Joy needs me.

The guard's voice adds another layer of tension to the room. He holds up a transmitter, though who needs to hear this conversation is beyond me. "The Royal Court has demanded his presence…"

"On whose authority?" My mom's response is measured, though an edge creeps into her voice. Her gaze flicks down to the transmitter and back up at his masked face.

"On the authority of Royal Advisor Arren Sai, ma'am." He

steps closer, looking down at her. "At this time, your son has been implicated in the murder of their Majesties."

"This is ludicrous!" Mom shouts. "That's not possible! My son—"

"Duchess, we have incontrovertible evidence taken from your son's belongings within your very home." This Soleil doesn't hesitate, holds his head high.

"My son…"

The rest of her words are drowned out as I continue standing there like an idiot a few feet away from the doorway and four Soleil. The only reason they haven't snatched me yet is because I'm a minor. My mind is torn in two, trying to do the acrobatics on how they found incontrovertible proof while also grasping for Joy. I would know if my Kindred were dead… I would know if she were in pain, right?

If she dies, I'll die. It doesn't happen to every pair, but my life would be nothing without her. We are too close, too important to each other. Or maybe it's just me. I'm too close, she's too important to me. I can't imagine…

Felix, Joy whispers in my mind as if she has been there the entire time. *Do you hear me? Felix?*

I try to answer but the words get trapped in my mind.

My mother squares her shoulders, stepping closer to me and toward the Soleil fearlessly. "You cannot—"

Dad's thrust into the room beside me by another Soleil who holds Dad's hands to his back. Despite the Soleil's hold, Dad's barely contained, as massive as he is. He's so close I could reach out and touch him. Something in his eyes tells me not to.

The guard nods to another. "Is the entire family accounted for?"

My happy father, who loves music and stars, wears a frown deeply etched onto his lips. His shoulders straighten like he's preparing for a fight. His gaze meets mine as an edge I've never heard before in his voice sends reverberations through the pit of my stomach. "You cannot take my son."

"Jesa, no. Stop." My mom's voice cracks as she holds her hands up in an attempt to calm the situation down. "We will *all* go willingly with you. This must be some mistake and... and Arren can clear it up. We will fully cooperate." She says it like she means it, like she's a negotiator, likes she holds some power over these guards in their precious royal uniforms.

But she just accepted.

That's when a few things happen at once. The guard clicks the transmitter off with one hand and levels a stunner at my mom's chest with the other.

"Mom!" I lunge forward just as the trigger's pulled and my mom's body slumps to the floor in a fury of shaking. Guards chase after me. One reaches out and I elbow him in the ribs. Another blocks my path, holding out holo-cuffs that shimmer with blue electricity. But I dart farther away, toward Mom. I need to see her. I need my mom to somehow be okay. She acts tough, but she's fragile. She's had heart issues before...

As I check to make sure she's breathing, Dad breaks free from his hold, knocking a guard to the ground in the process. Suddenly, his training and size kick in and I understand why so many guards were sent to pick me up. I always thought my dad was a lover and not a fighter, but right now he looks every bit ready for battle. And they just hurt his wife, threatened his son.

With one look at him, time seems to slow down. As the guards surround us, he snatches a baton and stunner from his fallen escort.

Dad's voice makes the time speed back up as he shouts, "Felix, run!"

Tears streak down my cheeks as Dad rams through the Soleil, crashing the table laden with delicacies to the ground. It's pure chaos. The Soleil leap back, sending all Mom's finery flying around the room, but creating an opening. I take it without looking back. I'm not a fighter, and right now Dad wants me to run.

I bolt through the Soleil who reach out at me and then turn to face the threat of my father. My silk slippers slide on the hallway floors. I'm running faster than I've ever run, toward our estate's emergency escape route Mom made me learn when I was kid.

Heavy footsteps follow.

"Get the heir!" I hear one of them say.

"Don't let him escape!"

I want to look back but I can't.

If I look back, I'm done. I won't be able to go forward, knowing what I'm leaving behind. If my dad will be okay. If my parents will be hurt, held, imprisoned, or killed. If the Soleil will use them to get me back here so they can murder me or take me in for murders I didn't commit. All of this for a throne I didn't even know could be mine and that I for damn sure don't want.

I push a table with a vase holding my mom's biallolilies—sharp purple flowers with spiky petals—out of my way. The glass smashes on the floor into a million pieces. I want to stop. I need to see if my parents are okay.

Instead, I tap the button on the side of the wall, my fingerprint quickly scanned, and a door opens. I rush through with two Soleil following behind, and bang it closed. There's pounding on the other side but no way for them to get in. This is a private escape reserved only for our family. It's been here for hundreds of years. This might be the first time any of us have actually had to use it.

The stone hallway leads down to a small hangar on the cusp of our estate. There will be individual ships assigned to each family member. In case of emergencies, we are expected to split up to our own safe houses on our own escape routes; that way there's a better chance of one of us surviving.

At the end of the hangar, there's a small black ship waiting for me, with my name printed on the gray stone floor in white lettering. A ship that's both luxurious and practical. A ship I've never flown before, but I'll cross that bridge when I get to it.

"Ferking move," I command myself. With one foot in front of the other, I run down the corridor underneath our home. The Soleil are no doubt scouring for this exit and soon enough they'll find it. But I've lost my parents already. I can't lose Joy, too.

If the Soleil don't catch me, they'll try to get me another way. They know my Kindred's name and location. Whatever security she has being my Kindred won't matter to the Soleil. They'll take her. They'll torture her to torture me, until she uses our connection to tell them where I am. And then they'll kill her just like they'll kill me. After they continue framing me for murder.

And if she dies... I'll die. I know it. Despite how hard we all tried, we're too close.

Ferking shut up, a voice in the back of my mind says. I'm unhappily aware it's my own. *Go get Joy.*

CHAPTER 4
JOY

"TAKE MY HAND, HONEY, WE'LL GET AWAY. THERE'S NOTHING LEFT FOR US HERE, NOWHERE SAFE TO STAY. THEY BURNED OUR HOME, SAID WE NEVER HAD ONE ANYWAY."

—DEJA REESE, "HISTORY BETWEEN US"

Fire and smoke obscure the sky. I don't know how long I've been sitting in a dirty lump on the sidewalk behind what used to be the bookstore. Thankfully, I was the only one inside when the ship exploded because now it's in shambles. My blue dress is covered in soot and streaks of dirt. Emergency services—Halins with a modicum of medical training and authority—march along the streets, telling people to go back indoors, but half the buildings don't even have roofs anymore.

Hali isn't strong enough to withstand another disaster. Not when The Second Chaos leveled nearly everything. It's a poor world in a rich system. We're only worthy of being flown over by the rich. And that's exactly what must've happened, to our own peril.

Even from here, I see the tail of a massive luxury liner sticking straight up in the air. The logo is vertical, but I know the Qadin crest when I see it. The nose is buried deep into the ground. It must have collided with Hali Cloud, the nightclub pavilion above. That's the only explanation for all this debris, all this mayhem.

People scream, running past. Where they're going, I have no idea. It's like a ship crashes and everyone enters a state of panic. I, personally, have no clue as to what I should be doing right now, but I don't think running around screaming will make any of this better.

I blink slowly, my stomach a jumble of nerves. Mum. Oh, *Gods*, what if she's hurt? I should probably go home, but will I lose my job if I do? We need this money. But Mum. Should I try to find my boss and see if it's okay to go? I'm sure he'd understand. Maybe he ran home to his own family.

My thoughts are nonsensical. Is this shock? Am I in shock? How does a person know they're in shock?

I look down at my feet and notice I'm missing a sandal. When did I lose a sandal? Like did it just hop off my foot? Did I kick it off somehow?

There's a sudden ringing in my ears.

I should check on Mum. Maybe our home is far enough away from all this…chaos. They probably just got a few shakes. Maybe my birthday cake fell off the counter.

What am I doing?

I need Felix.

For the first time in seventeen years, our connection's lost. *I'm* lost. Felix would tell me to stand up and go home. That this was just a tragic accident and there's nothing we could do. That the royal family is probably fine.

I tap my bare foot on the cement. Oh, *Gods*, what does this mean for Monchuri?

Joy!

Felix calls me in my mind but I can't see him. I only feel him.

His heart's racing a meter a minute. He feels unsure about... something.

Felix?

...coming.

I rise, walking away from the smoke rising into the sky as if that'll help the connection. I tiptoe around sharp rocks. *What?*

...my way.

I can't hear you, I shout in my mind. *Felix?*

Ready.

I shake my head, catching the edge of the lost sandal in my periphery. I creep over to it, avoiding the debris of fallen books and stone walls. It's halfway buried under a wooden beam that crashed down when the ship did however many kilometers away. When I try to yank it out, a slab of cement scratches my bare leg. I wish I had worn my one pair of pants.

Heavy breaths rush into my mind and I forget the sandal. Felix?

Joy. Coming.

Does he mean he's coming here? He's never been to Hali. We've never met in person. How will he find me? Wait. How will he get here? There's no way his mom would let him come to me; she forbade that years ago when he got his pilot's license. They probably let him hire someone to collect me. That's what rich people do.

Felix?

All my thoughts promptly shift aside as another explosion rumbles the ground and debris flings in the air. I run back toward the last strong beam intact in the shop before a big hunk of turbine thuds into the sidewalk. The ringing in my ears increases and I see people running but I can't hear anything except the high-pitched tone.

I fall back in between rows of empty bookshelves leaning against each other. My wristwatch starts to ping, and I stare down at it quizzically. A holo pops up, and Mum's face floats before me. She holds a hand against her chest, her face contorted in concern.

Her stern eyes stare into mine until she takes in the dirt, the blood, the debris around me. "Joy. Communication's down... all over. I know this is illegal but...not a lot of time." The comm cuts in and out but I understand what she's saying.

I squeak the most important question. "Are you okay?"

"I'm fine. Everything's fine," she answers quickly. "Can you come home? Is it safe?"

My gaze flicks to the fire blazing in the street. Houses and buildings destroyed. The downtown of Darben has been flattened. The Emergency Services still bolt by, attending the wounded. I'm scanning through the debris under the creaking wooden beam above me when I spot a guard in a golden mask and vibrant purple uniform looking my way from across the dirt road. Another one stops, as well. I've never seen any guards like this. I'm sure Felix knows who they are but without him in my head...

Red scanner bots detach from their belts and start drifting around the rubble. One scans me and then chirps once before falling back to the guard.

"Mum, there are some funky-looking guards here. Maybe they've come to collect me for Felix?"

"Joy. Be care...ful." Mum's voice cuts out.

"I will," I answer to myself. I take a deep breath, and maneuver through books and paper and wood to walk toward the guards. "Are you here because of Duke Felix Hamdi? He said—"

"Citizen, stay where you are." He holds up a hand and I stop a foot away from them. His voice sounds mechanical, though I know it belongs to a living, breathing man. "We must first confirm your identity." He flashes a light into my eyes and I look down, trying not to lose my sight.

I squint at him through the red light. "No problem. I'm Joy Mirari Abara. From Sector E-11?"

"Joy Mirari Abara, confirmed." He continues flashing the light and I step back in time to see him aiming a gold pistol my way. I stumble over a rock and my other sandal flops off my foot. What? My own voice is in my mind, telling me I'm in danger.

The guard's footsteps thump louder, closer. He's aiming again, while the other one reaches for me.

I twist around and zigzag quickly to the back of the store. Then I place my hands on the crumbly counter and hop over it. My dress rips up the thigh and I slide down to the floor in a heap. I press my back against the inside of the counter. My breaths are uneven and I gasp greedily for air.

These guards want to hurt me and I don't know why.

Should I ask?

Do they know where I'm hiding?

Dammit. What's going on?

Joy. Felix's voice is like a salve to my nerves. The connection's finally clear again. *Stay there. Just a second.*

The footsteps stop in front of the counter. I feel the guard's presence at my back. And then he starts walking again, this time around the counter. The back door is just a few feet away. Can I make it?

As he treads closer, I crouch down into a sprinting position. Now or never. With a jolt of adrenaline, I race toward the door, barefoot. Stones and sharp pieces of whatever poke into my skin. I wince, but I don't stop. The door is within my grasp when the guard's hand plops down onto my shoulder and levels a pistol at me.

I snake around and knee him in the stomach. My fist connects with his golden mask, and no lie, it hurts me a lot more than it hurts him. He staggers to the side and I reach for my own stunner beneath the band of my dress just as he is about to pull the trigger. I knock the inside of his wrist, sending the pistol scattering. And then I aim my stunner at his throat. Mum made sure I know how to handle myself. *Thanks, Mum.*

He goes down in a fit of shakes, and I can hardly believe my skills…or more likely he's not as good as he's supposed to be. Still, I drop the stunner and bolt to the door. I'm barely outside when a pitch of dust swirls up around me. Coughs wrack my body until the wind dies down. In the center of the debris, there's a bright tiny beautiful ship. And in front of it, on a slight ramp leading down, is my Kindred.

His hair is plastered to his face, his eyes wild. His silk

clothes askew. He reaches for me. He's beautiful. He's terrified. He's here for me.

A moment of awe passes between us and I gulp.

My heart feels like it's leaping into my throat and pounding
in my ears. It's just the two of us in sand and dirt and danger.
His breath whooshes on my face, and for the first time ever,
I feel him. He's real. We're real. I take his hand, marveling
at how mine fits into his. A tingly fire rushes to the surface
of my skin where our touch meets. His thoughts are all over
the place, impossible to understand, and so are mine.

"How did you find me?" I shout over the wind.

"I feel you." Felix pulls me toward him.

"Mum!" I step back, the panic rising to the surface. If the
Soleil came for me, surely they'll come for her. We have to
get her.

"Safe," is all Felix says. "Joy, we gotta go."

That's not enough information and he knows that, but still,
he's right. We have to go. We run up the short metal ramp
into the ship, into the cockpit. Everything's small. Not like
the movies or holo-shows. It's a fast planet hopper—luxury
class—and I hope it'll hop us out of here quick.

Through raspy breaths, I say, "You know how to fly this
thing?"

"Mostly." Felix sucks air through his teeth as he takes a
seat. There's only one in front of the console, but thankfully
oversized, and three folded up along the sides. This is clearly
a ship meant to be used for solo adventures, and short hops
with friends. "The autopilot helps."

I squeeze in beside him, and we buckle up using the one

belt. He starts pressing buttons and flipping switches, and he must know what he's doing because he got here, he found me.

My eyes widen and I point through the windshield. "Uhhh."

Guards assemble outside, their forms visible through the smoke and rubble. They aim their weapons at us, and this time I'm sure they're something far deadlier than stunners.

"Right. No problem. I just have to find the right one…" Information streams through his head and into mine. He read a book on this ship, about a year ago, to appease his mother, who felt he needed to be prepared for an emergency. Thankfully, for me, Felix has a photographic memory, and because he's in pure panic mode, his fingers twitching as he stares at the console, I access his memory.

I flick through the pages in his photo mind, and I hit the switch close to my right leg. The system powers on. I put some steel into my voice despite the guards opening fire upon us. "Autopilot, engage."

"Autopilot engaged," the comm responds with a sexy female accent. I look at Felix, ignoring the pings of bullets studding the outside of our ship.

Felix shrugs, cringing as each bullet strikes. "Don't look at me. She came that way."

A guard steps up, holding what I can only assume is a bomb of some sort. We can't be grounded before I've ever been in the sky.

Felix finds his voice. "Get us off Hali and out of the Monchuri system. Now!"

"Takeoff commencing," the comm purrs.

"Does that mean in a few seconds or—" The rest of my

words cut off as my head crashes back against the seat. We shoot off through Hali. Skyscrapers become small and space looms before us. The pressure makes my eyes bulge and I reach for Felix just as he reaches for me. Our fingers intertwine and I momentarily feel safe.

Like a bolt of lightning, we pass by ships, some bigger, some even smaller if that's possible, and the other Monchuri planets in our system, their colors vibrant and unique. I wish I had time to see them properly, to appreciate this moment. But it's all passing too fast and the console screen lights up. Those guards who tried to stun and kill me must be following. Maybe there are more of them.

"We've got company." Felix bites his bottom lip as he swerves the thrusters to the left. We slide in our seat, and his whole body's pressed against mine. There's no time to think about that.

"Who are they? Why do they want us dead? What is going on, Felix?"

He shoots me a glance as he hits more buttons on the console.

"Stealth-mode activated," the AI says. Cool air suddenly blasts through the ship and I stifle the shivers. My dress isn't warm enough for this.

"It's covering our heat signatures. We may still make it out of here…" Felix's confidence washes over me like a warm blanket, and briefly I forget the ships, the chase. Until he continues.

"They—the guards—look like the Soleil but they don't act like them. They think we killed the Qadins."

"The Qadins are dead?" I gasp, my hand flying to my

mouth. Oh, no. I'm cold all over again and my brain's think-ing too many things at once. "If they think… You said Mum's safe, is she? They—"

"Her Kindred got her off Hali." He swerves again, and my dress tears more up my side. By the time we reach wher-ever we're going, I'll be down to my undergarments. Before I can ask how he knows Mum is with Danio, Felix replays the conversation in our connection.

Danio's voice warbled as she said, "I'll hide Adora. I've had a plan in place because of my ex-husband for years. He's dangerous and if he had the chance…" She didn't finish the thought. "You get Joy. She's my daughter, too. Tell her we're safe. Don't worry about us."

Felix cuts the memory off. "This ship has a few minutes of untraceable communications. Danio was the first call I made."

"How did you—"

Felix eyes slide to mine before tracking the screens, the ships, our hunters. "Joy, you're my Kindred." As if that an-swers how he knew where and how to contact Danio and get my mum to safety. "There's protocol for things like this."

The ships are just tiny blips on the screen now, and we're safe. At least for the moment. "Your parents would never have a protocol for this."

He doesn't even glance my way. "I do."

And that's when I'm reminded that Felix is beside me, we're in the same place. When we touch, it's different and real and I can't just read his thoughts, I feel them. I feel his fear, his guilt, his…grief.

His mother's collapse flashes behind my eyes. His father's distraction and sacrifice sit heavy within my heart. "I'm sorry, Felix." I pull him into a side hug. "I'm so sorry."

"Yeah," is all he says, letting me wrap my arms around him before shaking me off. He's not ready to accept this, not yet. He's not ready to give in to the feelings that are threatening to crush his heart. It's not my place to push him. His parents are still alive. For now. We think.

"I'm being framed for murder, you, my Kindred are being chased by authorities, my parents are captured, and because I'm a royal cousin, we're in danger. Which means," he huffs, as the display starts flashing again and a siren blares around our ship, "that whoever killed them, is coming for me."

"Stealth mode, deciphered," the AI says cheerfully as if it isn't announcing our doom.

"Dammit." He takes the console off autopilot. "Use the holo-map. We have to find somewhere to go right now."

I flick the switch labeled Holo-map. Translucent planets and systems pop up before our eyes on the dash. Monchuri. Dosani, which is an unincorporated Monchuri territory, and way too close to home since we're being chased. Fer-Asta, home of the Juxto warlords, is a no-go, since they have an ongoing war with our system. Minor and Major Sidarra, beautiful oceanic wonders that are also close allies of the Monchuri system. Felix's father was born there, and there's no way we could hide with that kind of celebrity.

Then there's the ever-growing Ilori Imperial Colonies who worship Ozvios and we can't enter even if we wanted to; it's basically a death sentence for outsiders. They are master manipulators, immortal, rich beyond reason, and evil. They topple kingdoms and governments, sometimes with finesse, sometimes with force, and then they colonize. They survive and thrive on life energy and will stop at nothing until the universe is theirs. They're more dangerous than home at this point, and I hope I never have to meet one of them.

I suck in a breath.

"They'll expect us on Dosani. I mean, if we didn't know better, that's where we'd go, right?" I ask rhetorically as our ship swerves. "If we want a chance to figure this out, we should go where no one would expect us. Where we can fit in, and we can contact authorities to help us out." I point to a system where we're bound to be safe, at least for a while. One Felix has been to before once, and I recall fondly. "It's neutral and we can stay until we can negotiate our return."

"It might be neutral… I've heard rumors about the Ilori attempting to colonize it. But…" Felix scans the blue-and-green planet spinning on the holo, while his hands grip the thrusters. "It would be easy to fit in there."

"If we jump now, the Soleil will lose us, right?"

Felix nods. "If we jump now, we can lose them, but I think… I think maybe, we need to get in touch with Arren. I hate him. He's done some things… But he's loyal, he gave me an upload chip to personally get in touch with him—which I left at home—but he'll know—"

"No!" I shriek, surprising us both. Arren's the last person I want to see, the last person who will help us out. "Arren controls the Soleil. How do we know we can trust him?"

"I told you," Felix shouts over the console's alarm, which is slowly turning into a crescendo. "They don't act like the Soleil. They didn't sound right, didn't act right… Wouldn't take their masks off, didn't observe Monchuri tradition. You and I both escaped them, and there's no way that would've happened if they're so elite. Arren has to know what's going on."

I don't really have time to consider all of that. Real Soleil or fake, whoever's following us and planning on shooting us down won't stop till they succeed.

"I don't want to put our lives in Arren's hands. We don't know if he's been compromised." Lead drops into the pit of my stomach at just the mention of Arren. For years, I've been successfully keeping secrets from Felix about Arren, and his override, his treatment of me. If Felix knew…

"You're right…about Arren. But…" Felix pleads. And in his thoughts, I see Minor Sidarra. Where his father's family comes from. Where he thinks he could be safe. But it's not. It can't be. Not for him, for me, or for his cousins whom he'll inadvertently put in harm's way. I'm about to say as much when something clips our ship's tail. We rock to the side before plunging forward, suspended slightly over the dashboard. "They're going to shoot us down."

My fingers grasp the comms, and I hold down the button. "Get us to Ocara. Bring us to the hyperspace bridge."

The system chirps. "Shield's integrity is 61 percent, several components are compromised. A jump to the OM system will deplete all fuel resources. Proceed?"

Felix closes his eyes, and exhales. "Yes."

* * *

INTERGALACTIC TRAVEL GUIDE FOR BEGINNERS

Welcome, Travelers, to your guide to the universe!

Congratulations, you are traveling on the fastest, most advanced self-repairing AI-operated cruiser in the galaxy. Traveling to new systems* is encouraged by our benevolent royals, THE QADINS, and you make your kingdom proud

by gaining new perspectives. However, there are some rules that must be adhered to, or you will be prosecuted by Monchuri law.

It is imperative that when traveling to lesser-known worlds, you:

◊ DO NOT introduce Monchuran technology to the ruling beings.

◊ DO NOT speak Monchuran dialects.

  • All planet hoppers are equipped with three sets of heargos that will adapt to most world languages, written *and* spoken.

◊ DO keep all various registration and licenses within the ship's archive.

  • In case of a crash, the archive will be encased in impenetrable metal that can be accessed through the accepted familial code.

◊ DO remember that time is a fluid concept. While time is stable in the Monchuri system, it may pass slower or faster depending on your destination. Don't panic; your ship will always adapt and recalibrate its settings so that you always know your time.

◊ DO NOT leave your ship exposed to the native population.

  • In case of a crash, follow safety protocol detailed on page 15 of your guide.

◊ DO use the currency replicator located beneath quadrant 2 of the dashboard for necessities.

◊ DO NOT let local wildlife bite or lick you (learn about various creatures and their potency on page 42 of your guide) or infection may be forthcoming.

    • If exposed to illness, there are four medi-kits stored beneath quadrant 3 of your dashboard, including sleep tabs should you find rest difficult in the beginning of your journey or you need a reprieve from difficult thoughts.

◊ DO NOT take any produce or living organisms that could disrupt our ecosystem back with you. For more details, please thoroughly read page 23 of your guide.

◊ DO enjoy your brief stay, and register your planet hopper with Monchuri systems upon returning home for a full complimentary cleaning.

URGENT: In case of emergency evasive tactics, your planet hopper will halt gathering data and using online systems. To reactivate, you will need to complete a manual shutdown. Seeker tracking can only be broadcast from Maru-Monchuri. To disable Seeker tracking, you will need to input your familial code.

◊ TO REFUEL YOUR SHIP using Class B detritus, please read pages 48–55 of your guide.

*Currently, some systems are no longer safe for travel, especially though not limited to the expanding Ilori Colonies. On page 32, you may find a recent list of "safe" systems to explore.

CHAPTER 5
FELIX

The planet hopper is chaotic. Sirens shriek, and the sexy AI voice now sounds like she's been submerged into a fountain from all the constant noise. The damage isn't too bad, but I'll be surprised if we survive this.

My mom… My dad. How are they? Where are they? My second call on the comms was to my family estate. I was able to talk to Idu, who said my parents were taken, but alive. I wonder if they still are.

The open guide slides on my lap, and I grasp the edge before it falls. Joy handed it to me the moment we entered hyperspace, but I haven't managed to read much except for the ridiculous rules. I'm far too worried to let information soak into my brain right now anyway. I imagine that's why she gave it to me, that she's keeping me busy enough to distract me. I don't want to disappoint her, but I shut the guide, not bothering to read page two.

"Seventeen thousand seconds till arrival." The AI's voice warbles as the pressure intensifies and we flatten against the back of the seat.

"That's a weird measurement of time." My teeth chatter as my head swivels to Joy. Her watery gray eyes stare into the space beyond, her lips mash together as if she's solving the galaxy's biggest math problem. *If* we survive, it'll be because of her. Not me. I'm the spoiled, reckless brat she knows I am.

Despite her poor judgment of me, I was lucky to have been paired with the most determined person in Monchuri.

She shifts, her leg smashing against mine. There's only one pilot chair in this hopper, and the two of us are crammed into it. Every part of my body is touching hers. How have I been alive seventeen years without physically touching Joy until now? She feels soft and smooth and electric and warm and I want to curl up in her arms and let her hold me until the world makes sense. I'm always the weak one.

She tosses me a look. "Everything's gonna be just fine."

"Mmm," is all I can muster. She can read my panic and desire to be coddled. The Kindred is a blessing…but sometimes a curse.

That thought quickly dissipates the moment we slam to the right.

My arm swoops out to the side in front of her to keep her from falling forward into the dash. Fabric rips, and I look down at her blue dress. It's caked with dirt and I catch a peek of her black undergarments through the slit up her side. Her eyes bulge and I grip the thrusters tighter.

"To be honest, it wasn't your best dress anyway," I shout over the noise. She doesn't respond as her cheeks turn pink.

Instead, her eyes glue to the universe as we're forced to leave hyperspace, and a small green-and-blue planet floats in front of us.

"This isn't Ocara." It's a silly statement of truth, but it's all I can say. All I can do. "Where are we?"

The AI answers, though she sounds like she's really going through some trauma. "Terra."

Joy and I exchange a glance. Neither of us know anything about this planet—in fact, it was never mentioned in any of my classes, or apparently any of Joy's books. I swipe the guide in my lap… There's nothing about Terra for beginners. Oh, no, my head is spinning. My skin feels itchy and lukewarm.

"We left hyperspace too early." Joy twists around in her seat, staring at the other end of the tiny planet hopper. "Do you smell that?"

I sniff, catching the faint scent of burning plastic. My stomach roils and I stretch my legs out before me. "Something's… burning," I state through the haze that's coating my tongue and senses. The air feels thin, my lungs empty, and my ears pop. My world is a blur.

"Your asthma," Joy says, her hands fumbling to stretch out our seat belt to give me space. "Close your eyes. Deep breaths. Maybe put your head between your legs?"

"I'm fine." My eyes begin to shut on their own, as if following Joy's orders. Traitorous body. I've had asthma since I was born, and every once in a while, like when something's smoky or burning, it's like my body forgets how to breathe, and it's not like I had the time to grab my meds. "Just a little…" The words don't come to mind. What even are words right now? Where am I again?

We suddenly plummet forward.

"Felix!" Joy screams.

The dash starts wailing.

The blood rushes to my head and the loosened seat belt is clearly not up to the challenge of keeping me in my seat. I use my hands to push myself back, accidentally shoving the thrusters as far as they can go. After a few quick tugs, they refuse to budge. The scent of burning intensifies. Ferk.

My whole body is threatening to shut down at the absolute worst time. Using all the energy I can muster, I hit the console. Joy and I get locked into a harness that emerges from both sides of the seat and straps us in. "Joy."

The thrusters begin to quake as Joy grabs hold of them from me, trying to unlock them from their forward position. Terra looms in front of us, and no matter how hard Joy tries, she can't unlock them. This can't be good.

"We're being pulled into Terra's gravity. We have 0.5 percent fuel left," she mouths or shouts; I can't make sense with all the noise around us. "We won't make it to Ocara."

We continue our downward path when an explosion rings my ears. Our seat rocks forward, and the harness manually disconnects. I fall forward into the window. My head bounces off the glass, and for a moment, the edges of my vision blacken. My pulse quickens when I widen my eyes at the view in front of me. We're over a body of water.

I try to push myself back, but it's no use. Joy twists and scrabbles slowly toward the back of the ship.

"What are you doing?"

The cold from the window seeps through my silk garments, and I yelp as a metal flap dislodges from a floor compartment. I roll my body but it still collides with my leg. I gnash my teeth…and then the sirens stop. There's just the whine of the engines, the rush of the wind, and the promise of our impending doom.

Joy doesn't answer as she grapples toward something.

I maneuver around until I can edge toward the thrusters. I can save us.

"Almost there." Joy's overwhelming determination swells through our connection. And her terror, too.

She hits some flashing button along the wall, and the floor falls out beneath her as the ship turns completely vertical. She suddenly dangles awkwardly above me and the cockpit, holding onto the lever on the wall.

I continue my snaillike pace to the dash, praying the ground is still far off and no one will shoot us down. Joy collapses against the back of the pilot's seat.

"This is decidedly terrible."

After a few more inches forward, I grip the tip of a thruster in my hand. I try to pull it from its position but I'm not strong enough. Just then, Joy's arms land with a thud against the dash and she grips the other thruster to steer. Her legs wrap around the seat and her body's suspended over me.

"Not good."

I don't know if she says this aloud or in her head. Her face nears mine. The veins bulge in her forehead and for one brief, silly moment I can't help but think about how beautiful she is…

"What's not good? Joy, what's behind me?"

She glances at the window and back, her mouth opening and closing. "I'd rather not say."

I let my chin rest against the console. "Are we going to die?"

"One…two…three," she counts calmly but her thoughts scream uncertainty.

With one quick coordinated tug, we unlock the thrusters and fall forward. She lands beneath the dash while my feet fly over my head as my back bounces off the seat. I plop on top of her and stare into her terrified gaze.

"We need to get back into the seat," I say, breathless. "Now."

She scrambles to move and I push her up and forward. Once she's in place, she yanks me into her lap, and I slide off into the rest of the seat. I hit the harness tab, but nothing happens. Joy bashes on the tab, and it seems to unstick itself. It threads back over us, and we're so close, so tightly held together.

"Brace for impact," I scream at the AI, who doesn't respond.

The ship falls.

Our legs lift but our bodies stay in place. Joy hugs me. Everything rattles and cracks. There's noise, so much noise, but in this moment it's just the two of us as we hold each other.

The ground reaches up to meet us. The floor rumbles and we jolt in our seat. I know it's loud, but all I can hear is Joy's heart racing in my head. Bags burst from the floor and console to keep us safe.

But…the crash should've been so much worse. Instead, it seems like we're weightless.

Joy's lost behind those thick blue bags, and though I feel her arms around me, I feel too far from her.

We stay there for a few moments, heaving breaths in and out.

I gulp at the air greedily. Then the bags deflate and our

harness recedes back into the seat. Within a second, we're free and I pull her into me, wrapping myself around her. I know it's indecent. I know I shouldn't, but I'm terrified. And she's my Kindred. She doesn't complain. A haze of relief washes through the two of us.

When we pull apart, I notice a bag's caught on a latch beneath the console. My legs shake, and when I attempt to bend down, I end up falling forward into the dash and below it.

"Felix!"

She reaches down for me just as I mutter, "I'm okay."

I roll onto my back, and already miss the nearness of her, the reality of her. My eyes look up at the latches, all four of them.

Joy's silent for a few beats while I yank open the latches, one after another. Various items fall out of the compartments: a case of heargos, the tiny chips we need to insert into our ears; medi-kits, which I'll be needing shortly; sleep tabs; a currency replicator…

"What do we do now?" Joy's voice is small, filled with worry. Her mind reels from the day's events. Her day began with cake, and now we've crashed on a strange planet. Honestly, I don't know what comes next, how long we're supposed to run and hide, how we're supposed to fit in with whatever ruling beings are outside that hatch.

My parents… Her mum.

I take her outstretched hand and twine my fingers with hers as she lifts me up. The items jostle in my arms. The smoke and rubble form a thick haze in the ship, and we're reminded again that we aren't safe.

"We have to get out of here. The ship needs to repair itself." I push away with a groan. "We can wait around on this world, and then we get back to saving our parents."

For a second, we stand there staring as wires spark and dangle precariously out of place near the ship's hatch. The opening function might be broken. We're going to die in here if we don't get out.

My gaze swivels around the room as I think. *We* think.

Her dress is ripped all the way up her side, and my leg throbs. Splatters of teal blood cover my clothes and skin. The air smells like something's melting. Joy grimaces at the blood and my wounded leg, and darts to the hatch.

She hits the broken lever, over and over, with the travel guide. "We've got everything out of here that we need?" This she says more to herself than to me, but I assess the items in my arms just to make sure.

Medi-kits and heargos and currency replicator… There's nothing else.

"*Gods,*" she shouts. "Open!"

I'm about to drop the necessities to help with my screwed-up body when she lands a final hit that unlocks the lever. The hatch swooshes open and the ramp lowers onto Terra. A scent I can't quite place trickles in along with water. She reaches for the bent and battered guide before it can get soaked through.

Joy tosses a look over her shoulder at me and I give her a nod. "We're going to need that."

We don't have time to worry about where we are and what we'll step into. The ship is hot—too hot. Whatever's out there can't be worse than what's inside.

She limps onto the ramp, which is slick with water. It's floating. We're floating. I watch her go, clutching the guide, her mind whirring with all sorts of emotions, while I juggle the items. My lungs expand with all the fresh air—oxygen, thank the *Gods*—but my leg wobbles with each step I take. Pain, so much pain.

When I finally make it to the ramp, the water reaches my ankles. I grimace until the bright sunshine forces me to close my eyes. My home has three different suns and none of them feel like they are actively trying to kill me like this one.

"They just have the one sun. It's warm but I don't think it's lethal," Joy says, reading my mind. "Take my hand."

I reach out and her fingers thread through mine again. I almost don't care that the items sit unsteadily in my grasp—that they'll fall into the watery abyss we're somehow drifting on, as long as Joy tells me everything's okay. We walk together on the ramp that sways beneath our feet and it feels like forever, even though it's been a few minutes. When my soaked silk slippers touch damp ground, I hazard a peek at our new world.

"Give your eyes a second to adjust," she whispers. She would know; the sun on Hali is intense and hot. How she manages…

Then a thought strikes me. "Why are you whispering?" The world around me is green, with tall trees sprouting strange leaves. The air is humid, warm, wet. Unlike anything in the Monchuri system.

And there in front of us, through the tan-colored grass a few feet away, stands a tall being, same dark skin as Joy's, with their hands on their mouth, and rounded eyes. Before any of us can say anything, the ramp recedes behind us, closing the hatch, and the creature falls over into the grass.

"That's why I was whispering," Joy says. "Your observation skills need work."

I ignore the jab, and plod through the damp earth and through the seemingly endless nature in front of us. We stop in front of the fallen being.

"Bit dramatic, don't you think. Is it dead?" I stare at their rubber shoes and strange clothes. "It looks like us. Just like us."

"Maybe they're like Monchurans?" Joy wonders. "I think I've heard about beings that are just like us in the farthest reaches of the universe. New worlds created by Indigo's songs…"

"I don't remember hearing that. For all we know—"

"*You* didn't hear about that. You skipped that lesson for a concert on Jiva-Monchuri, remember?" Her hand leaves mine as she crouches down to touch the being's forehead. "Still breathing. It'll be fine. Probably shock."

I shrug. I remember the concert on Jiva, the planet at the end of our system. The lead singer was hot. His name was B'Vio, I think. He wore glittery black makeup and when he sang, his words swirled around my heart. That's about all I remember about that night. Joy, however, remembers everything. Every one of my excuses and missteps, for better or worse.

That thought vacates my brain as there's an eruption behind us. I twist to see our ship slowly sink into the watery swampland, bubbles rising to the surface. I'm surprised I'm not lunging toward it, my one escape from this world I don't know, the one way I can get back home to my parents. But there's nothing that can be done about that now. It'll be safe down there.

"Well, it should be able to repair itself." I feel oddly complacent about all of this. Maybe it's my own form of shock. Maybe it's fear. Maybe it's because Joy is with me. It really doesn't matter. At least we have the items we need. We'll blend in with these creatures and come up with a plan.

And then we'll find a way home. Joy's voice pierces my mind, and I'm relieved she's back in my brain.

"We could've been stranded somewhere worse," I manage, staring at the being as it begins to come to. "You, creature, what is this place?"

Joy shakes her head. *It doesn't understand you. The heargo.*

I nod, rummaging through the items until I open the silver pod that sits in the palm of my hand. Joy sets the guide on the ground before taking the pod and running her finger across the smooth metal. She drops it, marveling that gravity works the same on this world. The heargo case levitates in front of her, opening its seamless shell. Three miniscule black chips sit inside. Joy takes two and disengages the case. It seals itself and falls back into her palm.

She hands one to me, and I tilt my head to the side, slipping a chip inside my left ear. The pain is instant as it crawls on tiny mechanical legs down my ear canal and farther still until it imbeds itself and releases a painkiller. I shake my head to clear the sensation. Joy does the same. Our gazes meet.

"That's…weird." She gives a long exhale.

"It only gets weirder." I've endured the experience before on a diplomatic mission with my parents. I removed it once I got home; the idea of something burrowing into my mind that's not Joy is unwelcome.

The creature watches us from its spot on the ground. "I'm losing my mind."

"Ah!" Joy shouts. "We understand you!"

I decide to take charge here, my slippers squelching on the grass as I straighten my back. "Creature, identify yourself and our current planet location."

"They don't like being called 'creature,'" Joy attempts to whisper, but her equilibrium is off, so she's actually shrieking. "Be nice."

The being's head oscillates between Joy and me. I'm trying to keep breathing through the pain and confusion. My lungs aren't filling with enough air. Darts of pain from my leg shoot up to my brain, causing both Joy and me to cringe.

"Um…" it says uneasily.

"I apologize for my offense. Would you *please*—" I toss a sullen look at Joy "—identify yourself and our current location?"

It gulps air like a fish on dry land before answering. "I'm Rashid? A human? And you're in…in Rocky Apple Key, Florida, United States, North America, Earth?"

They must call Terra Earth here, I remark through our connection.

"Why is everything you say a question?" Joy asks, staring at the *human* named Rashid. "Are you unsure?"

"Uh, no? I'm scared?" Rashid's lips thin. "Shouldn't like… NASA people be here, or like government jets? You're aliens in a spaceship… How did you just arrive here like without anyone noticing?"

"Oh." She smiles. "Right, this probably seems overwhelming…and scary. Our ship was on stealth mode, um…

un…trace…able by tech. We," she slows down her words, "aren't from around here. My name is…sounds like Joy in your tongue and his name sounds like Felix. We come…in peace." She throws up her hands and honestly her smile has become a bit too wide, a bit too much. Rashid squeaks, edging away from us both.

I roll my eyes, trying not to laugh. "Don't mind her." The poor human's heart must be racing. They've been through an ordeal today, we all have, and it's time for everything to stop being so intense. Especially the pain in my leg. "So, human—Rashid. Would you be so kind as to tell us about yourself, Rocky Apple Key, Florida, Earth? And what is this NASA you spoke of?"

"Uh…" Their brows furrow. "Why, is your alien race invading, starting here? I've read enough comics to know this is a thing. You won't find any resistance. Please don't kill me. I—"

"No one's invading or killing anyone." Joy puts her hands up again, gingerly stepping closer to the human. "We just need a safe place to hide while our ship fixes itself and we get some fuel."

"And you want that place to be Rocky Apple Key?" Rashid scoffs, their expression incredulous. "Here?" They look around at the marshland, the trees waving in the light wind and heavy sunshine, the general warm nothingness of it all. *"Here?"* They point at a large green creature that crawls through the grass toward us. Joy gulps and skitters toward me, watching as the oversized pest scuttles by us, and then snatches the guide in its maw. It escapes into the tall grass, taking the only solution to fueling our ship with it.

"Oh, no!" She darts after it, but I reach for her arm, shaking my head.

"We don't know what else lies in this grass...what could infect us with its earthly germs. Besides, we'll be okay without it." Although I'm worried about not having the guide with us. I don't know what Class B detritus is. No idea.

Are you sure? she asks, her gaze locked on mine. *Did you read about the fuel? I can look for the information in your mind?*

I didn't read the pages about the fuel. But I'm sure we will be okay without it, I respond with a smile.

"See?" Rashid interrupts. "This is the most lizard-infested, uneventful town in Florida. No one comes here. We're all just waiting to leave."

"Sounds perfect," me and Joy admit at the same time.

★ ★ ★

One Year Ago

JOY

Felix, if you do not stop drinking right this second, you're going to be hungover for a week. I stomp my foot, though no one hears it, and jut out my chin.

Felix lolls his head toward me. He's surrounded by all of his chums and three of his last paramours. They can't see me, but he does. He can see me on my threadbare couch, sitting across from the window overlooking a dark Darben, not that I can see the stars through the smog.

Seeing him is the highlight of my night. His outfit is all shiny and black, worth at least a couple thousand melios—more than Mum and I pay in rent for two months. He's stretched out in the VIP booth, his black hair purposely disheveled, and his lips shimmer a glittery red. He smiles my way with those pretty red lips as our gazes meet.

"My Kindred's here!" he shouts above his crew, who are glued to his every word, every movement, every expression, wanting to grab his attention with their enraptured presence. The whole scene makes me want to vomit. "Say happy birthday to Joy, everyone!"

"Hi, Joy!"

"Happy birthday, Joy!" they scream and laugh and wiggle in their cushioned seats. The lights above flicker from one brilliant hue to the next, and beyond there's a dance floor full of pretty people, tossing their pouty faces toward Felix, who neither sees nor cares.

I sit on my couch, deciding on how I should tell him to shut this whole night down before I wake up in the morning to meet my possible-betrothed, Maxon, with a raging headache I don't deserve. I'm not supposed to get these sympathy pains, but I always do.

Don't look at me like that, Joy. It's been a tough night. He pouts like a child. *I thought with it being our birthday, we'd have better luck, but we bombed the audition.* His bandmates don't hear him, but they shoot him pointed glances. When he says *we*, he means himself because he got stage fright and ended up ill backstage. I don't correct him, though.

I huff, shaking my head. I wish I could smash his glass of amber liquid, but I can't. That's not how it works. I can't move objects. I can't reach him. I'm in my home, seeing him because I want to, because he wants me to. Air sails between

my teeth, whooshing into our teeny apartment. *Despite my…
adoration for you, Felix, you're a pain in my head.*

*Come on, Joy. We're sixteen. We have to celebrate and mourn
our dwindling youth while we can, right?* He takes a swig from his
glass and his friends cheer. A few seconds pass, and he looks
straight into my gaze. *And your betrothal.*

Well… I admit defeat …*I'll leave you to it, then.*

No. Please, he pleads. "You're the only person I want to see
on our birthday. The only one that matters." He mistakenly
says that last bit aloud, causing the chatter around him to stop
and his friends to stare our way. Well, his way.

If I can judge their soured expressions, I'd say they're of-
fended. But I can't read their minds, only his. And his mind…
It's thinking impossible things.

You are my everything.

Don't leave me.

Stay with me.

Run away with me. This thought repeats over and over and
over.

My own mind blanks at his honesty—Felix doesn't usually
do the truth without jokes—until the girl on his left leans
close, her makeup smudged, lips quivering.

"Wanna get out of here?" Her voice is raspy and seduc-
tive. She's gorgeous.

Felix shifts away from her, his gaze still on me. His thoughts
still on me. He's drunk and reckless with his heart and mind,
latching onto me because he's lonely and wants someone who
understands him like I do. He doesn't actually want *me.*

Have fun, I say, about to disconnect.

Joy, he whispers. *Please.*

I give him a sad smile, rubbing the stinging site of my birthday injection I got earlier today. The one that lets me turn down our connection unlike most Kindred pairs in the galaxy. *Don't drink much more. Tomorrow's a big day for me.*

So you can meet your future match? He says it with an air of disgust; his bottom lip curls. *You don't want that. I don't want that.*

Life, I say with a small smile, closing my eyes, readying myself to use the override injected into my veins and streaming through my mind, *is not about getting the things we want.*

CHAPTER 6

JOY

"SLIP INTO THE LONELINESS LIKE A SLINKY BLACK
DRESS, CRY YOUR EYES, SIS, BUT IT'S NOT OVER
YET. TIME TO BEGIN AGAIN."

—DEJA REESE, "BEGIN SOMEWHERE"

Once Rashid Williams, son of Ayana and Tony, starts talking,
he doesn't stop. It's been five minutes and he hasn't asked us
a single thing about being aliens or why we're hiding, which
I'd suspected would be a bigger thing, but instead he has been
telling us all about Florida.

He huffs, crossing his legs. "The thing about Rocky Apple
is that it's small. Like *small* small. I know every single person
on the island, and for real, they're all a little cray. You know
what I mean?"

I do not, in fact, know what he means. But using context
clues, I gather it means odd? Felix and I nod. We're spread
out on the grass under a palm tree—that's what Rashid said

they are—not far away from our sunken ship. The bright sun has dried our clothes, thankfully. I would love to draw this place, tell a story about it, if everything weren't such a mess, and Felix weren't so pale, his eyes glossy.

A disassembled medi-kit sits in my lap. He can't go on the way he is, and despite being born and raised on Hali-Monchuri, where I've never used technology like this, I'm the only one who can focus enough to put it together. My fingers twiddle a tiny metal piece that must go somewhere on this thing to start it.

"That's why I was out here. It's the one area in town where you can be alone." Rashid rubs at his eyes, which are a little red around the edges. Perhaps he was crying? "Home's not good right now. My dad's gone… And Johnny, he's my boyfriend, well, future boyfriend. He's an impossibly cute Māori nerd from New Zealand, and his accent is so adorable, but I think he's catching feelings for the art boy, Bradley. It's like, just a mess. And now I'm telling all my problems to a bunch of aliens."

"Hey," I say with a smile. "Aliens are good listeners, and I understand complicated relationships." I wink at Felix, whose breathing has become labored. He'll need meds soon. Felix tends to get tunnel vision when things get rough and his asthma acts up. He once cut his hand while trying to slice a starberry he pilfered from the kitchen before dinner and walked into a wall so completely that he had to go to the Qadin's personal hospital. That he's awake and pushing through the pain is a testament to his desire to not leave me alone.

His thoughts are all over the place, too jumbled, but I feel his emotions. He's scared and tired. And in aching pain.

"Umm…why are you here?" Rashid reaches over and takes the medi-kit and metal thing from my grasp. Before I can object, he sticks it into a slot I missed and twists it once. A blue light flickers, indicating it's on.

"How did you…?" My jaw drops as he hands it back.

"I run the AV Club. Johnny calls me a nerd…" His voice grows quiet and I imagine it has something to do with the art boy, Bradley. But it's not my place to speculate.

Instead, my fingertips run along the medi-kit, searching. The metal piece becomes a switch that I flip up. A robotic Monchuri voice fills the small space between us as it activates. Rashid looks confused, but Felix lets out a long sigh of relief.

"Hello, Travelers. Are you in need of assistance?"

"Yes," I answer quickly.

The voice quiets. "Scanning."

The kit moves from my hands and levitates around us, scanning its pale blue light over our bodies.

"There are three different life forms. Two Monchurans, and one Terran. Shall I dispatch aid to all injuries, commencing with the most crucial first?"

"Yes, please," I answer as Felix's eyes close. The kit travels first to him, employing robotic arms to clean his leg wounds before spraying quick-acting meds and three pumps of inhalation. It's not his emergency inhaler, but it'll have to do until we can either find one here or fix our ship and get to Ocara.

Felix drifts out for a bit when he's done. The blood and cuts are already gone and healed. I'm surprised by how quickly it works, how effortless… We don't have these on Hali, and this is just small tech. I wonder what their big tech can do. How many Hali lives it could save.

It travels next to me, cleaning and patching my cuts, also spraying medicine on my cheek that smells a bit like Kuumu bark from the desert oases back home. We use it in pastes for our hair, and sometimes for light maladies. Funny that the tech uses it. Funny that at any point Maru-Monchuri ever acted as if Hali had something to offer after The Second Chaos.

When the kit is done with me, I feel revitalized. Better than I've felt in weeks even. My skin feels firmer, I'm not thirsty or hungry anymore. It's only a temporary relief from dehydration and hunger, but I'll take it.

The kit swoops down in front of Rashid.

"What is it—?"

Its robotic arms latch onto his foot, moving faster than my eyes can follow, and then administers spray. Rashid faints.

Again.

"He's truly dramatic, huh?" Felix gives me a full-wattage smile. Some of his color has returned. Even his black hair glistens in the Florida sun. His brown cheeks sport a bit of stubble that'll stay short; he often complains about his inability to grow a beard. His piercing violet eyes flash at my appraisal and he sighs, stretching out his pain-free leg. His clothes, though silk and covered in slits, hang across his broad shoulders and taper in at his muscled chest. How is he still beautiful?

And then I remember he's my Kindred. He knows what I'm thinking, because I let him. While he's thinking of his parents, of Terra, of Rashid, I'm thinking about how he's beautiful. Not my mum. Not my worry or panic. I'm a monster.

I turn away from him, blocking out our connection.

"Rashid is… I like him," I admit. "Dramatic, sure, but talkative, funny, accepting despite our extraordinary arrival. He will be a good guide to fitting in with humans. If he has the time and inclination, of course."

"If he doesn't stop fainting, more like," Felix adds, nudging Rashid with his healed leg. His gaze finds mine, brows furrowed. "How is that sometimes I feel like your mind is blocked from mine…or that you aren't in my head?"

I inhale sharply, knowing his feelings without having to feel them myself. His arm twitches by his side, and I can tell he's wanted to ask me this for so long.

Felix is afraid. He handles change fine, but I'm his one constant. He needs our connection. He doesn't let anyone else in, and I guess neither do I, yet, I… I've learned to not need him in my mind the way he needs me. And recently, I've found myself using the override to give him space because I don't know how to be close to him the way I want to be—not when I've got to keep Maxon happy. I have to give up everything I've known while Felix can just go on the way he wants. Maybe this bit of privacy is better for the both of us. "Felix—"

"Did I faint again?" Rashid rolls his body to sitting, his eyes a bit glazed. "I can't *even* with this right now."

"You can't even what?" I ask, my head tilted to the side, happy for the subject change. "Were you injured, Rashid?"

"I twisted my ankle last week at cheer practice, wasn't a big deal." He shakes his head. "Is that what that thing did? It healed me? Because it looked like it was going to scan me and then make an evil copy of me that would destroy the world."

"Dramatic *and* ridiculous." Felix stands, stretching toward the sun.

"You're aliens! I don't know you or your...your strange items!" Rashid shouts, jumping to his feet. "And I'm not ridiculous or dramatic! You don't know me."

I roll my eyes at Felix, taking to my feet, as well. Normally, he's kind, well maybe a bit cold to anyone—everyone—except me, but panic makes him lash out. He's great at charming people when it matters, and his near-royal status means people always laugh at his jokes or shrug off his insults without actually ever listening to him. It's made him believe all interactions outside of mine are superficial, and now it makes him seem like a brat. I can't blame him; his parents raised him that way, but sometimes...

"Sorry, Rashid. Felix didn't mean to offend you." I straighten my back, knowing the next statement will be difficult to say. "We apologize for any inconvenience and would ask if you could please keep our arrival to yourself. We need to let our ship repair itself, and find some kind of fuel, which means we will need to temporarily remain on Earth for the safety of our homeland and kingdom. And...I know that is much to ask, but we will not be a burden to you or the human race."

Felix nods once, reaching out for my hand. I don't take it, though. *Your attitude needs to change fast or you're going to doom us.*

Rashid looks down at his feet, avoiding my gaze. It's his way, I think, of telling us he'll keep our secret but wants nothing more to do with us. I know that look well, from every single time people found out about Felix being my Kindred and then their disappointment when they'd realize I couldn't make them famous.

"Thank you, Rashid, for your help." I bow to him, hand to my heart as Hali-Monchuri etiquette dictates. "We will leave you now."

Felix inhales sharply at my display. "Thank you, Rashid."

Together, we walk away from him, through the grass and the palm trees, into the hot Florida sunshine…with nary a word between us. We haven't decided where we'll go or what we'll do when Rashid jogs up, hands on his hips.

"You can't just walk into town here. Not like that." He points to my scandalous dress. "What's your plan, other than waiting for your ship to be good?"

Felix cocks an eyebrow and I elbow him to shut him up. His thoughts may be jumbled, but I know when he's about to be sarcastic. "Well, we need to hide. Blend in and get fuel, and then go to Ocara."

"Ocara? What's that?" Rashid raises his brows, continuing without an answer. "And that's it? No hostile takeover or more alien technology that looks up to no good?" He towers over me with his dark brown eyes, his whole demeanor trying to be serious and imposing when in fact he's probably as soft as I am. I find myself wanting to hug him and tell him it's going to be okay. But I don't.

"Nothing of the sort." Felix sighs. "Earth has nothing to offer us but fuel and privacy."

"What he means is—" I toss a look at Felix "—we are not colonizers. We do not invade other worlds, and we mean humanity no harm."

All of which is technically a lie.

The Qadins did some fairly questionable things to amass their kingdom. The god Indigo may have created our system, but the Qadins, a prominent family of Maru-Monchuri, seized control of it shortly after The First Chaos. They manipulated everyone into not only granting them power, but a crown in order to prevent another chaos. Once deemed royal and mighty, they formed an army to invade the other planets in the Monchuri system. They stole resources and threatened war unless those planets agreed to be colonies in their kingdom. No one stood against them.

"Promise?" Rashid stares at Felix. As if he doesn't trust him out the two of us. But given Felix's treatment, it makes sense.

"Promise," Felix says with a slight bow.

"I hope I don't regret this," Rashid mutters to himself. "If you walk into town, people are going to question you. Everyone knows each other. It's an island. If you want a place to hide, you can stay with me. I can tell people you're my cousin," this he says to me, "and you're a foreign exchange student or something."

"Why?" Felix and I ask at the same time.

"Why do *I* have to be foreign?" Felix narrows his eyes.

"Uh, because your accent is super foreign and your brown skin a different kind of brown?" Rashid shrugs his shoulders like that was a silly question. Maybe it was.

"Why would you do this?" I shake my head. "Why would you do this for strangers, for aliens? You don't know us. You said it yourself. We could burden you. We could be villains."

Then Rashid laughs. A bright, beautiful thing that has me instinctively smiling in return. "Jury's still out on him." He points at Felix, but then chuckles again. "For real, though, two aliens show up in a ship on fire, looking as bad as you do, and then your ship sinks? Nah, you aren't villains. You're running *from* villains, right? I mean, who even says villains, like really?" He laughs again, running a hand over his tightly coiled hair. "I'm doing this because…" He stares at something in the distance. "Because my dad hasn't come home since my mom died and he was supposed to deliver her ashes to her family, and I'm tired of being alone all the time…and I get it. The need to hide from the world."

A beat of silence passes between us.

"How can we repay you? How can we help you?" I ask. The idea of this human, who just met us, taking us in, offering us shelter and safety out of the goodness of his heart is too much. Too easy. Too nice. People are never that nice and giving. Not without a price. "We have nothing."

"Let's just say you'll owe me one. And don't fuck up my house. Deal?"

"Deal." I smile as I fall into step beside him, though I'm unsure what *fuck* means. "I will find a way to repay you, though. I promise."

"Yeah, well. Maybe you can help me out in my summer class. Astronomy." When we stare at him, mouths drawn, he tilts his head to the side. "If anyone has the fuel for your ship, it's Mr. Gibston. He used to work for NASA, but now he teaches an extra science elective at summer school. Dude's super busy and sorta depressed like all the time, but I think I can sneak you into class tonight." When our brows furrow, he continues, "One of my classmates had to take their siblings with them and Mr. Gibston said it was fine to bring guests, as long as they aren't disruptive and they like school."

"School?" Felix's voice rises. "What do you mean school?"

"High school…" Rashid stops. "Don't you have school in space?"

Both Felix and I stop in our tracks. I don't like where this discussion is going. I've heard about school…in rich places like Maru. But Felix didn't have to go to something so public. Nobles get private tutors and stuff. Hali doesn't have school. We read outdated books to teach ourselves. I got lucky because I could just listen in on Felix's private lessons.

Either way, though, this is cause for concern. And what do we know about this Mr. Gibston?

Rashid's smile changes into something wicked. "Oh, this is going to be fun."

★ ★ ★

The Inkara Royal Palace of Maru

For Immediate Release

Royal Advisor Arren Sai, now Steward, has assumed control of the Monchuri Kingdom while authorities, including the Soleil, dig through the rubble on Beyla- and Hali-Monchuri.

Steward Sai and the Monchuri system are devastated by the violent murders of the royal family. He assures the public that during these difficult days ahead, he will do his utmost to maintain peace and stability within the kingdom, searching now not only for justice, but the rightful heir.

Updates to come.

CHAPTER 7
FELIX

Rashid lives in a house that's far too small. And far too blue.

As we stand outside, I try not to devolve into panic amidst these moments of uncertainty. I try, though I just want to go home where my parents are safe. I want to see them. I want... all of this to go back to normal. Except Joy.

The small blue house looms in front of us. Though it should be a reprieve after having walked through disgustingly tall dead grass that somehow had a damp surface, which seeped through my slippers. The walk was long and boring; we didn't see another human nor any extraordinary wildlife to break the monotony of yellow. Something hissed at one point and Rashid, the strange human that he is, insisted it was just a harmless water snake. Whatever that is.

I find him very suspicious for several reasons. His pants only fall to his knees and are strangely shiny. His shirt says something about cheerleading...which sounds like either an odd dictatorship or a cult that caused him physical harm. He called someone his *future boyfriend*, his father is gone, and he admitted that he's lonely to us, complete strangers. The only conclusion I can draw is that humans are nonsensical, making rash decisions such as taking two aliens into their home and offering aid.

Worst of all, we have no other options.

If Joy shares my doubts, though, she doesn't say. Her mind seems cautious but curious, and dreadfully quiet.

Her eyes go round and her jaw drops as she stares up at the human's house. As if she's never seen something so beautiful in her life. As if she's never seen the splendor of Maru. If I didn't know her better, I'd think she was lying.

Look how big and blue it is! What beauty. She's genuinely impressed. Compared to her tiny apartment that reaches epic temperatures during the day and has a view of hazy smog, this is grand.

It stands on stilts, has some sort of transport machinery on the ground floor, the white windows have flowers growing out of boxes, and water sparkles beyond the entire structure.

Neither the house nor the location, so close to water, is very practical. *Of course* we'd land somewhere unsafe. What if the water were to rise? How strong is the foundation? What will our accommodations be like? Damp like everything else on this planet thus far?

You're spoiled, she whispers in my mind.

Rashid climbs the rickety white steps to his home and then turns as he opens the front door, which is studded with the skins of unfortunate crustaceans—we have some similar creatures on the man-made coastal planets of Ara Kadia.

They shed their skin and find new ones within the silver sands. People collect them, and I suppose humans do, too, although I can't fathom why.

"Come in before the neighbors see you." He ushers us up and inside within seconds, shutting the door behind us.

The air is instantly cooler, and the sweat lingering at the nape of my neck begins to dry. I let out a sigh of relief. And then I look around.

The space is open and small. A massive sofa takes over half the room, and a large…screen of some sort sits across from it. To the left, there's a servant's kitchen—though I see no servants—with earthly produce sitting on the counter, stools beneath it, and beyond, a door leading out to the shimmering sea. It's quaint. There are five closed doors, which I imagine are tiny bedrooms and washrooms.

At least I hope they are.

We've spent too much time establishing that we aren't villains, but what if Rashid is one? What do we really know about humans?

Not a picture of his passed mother anywhere in sight, Joy says, peering around. *Perhaps he is merely grieving and lonely.* Her lips curve and brows rise.

Rashid smiles, opening one of the closed doors by the couch. Inside, there's a strange mechanical hum, and out bounds a tiny black four-legged animal.

"This is Chadwick," he says, scratching behind the animal's left ear. "He's a good boy, yes he is…"

I toss Joy a look, one that says, see, humans are ridiculous. She shakes her head and turns away from me. For whatever reason, I've upset her and I don't know how.

"What kind of animal is this?"

"Oh, right..." Rashid chuckles. "Right. Aliens." He puffs out air slowly. "It's a cat. A very good cat. My mom's cat."

Ah, the mom who died. I should say something nice. I know that's what Joy wants me to do, although death isn't an experience I understand. But then I just left my mother and father behind and I'm unsure if they're okay...or what will happen to them.

"I'm sorry," I say, my shredded silk slippers sliding on the tiles. "I cannot imagine your loss."

"Thanks." Rashid keeps running his hand across the cat. "It's only been a few months. I don't..." His voice trails off and no one attempts to fill in the gap.

I look to Joy for approval, and she nods once, though I sense she's still annoyed. I seemingly cannot make things right between us. What more am I supposed to do?

"Anyway." Rashid stands and the cat scampers over to Joy, rubbing its face against her legs.

Joy stills, an expression of terror crossing her features. I'm about to remind her not to let the creature lick or bite her as per the guide, but Rashid cuts me off.

"Let me find you some clothes. Are you hungry? There's food in the fridge. Make yourself at home."

"If it's not too much of a burden." Joy gives him a tight smile. "We don't wish to inconvenience your life."

"You're not, promise." And with that, he disappears into the room, the door shutting behind him. Joy and I stand alone, with the tiny cat, in a foreign home, on a foreign planet, half-clothed, and hungry, though unsure of what a fridge is and what constitutes as food here.

Joy bends down and tries to replicate the way Rashid behaved with the cat. It responds well, emitting a tiny motor-like sound from within its vocal cords, and Joy smiles.

"Don't let it lick or bite you. We don't know how it affects us...like the guide said."

"I like this creature," she says, ignoring me, her voice changing into something lower, as if speaking to a baby. "Yes, I do. I do, very much."

"It is one thing to emulate the human," I say with a shake of my head. "I wonder if humans believe they own these creatures but in actuality, the creatures own them?"

She shoots me a glare. "I can't believe I have to say this to you, of all people, but stop being so...uptight. You're even talking weird."

"Me? Uptight?" I whisper angrily in our own language. "We aren't even supposed to be here. We know nothing about Earth or humans. And yet here we are in some human's house, possibly staying with him until our ship's ready. And we have to go to *school*?" I shake my head, my hand thrusting out for hers.

Her hand feels warm and right in mine, and for the second time since we've met in person, something erratic tingles in the pit of my stomach. I don't know what it is. I love it. I hate it. I don't want it to end.

But it will. The moment we leave Earth and return to our own reality.

"Earth is foreign to us, Joy. This human...he may be kind and generous. But we don't know him. Our ship sank into that disgusting water and we don't know how to get it out... At first, I thought it was fine. Now..."

"I know you're scared. And you know I'm scared, too."

Joy steps closer to me and puts her head against mine as our hands fold between us. "But we're together…"

I close my eyes, relishing her smooth skin against mine. This is the safest I've felt all day.

"Do you trust me?" she asks, her voice small and sweet.

"Always," I answer as my breathing slows, my heartbeat matching hers like it has since we were born. This is new and bizarre. To be here with her in the same place. To have her tell me her thoughts instead of speaking through my mind. To hear her voice aloud in a foreign world.

"Rashid will help us. We will go to this…school and ask this Mr. Gibston for fuel. And then we'll go to Ocara. We'll contact Arren and find out what happened, explain the misunderstanding. We'll free your parents and go home."

I take a deep breath and let out a long exhale. "Then that's what we'll do."

"Good." She moves back, giving me a smile. "And until then, let's try to not have long conversations in our heads with our connection. We don't need it when we're in the same place, and we don't want to make the humans uncomfortable."

I furrow my brows. "They won't know or care, Joy."

"We don't need it."

"I need it." I step into the gap between us, just to be close again.

"Felix," she whispers. "I feel your emotions as strongly as I feel my own. That'll have to do for now."

"But how can we stop doing something we've done since we were born, Joy? We—"

Rashid shuts the door, startling us both. "Sorry to interrupt," he says, his hands full of items. "I've got some clothes, but you're both a bit tall so these will be awkward. If I had some cash, I'd buy you some."

"Whatever you have will help," Joy says, moving farther away from me. "And we have a currency replicator."

Rashid tilts his head, handing us both piles of garments. "What's that mean?"

"It means," I say, rifling through the same sort of shimmery shorts Rashid wears, and a worn shirt sporting a hole under the arm, "that we can buy our own clothes if we have a few pieces of your currency."

"Damn, y'all got capitalism in space?" His eyes light up. "How much can you make?"

Before Joy can answer, I cut in. "According to our guide, enough to blend in but not stand out."

His lips twitch. "So what you're saying is, you're not finna have a good time?"

"What I'm saying is, we'll pay for what we need, and no one will question our humanity…or lack thereof." I stand tall, making sure my words are understood.

"Damn, alright." Rashid shrugs. "Just saying, if you can replicate dollars, you could stay someplace better than this."

"This," Joy says with a smile, "is perfect. We are grateful for your hospitality."

"Okay…" Rashid quiets, scratching his head. "But if you got a money replicator, we should go to the mall. And grocery shopping before we go to cheer practice and then class. We haven't had fresh food in weeks. Dad got laid off after the pandemic, took off a few weeks ago and hasn't been back, and money's tight since the diner reduced my hours. I've just been eating frozen pizza."

I have no idea what that means, but buying necessities is something we should do as soon as possible. My eyes dart to Joy and she nods as she touches the produce on the counter, only to find that they are fake.

She attempts a smile. "We just need money."

Rashid fishes out a piece of green paper from his pocket and places it on the counter behind us. "Here's my last twenty, make all you want. We'll need gas, too. I'll explain prices and stuff in the car."

I turn the replicator over in my hands. This should be easy. And I'm properly motivated, even if we're only here for a few days till we can fix the ship. At least we'll have better... everything.

Joy's gaze meets mine, and already she's back in my head. *Are we sure we should be shopping when we could be figuring out a way to find comms here? Should we wait to meet this Mr. Gibston, or just track him down now? I don't like the idea of waiting...*

We must be patient and careful. We don't know this world, their technology, their culture... Shopping will help us learn about them. We can't rush this.

I hope you're right.

I don't say that I hope so, too. But if the ship needs to repair itself, we need to be patient anyway. And this could be a moment to slow down before the next storm.

Rashid shows Joy where the washroom is so she can change. Once she's out of the room, he bumps my shoulder.

"So what's the deal with you two? Brother and sister or something else?"

The words sit in my throat, unable to move. *Something else.* Something so much more than what a human could comprehend. Something I can't tell Joy, something I can barely admit to myself.

I ignore the question. "What are these clothes?" My fingers touch the material, and yet I don't understand what they could be made from that would leave them so shiny and strange.

"…shorts, a T-shirt, some clean boxers if you need them, and socks?"

"I don't like them," I say at once, turning them over in my hands.

"Well, sorry to disappoint you." He huffs, and I know I'm being rude, but I can only handle so many terrible things in one day. "You can buy new stuff then, but you should probably wear them till we go shopping, feel me? People don't walk around in silk whatever-it-is-you're-wearing around here."

"Because they lack taste," I mumble under my breath. "There's a difference between fitting in and ill-fitting."

"And you called me dramatic." Rashid chuckles, heading back to his room. "Get dressed and we'll go."

As I step out of my pants and slide into these scratchy shorts, I can't help but think this is just the beginning of a bad trip. My parents are imprisoned, or worse—no, I can't believe that—and Joy and I are wanted for murder. Monchuri must be a mess.

And here we are, stuck on this strange planet, about to have a bit of shopping levity—which admittedly may improve my mood as my entire life falls apart.

★ ★ ★

Six Years Ago

FELIX

Our home is cold and I'm hungry. I can't decide if I should sneak into the kitchen for a second helping of dessert or if I should just wait for sleep to find me.

The former sounds better.

I wonder what Mom would say and then I remember she's not here.

Mom and Dad left for a business trip two weeks ago and commed this morning to say they won't be home for another three weeks. That's the fourth time this year they've been gone for months without me. Idu says this is normal for kids of diplomatic parents, but that's not true. Other diplomats' kids go with their parents, call it hands-on learning. When I mentioned this to them, they said I needed stability to focus on my studies. That I'm already falling behind my peers—which isn't true; Joy helps me study. She won't let me rest until my grades are fine. Probably because she loves learning through our connection, and she likes being the best.

Anyway, the way I figure it, if they can't tell me the truth, they don't deserve my *adhering to a healthy balanced diet* while they're away, either.

I swing my legs over the side of the bed and creep out of my room. The halls are even colder. It's like the staff turn off the heat when my parents aren't here to save energy—though we don't need to. My bare feet pad onto the warm tiles of the servant's kitchen as I follow the scent of the cabva cake—spicy, citrus honey cakes that are sticky perfection—I had earlier. My fingers graze the edge of a shelf along the back when I hear Idu's dulcet tones.

After a few soft steps into the shadows of the shelves stuffed full with the prepped ingredients for the next day and the leftovers from the evening, I stop. On my tiptoes, I peek through two pans of the sticky, flaky cabva cakes, the scent drifting up my nostrils and making my stomach rumble.

Idu and a few other maids sit at the kitchen table, swathed in the light from the ovens. They're drinking something red from our fancy glasses Mom says we aren't allowed to use, and smoking something that's a lot stronger than Dad's secret stash of ciggys, while sitting at the kitchen table.

"We have to keep it down. The boy's tutor comes into the kitchen at night and we don't need her in here," Idu says, shaking off her laughter.

"Why do they leave the poor thing here?" one of them asks, slurping from their glass tumbler.

"King Jevor's concerned about his Kindred." Idu sets her glass down hard, the red liquid sloshing out onto the wooden table. She whispers it harshly, as if speaking the truth aloud is a crime. "He thinks if she's privy to Qadin politics, she'll tell the wrong people on Hali, might stir up another revolution. It's dangerous."

"Why don't they just break the connection? Is that even possible?" one of the maids asks, though I don't know which one.

"They'd have to have an operation that could damage the poor boy." Idu's quiet for a moment. "The only other way to break the connection is if one of them dies. They'd have to kill her."

Someone sharply inhales. "They wouldn't do that. Not to a child."

"Oh, yes, they would. King Jevor has considered it more than once. Advisor Arren suggested there's a gentler way, but Duke and Duchess Hamdi refused. They say it'll scar Felix for life. Her Grace said it wasn't a solution. King Jevor said it would have to be if they crossed the lines of impropriety. If the boy falls in love with her and is unable to keep their lives and politics separate, she will have to be eliminated."

There are shocked gasps, including my own, which I muffle under my hand. They would kill Joy? Because I love her? No. They wouldn't do that. Mom wouldn't allow them to do that.

Would she?

"King Jevor said he'd send Arren to make sure that they never form an attachment stronger than Kindreds."

"How can they even do that?"

"They have their ways," Idu says, and then there's silence. "Arren's a loyal hound, and he'll do whatever the King asks."

That's when I decide to run. I run back to my room, down dark glittery hallways embossed with intricate golden designs that are meaningless shows of wealth. My legs feel wobbly, and my breathing is rushed. I can't make sense of everything I've heard. Or maybe I can and that's why my heart is breaking.

Once I'm back in my room, I shut my eyes, gulping air, just as Joy awakes in my mind.

She yawns. Her voice is full of sleep and as soft as my silk pillows. For the first time in my life, her presence sends a pang of panic in my gut. "Why are you awake?"

"Couldn't sleep," I squeak, gingerly shutting the door behind me. "I was hungry."

"But you aren't eating anything." Joy's lying on her couch, concern in her half-lidded eyes. "What's wrong?"

"Nothing." I climb into my bed, my heart hammering against my chest. "Go back to sleep."

"You aren't telling me something." Now she's fully awake, hands on her hips. "You always tell me your secrets."

I pull the covers over myself, my hands trembling. "There's nothing wrong. I just miss my parents. Gets scary in this big house alone."

She sighs, her arm falling to the side of the couch. "I know you get lonely, but I'm always here for you. Always." She gives me that big silly smile of hers that's cheesy and shows all her teeth. The one that makes me happy…that always lifts my spirits even when I'm at my lowest.

"Like that helps," I lie, adding an edge to my tone that'll make her hate me. "You're just my loser Kindred. You're a mistake. I should have been paired with someone smarter and funnier and who could help me understand what it means to be noble so I wouldn't disappoint my mother so much. I shouldn't have been paired with some poor girl from a poor planet."

"Felix." Her voice cracks with hurt. "Why are you saying this?"

My fingernails dig into the palms of my hands under the blanket. "Because you telling me that you'll always be here for me means nothing. I wish you were somebody else. I wish I never got stuck with you."

Joy sniffs, her eyes averted. "I'm sorry you feel that way."

My anger seeps into my words, aimed at Joy when it should be aimed at everyone but her. *Anyone* but her. "I hate you."

"I…" Her form flickers once and then she's gone. Closed her eyes and closed her world off to me. I feel her pain, her confusion, her anger. They spiral around in her like a storm, all because of me.

And I hate myself. And I hate my mom for letting King Jevor threaten to kill Joy if I love her. And I hate that I know in my heart that I love Joy more than I love them or even myself. She's sunshine and smiles and beautiful and smarter than anyone I know.

I'll apologize later for what I did, but she'll remember this. It will sit between us like a wedge and nothing will change it. It has to be that way. I'll have to make her hate me a little. So that we both can live.

Because if anything happens to her, it will be the death of me.

CHAPTER 8
JOY

"WEARING OUR SUNDAY BEST ON A MONDAY, CUZ
AIN'T NOTHING PROMISED ON TUESDAY."
—*DEJA REESE, "LIVE YOUR BEST"*

Felix figured out the currency replicator, and now, according to Rashid, we're somewhat rich. Which means I'm already living a better life on Earth than back home. Mum would be jealous... I clear my head of the path that thought could lead down.

No, we're shopping, and I want to buy a pretty dress—if I could just find one my size.

"Why did that salesperson say I needed to get clothes for 'plus-size' girls?" I ask Rashid, carrying three bags full of shoes, sunglasses, and pretty trinkets that serve no purpose at all, but I love them. Like Felix, I've learned that I, too, like to buy things I don't need when stressed and worried about being blamed for royal murders, and his parents...

"She meant that you have to get bigger clothes, like me. Don't worry. There's some good shops. I'll show you." Rashid winks my way. He's walking along when I stop at a window filled with screens, all ranging in sizes from large to gigantic. They must need electricity to run, like how old Hali tech used to run before The Second Chaos. Now everything's powered through stardust, which is more sustainable and cheaper. I bet electricity costs a fortune.

On one of the screens, there are people who look like me and Rashid, rubbing their eyes, screaming fearfully.

"…Protesters were tear-gassed and pushed out of the path for the President's upcoming photo op… Several were injured and hospitalized after officers are seen brutalizing the, by all accounts, peaceful crowds."

And on the next screen there are people in headscarves like in Maru-Monchuri, covering their faces and crying. People who look just like Felix. A message across the screen reads Refugees.

Before I can understand what's happening to them, Felix struts out of a store with one oversized paper bag and a brand-new outfit stretched beautifully across his body. And just like that, the thoughts about human news fly from my mind. He smiles as he shoves Rashid's clothes into a trash can.

"Hey!" Rashid cries, lunging forward. "Don't throw away perfectly good clothes."

"They've expired and look impervious to cleaning." Felix catches his hand and shakes his head. "And if you want your future boyfriend to be your present boyfriend, then you've got to put in some effort. Like these… These are proper clothes." He waves his arm up and down. His pants are dark blue and fitted. They look both thick and like a second skin. His white shirt, also very fitted, has two open buttons on the top and the sleeves rolled up to his elbows. His unbrushed black hair flutters off to the side as if there's some magical wind machine focused entirely on him. Humans stride past, their eyes roving over him hungrily. One even mouths, *Oh, my God*, to their companion.

Felix Hamdi has arrived on Earth, and this can't be good for humans.

"How much money did you spend?" Rashid eyes him with the same appreciation.

"What is money when you feel confident in yourself and your outward appearance?" Felix cocks an eyebrow. Though there's humor in his countenance, there's still panic circling his head. He's trying so hard to stay calm, to have fun. Most likely for my benefit.

Rashid mashes his lips together. "That's some rich people shit."

"Yep," I agree, shaking my head. "He's never lived without currency. Never had a job. Never—"

"You're being very judgmental." Felix taps his new black shoes on the tiles. "We have money now, so we should use it wisely."

Rashid tuts. "I thought you said you'll only use enough to blend in, not stand out. You're standing out."

Felix's brows furrow. "If I stand out, it's because I look good. And now it's your turn, both of you." His gaze travels over our same shorts and shirts and rubber shoes.

Rashid looks down at his raggedy sheltered feet. "I can't

look the way you look. My body wasn't made to look like a supermodel. More like an oversized potato."

I stifle a chuckle, though I'm not sure what a potato is. "Maxon called me round, so…"

We will not utter that name on this planet. For a moment, we can be just Felix and Joy, Felix's voice whispers in my mind. He fixes us with an infuriatingly beautiful smile. "That's nonsense. You are both extremely lucky to have me. After this, I want no more of your judgment—" he points to me "—or drama," he says to Rashid.

An hour later, I'm in a mint dress that brings out the darkness of my skin and makes me feel better than I've felt in ages. Felix picked it out. He's a professional at shopping and at accentuating his natural good looks. I always thought that since he has a personal tailor at home to make his clothes, stores were beneath him and his ilk. Yet, it seems he has been waiting for this chance to spend more money, live lavishly, and find variety. If only to distract us.

Because of him, though, my arms are laden with bags full of things I can't wait to wear. He not only found the shops for "curvy" girls like me; he went through each rack, each dress, making me laugh the entire time. The shopkeepers were smitten as he held up swaths of clothing to my face and said, "Perfect." As if I'm perfect to him.

I know we won't be here long, that this is just a pit stop on the way to Ocara, but I'm happy. This is an adventure like one of the many books I've read and dreamed about. And here, I'm not Maxon's betrothed. I'm not poor and working to support Mum and myself. I'm not Felix's sidekick or voice of reason. I'm his Kindred.

Rashid waves hello at someone who passes us by, startling me from my thoughts. He seems so unlike when we first met him. He's wearing actual pants, and a shirt that says *Star Wars*, which sounds scary and fun from his quick description. And he even got his hair trimmed. Felix had his done as well, but the stylist said she didn't want to change much and ended up cutting maybe three strands.

A beautiful Black woman named Bernice looked at my hair and said I *needed* a big chop. She cut my curls down to my ears, now studded with dangly metal accessories called earrings—which hurt a little, if I'm honest—and then bunched them up and put a little flower on the side. For the first time, my face is more visible, my curls full of life, my skin more radiant, and my smile wider. She gave me products to maintain it, too. Such things exist on Hali, but only for exorbitant costs none of us can afford. Most have never had their hair cut professionally before; I never had. Mum cuts my hair over the trash, and it's never truly straight but she tries.

Bernice treated me as kindly as Mum and the Hali elders, and I think this may be a part of their culture. Or "our" Black culture, as she stated. She gave me her cellular number—which I took, though I don't know what to do with it—and something called a Tweeter handle, and told me to get in touch if I needed anything. Humans are kind, I think. A pleasant distraction.

I will miss this place.

Felix keeps eyeing me over his frothy drink in a plastic container.

Beautiful Joy, his thoughts repeat. And I find myself trying to stop blushing. We agreed—well, I said that we shouldn't use our connection, and here I am, listening in as always. I shake my head and slurp my own drink. I got a *smoothie* with fruits called strawberries and coconut. With new outfits and attitudes, I can't help but look at this like a temporary vacation from everything.

If only...

If only we knew whether Felix's parents are okay. He replays the image of his mom falling, his father telling him to run. In his heart, he knows they're alive, but in his mind... he can't help but feel they may not be for much longer if he doesn't negotiate soon.

Mum must be panicking. Felix spoke with Danio and Mum's probably with her, but what if something went wrong?

Oh, Gods.

That's when I begin to feel sick to my stomach. I spent hours—we spent hours—enjoying ourselves, playing dress-up and spending money while our parents could be in pain, worried, pacing their homes, not knowing where we are. The world around me blurs and I look at the only thing that's ever in my focus.

Felix.

The color drains from his face. Guilt swims in the pit of my stomach as I realize I've soured his mood, too.

"Joy," he says quietly. "No."

"I'm sorry." I stop, putting my head against his shoulder. "But what if they think we're dead?"

His confidence cuts through my panic. "Then they're safe."

"And if the...the Soleil think we're alive?"

He lets out a long exhale, his chest expanding against mine. His shirt shows every muscle, every detail. I avert my gaze.

"Then they'll be looking for us, and they'll use our parents as bait. Either way, they're safe."

"You really believe that?" The words tumble out of my mouth quietly. Back home, I wouldn't have to ask. I would just know. But here… I don't know. His expression is different in real life, his body warmer, his emotions a jumble the closer I am. He's the person I know better than anyone and yet the biggest mystery to me in this moment.

"I do." He nudges my head back to stare into my eyes. "There's nothing we can do at this moment to save our home. If there was, we would've done it. You know that." His chin dips, his eyes landing on my lips in thought. "Right now, we're allowed to just…be."

Feelings I can't understand swarm Felix's mind. Even in our closeness, I can't read him like a book, though if he were one, I'd have read him twice. "Are you sure you're okay?"

The corner of his lips quirk. "I'm okay as long as you're with me."

I find myself smiling in return. "What would you do without me?" I've asked him this since we were kids. Sure, Felix has acquaintances, but no friends. Although people flock to him, he's not a people person. I am, despite the lack of opportunity. If it weren't for me, I don't know how Felix would navigate his world. How he'd manage his loneliness outside of his several lovers.

He only touches the strap of my dress with his free hand, his soft fingers tracing the imprint in my skin, featherlight. "What would you do without me?"

I gasp softly. A million feelings flood my brain and wash over my body. I find myself leaning into his touch, despite knowing this isn't allowed. He doesn't care about me like that. He's desperate to change the subject, to not be consumed by guilt and worry. But then why do I want to believe this is real? Why do I like the way he touches me?

The corners of his lips lift, and his gaze intensifies briefly before he pulls away. "It's very easy to goad you, Joy."

I smack him, stifling the hot blush that creeps up my cheeks. "You're a mess."

"It's weird being here with you in person, touching you like this. When all of this is straightened out, we'll go home, go back to normal and—"

"I'll continue my engagement to Maxon," I cut in, stepping back from him. "All will be as it should be."

That earns me another smile that causes flutters in the pit of my stomach. "You know, what if—"

"Hey, Rashid." Some blonde with blue eyes and a shirt that matches the one Felix just threw away strides up with a bevy of similar-featured companions. Felix and I shift apart. "Didn't expect to see you here!" The friends chat amongst themselves, giving us friendly glances. "And holy shit, you look incredible. Did you raid Hollister or something?" the blonde says and the friends laugh along playfully.

"Hey." Rashid's voice takes on a strangely high-pitched, cheery tone. "How are you, Sarah? Brittney, Kate, and Tara?"

"We're good," Sarah answers for them. Then her voice falls, some emotion swimming in her gaze as she steps closer to him. "Um…how are you doing, though? Are you…okay? Is your dad back? You know you can always talk to me, right?"

"Yup." Rashid glances off, and I wonder if he really is okay. Sarah doesn't linger on his dismissive answer, adding a little more excitement into her words. "'Bout to meet up with Johnny and Beck before practice."

"Uh...cool." Rashid steps back toward us, nearly dropping his bags. I see the word *cool* doesn't mean cold, but rather nice. I make a mental note of it.

"Who are your friends?" Sarah asks, tossing her hair to the side. Her blue eyes glue to Felix. "Haven't seen you around before." Her lips twist, and she runs a hand down her bright pink skirt.

Felix smirks, just for the fun of it. Goodness knows that if he's flirting with me, he's in need of further distraction.

"This is um, an exchange student, Felix—he'll be coming here in the fall and wanted to check out the area. And this is my cousin, Joy." Rashid shrugs. The lies coming off his tongue are quite convincing.

"I didn't know they named boys Felix in like...what, Pakistan or something?" Tara, the beautiful red-haired girl, says flippantly to either Brittney or Kate.

"Does he speak English?" Brittney or Kate asks.

"Oh, my God, Tara, you can't judge a person's name by their ethnicity. That's super racist." Sarah shoots a look over to Tara, whose cheeks suddenly match her hair.

"I speak English," Felix says, nibbling his bottom lip. He's such a show-off.

"Oh...um, cool." Sarah seems stunned, eyes wide, mouth open. Felix Hamdi is going to ruin these poor humans—all because he can and it brings him fun, not because he cares. Again, he's the absolute worst, which I leak out of my mind into his, earning a light chuckle from him.

I step away, enjoying the lack of attention. No one seems

to care about me. It's like I don't exist. It's like being home in Hali...nonexistent. I don't matter, not to the rest of Monchuri anyway, except for Felix.

Sarah straightens. "You should hang out with us. We can show you around and everything. Are you visiting the Keys for the summer? Oh, my God, you're going to love it. Is he coming to astronomy class tonight? Or cheer? We have full-day practices for the tournament at the end of August."

"Yeah, he'll be there," Rashid answers, running his hand over his fade. "Anyway, we should get going..."

"Oh, really? Johnny would love to see you." Sarah's tone changes, something sneaky edging into her words. There's a sparkle in her countenance, and her body is rigid, posing awkwardly. She wants something. And to my own absolute surprise, I'm impressed with my newfound ability to read human nonverbal cues. By the end of all this, I'll be an expert on humans. Maybe I'll write a book about it. A children's book... And it'll include human food. Like these delicious shakes but also something called *cookies*, which I desperately want. Dammit, the hunger has come back with a vengeance. "I'd love to show you around, Felix. I'm sure you'll want to meet everyone."

There it is. Felix. The bane of my existence. The reason I'm standing here ignored, annoyed, and famished.

"We really should be leaving." I step in, nudging my shoulder against Felix's. "But we can't wait to spend time with you all later. Nice to meet you, Sarah." We don't have time for this. I'm hungry, I'm tired, and our parents are galaxies away. We're accused of murder. We had our fun for the past few hours as the ship repairs itself, and now all we need is fuel.

"Oh, okay." Her lips pout, and her eyes glue to my contact with Felix.

Humor rattles around Felix's mind. Rashid tosses me a look that I'm sure proves we're cousins to the other humans.

"Nice to meet you all." I smile. "And I love that bag," which I honestly mean. Sarah's face brightens and with that, I drag the two of them back toward the outdated human transport. I polish off the last of the drink and toss it in a garbage can.

"I see your patience is wearing thin…" Felix laughs, gently placing his bags in the back seat of the transport. "Are you hungry? You know how you get…"

I give him a side-eye. "We have priorities."

He purses his lips. "Joy, I haven't—"

"What's that?" Rashid's eyes widen, his hands clapping over his ears. "Is that…you?"

Felix and I turn, our gazes meeting as a tiny high-pitched squeal begins to ring in our ears.

"Ferk," Felix shouts over the crowds of people dropping items, screaming and shouting. Panic emanates off him in waves and sinks into the pit of my stomach. The humans clasp their ears, some falling and rolling on the ground.

It must affect them more than us. And that's a problem.

I stare at Felix. "What is it?"

"Seeker," he answers, his breathing shallow. "I knew they'd do this, even the guide said to expect it, but I thought we'd have more time. It sends radio waves through the body to determine origin species. Obviously to the humans, it's intrusive, but for us, the waves bounce back."

"Felix. I— How far away is it? What do—"

Felix runs a hand through his feathery hair. "They must be broadcasting through systems in waves to find us."

I grip my bags tighter, as if that sound threatens to take them away. To take me away. To take this temporary peace we've found away from home. "What do we do?"

"We need to…" Felix lets out a long exhale. "We need to disable it."

My jaw drops, and the feeling of terror swims around the pit in my stomach. "But how?"

"It's looking for our ship. It's looking for us. And I think…" He trails off, and his thoughts of the manual stream through my mind. "I think our ship has a way to stop the signal."

★ ★ ★

MONCHURI MORNING NEWS NOW!

Transcript featuring L'avi Jonu and Nyla Harkibi
of *Good Morning Monchuri*, filmed in front of a
live studio audience in Maru-Monchuri

LJ: Now in Breaking News, Seekers have broadcasted across the universe to find escaped murderer, Duke Felix Hamdi. His parents have been remanded to custody until their son comes forward.

NH: This is just…unbelievable, unprecedented, really, that we reported his birth and now we're reporting the death of his victims, our esteemed royal family, the Qadins *(voice cracks)*.

LJ: I… I'm devastated. We all are. But is there proof? These are two seventeen-year-old kids. It seems so unlikely they were able to not only conspire against the Qadins, but also succeed in assassinating them.

NH: What we know is that Felix Hamdi was next in

line for the throne, thus he had the motive to have the Qadins killed. Officials from the Soleil state that they found an upload chip within the Duke's belongings detailing how he met with—and paid—assassins on Outpost 32 to hack the royal cruisers and cause them to crash. Several witnesses attest to seeing Duke Hamdi at the outpost, though they cannot confirm whom the young Duke met. There's also a strong possibility that Felix's Kindred, Joy Abara, helped plan and coordinate these attacks. This would not be the first time a Halin attempted a coup or revolution.

LJ: That could explain why the second ship was shot down over her home of Hali-Monchuri. The death toll there is…beyond compare. An already impoverished world struck now by insurmountable tragedy.

NH: I know. Just terrible, especially since Joy may have manipulated the impressionable Felix. *He* showed only goodwill toward our people. But as a member of the lower class, Joy had everything to gain by Felix's elevated rank. We knew their pairing was disastrous from the beginning, but no one could have imagined *this*.

LJ: And she's missing as well, right now, casting more suspicion on them both. She is believed to have fled the system with Felix.

NH: Is that why Royal Advisor—now Steward—Arren Sai is searching for them?

LJ: Steward Sai issued a statement just a few hours ago. Let me read it… "As we mourn the loss of our beloved royals, let it be known that I do not believe Duke Felix Hamdi, nor his Kindred, Joy Abara, are responsible. These are two very scared youths, who felt as if they had no choice but to flee their homes from these horrendous accusations. He had no idea he was the heir to the throne until the Qadins were murdered, and undoubtedly believed he and his Kindred are in danger of befalling the same fate. Therefore, I've allowed the Soleil to broadcast Seekers through each and every galaxy to locate our Duke and bring him home."

NH: What do you think about that, LJ?

LJ: I think Steward Sai genuinely cares for the Duke and wants to see justice. But we don't know Arren. He's not our King. He's not the Soleil, who worked exclusively for the Qadins for centuries. So I tend to believe the Soleil more, if only because they said they found proof and they are more motivated to find justice for our rulers. But I guess we won't know anything until the Seekers give us a location and we're able to know the truth.

NH: Do the Seekers have any particular destinations where they could be hiding and where citizens should avoid?

LJ: As of now, we know they haven't traveled to any of our allies. It's likely they went to systems or planets that are infantile in their technological capabilities or are diplomatically neutral, such as Ocara, XiGra, and Andarra.

NH: And Joy's parents, are they in custody, as well?

LJ: Joy's mother sent in an encrypted message proclaiming her daughter's innocence, but has left her home. Authorities are currently looking for her, and if you, our viewers, have any information about her whereabouts, please contact the Soleil. Their comm-wave will be broadcast below, system-wide.

NH: And…we're just getting word that the Soleil, on their own volition, have authorized a holo-vised hunt for the first time in Monchuri history. If you have a ship and wish to partake in a universal search, you are invited to do so by the Soleil and should contact our station to be entered. But it should be mentioned that Felix Hamdi and Joy Abara are considered armed and dangerous, and could have accomplices. A reward of… Am I reading this right?

LJ: *(inaudible)* I… Yes, you are.

NH: An award of five…five billion melios will go to those who are able to capture the murderous king-to-be and his Kindred.

LJ: And it's very important, as per Arren and the Soleil, that they are brought in alive.

CHAPTER 9
FELIX

As Rashid stands there along with the other humans, clutching his ears and staring up at the sky in confusion, Joy throws her bags into the back seat. She's not talking, but fear rolls off her in waves. She doesn't know what I plan to do, or if I know what I'm doing.

Frankly, neither do I.

"How long does it last?"

"As long as it takes to find us." I walk around the transport and tug on Rashid's sleeve. "Might I pilot this vehicle?"

His brows furrow, his voice as high as the radio wave signal. "Do...you...even...know...how?"

I try not to let disdain edge into my words. "I piloted a ship here, I believe I can *drive* an outdated human transport. You just use that wheel and press those pedals and go, yes?"

Rashid hands me the keys and I give a short nod of my

head to Joy. She shuffles Rashid into the back seat among all the bags, closes the door, and slides in beside me.

"How are we going to do this?"

I bite the inside of my cheek, thinking. "We need to get inside the ship. It said—"

Joy closes her eyes, mind whirring. "We can disable all Seeker tracking in case of emergency using your familial code? But what exactly does that mean? And how do you know so much about Seekers?"

"It's how they track celebrities." I shrug as I begin the transport's transmission and the engine revs to life. It's very old and clearly has mechanical issues as the sound it makes is anything but smooth, and unnaturally loud. I move the stick in the console as I'd seen Rashid do, into the *R*, which I think means "ride," and ease my foot on the gas pedal. It's like piloting one of those ancient speeders on Beyla-Monchuri.

We're all startled when we shoot backward, nearly hitting a parked transport.

"Not to worry, just testing," I lie. Joy smooshes her lips together, holding tight to her buckled belt.

Please… Be…careful, she says through our connection. It's a bit distorted, perhaps by the Seeker, but her voice is always welcome.

I move the stick into *D*, for "direct" I imagine, and then swivel the car around, avoiding the humans cowering. Thankfully, Joy's mind is open to me, even if she's hesitant. The streets are in her brain—she pays attention to nearly everything. And always has an escape plan.

I understand why. While my family name keeps me from danger in Monchuri, Joy's dark skin and gender often put her in an uncertain state of peril back home. She's always prepared to run, hide, fight, and fear.

"Hey! You have to drive on the right side of the road!" Rashid cringes as his voice pierces my ears like a siren.

"Yes, yes," I mutter. Most transports have been strewn across the road, their drivers bent over the steering wheels, clutching their ears. The Seeker can't last much longer. I think. I hope.

"Does it hurt?" Joy's gaze darts to Rashid. There's a quiet to the world around us while the humans suffer. We're the only ones on the road, racing to an alien ship embedded in their marshy wasteland. We're fine. I think. I hope.

"Yes," Rashid answers from the back seat. In the mirror attached to the roof of the transport, I glance back to see a trickle of red liquid—blood, I think—dripping from his ears.

The Seeker is slowly killing them, their bodies are too fragile for this. We've got to stop it.

"Joy." We take a road that has a sign reading Rocky Apple Key before coming to an fork in the empty road, and I don't know which way to go.

Left, she answers with her mind, panic rising in her words. *The water will be on the left.*

We'll save them. Only a few minutes.

Please, is all she says. Joy's tender heart is going to break if a single human dies while we're here. Mine will be filled with anger. The Soleil have locked up my parents, maybe they even killed the Qadins, shot our ship down over this… place, probably are pulling Arren like a string, and now they're going to harm humans just to cover up their crimes? Nothing about this is fair.

I direct the transport through a field of tall grass, the one I recall walking through upon arrival. The transport bumps and groans.

"You can't just drive through a field!" Rashid's got one eye cocked open, his face is pale, and he's slumped over in the back. Still, he just has to bother me.

"Shush, human," I call back to him. I sneak a peek at Joy.

"There. The ship's there—I remember that weird floppy tree." She points through the grass at the abnormal tree. "Stop the transport!"

I twist the keys and the engine dies. We unbuckle our belts and bolt from the car into the marshy soft land. There's nary a sign of our ship, not a dent in the land, not rising bubbles on the surface to tell us where it was.

Still, Joy kicks off her shoes as I tug at the buttons on my brand-new shirt and toss it into the grass. With a small look at each other, we wade into the water. My hand reaches out to hers, just for a squeeze, just to tell her I'm with her, that we'll do this, that we're okay as long as we have each other... and then the water comes up to our necks, and we dive below.

The water is murky and full of small creatures.

Fish, Joy says.

How do you know everything? I mutter. Indigo, I am lucky she's mine. My Kindred.

Here, she says. The hatch has closed and the moment her fingers touch the edge of our ship, a blue light begins blinking. *It won't open.*

I swim closer, placing my palm against the smooth metal. The blue light solidifies, and a bubble of oxygen forms as the hatch slides open. I reach out and yank Joy into the bubble with me, inhaling greedily as the water inside the ship gets sucked out through holes I hadn't seen before on the bottom of the walls.

"Welcome, Hamdi. Oxygen level restored." The AI's voice is sultry once more.

"Thank the *Gods*, she works again. That means the ship's repairing itself well, right?" Joy wonders aloud, and I wish I had an answer.

Our feet find purchase on the ship's floor. It's completely dry. And though the scorch marks remain from the sparks and the impacted wires, the console is still intact. The lights still flicker, and there's still a bit of damage around the thrusters, but it's not on fire and that's good.

"Disable Seeker tracking," I command quickly.

"That function requires a familial code and restarting the system. Proceed?" A sleek black panel emerges from the console and sits there, waiting for…something.

"But what does that even mean?" Joy grips the thrusters hard, staring at it. "We don't have time."

Water drips down my chest and I catch Joy looking before she turns away.

Put your hand on the panel? she asks, her energy bouncing all over the place. Panic rolls off her in waves.

I touch my hand to the panel and wait. Nothing happens, though my hand does feel colder.

"That function requires a familial code," the AI repeats.

"I don't have a ferking code. I don't—"

Joy blows out a steady stream of air. "If you had a Seeker on you, which you do, and you needed to stop it in case of an emergency, which this is…you'd need your DNA or something. That holds your familial code, right?"

"But I'm adopted. I don't have the Hamdi familial DNA or whatever." I furrow my brows, my foot tapping, hand shaking.

"Yes, but no doubt, they had this ship waiting for you, just in case this happened. It never said it had to be Hamdi." And before I can think of how she figured that out, she takes my hand in hers, staring deeply into my eyes. "Trust me?"

Always.

She moves quickly, and rips a piece of hair from my head. We both cringe and I know, in that moment, that she feels what I feel. How did I never know that before? Because she's never really gotten hurt. But if she feels what I feel—is it only pain? What if…

Felix. The panel.

I take the hair from her grip and place it on the screen. The screen shifts into tiny metal pieces and the strand sinks in, disappearing. The panel lights up.

"Qadin familial code accepted. Seeker tracking will be unable to locate FELIX HAMDI QADIN on planet Terra, Milky Way system."

"Repeat process with Kindred, Joy Abara," I demand of the AI. The screen shifts again and I gently pluck a hair from her scalp, touching the silky soft coils with my fingers. Touching her hair feels intimate and strange and I don't really want to stop. But I have to. I place her hair on the screen and it disappears again.

"Congratulations. Felix Hamdi Qadin and Joy Abara are now untraceable." The AI's voice is nearly a purr, yet neither of us care.

We both let out a sigh of relief and glance at each other. And then the information sinks in. Her eyes narrow.

"Qadin?"

"My mom mentioned something about it but…" is all I can say. I'm related to them somehow, which is why I'm an heir. Which is why I'm accused of murder and being hunted?

Joy drops the subject for now, though we both know it'll haunt us later. "So…the humans won't have that ringing in their ears now? They're safe?"

"The Seeker will stop broadcasting on Terra now that it doesn't get any ping-backs from us. The humans should be fine—I think. I don't know…" I exhale slowly. "Problem is, the Soleil will know we're here in the Milky Way. The Seeker was on too long."

"So our time is running out." Joy's shoulders slump as she tilts her head to the side. The movement draws my eyes to her shoulder, to the strappy dress stuck to her skin and down to the fabric clinging to her body, her chest. Something warms in the pit of my stomach.

I've seen Joy naked before now, although not since we agreed to give each other privacy. Still, I know her body as well as I know my own. I know every single line in the palm of her hand, every mole that dots her back. And she's not naked, not now. And yet, this time…it's different.

Everything about *us* is different here.

Her cheeks flush, and if she knows what I was thinking, she doesn't say. Instead, her thoughts are confident that I could never be interested in her, that when I'm lonely, she's the easiest cure.

She doesn't know all my secrets.

I'm beginning to understand something about Joy I hadn't known in our seventeen years together. She's been holding back. Not just her thoughts, but her feelings, emotions, physical reactions. Kindreds can do that; I do that sometimes for very specific reasons, but why has she?

She doesn't let me speculate anymore. "We should find out the extent of the damage to the ship and how long it needs to repair, find out what kind of fuel we need, and then go back up to Rashid. He's got to be terrified. All the humans must be. Their leaders may investigate, maybe even track it here to us, to our ship. They might—"

"Joy, this planet doesn't have the technology or knowledge or capabilities to understand what just happened. I mean, they didn't even see our ship crash. No one has come here and it's been hours." I interrupt her panic. "But we do need to hurry up and get out of here."

Her eyes round as she smooths back her wet curls. "The Soleil are coming, aren't they? They'll find us here." *They're going to kill us.* There's no more panic, only resignation, as if she always expected this.

No, I answer, pulling her into a hug. "They may know we're here, but they don't know *where* yet. We disappeared. It may not take them long, but it'll give us enough time to go."

She pulls back to look into my eyes, concern threading her brows. Her mind screams a million questions and thoughts, all too many for me to focus on. I settle for the answer both of us want to hear.

"They won't find us. They'll send the Soleil, but they won't succeed. Now that they think we're in the Milky Way, they won't even consider Ocara. We just planted a false lead." My hands run down her cold arms, and there goes that weird, flippy feeling in my stomach again. Oh, why does that feel so good? Why does she feel so good? She lets me hold her, for which I'm especially grateful. "But we have to hurry up and get fuel."

★ ★ ★

Nine Years Ago

JOY

"Do you know why you're here, Joy Abara?"

I straighten my back against the rigid chair, my feet dangling beneath the white table. My mandatory checkup to test my intelligence and usefulness to our system isn't going well. "To a-a-affirm my loyalty to the Monchuri Kingdom and our es-esteemed King Jevor."

"Yes, this is correct." The adjudicator, Arren, purses his lips, his golden eyes staring down at me with disgust. I'm used to the expression by now, especially when everyone outside of Hali looks at me this way when they stop through to "aid" our poverty. It's like my dark skin, curly hair, and worn clothing personally offends their sensibilities. "But this time, we have a new objective for you."

I try not to let my surprise show. We do these checkups three times a year in this white room with white furnishings and white walls without fail. A missed appointment is punishable by law. My mother isn't allowed to come in the room. Normally, by now, I'd have been given an examination. But nothing about today seems normal.

The adjudicator bends down to pick up a suitcase. He slams it into the table, startling me. His fingers trace the edges of the metal, until the case activates and slides open, showing a translucent skullcap with five blue worm-like wires within. I have no idea what it is, but the sight of it makes me squeamish.

"This is a manual override of your Kindred connection. It can train your mind to decline incoming messages or stimulation from the Duke's mind before they are received by your neural receptors. Do you understand?"

I shake my head. "N-no."

He laughs. "Of course not, you're eight years old and live in this…this hell—this impoverished planet." He smirks at himself for being clever, and at me for my foolishness. "At this exact moment on Maru-Monchuri, your Kindred, Duke Felix Hamdi, is undergoing an educational and spiritual treatment where he electively loses consciousness, which is why you're incapable of communicating. During this brief window of time, we will teach your mind to protect the Duke from any pain inflicted upon you. We will teach your mind to give the Duke his desired privacy, and to lessen the effects of certain emotions that will keep you from forming any bond that would be deemed inappropriate. Do you understand now?"

This time I nod. He wants our connection to be weak. He wants us to not love each other. But does that mean I won't be able to talk to him anymore? Will I still have my best friend?

"Good. Your mother has already signed, now I just need your signature." He jerks his chin and a holo-sheet appears, hovering in front of my face, a red line blinking where I'm expected to sign. He and I both know that I have no choice but to sign. He made sure of that by separating me from my mom. She probably doesn't even know the extent of what I'm agreeing to.

I sloppily sign my name and the sheet graphically folds itself before disappearing. "Following this session, you will receive an annual dosage of override serum, which will keep the training principles you'll learn today in place."

"Okay," I say, swallowing down the panic.

"Very good. You're making the right decision." He gives me a sweet, rotten smile. "The Qadins have given this consideration and determined, with the approval of the Hamdis, that this is the best course of action for your Kindred connection and have even offered a stipend to be paid to your mother monthly to support your…needs. But it would behoove me to say you that you are forbidden to tell the Duke about this meeting, the manual override, or the injection, you understand. Failure to adhere to the rules will result in… familial punishment."

I gulp, my fingers twitching on the table. "I understand." They'll hurt me or Mum if I tell Felix. They'll lock me up and throw away the key. I've been threatened before by Arren. This time is no different and the stakes are always the same. I know better than to disobey.

"Great." He walks around the table till he's standing behind me. The wires wiggle, until they find the right position, I guess. He gently places the cold cap on my head—not, I imagine, for my sake, but for the safety of his precious technology. "There will be no permanent damage, but this is going to teach you how to block your connection. Now, this will hurt."

And then my scalp feels like it's on fire, and pain radiates through my body and mind, and my back arches against the chair. I scream.

CHAPTER 10
JOY

"I SAW HIM STANDING THERE, BROWN SKIN DRIP-
PING, AND I SAID, BABY, WHERE YOU BEEN?"

—DEJA REESE, "SHOW BLACK LOVE"

"What fuel do we need?" Felix asks for the second time.

"Please follow your detailed guide's instructions for refueling practices," the sexy AI, the state-of-the-art, fastest ship in the galaxy repeats once more.

"A weird lizard stole it!" I yell, though the AI doesn't care. "What is Class B detritus?"

"Class B detritus is the necessary fuel for this Hamdi spacehopper to operate at an optimal level."

"Completely unhelpful," Felix mutters. "Where can we find Class B detritus?"

The AI doesn't miss an annoying beat. "You can learn more about Class B detritus in your detailed guide."

I let out a long groan. "How much time does the ship need to be fully repaired?"

This time she pauses before answering, as if she actually cares about this. "Your HAMDI hopper needs one hundred and eighty thousand seconds to repair its hull, console, and engine. Thank you for your patience."

"How long is that even?" Felix flexes his fingers. "Come on, let's go. We'll figure this out."

We leave through the hatch, and after swimming around briefly, trying desperately to see the guide through the murky water, we give up.

How hard can it be to fuel a ship? Felix says, and I swear he just provoked all the Gods by asking that.

Rashid's waiting for us by the edge of the water when we reach the surface. He's got his hands on his hips, and a wild gleam in his eyes. "So are you going to tell me what that was?"

My gaze slides again to Felix's bare chest as he wades through the water toward the grass.

What is wrong with me? He's my Kindred. I can't be looking at him that way. Legally, I'm not even allowed to. He's off-limits and he's sometimes the worst. Like when he drinks too much and burps while sleeping, startling me awake. Or even an hour ago when he strutted out of that shop, looking like a heartbreaker. Which he absolutely is.

I shake off the thoughts. I hope he didn't hear that.

But if he did, he doesn't show it. He reaches for his discarded shirt and drapes it over his shoulder. Even Rashid looks temporarily stunned by Felix's bare chest.

I flash Rashid a smile, and we both soundlessly chuckle.

"Well, that was unfortunate," Felix says, sinking his feet back into his slip-on black shoes. "How are you, human?"

"Rashid. Just call me Rashid or Raz. If you call me 'human' in front of others, that'd be suspicious, you feel me?" Rashid lets out a long huff. "We should go. I'm sure it's all over the news by now."

"Can we get food? I'm starved." I shove my feet into the sandals and smooth back my short curls.

"Yeah, of course," Rashid says. "We just—"

"Hey, is everyone okay over there?" A human with broad shoulders, dirty blond hair, and an easy smile that makes my brows rise strides toward us.

Felix shifts, trying to block out the sunshine from his eyes. "Oh, great, another needlessly friendly human."

I elbow him in the chest, forgetting that he's still not wearing a shirt. Ugh.

"Did you crash because of that radio-wave thing?" The human stops in front of us, regarding the car, which is perilously close to the water's edge. "Need help?"

When the human turns to me, I suck in a sharp breath and nearly choke. They have beautiful green eyes and their smile threatens to melt me like chocolate.

"Nah, we're fine, Owen." Rashid sidles up to the human. "Joy, Felix, this is Owen. He's Mr. Gibston's son, the teacher I was telling you about? Joy's my cousin, and Felix is a foreign student checking out the area for the fall. They're both staying with me."

Owen shoves his hand out to me first, not Felix, which for some reason I expected because he's Felix Hamdi and people always pay attention to him first.

That's when I realize I'm supposed to do something with his hand. Oh, *Gods*, what am I supposed to do? And oh, no, I'm soaking wet and all of my roundness is on display.

"Hi, Joy."

"Hi," I say, thrusting my hand out and slapping his. Did I do that right?

He laughs, the sound melodious. No, I did not just think that. "You're right, shaking hands is weird, especially after the pandemic, right? And hi, your name's Felix, right?" He waves his hand instead, but then his gaze settles back to me. "Are you okay? That noise… Dad and I are riding around town checking in on everyone. No big accidents, but Mrs. Graham down the way had to go to the hospital. She fell and bumped her head on the stove. When Dad checked on her, first thing she said was 'don't let my cookies burn.'"

"Is she gonna be alright? Was it serious?" Rashid's eyes bulge as he throws a hand over his chest.

"Nah," Owen says, still looking at me, "she's gonna be just fine. Suspect the cookies will still be warm when she gets home." His lips quirk and his hand twitches by his side. "I'm sorry. I'm being weird. It's just…you're really…um…do you need a towel? Are you cold? Let me run back to the truck. I'm sure I've got something." And with that, he jogs back through the grass and momentarily out of sight.

"Well, he certainly cares about *your* well-being." Felix cocks an eyebrow. "He has eyes for you." Some emotion lingers in those words and his mind, but whatever it is… I can't quite place it.

Rashid chuckles. "Everyone loves him at school. He's the captain of the debate team, plans on going into art school for architecture or something in Rhode Island, apparently a great kisser, and never wore a shirt he couldn't fill out." That last part he mutters aloud dreamily.

"Okay," I squeak a bit, not knowing what half those things are. I attempt to pull the fabric away from my chubby stomach and thighs, though it doesn't help one bit.

Felix taps my hand away. *You cannot hide your perfection, no matter how hard you try.*

A blush creeps up my neck and cheeks and suddenly it feels so much warmer outside. *Shut up, Felix.*

Owen stalks back, carrying a blanket. He maneuvers between me and Felix, who reluctantly steps aside, amused. "May I?"

I say something inaudible and he drapes it around my shoulders without touching me. Never, in all my life, has someone like him offered me care and support. Boys back home wouldn't dare, not at my age when I could be betrothed to someone. And Felix wouldn't. Not because he doesn't care about me. It's just, he can read me—he knows I'm not cold, and he's seen my body in all of its glory more than I'd care to think about. Any embarrassment between us died a long time ago, although we still have awkward moments.

But this boy. He doesn't know. And he's caring and kind. Monchurans could learn this from humans.

"Do you all need help getting home? The car working okay?" Owen's voice is soft and he still stands so near to me.

"Actually, the transp—the car is fine. We just thought it'd be fun to take a swim because of that weird sound hurting our ears." Felix wraps an arm around my shoulder.

"Yeah, it's wild. On the radio, they said they're investigating, but most likely was a satellite issue, and it had something to do with a solar flare? There's a lot of theories, but everyone says it wasn't serious. Including Dad." Owen steps back, as if seeing Felix's arm around me has shifted his opinion on his own proximity. Ugh, Felix.

I let Felix's arm fall and graze Owen's hand. "Thank you for your generosity."

"Of course, yeah. I guess we should all be going. I'll see you at astronomy lab?" This he says to Rashid.

"Actually, would I be able to chat with your father about a project?" Felix tries not to sound desperate, but the question sits there like a stone between us all until Owen shakes his head.

"I'm not sure. Dad's checking on people and then he's got some conference call about some rocket thing and then class tonight. He's…uh, preoccupied." Though I don't know Owen, there's a bitterness in his tone, and his shifty eyes tell me he's not being entirely honest. I'm learning today that people, regardless of their world, have troubles with their parents. And I wish I knew how to make it better for everyone.

I wish I could tell Mum that I love her and miss her and I'm sorry for this whole mess. I hope she's okay. Danio would never let anything happen to her. And I hope Felix's parents are fine, too. I know they hate me—well, at least his mother does—but they love Felix with their entire hearts and…it'll break him if anything happens to them.

"Oh, well…perhaps we'll have a chance to talk to him tonight." Felix is displeased for several reasons, but mostly that this can't be done in a timely manner.

"Yes, we'll see you, then," I say awkwardly. "And here's

your—" I attempt to take the blanket off, but Owen moves back, already turning away.

"Keep it. The last thing you'll want is to catch a cold." He gives me another smile that warms my insides, and then strides back through the field.

I stand there watching him until Felix puts a hand on my shoulder. "Weren't you starving a moment ago?"

"Uh, yeah. Yes. I am, yeah." *Gods*, I'm a fool. Maybe it's because no boy has ever looked at me like that before. Like I'm his equal and that there's nothing holding us back. No weird history between us or…or…a bundle of paramours. Maybe because it's just easy to like someone new that I won't know long.

I decide then and there that I want to draw him. Owen, I mean. He's got such a beautiful face. And since I've never drawn people before, well except Felix, this would be fun. If I survive this whole thing.

Felix cocks an eyebrow, though his lips fall into a frown. "Well, shall we get something to eat?"

I nod and am about to slide back into the transport when Rashid says, "I'm driving, and you're going to watch if you ever want to drive again." Felix rolls his eyes. Sure, he almost crashed the transport, but he didn't, and in his mind, that's all that matters. "Since you're both wet messes of weirdness, we'll order takeout for lunch and groceries. I should have enough money in my account. As long as that currency replicator you got still works and I can deposit more later."

"I'm sure it does." Felix jumps into the front seat beside Rashid. "We need a rest, a nap. Wouldn't you say, Joy?"

"Um, yeah," I say to no one in particular. "Yeah."

I stand there another moment more, the blanket swaying in the slight warm breeze. My feelings are all over the place and… I'm not sure why. Maybe it's that I've met Rashid, who may very well be the nicest person I've ever encountered, or Sarah and her friends, who were all incredibly beautiful and bubbly and different than people back home, or Owen, who inspired me for the first time in forever and made me feel seen after years of invisibility… Even Felix feels different. Our friendship is different. My hands shake and my stomach grumbles.

Why do I feel like something transformative is happening to me?

★ ★ ★

"I like this pizza thing." Felix shoves another triangle of cheese-covered bread into his mouth. "And I really like human music, especially this starry band I heard, and this outdated music player you've got. I should get one before we leave… It's so…vintage." Felix gives the best backhanded compliments.

"What kind of music is this?" I ask, moving my shoulders to the beat. Felix and I both love music. He loves it with every fiber of his being, which is why he naturally makes it, while I'm just a fan. But this music hits my heart a bit different than songs back home. Maybe because it's so…dreamy. Maybe it's because I'm different now.

Rashid freezes, the slice of pizza dangling in front of his lips. "I keep forgetting you're aliens. Like, no human anywhere wouldn't know Taylor Swift. Every song she drops is a certified bop."

"I don't know what that means, but I like it. A lot." I hum a little, not knowing the words.

"If you like her, I have a feeling you'll love Deja Reese. She's a cross between Beyoncé, Lizzo, and Taylor Swift, poppy with catchy hooks, all about Black empowerment—hashtag Black Girl Magic, and has like voodoo priestess living in the NOLA woods vibes. Listen—"

I like it, too, Felix murmurs, though he won't admit it to Rashid.

He hits a few buttons and the music switches to something different...but similarly beautiful. The music thrums through my body and through my mind and I find myself moving gently to it. It's perfect.

"You already know me too well." I smile at Rashid as my fork picks at the edge of the vibrant green lettuce sitting on my lap. We didn't bother with sitting at a table or unpacking our bags once we got back to the house, but we both showered and changed into dry clothes. Mine's a long shirtdress that falls a bit shorter than I'd like. Only I seem to care, though.

I've eaten the pizza, and salad, which may be nutritional but tastes like something given to small nocturnal animals.

I pluck up the cup filled with something called soda, and take a big sip. The bubbles burn my throat and make me want to burp, which I won't do in front of present company. Despite these strange sensations, I think I like it. I take a smaller sip this time and enjoy the flavors bursting on my tongue.

Felix yawns and looks over at me, causing me to yawn, too. "We should take a nap."

"You're right, this has been the longest birthday." I rub the sudden sleepiness from my eyes.

"It's *both* your birthdays?" Rashid swivels his head between us. "Are you like…twins or something? Cuz that's not the impression I got at all."

"No," I answer uneasily, shifting my bare legs on the cool tile. "It's like… I mean, we're… It's just…"

"We're Kindreds." Felix puts his cup down on the small table. "We were paired at birth." This last part he says as if it makes perfect sense, which I'd gather it does not to a human.

"Paired, like you're meant to marry?" Rashid stares at us both, his brows knitted together.

I laugh, piercing the awkwardness of the moment. "No, no. We're not getting married or anything like that. It's like we're family or…or…the closest of friends."

Felix grimaces. "We're more than family or friends. She's my Kindred. We share our thoughts and failures and triumphs." He's quiet for a moment, his gaze far off. "She shares my life with me."

"You mean you talk to each other or…?" Rashid stares at us, openmouthed, for another moment.

"She knows what I'm thinking, can see me far away… We share everything." Felix glances lazily around the room, as if bored. "I suppose it's a bit complicated to humans."

"Yeah." Rashid rocks to his feet and takes away the remnants of pizza and salad. He tugs open a can and plops it into a bowl on the floor, causing Chadwick to run to it. "I can't imagine sharing my thoughts and life, from the moment I'm born to my death, with someone else. I don't know… It seems like a lot for someone you aren't going to marry or like, be with, romantically."

"It's not," I find myself answering quietly, glancing as

the cat gobbles down its food. "It's a gift. Sharing intimate thoughts doesn't have to lead to romance."

Rashid's lips shift to the side in thought. "I guess." And then a loud yawn reverberates through his whole body. "Yeah, I'm exhausted, too. Florida afternoon sunshine makes you tired." He smiles before rubbing his eyes. "Since you share each other's lives unromantically, I'm sure you won't mind sharing the spare bedroom? Both of you are a bit too tall to sleep on the couch, and I'm not about sleeping with anyone. No offense, Joy."

"None taken." I chuckle.

Rashid runs a hand over his tight short curls. "Practice is at 4:00 p.m., so I'll wake you at three thirty. Cool?"

"Cold." Felix groans as he rolls to standing. He holds out his hand for me, and I take it, slowly coming to my feet. "Come on."

"You better not snore," I say, pulling at my oversized shirt-dress. I'm suddenly very, very nervous.

PART II
WHEN ON EARTH,
LISTEN TO DEJA REESE

CHAPTER 11
FELIX

My arm's wrapped around Joy's waist while she murmurs softly in her sleep. She made a pillow barrier in this too-small bed for us to give each other space, but that was quickly disregarded as she crossed over to my side and snuggled close to me. Her head lays beneath my chin, her body meshed against mine, and I've never felt safer in my life.

It also makes me feel things I thought I'd buried deep inside myself. But it's useless. Joy would never think of me the way I think of her. She knows all my flaws, all my faults, every mistake and bad decision I've made. How could she see me as something or someone else, when she's seen me one way for our entire lives?

She begins to mumble louder, her eyes squinting with some imagined pain. Her lower lip wobbles, and a warm breeze makes a curl flutter across her cheek. Earth's solitary sun continues to rage through the window outside, offering more unnecessary heat.

"*Shh,*" I whisper, my fingers grasping her a little tighter. I nuzzle closer, grazing my lips against her forehead, but instead of kissing her—as I've imagined doing a million times—I stop myself. I stop myself even though her scent—like water lilies floating in our pools back home and something wholly Joy—tugs at me like gravity.

I can't decide if I'm being a good Kindred to her, or if I'm doing this for me because I love torturing myself. I've been selfish so long it's hard to tell. Still, I can't help myself. My kiss lands softly on her smooth sweet-smelling forehead and lingers there.

Some life-altering emotion flips in my gut. And then I feel something I haven't felt in a long time…the gentle warmth of my own kiss on my own head.

But how?

A smile stretches my cheeks and I let out a small gasp.

I didn't know. We've never been so close as we are now. I never knew I could feel things like she does… When she plucked my hair earlier—was that really just a few hours ago?—she felt my pain. But I never felt hers. Not since we were really young. What changed?

There's a light knock on the door.

"Hey," Rashid calls, "time to get up and ready for cheer practice. I'd let you stay here, but the thing is—"

"Rashid, might we wake up before needless conversation?" I stifle a yawn and peer over at Joy, who has just awoken and is giving me the side-eye. "Sorry, I meant to say, I'm not in receiving mode for information just yet. My apologies."

"Yeah, okay. Just…be ready in twenty."

And with that, Rashid disappears, leaving me cradling a wriggling Joy.

"Good afternoon, Kindred." I give her my most cheeky smile and cock an eyebrow down at her. "You had a nightmare. How are you feeling now?"

"I'm fine," she squeaks, rolling away from me and nearly landing on the floor. "We have to go to cheer practice? What do they do there?"

"Yes. I'd argue there's no good time to *learn*, but it would be interesting to learn more about the humans while we wait for our ship." I swing my legs over the side of the bed and walk into the attached bathroom. Joy picks through her bags of clothes while I attempt to brush my own teeth using a toothbrush Rashid told me I'd need. Technology really doesn't do enough on this planet. Next, I'll have to moisturize my own skin. Humans must work so hard just to make their bodies presentable. "Wear that flowy yellow top with those dark blue shorts. Yellow makes your skin shine like the sun," I say, squeezing toothpaste onto the blue brush.

"Thanks," she answers and I find myself smiling. Joy's a bit of a mess when it comes to taking care of herself. Always has been. Before today, Joy always dressed as if she wanted to fade into the background when she's too beautiful not to be in the spotlight. And now I can finally help her in real life, though not nearly as much as she helps me.

"Are you excited to see *Owen* again?" I don't bother looking at her facial expression to know she's making a sour one.

Her retort comes back quickly. "I don't know, are you excited to see *Sarah* again?"

I scoff. "Are you a wee bit grumpy, *beje*?" I use the Maru term of endearment that means *joy of my heart and life.*

"Do not call me that, Felix! That's what old people say to their significant others, and we are Kindreds." She peeks in the bathroom, wearing the outfit I suggested, her hair sticking up all over the place. "And hurry up, I need to do my hair."

I spit the remainder of the toothpaste out of my mouth and rinse the sink. "Yes, my Kindred."

She pinches her lips together. "Not that either in public." She walks over to the sink and sticks her whole head in, letting warm water drizzle over her hair briefly.

"So what can I call you? My darling, my love, my wet-haired paramour?" I hand her a towel, which she quickly wraps around her head.

"None of those. Now go get dressed. He said twenty minutes and it's been a while. And you know how it takes you forever." She shoos me away, dries her hair, and then runs some strange human gel through her hair, though it's still wet. I know I'm supposed to get ready, but why does she have to look so pretty?

And then I remember that we need to fuel the ship. Ocara. My parents. Her mom. I can't keep forgetting the urgency because I'm finally face-to-face with my Kindred and I'm suddenly realizing that here, in another world, there's no one to tell me I can't feel the way I feel at the moment.

Not to mention, because of the Seeker, all sorts of people are coming to find us.

While Joy hums a cross between a human song and one of her hymns, brushing her teeth, I shimmy into a pair of dark blue pants, and button up a short-sleeved shirt dotted with spiky fruit called pineapples. I pop back into the bathroom, where Joy's looking at herself in the mirror. I run some of her product through my hair, catch her gaze, and wink.

"Remember, we're trying to fit in, not break some poor human's heart."

"This *is* me fitting in." I run my fingers along the stubble on my chin. It's always stubble, never a beard. It stays short and refuses to grow. How will anyone in Monchuri take me seriously if I can't look like an adult? My dad… My mind flashes to him, his kind eyes, panic across his face as he sacrificed himself for me. And the look of anguish as Mom fell.

Joy places her hands on my cheeks and stares up at me. "We're working on it. That's all we can do." I let my face fall into her hands, savoring the touch. She blushes.

"It's different here." I cover her hand with mine. "You're different. There's something about our connection that has changed…"

She steps back, giving me a lopsided smirk. "Not flirting for literally a few hours is killing you, isn't it?"

My heart sinks. She thinks I miss—I need—flirting with someone else, being touched by someone—anyone—else to be happy. Her opinion of me is so low. I've done everything I could to keep it that way, to keep her safe, maybe a little too well.

"You look good." She smiles, the moment already lost. These little cuts never draw blood, but leave me scarred just the same. "You ready?"

I pucker my lips and gaze at her. "Look at me, don't I seem ready to you?"

She laughs, her head shaking. "I'd be lost without your arrogance."

I try to smile back, though my heart hurts at the attempt. We join Rashid in the kitchen, where there's some bars of what I assume to be food strewn across the counter. Chadwick jumps up onto the same counter to bellow for, what I suspect, is his own ration of food.

"Good afternoon, sunshines." Rashid turns and fills a bowl with water, which Chadwick eyes with disdain and then saunters away. Cats are strange. "I thought I'd take you on a quick tour of the school before practice, so that way it actually looks like Felix is interested if the others ask."

"Thanks, Rashid." Joy smiles. There's an undeniable excitement in her eyes. "So what happens in human schools?"

"During the summer? Not much. We have cheer practice, astronomy once a week, and access to the school library. It's mostly deserted, but we have a really big school, and during the school year—"

He continues on about the school and its many dreadfully boring functions as we leave his house, get in the car, drive for fifteen minutes, and find ourselves standing outside a sprawling tan building, sweltering in the disgusting heat. At this point, we know far too much about humans and school and I wish I could reclaim my time.

Joy lifts her chin and slaps me in the shoulder. *Look at that! It's so grand.*

It's a distraction.

We climb up the chipped stone steps and through a plastic archway that clicks once each time we pass through.

There's a guard of some sort sitting behind a tiny desk in a blue uniform.

"ID?" they mutter perfunctorily, while sipping from a strange cup filled with a scent that reminds me of mocha. Rashid places his cheer bag on the table, letting the guard inspect his meager belongings. "You two don't have ID?"

"We're visiting?" Joy nearly stutters.

"I was just giving them a tour...before practice. You know me, Ronni." Rashid tosses us a glance and we both nod. The guard cocks an eyebrow.

I give them my sad eyes that usually works on guards and other people who don't want me to have fun. "I really wanted to see what schools are like...in Florida. They're far more beautiful than the ones back home—"

"And friendlier," Joy chimes in. "The guards at my school yell at us, very...meanly."

I try not to laugh at Joy's attempt at smoothing over the situation, because there's no way that'll work. *Meanly? Really?*

But the guard actually smiles at her. "Eh... Normally this sort of thing's not allowed, but since it's the summer, I'll make an exception. Just keep to the gym or library, nothing in between." They say something inaudible and we're waved through this new checkpoint. The guard's perfume hits my nose and I have a strong urge to sneeze or possibly run away, I can't tell.

Once we're alone and trudging down a long desolate hallway studded with blue compartments featuring old-fashioned turn locks, Joy finally asks the question she's been holding in the entire time.

"Why must that guard inspect your things and require ID for you to get inside the school?" Her lips purse thoughtfully, and she slows her steps a little, giving Rashid time to answer.

"School shootings." Rashid says it like we understand; but when he notices our puzzled expressions, he stops. "So…in the US, it's legal for people to have guns because of the Second Amendment—a law in our country. But that means some kids have access to guns and for whatever reason, bullying or whatever, they come to school with them and then…they shoot them."

"They hurt others?" The breath leaves my lungs in a large whoosh.

"As many as they can, I guess. It's happened a lot in this state." There's a sadness in Rashid's tone. "They take precautions so it won't happen here. Drills and stuff."

"But… I don't understand. Why would…why would a human resort to such violence? Why would they hurt children? Children are supposed to grow up enjoying the beauty of the universe, not fearing for their lives." Joy feels a wild panic, her eyes roving down the hallway suddenly. "Why are there not more protections to keep guns from those who would harm?"

"Welcome to America, where old white men want to protect their interests more than kids." Rashid laughs mirthlessly. "Wait till you find out how they treat Black, Asian, and transgender folks. Our history's fucked up."

"Sounds like The Second Chaos," I say, pushing my shoulder against Joy's. Neither of us have experienced violence before yesterday, never known people who were murdered until the royals, and the thought of more…? The thought of evil lying in someone's heart? While I tend to believe the worst in most people, Joy wants to believe the best, especially in humanity as she's seen the worst of Monchuri.

As it is, if she keeps thinking of this, she'll never calm herself. And her anxiety doesn't need the fuel, not that she'd admit to being anxious.

"What's that?" Rashid's head tilts to the side.

"The Second Chaos was…a class war," I say slowly. "It overtook our whole system."

Joy looks away.

"Like *Star Wars*?" Rashid's eyes round, and the thought of school shootings has dimmed a little in Joy's mind, for a moment. Now it's replaced by disappointment. "Like the Empire versus the Rebels or as some say, the Rebel scum! Like X-wing starfighters and lightsabers? Like Jedi versus the Sith?"

"That sounds ridiculous." I let out a long sigh. "Humans are nonsensical. You can't compare fiction to reality."

"Whatever." Rashid scoffs and I laugh. I may end up missing him, or at least teasing him a bit.

Another student with an oversized backpack and light brown skin walks by, their gaze flicking to Rashid.

"Hey, Raz!" they say, a big smile stretching their cheeks.

Rashid's cheeks pinken, and he raises his hand awkwardly. "Hi," he gulps, his voice wobbling. "Johnny. How are you?"

The future boyfriend, I say into Joy's mind. *Cute*.

Very cute, Joy agrees.

"Good! See you at practice in a bit." Johnny stalks by, leaving poor Rashid flustered. What Rashid doesn't notice is the way that Johnny turns back to smile and shake out his hands.

Rashid's lips twitch. "We should get going before the going gets got, you know what I mean?"

Neither Joy nor I know what he means, but we follow him down the hall and through a dirty glass corridor. A musty scent wafts by me. I sneeze unceremoniously, earning the attention of a tall human with a very large head of pastel pink hair pulled into two round buns, who stops looking at their sheet of paper and stands in front of us.

They look up, shocking me with their crystal clear blue eyes.

"Hey, Rashid. Hello, newcomers. I'm Miss Rae. How can I help you?" Their cheeks stretch into a friendly smile.

"Um…" Rashid shifts on his feet, his hands fidgeting at his sides. "I'm just giving my cousin and a possible exchange student a tour of the school before practice. This is Joy Williams, and Felix…uh… Felix?"

"Idu," I offer, my mind drifting to our maid and the one constant besides Joy in my life. I wonder if Idu's okay, if she's alive, if they're holding her, too. Joy's gaze flicks to me and I know to shove those thoughts aside. We will fix this.

"How do you like it so far?" They smile again.

"Fine," Joy and I say at the same time.

They regard us carefully, their brows furrowed, but don't say a word. Rashid shifts from foot to foot. I almost wish I could connect my mind to his and tell him to calm down. As it is, though, he doesn't take well to being told what to do, especially by me.

"Well…we'd better get going," Rashid says, nodding in the direction of the nondescript hallway.

Miss Rae's smile resurfaces. "Okay, well, I'll see you all at practice, then…" Their voice is unnecessarily jovial, but it's welcome nonetheless.

"Have fun." Their brows knit together, and they stare at the both of us again. "I hope you'll enjoy…Florida." And with that, they stalk off.

That was weird.

Rashid leads us toward rooms separated by genders.

I stop outside the door labeled Boys Locker Room. Whatever that is. "Can't you just…take us to this teacher now? We're wasting time." I don't mention that the Seeker alerted our earthly presence by now, and the royal guard may very well be on their way to collect us and bring us to their desired justice.

Or kills us, Joy chirps in my mind, panic rising again.

They won't kill us. I'm a Hamdi, possibly a Qadin—I don't know, but my name alone means I will get a chance to prove my innocence.

Except when you were in a ship with me and they were okay trying to shoot us down. Joy shakes her head, and Rashid's eyes dart between us. *Maybe they'll just kill me.*

"No, they won't," I answer aloud. "I won't let them." But I can't help but feel they may very well try to kill her. It wouldn't be the first time.

"Mr. Gibston's not here yet. And I couldn't leave you at my home in case my dad comes back." Rashid shrugs his backpack off his shoulder and palms the handle of the door. "He'd flip if he found two strangers in his house, and he never checks his phone. You'll meet Mr. Gibston today. He'll pop into practice, and we have his class tonight."

These humans are going to get us killed.

★ ★ ★

Four Years Ago

FELIX

"Felix Hamdi," Arren says, hands gripping the edge of the chair across from me hard. "You may have caused an intergalactic catastrophe! Do you know the damage that will have to be repaired? How many years we spent forging this friendship with XiGra, only for you to upend it overnight?"

His voice is three pitches higher than normal. Arren's the head of relations for the Qadins. Which relations those are, no one seems to quite know outside the tight royal family. He shows up on holo-shows, always in his pressed, fitted blue suits, yellow hair parted to the side. Whenever he's with the royals, he has his arm around Princess LaTanya, whispering something in her ear. She always looks uncomfortable with it. In fact, *Holo News* likes to rate uncomfortable topics by memes of LaTanya's face, called Levels of LaTanya. It's funny and more than a bit sad.

"It wasn't that big of a deal. I thought having a party to celebrate the one hundred years of peace would be a gift." I shrug, a small smile playing on my face. Yeah, okay, the party wasn't *just* a party. In fact, it did get a little out of hand, and how would I know the foundation of the XiGran palace wasn't built strong enough to accommodate a dancing herd of Calefs, with their massive orange bodies and hooves that can smash through stone? Better question, does Arren know how hard it is to train Calefs to dance? How many years *that* takes?

"You destroyed his west wing. He has to relocate—"

"Temporarily... And I mean, I kind of did them a favor. Did you see how old and drab it was? It *needed* renovation. It was so cold and dark and ugly in the halls, and I swear I saw swaths of silverambles crawling everywhere. When you see one, you know your palace is infested." That last part's true, too. The pests were gnawing on the royal portraits, and everyone knows silverambles live within the stone. Getting rid of them is next to impossible unless you rebuild and clean. I would say this was a happy accident, really.

"King Yecki is furious. Do you know how long he has wanted to meet you, embrace you and your parents in his home? He wanted to strengthen your relationship, get to know you personally. Not agree to let you throw a concert party that totaled his palace." Arren lets out a long line of curses that lifts my eyebrows. "Did your Kindred have anything to do with this?"

"What? No." Things are weird between us. We just turned thirteen, and it's like Joy wants nothing to do with me. I get it—our lives are going different ways, but why... Why doesn't she want me in her life? Sometimes I feel like she's blocking me out and it hurts. "Joy's... She's not around often."

"Good," Arren blows out a whoosh of hot air. "But still, the Qadins demand punishment."

I sit up, worry turning the contents of my stomach. "Punishment?"

Arren smirks. "A Kindred connection is hard to sever. It cannot be hacked. The Second Chaos required privacy from the government, and extra voices within it. Freedom of speech that cannot face the consequences of our laws. We're attempting to find a way to temporarily disable it…" His hands loosen on the chair, his shoulders drooping a bit. "But the Qadins still know the most useful tool in…achieving compliance is to use this connection for their benefit. Look."

A holo emerges from the center of the table. On the screen, I see Hali-Monchuri, with its blindingly bright sunshine, poor housing units, dirty streets, and dark skins not much darker than my own. And I see Joy, sitting at a table beneath a rotted tree, with a ratty blanket strewn beneath her, a book held in her hands. Her lips are parted in wonder as her eyes rove across the pages. Reading and writing makes her happy, makes her forget about the world. Maybe even makes her forget about me.

Then the scene zooms out, and I see… I see faceless soldiers in purple and gold—the Soleil, I think they're called—surrounding her. Too far for her to notice, far enough for me to see they've got her in their crosshairs, their weapons pointing at her. I try to connect to her mind.

Joy, I scream. *Joy, you're in danger!*

"Have you tried to reach her yet?" Arren laughs, and I know it's genuine. He's an evil bastard and now I know why LaTanya hates him. "Not connecting?"

He places a small white cube on the table. It blinks a small frantic green light.

"This costs a small fortune, though the Qadins allowed me to borrow it for a few moments if only to make a point. Every minute costs a hundred thousand melios, but it can temporarily disturb the connection. So let me use it wisely, huh?" He presses a finger to his ear. "Advance."

The soldiers creep closer while Joy's head's still in her book.

"Stop," I whisper, my eyes flicking from Joy to Arren. "I'll do whatever you want. Don't hurt her."

Arren's face falls, but he still presses that finger to his ear. "Aim."

"I will personally apologize to the Qadins and to the Xi-Grans. I will offer my services to help them repair their palace. I will—"

"You will." Arren's tone is low and full of authority. "You will know your place in this world and others. You will never disobey the Qadins again. You are powerless, do you understand now? You can be seen but not heard. You can never embarrass them again."

"I promise," I say, my voice shrill. "Let her go."

"Oh, how easy you are, Felix Hamdi." Arren stares at the screen. "Give him something to remember."

One soldier fires his weapon at the tree, and Joy screams, dropping her book and jumping out of the way as it explodes and falls on her blanket. She stands there in abject horror, a hand pressed to her chest, eyes wide at the trunk of the tree that could have killed her had she not moved in time. Had I not sworn to do whatever it takes to keep the Qadins happy. Even if it means living silently in fear the rest of my life.

"I take no joy in this," he says. "It is my job, my duty. The Qadins want you to know your mistakes have consequences, and I agree. Because the next time we do this exercise, Felix, I promise, she will have to die."

CHAPTER 12

JOY

"SHE SAID SHE LOVED ME, BUT THEN LET ME LIVE
IN AGONY."

—*DEJA REESE, "LOVESICK"*

I'm sitting on the gymnasium floor beside Sarah, who looks especially adorable in bright pink matching athletic gear. I give her my most charming smile. Being friendly with humans isn't necessary, especially since we won't be here long if all goes according to plan, but being nice makes me feel better. And I was rude to her before. Hunger does that to me…

When she unpacks her bag, her cellular device—a phone, is what Rashid called it—rings once, and to my absolute surprise, it's Taylor Swift. She shuts it off, but keeps touching the screen with her fingers with a frown.

"You like Taylor Swift?" I ask her excitedly, forgetting to ease into conversation. "I really like her song, 'Lover.' It's so romantic. And have you heard of Deja Reese? I love her work."

At first, I'm unsure if she heard me or if she intends to ignore my outburst, but then she scoots closer to me. A floral fragrance hovers around her, and I momentarily enjoy the scent. "Are you kidding? Taylor's my favorite. *Reputation, Lover*, and oh, my God, *folklore* and *evermore*, and then her redoing her masters, and more. I took the whole aesthetic of those albums and made my room like a shrine to it. I'm super into cottagecore." She beams and I find myself wanting to be her friend.

I had friends, more like acquaintances, on Hali. But we could never develop a deep connection. We were competing for a good betrothal, all struggling to put food on our tables, and do better than our parents. Poverty, expectations, and knowing one's place in Monchuri made it that we were incapable of much more than trying to survive our circumstances. Here things are different. Here, I can just be Joy.

Sarah continues, not privy to my inner thoughts, which is nice. "Deja Reese is glorious. She's so different, and the way she transcends genre… She's having a concert in Key West on Saturday night… Are you going?"

"Concert?" I know what they are; Felix has been to several of them, and performed in a few, too. But Hali-Monchuri doesn't host concerts. Sometimes people illegally livestream from their holo-handys, but if caught, the punishment is a hefty fine and street cleaning.

"Yeah. Some of us on the team are going. We bought the tickets right before they sold out. If you haven't got one now…you're not getting one, then." She shrugs, dropping her phone into her bag.

"It's okay, I don't think I'll be staying all that long anyway." I give a tight-lipped smile and am about to let this failure of a conversation drop when she taps her polished fingers on her phone to get my attention.

"So like…what's up with that exchange student guy?"

Oh, here we go again. Both our gazes dart over to Felix, whose head is hanging down, arms folded around his knees as if he's about to go to sleep. In fairness, I've never seen him doing something he doesn't want to do for this long. "Felix?"

She scoots a little closer as others bounce on the cushy mats and stretch their limbs.

"Are you into him? Cuz he seems into you. I mean, the way he threw his arm around you yesterday, I felt there was something between you two…" She nibbles her red-lipsticked bottom lip, her yellow hair tucked under her chin.

I don't know what comes over me in that minute. Why I say what I say. But the moment the words drop out of my mouth, I know contradicting them would make me look silly. "Yeah, we're…involved."

"Yes, girl! He's so fine. You're lucky."

I bristle at the implication of that. Because he's beautiful and I'm not? Because he's thin and I'm not? Felix is decidedly quiet in my head, so I just ask. "Why?"

"Oh, I mean, just look at him…" Her head swivels to re-gard Felix, who's now giving us a lopsided smirk. He heard me. He must've. And now he's just amused. "He's like… I don't know, he reminds me of like a less-tatted Zayn during his One Direction days—I went through a phase of listening to ancient pop." She laughs at herself. "Now he's all just old and sure, some of his new songs are good, sexy even. But, yeah. He looks like he could do bad things, you know?"

I pause for a few moments, trying to sort through all of that information. "Felix or this Zayn person?"

"Felix. I bet he gives the best kisses, right? He's—"

She has a high opinion of me, Felix's voice whispers into my mind, cutting off my attention from poor Sarah.

Too high, I retort.

How would you know, beje? When's the last time you were kissed?

I jut out my chin, staring daggers at him. *Maxon kissed me once.*

Oh, really? His brows lift, and his jaw sets. He's not angry, but waves of emotion that I can't quite place wash over our connection.

I never told him, didn't let him feel what I felt. I blocked him out of the moment, using the override. My private moments and disappointments should be mine alone. And that was certainly private and disappointing.

And how was it?

Before I think better of it, I envision the scene. Standing in the bright courtyard outside the Temple after morning prayer. Everyone was there in their best clothes, meeting their betrotheds. Maxon was standing in front of me in his tan silk tunic embroidered with a red design of the sun along the cuffs. His brown skin sparkled in the sunshine, and when I leaned in to curtsy, the traditional Temple greeting, he smelled like sickly sweet honey, as if he showered in it. Mum and I couldn't afford honey; it was far too precious. This was his display of wealth and it worked.

Maxon smiled at me, his locs swinging down as his fingers quickly held my chin up to his face, and he bent forward to kiss me. His lips were rigid, unyielding, and wet. My whole body cringed, and I felt a coolness spread in the pit of my stomach. Thankfully, it was over quickly. He stood straight, peering over his shoulder at his father.

"A bit round," he said, his eyes roving over my body in the light summer dress I'd borrowed from Mum. It was her pregnancy dress and the only one I could borrow that fit me. "Pretty, but not enough to dull my star. She'll do. Let's take our vows now, so we needn't concern ourselves more later."

The memory snaps out of my mind and Felix snorts. *That's the worst first kiss I've ever seen. He didn't even wrap his hands around your waist, pull you close, tell you how beautiful you are, explore your—*

Cut it out. And just like that, I focus back in on what Sarah's saying, ignoring him. Though he has stopped speaking, and instead is giving me the sneakiest, most evil smile ever.

You're blushing.

Shut up!

"—I'm so done with boys right now. They're all the same, and Felix, he looks like a good one. Like he cares. Boys here don't care about me. They think that because I cheer that I'm easy or something. Anyway, I'm waiting to date again till college. If I get into one." She chuckles, and waves at a friend that settles onto the mat beside her.

Sarah begins a conversation with her friend about new routines—I think—and I'm somewhat grateful for the reprieve as that was a lot of information to process at once. The massive room with wooden implants in the walls and strange hoops hanging from the ceiling hushes when Miss Rae stalks in. They smile as everyone quiets down and sits on the mats to listen.

I wish I had that presence and confidence.

It's overrated, Felix says in my mind. *Just because people listen to you, doesn't mean they care about you.*

Always the pessimist, I respond.

Johnny rushes in behind Miss Rae, and scoots in beside a beaming Rashid on my right. Though he whispers, I still hear him crystal clear.

"Hey."

"Hey." Rashid's voice wobbles. His body stiffens and mashes against mine. I tap his knee, hoping to give him strength to ask the beautiful Johnny out. He helped us when he had no reason to, and I want to help him as much as I can before we leave.

"First things first." Miss Rae's voice pierces through the oversized space, demanding attention. "Mr. Gibston wanted to talk to you all before practice about astronomy class tonight. Mr. Gibston?"

Mr. Gibston bears a striking resemblance to his son, Owen, with his straight yellow hair, tall and solid stature, and green eyes, which I see even from here. Those same eyes are ringed with dark circles, and his clothing looks rumpled, as if he pulled the clothes off the floor.

"So tonight, we're going to talk about Superman… How, if he could leap, shoot lasers from his eyes, fly, and lift impossibly heavy items on this planet whereas he couldn't on Krypton, what differences there must be in not only gravity, but density of these two worlds. These are the thoughts I want you to contemplate before class."

"I think that'll be good to think about during practice, too, right? Let's get up and stretch and be like superpeople!" Miss Rae waves their arms and everyone bounds onto the mats in the center while Felix and I sit on the side.

I see humans always use fiction to understand reality, Felix murmurs.

Fiction makes reality more fun, though. Stories make sense of our worlds.

Or, he says perceptively, *they use these comparisons to obscure their own reality, to liken that which they do not know into something simpler.*

I sniff. *Why do you hate Earth so much?*

Why do you want to like Earth so much?

Because our home hated me.

But I don't. Not at all.

I shake my head. *You're my Kindred, of course you don't hate me.*

His gaze pierces mine. *You're more than a Kindred to me, Joy.*

I turn suddenly, my mouth agape, staring at him a few feet away.

"Hey, my dad's got a few minutes. You wanted to meet him, right?" Owen suddenly stands before us, and I'm surprised by how he arrived here, how long he's been standing there, and the hand he's holding out for me to pull myself up. I try to block Felix from my mind, only to find the barriers aren't there. I still hear him, his thoughts whipping around in panic and relief and something I don't understand…like music set too low to hear, but still the white noise is there.

The manual override… It must not be working anymore.

Because of the missed injection? I don't have time to consider all of the possibilities or what it means to share my thoughts and physical reactions with Felix after years of choosing to separate.

I take Owen's hand with a weak smile. "Th-thank you."

"Of course." Owen's green eyes find mine. "Are you okay? You look like you've seen a ghost."

I laugh. "I'm okay. I'm fine."

"Owen," Mr. Gibston commands, waving him over. "Can you get the equipment?"

"Yeah, sure." Owen steps back from me. "See you in a few?" I nod before he takes off jogging through the gymnasium.

Felix…

You know what I meant, he says, and flashes me a toothy grin. The moment is over but the thought remains. Something in us has shifted. And I can't understand what just yet. *Let's talk to him. Maybe we can get his help and get out of here sooner than later.*

We saunter across the mats and pass by Rashid, Johnny, Sarah and her friends as they stretch and talk and bend their legs in strange ways. We make it to the edge of the room where Mr. Gibston's still talking to Miss Rae. And we wait until they're done. Not exchanging thoughts or plans through our connection.

We remain quiet until Miss Rae leaves, giving us a wink. There's something unusual about that teacher, but then humans are generally unusual.

"Sir, might we have a moment of your time?" Felix uses

his uncharacteristically polite voice, which I've only heard a few times before. He stands proper, facing this Mr. Gibston.

"Aren't you supposed to be practicing? I don't want Miss Rae saying I'm distracting you. Isn't the tournament coming up?" Mr. Gibston folds his arms over his chest, pursing his lips.

"I'm not a cheerleader," Felix replies angrily. "What even is that?"

"Sorry." I step forward, giving my usual apologetic smile to cover for Felix. "We don't want to take too much of your time. But we need your help with a special project. Um… well, we need to know how to fuel a…" *Ship, they have those. Say ship*, Felix says. "…ship?"

He stares at us for a long while as cheerleaders line up in formation behind us, their tones excited and cheerful, happy. Meanwhile, Mr. Gibston's face turns a strange violet color, something I'm not sure is typical for humans.

"Is this some sort of sick joke?" His edgy tone sends goose bumps up my arms and I step back toward Felix. "What, you heard I used to work for NASA, and now you want to build some science project?" He looks at us with fresh eyes. "Do you even go to school here? Who put you up to this? Tell me."

"I assure you, no one—"

"I'm not a joke." Mr. Gibston thrusts his arm out, pointing toward the door. "Excuse me."

Felix and I exchange a quick glance as the man stalks off, his footsteps loud and thunderous. Once he's outside, we take a deep breath.

"Well, that didn't go well." Felix lets out a long exhale. "What do we do now?"

"We go to this astronomy thing tonight and try again? But I don't know... He looked really angry." I shift my sandals on the squeaky floor.

Felix reaches his hand out to me, intertwining our fingers. "There's no other way and time is running out."

Just then, Rashid runs over, sweat coating his face as he holds out his cellular device. "Guys, there's something you need to see."

★ ★ ★

MONCHURI MORNING NEWS NOW!

Transcript featuring L'avi Jonu and Nyla Harkibi of *Good Morning Monchuri*, filmed in front of a live studio audience in Maru-Monchuri

LJ: Good morning, Monchuri! We have incredible news, but first let's talk about the reports that came from the palace late last night. Felix Hamdi and his Kindred, Joy Abara, have been located on the planet Terra. Although their exact whereabouts haven't been identified yet, we suspect a full-planet search to be underway now that the Seekers—radio-wave locators—have proved useful.

NH: What do we know about Terra? Why did they choose that infantile system? How did they hope to fit in with the earthlings?

LJ: From information gathered by the Monchuri Academy of Science, we understand that Terra is a relatively new planet, with one solitary sun, and on the brink of the first trials of climate change. Terrans resemble our own anatomical composition, although are more fragile, lack proper healthcare and technology, but do have a similar atmosphere to ours.

NH: Don't tell me the science stuff, L'avi. Tell me about the earthlings! Are they hot? *(audience chatters)*

LJ: I think discussing the aesthetics of the *humans*, as they're called, so soon after our beloved Qadins were taken from us is in poor taste…but…according to satellite feeds, there are some very decent-looking humans—if a bit bland.

NH: Oh, *really*, bland?

LJ: They have very standard eye colors like blue or green or gray, though some are lucky to be blessed with various hues of brown, and their skin colors are similar shades to our own. The only interesting part about humanity is their lack of knowledge. They have a limited understanding of the outside world, have barely scraped the edge of the universe…and given their political turmoil and climate, I suspect they won't last another millennia.

NH: That's so sad…but not the first time we've seen this happen with one of the newer planets in accidental systems. They tend not to learn outside themselves, preferring to focus on their own individuality, and then end up destroying each other and their planet in the process. And that is why it's important that unity among the stars, like our Kindred Program, is necessary for survival.

LJ: So true. We've seen it happen to even the most beautiful of worlds and it's a shame. My only worry is that by Felix traveling there, he could damage the struggling world even more.

NH: It's very selfish of him to have gone to a planet

that cannot protect itself, in case he needs to be captured by force. How did they react to the Seekers?

LJ: We've been told that global governments said there was a... *(laughs)* ...military exercise gone astray. And then the humans...believed this.

NH: How gullible! *(audience laughter)* Well, on a more interesting note, will we be monitoring the search for Felix Hamdi and his murderous Kindred accomplice, Joy Abara?

LJ: Yes! That's the incredible news. The Soleil have found and recruited three hunters to find the Duke. They are equipped with holo-handys to record their vitals and movements, and maps of the tiny planet Terra. The winner will become the Steward's personal guard at the palace of Maru. So you know what that means...

NH: The hunt will be holo-vised! *(audience cheers)*

CHAPTER 13
FELIX

Rashid hands us his handy with a video playing on its ancient tiny screen. Words scroll around the stream saying *Breaking News* while dramatic music sounds in the background. Oh, humans.

The view changes to a person in a red suit sitting behind a desk, flashing us a big smile. "We have a major update about the *ring* heard around the world this morning. The US government has labeled it a training exercise gone awry and assured us not to worry, but we now know the location of the signal that plagued our ears."

"That's right, Jean," another person says into a black device, also smiling. "While most of the world only had to deal with the signal for a few seconds, southern Florida suffered the longest, up to seven whole minutes. Residents of Dade and Broward counties were admitted to hospitals today following bloody noses, minor accidents, and some loss of consciousness."

"Oof, poor Florida!" the other smiling face exclaims. "Glad there were no major injuries."

"No major injuries at all," the second speaker confirms. "And the US military gave an official statement promising to investigate the Florida coastline and make sure nothing like this happens again—"

Rashid takes his phone back and stares at us expectantly. "I feel like that's probably not good, right?"

Joy smooths a hand down her dress and I take a deep breath. Well, at least the humans aren't completely clueless, though I wish this didn't put even more pressure on getting Mr. bloody Gibston's help.

Honestly, he should *want* to help. Especially since he has the desire to understand the outer reaches of space.

Finally, I interrupt their panicking with cool, calm logic. "Humans are the worst. How do we find out what happened to this Mr. Gibston and appeal to his—hopefully—better nature so we can get out of here before our ship is discovered?"

And that's how we find ourselves an hour after practice sitting on the deserted library floor, borrowed computers on our laps, searching for any information on Thomas Gibston and why NASA let him go. Rashid said I cannot demand he help us because my dukedom means nothing to humans, so we actually have to ask him, which is further proof that Earth is nonsensical.

Deja Reese croons about love through Rashid's handy while Joy reaches for her bag of "stress" chocolate she bought from the vending machine. I thrust out my hand, waiting for some, which she reluctantly gives me. I shove them in my mouth quickly, enjoying the questionable flavor.

"Y'all have chocolate in space?" Rashid asks, watching Joy take another handful of her candy.

"Of course, we do, although it's much better than this. What are these, chocolate-covered dried fruit?" I swallow, shaking my head. Of course, Joy would find perfectly delicious chocolate with a strange twist that almost makes it healthy. Joy can never just like terrible things.

"They're chocolate-covered raisins and I love them, thank you very much." She narrows her eyes on me before returning back to the screen. I lean over and snatch the yellow bag, eating mouthfuls of the sweets. I happen to like them, too, although I could go for something else.

"Are you sure we can't have some alcohol? That usually calms me down when I feel like something's out of my control. Or I'm despondent about the day's events." I nudge Rashid, who's chewing on the tip of a pencil, his eyes glazed over in thought.

He comes back from wherever his mind went. "Alcohol isn't legal at our age." Rashid gives me the side-eye, putting the pencil down. "I swear to God, what have you been doing with your life? You've never been to school, you drink, you can't pay attention to things that don't interest you, and you nonstop complain about literally everything."

"I've led an interesting life." I shrug, and Joy laughs. "Far more interesting than you two."

"Shut up," Joy and Rashid mutter at the same time.

I smirk, getting back to the research. Tech may be seriously behind here, behind even the most tech-reversed planets in the galaxy, but I like the retro-ness of these computers. It's like traveling back in time. I'll take this with us when we go home, if only to show my parents that such things exist.

My parents... Dad. Mom. Idu. The palace. I wonder if Monchuri is okay without the Qadins. If there's a power vacuum. If Arren has filled it for now...

Once more, I type *Thomas Gibston, fired* into the search engine called Goo-goo or something. The results pop up on the screen, and I sift through them, again, not finding anything at all helpful.

"Nothing. I can't believe you don't have infobots to look things up for you. I'd respect humans for their do-everything attitude, but it's all so tedious." I take another handful of chocolate raisins and huff. "We only have two hours before we're supposed to see him for this 'astronomy' meeting. I want to be able to understand what inspired his anger and how to prove to him that we are serious about needing his help."

"Well... I probably should've said that Mr. Gibston's really, really smart, like whoa smart. But he's also... He's sorta a mess. Last year, Mrs. Gibston left their home—I think she was tired of Rocky Apple and always wanted more, and with Mr. Gibston's change in revenue, he couldn't give her the life she wanted...? And Owen wouldn't leave his dad behind. So he stayed, and things are tense. I should be minding my business like my momma used to tell me, but that's what I think—well, pretty sure—happened."

"That's all very interesting, but what does it have to do with us?" I shrug when Joy snatches the bag back and gives me "the look."

"The reason I didn't just bring you to his rinky old house

across town when you got here is because…well…he's not…
He's not always… He's not like he used to be." Rashid takes
a second to elaborate while Joy and I await his news patiently.
"He's depressed. Major depression. And instead of getting help
and counseling, he drinks. I mean, I shouldn't even know
about this, but Owen told me one night after his dad pushed
him away. Same way my dad did till he went on that cross-
country road trip with Mom's ashes…"

Where do we even start with all of that?

"Why didn't you tell us all of this before, Rashid?" Joy's
temper rises, surprising us both. "We're putting our future in
the hands of this teacher… We don't know him. We… Our
parents are relying on us. Our system wants us dead, and they
tracked us here. To this planet."

Rashid's eyes widen. "What do you mean? More aliens
are coming?"

"Yes," I say calmly. My hand finds Joy's on the floor, and
I thread my fingers through hers, willing her anger to dis-
sipate. Her skin is smooth and warm and my heart pounds a
little faster with the contact. "We probably only have a few
days to get off this planet before others come. I promise you,
they won't be as kind or docile as us."

Rashid scrambles to standing, his laptop sliding off his lap
in the process. The library worker, who let us borrow the
machines, shushes us and retreats into her office, shutting the
door. Rashid lowers his voice. "What will they do?"

"Find us," I answer.

"Kill us," Joy says, panic curdling the milk chocolate in
her stomach and I squeeze her hand harder.

"Will they kill me?" Rashid's voice falls softly, his hands shaking by his sides.

"No," Joy and I answer at once. "They won't hurt humans. I mean, why would they? They don't care about you."

Rashid nods and begins pacing. "So we need his help now."

"I feel like we've been telling you that since we arrived." I close the laptop and let out a long exhale. "We dressed up, we shopped, we watched you jump around on mats, we are doing everything we can to fit in. But it means nothing if our ship doesn't get fixed."

"What can I do?" Rashid pauses and stares at Joy and I as if we know all the secrets to the universe. As if we have the solution to this massive problem that lies at the bottom of a marshy swampland in Rocky Apple Key, Florida.

"You can help us find out what happened to Thomas Gibston and help us get there tonight," Joy answers for me.

Rashid sits back down and picks up his computer. "Alright, let's do this."

An hour later, after searching and consuming takeout from a diner down the street, which consisted of something called pancakes, eggs, and waffles—Joy's new favorite, especially with gobs of fruit and cream on top, we have our answer. We stumble upon an uploaded video from some NASA scientists talking about one of their coworkers and his wild theories.

Rashid rubs at the exhaustion in his eyes. "Thomas Gibston believed in aliens. Better yet, he believed that there were galaxies out there with advanced life. He wanted to allocate funds to...do something really technical. I don't know, I'm not an astrophysicist, but it sounded intense and expensive. They said no."

"This human space program took away his job for believing in...us?" Joy purses her lips, stretching her legs on the floor. "That's silly."

"Yeah, well. Humans are... You know what, it doesn't matter." Rashid drapes a black sweater around his shoulders. "But we do have to get there soon if we want one of the good telescopes."

I rise to my feet and extend a hand to Joy. "Want to pretend we don't know the universe?"

She cocks an eyebrow, taking my hand. "I don't have to pretend. I didn't get uploads like you."

I tug her up and close to me, our noses nearly crashing into each other. My gaze lingers on her beautiful soft lips, and I suck in a breath. My stomach flips again, telling me that I'm completely where I want to be and yet terrified. A blush creeps up Joy's cheeks. She looks away, stumbling back, and I resist the urge to bite my lip and pull her back toward me. To taste those lips and feel everything I've wanted for far too long.

I told her she's more than a Kindred to me.

Does she think about it?

Should I even think about it?

Is she reading my mind right now?

Instead, she yawns, and tosses our garbage in a bin. "It's late, but I suppose it's a long wait for the sun to set here. For the stars to shine and light up the night sky."

A cheesy line rushes to my mind and into hers. *You light up my night sky.*

Stop flirting!

I smirk as Rashid slips his phone into his pocket and puts

the laptops back on the library desk. The worker left a while ago but trusted Rashid with the equipment. "Right, so—"

"Come on, the football field's not far away…" Rashid leads us out of the library and through the halls as Joy holds my hand absentmindedly.

As we walk out into the evening, the stars flickering above, the cheer team now dressed in jeans and T-shirts, slurping shakes and laughing about nothing important, I try to collect my feelings. Something's shifting between Joy and I…and I… I want it to. I know I should be the Felix she loves and hates, who is confident and just wants to go home. Go back to normal. But… I don't know if we can. Worse, I don't even know how we'll get home without Thomas Gibston's help.

★ ★ ★

The field is quiet. There's only ten or so of us spread out among tools called telescopes that look like an arts-and-craft project I did when I was five. Even Joy looks unimpressed, and she's easily wowed.

Rashid meanders toward Johnny, who gives him a big cheesy smile and tells him he saved him a spot. *Ah, young love.* While Owen, the obnoxiously hot human with a hero complex, swoops in beside Joy and gives her his extra sweater, though she says she isn't cold, and there are beads of sweat dotting her scalp. That's the problem with Joy. She either attracts assholes like Maxon or boys who think she needs saving. She has to know by now, as she's known me our entire lives, that I'm neither.

But first, I need to save our world and my parents.

I stand close to Mr. Gibston, whose breath whiffs of alcohol. Amazing, really, that alcohol smells the same, so far away. Amazing that even though it's been days since I drank, the scent of it makes me ill to my stomach. I've used it as a tool to bury my feelings over the years, not because I enjoy it. Not because I needed it. I just found that it was one way to hide my feelings for Joy.

And now I'm here, letting all those feelings and worries rise to the surface, realizing I was reaching for drinks I never actually wanted.

"So, over the course of the year, we've come out here every few weeks to navigate the night sky, to see the changes during the seasons, to identify the constellations, and to discuss our place in the universe. Tonight, I would like us to explore the unknown, like Superman." His voice carries over the field, and I stop to stare at him, spotting the hurt behind his eyes and words, but love for the stars.

That might be the only way to get through to him.

I glance over at Owen, who's showing Joy how to use the equipment. The taste of soda in my mouth sours and jealousy rises to the surface as I gently unscrew the cap to the telescope. How do I keep her from knowing out here? How do I bury these feelings again?

I should let it go. She's my Kindred. I should be happy that I get to spend my life with her in my head. I should care less about my own selfish desires. With another glance at her smiling face, I decide there's never going to be a right time for us. She deserves so much more than me or that douche-nozzle Maxon.

Maybe this pretty human boy will make her realize that.

There's a light breeze that carries the scent of salt and grass. I inhale and regard the cloudless sky. I put my eye to the looking glass of the telescope and stare up. It's too weak to see much beyond their own system; perhaps the machinery is basic for a school class. With a deep sigh, I swivel the body of the telescope and adjust the lens to see their solitary moon. It's pocked with craters and so tiny.

I find myself thinking about Indigo and how they created Monchuri just through music. If Monchuri was created by a God, who created this world? Who created the humans? Why would they create them and then abandon them to their own devices? How can they ever understand the universe if they cannot understand their origin?

Suddenly, I feel sorry for Earth and humanity. I want to hate them, to look down on them. Because I miss home and want to believe in the worlds I lived in. But I can't anymore. We had Indigo. We knew our history. Humanity only has itself, and clearly they don't know how to handle it and take care of their world.

My eyes catch on movement circling the Earth's single moon. I peer closer and see it again. Panic rises up my throat and I swallow it down. Joy tosses me a brief glance, and I tell her I'm fine. We're fine. Because if I were a human, I would think we were.

But to me, a duke from Maru... I'm used to seeing them up in the sky, catching my every single move and mistake. The metal is supposed to act like a mirror, unobtrusive and sneaky. Most would think their eyes are malfunctioning... it's so small and innocuous, spinning its little body around, following something or someone.

In our world, they're called holo-lites...they transmit videos and images on live holo-vision. Which means another Monchuri has landed on this planet to find us.

Who knows the propaganda they've spun back home, who knows how angry the citizens are or how scared. What I do know is that if I can see a holo-lite, we have even less time than I thought.

I sneak a peek back at Joy as she laughs at something Owen said. She doesn't need this right now. She needs levity, and I can't give that to her. Our ship's sunk in slimy water, and it needs fuel. We're being chased by an elite royal army. I can't tell her that they're here, not yet, so I shove the thoughts aside.

"Mr. Gibston," I call out, "I think I've found a bit of the unknown."

He tosses me a look over his shoulder as he finishes up helping a student assemble their machine, and hobbles over, huffing loudly. I expect him to still be cold and upset about earlier, or to point out that I'm not a student and shouldn't be here, but instead he seems a bit tired. He limps a little on his left leg and there are dark rings around his eyes, even in the moonlight. His blond-gray hair flaps in the wind and he steps beside me, running his hand through it.

"So...what have you found?" There's excitement in his voice, though he can't actually think any of these human students would find something wholly new and unknown with this old equipment. "Let's see."

He bends over the lens and looks in.

I wait till he's adjusted before I answer. "You'll notice a shiny, if a bit small, metal structure on the right side of the moon. I'd say at a forty-seven degree angle. You'll need to watch it for a bit. It's meant to be invisible."

"I don't—" he begins, and then he must see the glint of it. "I'm sure this is some sort of malfunction." He laughs. "I assure you, these things happen all the time."

I lean in closer. "Your eyes are not deceiving you."

"Wait a minute." His voice wobbles before he stalks off toward his own machine, which is noticeably much better than the ones we're using. He waves me over. "It might've been just a faulty telescope. It's really quite normal to think you've seen something unusual when it's just a piece of sand or dirt on your lens."

He bends down again and I amble closer, waiting for him to tell me I'm wrong again. Humans cannot understand that which they do not know.

"It's probably just a satellite. I'll call it in and they'll reaffirm it…"

"I wouldn't," I say quietly. "The last thing anyone needs is for there to be a panic."

A response doesn't come. He rushes around his equipment, hitting buttons and making strange noises. "What is that?"

"That," I answer, leaning by his ear, "is a Monchuri hololite. Made to be unseen by great big…telescopes and advanced technology, but noticeable with flimsy equipment they'd never have guessed humans would use."

"Holo…light…?" he asks, turning to me. "You're that kid from earlier. Still making jokes?"

"Come now, Thomas Gibston." I chuckle, watching his face fall and his shoulders hunch. "You knew aliens existed— you believed in us before we ever believed in you." I step closer to him, his face paling to the color of the moon. "Are you ready to explore the unknown? Because if so, we could really use your help and fast."

And then his fists clench at his sides and as his mouth drops open to accuse me of pranking him, his eyes roll back in his head and he falls face-first onto the grass.

Students call out his name and go rushing to his side, and Joy pierces me with a gaze.

What did you do?

I showed him the truth. I shrug, watching Owen abandon Joy to crouch over his father, dab at the blood dripping from his forehead, and search for his pulse. *Humans are so dramatic.*

CHAPTER 14
JOY

"JUST A LITTLE BIT OF FUN, BABY. DON'T MEAN
NOTHING, BUT BETWEEN YOU AND ME... I'M SEEING
HOW FAR I CAN GO TILL YOU SAY SOMETHING."

—*DEJA REESE, "SAY SOMETHING NOW"*

After helping to pack up all the equipment, Owen took his
dad home in a rush, stating that his blood sugar was low despite Mr. Gibston's assurances and attempt to question Felix.
I'm not entirely sure why Owen pulled him away, but there
was nothing we could do. Rashid reluctantly broke apart from
Johnny and drove us home in silence.

Felix and I barely spoke. He was stewing in hopelessness,
but still believes we'll be fine.

We will have to try again tomorrow, he assured me. *There's
nothing to be done now. We wait and be patient.*

Back at the house, Felix returned to researching on a computer, listening to dreamy pop music through headphones,

while Rashid's been flicking through television channels. To my surprise, many of the programs feature people who look like us.

"These are fictitious shows?" I plop down on the couch next to him and he wraps an arm around my shoulders, drawing me closer. Just the gesture, unprompted, melts away some of my worries about Mr. Gibston and our rush to get to Ocara. And I wish, suddenly, that I had been gifted a brother like him. I wish I could take him with me to Monchuri. I never knew I needed him until he entered my life, and I don't know how I'll go on without his presence. With Maxon and my life once everyone realizes we didn't kill anyone...

"Yeah. Some of them are good when they aren't making us look like drug dealers or put our dads in jail." He shakes his head, letting out a long exhale. "Do you have shows back where you're from?"

"No. Not on my planet. On Felix's, though, they do." I snuggle against his side, breathing in his scent of something floral. "Most of us don't even have holo-visions back home. Technology is frowned upon. Our leaders believe the only stable things we have—or should have—are our traditions."

"Damn," he replies. His finger hovers over a button as the news lingers on the television. More headlines about Black lives not mattering, people shot or killed or dead from illnesses. All miserable. It makes me sad about the state of this world, about Rashid's safety. He is young, and Black. Paler humans must think he's dangerous because of this. It's no different than home, but still disappointing. He cuts through my thoughts with a smile. "Wanna watch my favorite movie? I think you'll love it. Imagine a country full of Black people that never got colonized, that was rich in resources and had equality."

I nod. "Yes, please. I'd love to see such a place."

And that's how we spend the next few hours late into the night. Watching *Black Panther*, in awe. I'm so rapt by their beautiful dark skin that shimmers like mine, the way they treat their ancestors and elders, embrace both technology and tradition that I forget the world around me. Mum would've loved this. Just the thought of her threatens to unravel me, so I stop myself. She's safe. She's with Danio. I have to believe it.

Not until the music at the end do I realize that Rashid has tears in his eyes. "It was my mom's favorite movie, too. She took me to see it in the theater."

"What a world it would be if we could live like this." I hold him close, letting him cry into my chest. I want to take his pain away, but no one can take loss away. No one should, either. As the movie credits roll by, he drifts off to sleep. I lower a blanket over him and turn to Felix, who sits at the kitchen island across the room, eyes locked on the screen.

He looks up at me as I step beside his stool. "I've been reading about Earth and humanity for hours, trying to understand them better, I guess. That might be the key to getting Mr. Gibston's help."

I take a deep breath. "And what did you find?"

"Besides really good music by this starry band I like a lot, I found that they hate people like us, Joy. They think people, with our dark skin, are inferior—"

"Back home, they think the same, Felix," I respond softly. "You didn't see it because you're protected, you're noble."

"Maybe," he continues, undeterred. "But they select bad leaders."

"At least they get to select their leaders." I bite my lip, trying not to start a fight. "The Qadins ruled for centuries…"

"You're right. But here, they care more about money than each other. They are so…self-focused they don't realize the world outside themselves. With the exception of our new friends, on the whole, humans, humans like Thomas Gibston, are—"

"Imperfect and flawed. Like us." I put my hand on his shoulder. "Their existence is new. They're learning. In time, they will grow. Like me and you."

He lets loose a long ragged breath. "Joy…"

"We should sleep," I cut him off and take his hand in mine. He lets me pull him into the bedroom. We go through the motions of getting ready for rest, and it's not until we're in the bed that we speak again.

I look over at him, and he lies awake, anger at Earth, concern for his parents, and worry circling his thoughts. He's unsure of the path ahead. So am I.

I run my hand over the fluffy light purple blanket we picked out at the mall until the edge of my hand touches his. He takes it and lifts it to his lips, placing a gentle kiss. My insides warm and I clear my mind of all the thoughts that would make my mind uncomfortable for him.

Instead, I jump up and walk over to the dresser where there's a picture frame lying flat. I pick it up, my fingers gently roving over the embossed grooves and place it facing out. In the picture, Rashid smiles. He's a few years younger than now, his hair close-cropped with a fade, and he's wearing another cheerleading shirt. On one side, a man I assume is his father wraps his arm around him. They don't look much alike, except for the thick eyebrows, height, and jovial gaze. But on the other side, I know it's his mother. Their smiles match, they have the same nose, the same chin. She's beautiful, and now I see it—so is Rashid, with long eyelashes and something genuine in their expressions.

They all look so happy, standing in front of this house with a big red bow on the door. This must have been a new start for his family... Before it all fell apart. And she died. And the father left. I wonder what it would take to get him out of that room and into the world again.

"Don't think what you're thinking." Felix props himself up on his elbows. "You can't fix a family, Joy. We can't fix humanity. And we have a bounty on our heads. They're here, the humans are probably looking for our ship... We don't have time. We don't even..." He stops, standing up and crossing the room to me. "We have a few days at most before they find us."

"Rashid's lonely," I say quietly, staring at their faces in the photo. "He invited us into his home, shared his life with us. I know humans are...chaotic, but he deserves so much more than what he has. We owe him more than we can ever repay. He's alone and grieving, and we have to help him."

Felix exhales, looking down at me. "How?"

"I don't know." I purse my lips. "Somehow."

"Come to bed." Felix reaches for my arm. "Let's not think any more about this world and its problems we can't fix. The only thing we can do is get this teacher to give us fuel. Do you want to take the sleep tab from the medi-kit?"

"No, I suspect that would render me useless for a few days.

Besides, I…um…want to pray before bed." I imagine he'll think I'm silly for praying when he doesn't believe prayers work, and suddenly I feel embarrassed. It's deeply personal. My prayers are usually mine and mine alone.

"Do you want company?" There's an earnestness in his gaze. "I would like to join you."

Something about his voice makes me nod. He is my Kindred—I can share all parts of myself with him, even this, even if he doesn't believe the same things as me.

He steps over to my side of the bed. We gently fall to our knees, close our eyes, and press our hands to our hearts. A flurry of ancient Halin leaves my mouth, and surprisingly his as well, as if he knows what the words mean. Any embarrassment I felt before is replaced by happiness and acceptance. I never prayed with anyone but Mum, and this…this feels nice.

We pray to Indigo for hope and protection from those who accuse us of murder and treason. We pray for love, and my mind lingers on Felix at the mention of the word, though it shouldn't. I'm betrothed in the Gods' eyes to Maxon. That is what Hali wants of me, though, I doubt Indigo would care. I shake the thoughts aside.

After, we slide back into the bed, turning off the side lamps in the process. I don't bother creating a pillow barrier again, especially when I'm the one who breaks it. We've slept together for years mentally, physically should be no different. I feel good, safe, happy around Felix. I trust him. I know him as well as I know myself.

I snuggle up to him, letting my head fall into the crook of his neck. His chest rises and falls, up and down, slowly, until he falls asleep and I follow straight after.

In my dream, I'm in a dress made of midnight and stars and I twirl around and around in a white room. The white room where I had my first override treatment and injection. Where Arren would badger me until I did exactly as he said and I screamed when the cap full of wires was placed on my head and the pain radiated from the tips of my fingers to my toes. It flashes through my mind as I twirl around and glitter flies up in the air and speckles the white walls.

Still, I snatch glances of him, where he would stand, yelling at me. Scolding me. Holding the suitcase that brought me pain and isolation. My feet move faster and I'm dizzy and scared.

Then Felix is there, his hands on my waist, staring down into my eyes. A smile stretches his cheeks and where his touch meets my skin, I feel delicious electricity. Excitement pools in the pit of my stomach, moving around like an ocean, the waves crashing one over the other.

"Are you real?" I find myself asking. "Are you here?"

"I'm always real. I'm always here," he answers, twirling me slowly. His suit matches mine, all stars and dark blue and spiraling galaxies in between. Planets we've seen and those we haven't in the outer reaches of space we've not yet explored. "Does it matter, my love?"

"No…" I glance at his lips. Those lips that have kissed a million lovers, but never mine. Not even once. And yet I know, in my heart, that they were meant for me. I look away because even in a dream, where nothing is real, I'm terrified. And if I do this now, will it ever be enough?

But if I don't do this now, will I ever have a chance? We have laws against us. We have a system looking for us. When we go back, will we even survive? My brain starts to think about other impossible questions that have no answers and yet none of it sticks for long with him so close. Smelling like the ocean and stardust.

"Do you want me, Joy?" Felix leans down, the tip of his nose tickling mine. His hot breath skitters across my skin like a soft caress.

The glittery walls darken. The stars move from my dress and his suit and solidify all around us. There are too many and the room is too small. A wild wind pulls at my hair and the hem of the fabric. I tug Felix closer. My hands grip the sides of his face as he stares at me like nothing is happening. As if there's no danger of the universe tearing us apart.

There was never going to be a happy ending. There is no safe place and moment where we can just be. There are rules and danger and worlds between us.

"Felix," I shout over the growing wind that batters the walls. "I love you."

"I know." And then the floor drops out and the walls crash down and we're floating in space. The air's sucked from my lungs and we're going different ways. No matter how hard I reach for him, he's taken from me and I'm alone in this nothingness.

I bolt awake, wiping at the sweat pouring down my face. Felix is still curled up around me, and his heart is racing. Somehow, he didn't join me in my dream, and thank Indigo for that. Maybe he's dreaming something better, something happier. There's a small smile tugging at his lips. He's at peace, at least for a moment.

With a quick twist, I extract myself from his embrace and place my warm feet on the cool tile. A hot breeze streams in through the screened window and I inhale, letting my senses wake up. In and out, though my heart hammers against my chest.

Deftly, I pick up a laptop from the side table and creep to the edge of the bed. Before I even see the screen, I lower the brightness to not wake Felix or burn my eyes. I run my fingers down my jaw and chin, hoping my heart will stop pounding at some point. When I can finally focus, I begin researching how people overcome grief. Which leads me down a path of some exercise called counseling. I want to help Rashid. I want to stop myself from thinking about what I said and what my dream meant.

Because I fear, my worst nightmare is true, has always been true. I'm in love with Felix Hamdi. My Kindred. I've known for years this couldn't happen, I've done everything I could to keep myself from falling, and now... Now, it's going to kill me.

★ ★ ★

We spent all morning in the gym. While Felix thought of the many ways he could get Thomas Gibston on our side, I taught one of the cheerleader's little sister, Livi, how to draw planets and stars. My heart nearly burst with purpose.

Rashid pulls my arm through his while Felix follows behind us, thinking a million different thoughts and humming his new favorite human songs I haven't listened to. Rashid pulls snacks from his backpack just as Livi bolts toward me, holding out a piece of paper to me.

"Thank you for showing me to draw stuff, Joy. I made this for you." I take the piece of paper from her grasp and stare down at it with a smile. It's me and Livi in a rocket, cruising around space. The colors pop with glitter and at the bottom it tells a story about unicorns. I laugh.

"Thank you, Livi," I tell her, and she darts off into the sunshine.

A silly smile lingers on my face as Felix's voice pierces my thoughts. *I've never seen you look so happy, Joy… I want… I wish you could follow these dreams and make them your reality after all of this.*

After all of this, our lives will still be stuck, Felix. My dreams will only just be dreams.

He doesn't respond, which is just as well, as we have more important things than dreams and drawing to focus on. Moments later, Owen finds us and says his father is at home sick. "He's not well. Talking nonsense and all that. I'm worried he caught a virus or something…"

Felix and I exchange a glance.

We should go to him, I say, nibbling on a granola bar Rashid packed for me. It's got chocolate and dried fruit, my favorite. Although it hardly seems healthy, despite the label saying so.

I'll go, Felix responds, shoveling something called a taco into his mouth. A bit of sauce dribbles onto his bottom lip and my eyes glue to it. He slides his thumb across, watching me watching him. I shake my head away.

Not both of us? I wonder if he knows what's happening inside my mind…if he's keeping his distance now because he's upholding his propriety. All his flirting and cheekiness was just for fun and I let it get to my head like a fool.

Was the override keeping me from these feelings? Did I want it to?

I'm a mess.

No, he answers. *I think I understand Thomas Gibston a little better than I should. You are too kind and too patient, but I will get through to him. Leave it to me.*

"Joy, are you okay?" Owen's voice lifts with concern. He seems so worried about me. Since the moment we met, he treats me like I'm fragile, although he knows absolutely nothing about me.

"Of course," I answer with a smile, though I find myself somewhat annoyed for some reason I can't quite place. "Why wouldn't I be?"

Owen leans in, his gaze traveling over my face and lingering on my lips. "You just seem...stressed." He peeks around us, his voice falling to above a whisper. "I'm sorry for being weird, it's just... I like you."

He's sweet and far too nice to a stranger like me, but my feelings are all over the place and I don't know what to make of them. No one, except my Kindred, has ever treated me with such kindness before. Maxon certainly didn't. Still... my Kindred is the one who... Better not finish the thought, especially when my thoughts aren't my own.

"I like you, too," I say quietly. I like most people and he is very attentive and caring. "And I really am fine, thank you for asking."

"Hey, Owen," Rashid butts in, "do you think you can give Felix and Joy a ride home today? Practice is going till six." He glances at me, asking for approval, and I nod that it's okay.

I wish I could take Rashid with me everywhere. We understand each other without needing a Kindred connection. I will miss him when we're gone and I hope we'll have helped him, made a lasting impact in his life that will make him remember us, too.

"Actually, I have plans this evening, too." Felix gets up to throw his trash away. *And you can distract the wonder-boy son, yes?*

"Yeah, of course I'll give Joy a ride home. No problem." Owen's face lights up, and I return the gesture. "Maybe I can show you around Rocky Apple, if you haven't been sightseeing yet?"

Say yes... I need time with his dear old dad. Though Felix says it nonchalantly, I feel a surge of...something in him. Anger? Worry? I can't tell, and normally he is an open book to me.

"I'd like that." I flash Owen my most innocent grin, and then the cheer practice break's over and I'm saved from any more socializing for a few hours.

Felix chuckles through our connection and I desperately want to smack him. He's infuriating and... I can't think of Felix. That's what I tell myself. If I don't think about him, he won't know, and I can pretend nothing in me has shifted. It's for the best.

When I walk out of practice, Owen is waiting against his car right out front. The sun shines down on his yellow hair that's slicked back of its own volition, I'd imagine. His muscles strain beneath his white shirt as he flicks on his phone. As if he's doing something strenuous on it.

He glances up as I saunter closer, and his green eyes look like the fountains of holy water in Maru-Monchuri. Beautiful and crystal clear, flowing through public spaces to mesmerize but just out of reach. The water isn't real; Maru has no oceans or lakes, just pools with water that's lethal to ingest. It's so Maru—pretty but poisonous.

The first time I saw a pool through Felix's mind, I was twelve and I wanted to swim in it. To feel free and weightless, have cold unjudging water surround me, and be unbound from the role I must always play. Felix said I didn't need a pool to feel any of that. One day, we would both be free and weightless. One day, we'd break from the roles we were born to play, and we'd change our fate. Back then, I thought he was optimistic. But now…

I clear my mind as Owen smiles up at me through his eyelashes. "Are you ready?"

"Let's go," I reply, throwing my backpack in the back seat with his and sliding into the front seat. "Where are we headed?" I buckle my seat belt and watch as he puts the keys into the truck's ignition.

"I decided I wanted to take you somewhere you've never been… Well, I hope you haven't been there." He buckles in and turns the knob on the radio, which is, of course, playing Deja Reese. I resist the urge to sing along because that'd be weird, and we don't know each other that well. But Deja Reese understands my soul. "It's a bit of a drive, though. You up for it?"

Will be gone a while, good luck, I tell Felix. "Absolutely," I tell Owen. "But where?"

He pulls out of the parking lot, and then follows the signs toward bigger streets, called highways, I think. "There's this beach a few islands over that's usually deserted this time of day. My mom used to take me there. We can stop and get ice cream first and then go swimming."

My stomach feels like lead. Of course I can swim, Felix knows how to so I know how to, otherwise I would never be able to get back on the ship. "Oh, I didn't bring a bathing costume. I'm sorry, I didn't know we'd—"

"You're wearing underwear, right?" he asks, his lips curving playfully as his gaze roves over my dress and straps.

"Yes, of course, but—"

"That's all we need… Don't worry, I won't do anything creepy." He laughs as the joke thuds between us. I cringe, and he catches my expression. "I'm sorry, I don't want to make you uncomfortable. It's just… I have a huge crush on you and I just wanted to spend some time together. I have a spare T-shirt, probably has some grease on it somewhere, in the back seat."

"It's okay, I'm okay," I say just before the breath leaves my lungs in one giant rush. A crush on me? What does that mean? "It's okay." I smile. The truth is…it actually is okay. This is all so new to me. To be liked for who I am and not what my Kindred connection can offer. By someone who doesn't insult me while tethering my life to his. It's nice. There are no expectations. There's no pressure. Nothing will happen; I'm leaving this world soon.

Mum's not here to tell me Owen can't provide me stability we so desperately need, and despite the holo-lite in the sky last night, there's nothing I can do right now to get off this planet. There's nothing I can do to prove to our home that Felix and I aren't murderers… No, right now, I can forget all my worries and terrors, missing Mum, and my betrothal to Maxon who will never love me. Or my Kindred, who I can never love.

Right now, I can just be Joy. A teenage girl on a foreign planet, swimming with a boy in the sun.

★ ★ ★

MONCHURI MORNING NEWS NOW!

**Transcript featuring L'avi Jonu and Nyla Harkibi
of *Good Morning Monchuri*, filmed in front of a
live studio audience in Maru-Monchuri**

LJ: Good morning, Monchuri! We have exciting news coming from Terra. To recap last night's broadcast, all three hunters arrived on the green-and-blue planet, though one was injured on impact—which leaves only two in the running.

NH: Boo! They sure got there fast, though I was really hoping for more drama, more hunters, more tension. But even two skilled hunters like DiOla H'ue and Brak Merlbin are enough for the likes of our murderous Duke and his Kindred. That said, what do we know about our hunters? Can you give us an overview, L'avi?

LJ: Sure can, Nyla. First up, we have DiOla. She hails from Braxis-Monchuri. Now you don't all want a history lesson—

NH: *(laughs)* Do we have to? Can't we just get to the good stuff!

LJ: It'll be quick! Braxis-Monchuri is home of the golden warriors that still send their firstborn sons to the Soleil. After The Second Chaos, when Braxis allied with Hali-Monchuri, they signed a treaty with the Qadins that they would supply the Soleil for the next century. So, these sons are trained from early childhood onward. They're not only skilled in all facets of combat, but they are expert trackers, too. Now, DiOla is not a son, but she—along with most Braxis children—trained alongside the Soleil.

NH: Oh, wow, that means DiOla will definitely find our wayward fugitives.

LJ: That's right. And DiOla was the top of her class, experienced for twenty-plus years, and was once the head of personal safety for our beloved, sorely-missed Princess LaTanya.

NH: Hopefully, she'll catch them soon.

LJ: Hopefully. There's also Brak Merlbin, from Kippilu-Monchuri. He's one of the most experienced and decorated warriors in our system, selected by King Qadin to direct the royal army. He's ruthless and determined. Brak is double DiOla's age and I have a feeling he'll kill her for the glory. Or she'll kill him to make a name for herself. Everyone desires justice, at any cost.

NH: You're right. Moving on, do we know our hunters' locations at the moment?

LJ: Yes, let's check the map…

NH: There's so much water on this planet, how gorgeous. If we had the time, it would be a good planet to exploit, or at least include on our vacation destination database. Although, yes, it has humans, it would be really quite easy to commandeer their land.

LJ: Nyla, that's called colonization, and usually we frown upon that. I can imagine, though, this is something the Ilori are developing right now.

NH: Yes. To the Ilori Empire, if you're watching, instead of trying—and failing—to colonize us and cause discord here, why not make a new vacation destination? After this, we'll all need beautiful quiet paradises to rest and mourn our befallen Qadins.

LJ: You're right that we all deserve time to mourn. Anyway, Brak and DiOla are on the North American continent. But on two opposite sides. It'll be fascinating to see these two converge.

NH: It'll be fascinating to see the Duke and his Kindred pay for their crimes.

CHAPTER 15
FELIX

Thomas Gibston lives in an old faded pink house at the end of a street, according to the directions Rashid gave me. The paint is chipped in places, and the sun has bleached the color in others. The grass is overgrown around the house as if it'll swallow it whole, and the light blue front door looks rickety and warped. There are also all sorts of telescopic equipment strewn across the front path and a massive sundial beneath leafy vines to the side. His truck, identical to the one Owen drives, sits outside the home, shiny and bright unlike everything else. Owen shows the signs of Thomas's descent into depression while this house shows the signs of Thomas's neglect.

The sun beats down on me, and sweat pools on my neck. Well, there's no time like the present. With a deep breath, I trudge up the broken stone pathway, maneuvering around broken bits of machinery to the door, and knock.

"Who's there?" The words slur as he yanks the door open

and stares at me with a pair of glasses that look like a relic from yonder year. If humanity even has a yonder year. "It's you. What are you doing here? It's inappropriate for you to be here."

"I thought it best for us to talk." I put a little sweetness in my tone, though I'm desperate and annoyed and this man is frustrating.

Time is running out. The humans are looking for our ship, the Soleil are undoubtedly on this world looking for us, and we need fuel. He should be excited to help us solve this small yet incredibly annoying problem. We are proof that the universe is large and full of life, and he was right.

"I'm not interested." He attempts to close the door, but I wedge my foot inside and push forward.

"It wasn't really a question, Thomas. Do you mind if I call you Thomas?" I shut the door behind us and inhale a strong whiff of dust that makes me sneeze. All the windows are closed and the room is boiling hot. He stumbles back onto a raggedy old chair, clutching a book to his chest. His hair pokes out all over the place, not fashionably disheveled, and the cut from last night still grazes his forehead.

I stride across the room, opening the drapes and find an air-cooling machine. I hit a few tabs until cool air blows out and then I take a seat opposite Thomas. The room is a library of sorts. No television as the humans call it, but books stuffed onto shelves, in piles around every piece of old furniture, and maps of the night sky hung between the cases. Everything's thickly coated in dust.

"I know this is all a bit overwhelming for you. This existence of us."

"I don't know what you're talking about, but I think it would be best if you left." His hands shake and his eyes dart to the door.

"Thomas, I'm afraid I'm losing my patience. Our ship crashed here as we tried to escape our system. Believe me, Earth was not our first choice." I pause, the sweat starting to cool on my skin as Thomas stares at me wide-eyed. "That said, that radio wave that permeated Earth was a Seeker from my system. They're searching for us, and they're coming here. It's no longer safe. I need help fueling my ship. A ridiculous creature stole our guide and I don't know what Class B—"

"You're putting me on," Thomas interjects. "For years, they all laughed at me and when they couldn't find a new joke, they created one. Do you have a phone on you? Are you recording this? I'm not some punch line." There's real pain in his voice, and I understand it.

I know what it's like for people to either laugh at you for not being the way they want you to be, to treat you like a pretty joke they can manipulate, or expect nothing of you and think you have nothing to offer. My words never mattered as much as my name. At this point in my life, the only person who hasn't treated me this way is Joy. She listens. She cares. She's the only one who just lets me be and doesn't judge me. Well, doesn't judge me without reason.

"No one's laughing." I hold his gaze. "Our ship crashed near Rashid's home into a swamp. It's underwater, and your soldiers are looking for it. I have no idea how to fuel it under there. Or what fuel we need. The ship said—"

"The ship said?" Thomas sits up. "Your ship...talks?"

"Of course it talks, Thomas. How else would I know it's

broken and needs fixing?" I shake my head, chuckling at his lack of sense. Humans. "There's an AI system inside, every ship has one. Admittedly, ours is very…unusual."

"I don't… I can't. I can't help you," he finishes, standing up and opening the front door. "My mental health isn't where it should be, and I can't trust anything you say is real. I can't believe this…or you."

I inhale but I make no move to get up. "I've read about Earth since we arrived here. You believe that either Earth was created by a God, or that it was the Big Bang. On my home planet of Maru-Monchuri, we combine our religion with science. There is not just one God but many. Those that create like Indigo, those that destroy like Ozvios, those that fade and those that shine, like stars. Our system is much older than yours.

"I'm telling you this because—" I stand, walking over to where he holds the door "—we aren't so different. Our worlds, I mean. Earth was created like all planets. Bacteria colliding with stardust, and a sun, gifted by Gods, or that was just divinely located and happened to offer the opportunity for life."

Thomas shakes his head. "Our science says differently."

"Your science is immature. Much like your technology." I take the medi-kit from my bag and hand it to him. "Try."

He takes it from me, letting the door shut. His fingers trace the lines until they touch the button and the light blinks. The kit opens and speaks in proper Monchuri.

"Hello, Travelers. Are you in need of assistance?"

I translate for him, but it seems like my words haven't registered.

"Scanning now. One human." The lights travel over Thomas, stopping on his forehead. "Shall I administer aid?"

"Yes, please," I state. The medi-kit makes short work of it, spraying his cut with healing liquid. It mends itself as if it were never there and Thomas still hasn't moved. The medi-kit folds back together and lands in the palm of my hand. I tuck it back in my bag and watch Thomas as he feels his head, his eyes widening more.

"What have you done to me?"

"I've given you a tiny taste of our technology." I stand in front of him, letting my desperation leak into my words. "And now it's time for you to help me, Thomas. You're our only hope."

Thomas gives me a strange glance at my words, but doesn't respond. A few moments of silence spans between us as he stares some more at the medi-kit. Eventually, he meets my gaze with a long exhale. "What do you... How do you... Is this real?"

"I'll show you."

Ten minutes later, we end up in the field. He was too overwhelmed and possibly a bit too inebriated to drive, and I was just a bit too keen to drive that tall red truck across town. Although I nearly hit a mailbox and another tiny transport that was driving far below the speed limit, Thomas didn't complain once.

Of course, since we stopped the truck, he's done nothing but complain. The sun's too hot, the visibility is too weak in the murky water, he's not sure he believes there's a ship down there. Why is he here again? Am I actually joking? Is this a prank by his former NASA coworkers?

"Even if what you're saying is true, I've helped build rockets, not spaceships." Thomas stands at the edge of the water, peering down at the ship, though he doesn't know it.

"It's basically the same thing," I say, kicking off my shoes. I think of a movie reference for him I'd gleaned when researching Earth. "Like fixing a hoverboard."

"We don't have hoverboards. Do you have hoverboards?"

I pause, looking over at him. "No, because they're outdated, Thomas. We've replaced them with holo-boards... Anyway, only kids ride them."

Thomas's mouth is open. "I don't believe you."

I roll my eyes. "Are you coming into the water, or are you expecting me to drag it out with my bare hands? Because although I am an alien to you, I don't have super strength like your fictitious comic book heroes. Apparently, the density in the Monchuri system is too similar or whatever. No powers, just otherworldly good looks."

"Oh, you're one of those." Thomas carefully unties his shoes and takes them off one at a time, tucking his socks into each corresponding foot. "Young, arrogant, and entitled."

"I've been called everything you can muster by people who have far better taste, far more money, and less of a penchant for alcohol than you. I was born to make myself quiet, uphold my name, think myself mighty—even if it's not true at all. Though, I am delightfully good-looking, I think we can agree on that."

He reluctantly purses his lips as I step into the warm water, my pants clinging to my legs.

"There's only one person whose words can cut me, and it's not you." The water's warm and I wiggle my toes in the marshy dirt below. "Now, Thomas, forget everything you think you know about your world and your technology, stop being so close-minded—it makes you seem older than you already are—and be prepared for something wholly new."

"If…anything happens to me…" Thomas unbuttons his shirt, leaving a sleeveless white one below. His voice is stern, but his whole expression is alight with curiosity. "I'll…"

"Nothing will happen to you. You have my promise." With that, I slip beneath the surface and my mind travels to another place unexpectedly.

Joy's in cooler water, her arms dancing on the surface as it encircles her. Her mind is full of wonder and peace. Weightlessness. Owen swims beside her, talking about…who even cares. How can I focus when she's in her underwear and she's smiling so sweetly…

Joy. I say her name with reverence. *What are you doing?*

Her face drops as she sees me in the water across from her, swimming but somewhere else. *You told me to distract him. I'm distracting him.*

I hold the feelings from bursting out of my chest as I work to keep air in my lungs. *I didn't say get naked and take him to the ocean.*

That was all his idea. Said he wanted to see me wet again. And I'm not naked.

Thomas finally enters the water and I inwardly groan. *That's a line if I ever heard one.* I swim closer to our ship, eager to get this over with. *You don't even like him.*

You don't know that. He's really nice and kind and observant. She grins at Owen as he dips below the water and scoops her up by her waist and throws her. She screams and sinks, laughing…

Do you want him? The question shoots from my mind to hers as I catch glimpses of her bare legs, her chest, his face coming closer. Their laughter. No baggage or bad memories between them.

I'm doing what I said I would and I'm having fun. I'll see you to-night and we can talk, okay? She's dismissive, and twirls around in the water as the sun begins to descend in the sky.

What about Maxon, Joy? What about... I can't finish the thought. Can't ask the question I want most to ask.

She ignores me anyway and Thomas slides up next to me as I open the hatch and we're engulfed in the bubble of air. Thomas mouths something as we're pulled into the ship and the hatch closes, leaving us soaked on dry flooring.

"Welcome, Hamdi. How may I help you?" The AI's sultry voice speaks in posh Monchuri. Thomas looks a bit green at the edges.

"Switch to the human language known as English," I command, inhaling the oxygen and trying not to think of Joy and that human boy who doesn't deserve her.

"Affirmative," the AI responds in English, her tone still come-hither. "How may I be of service?"

I look at Thomas, who's standing there with his eyes glazed and mouth dangling open. At this point, I'm worried his jaw doesn't work. Humans are fragile.

"Well, Thomas. How may she be of service?"

For a few stunned moments, he silently freezes in place, but looks at every, single detail in the ship. He now realizes I'm real, the universe is vast and full of advanced life...everything he was forced to disbelieve is in front of his eyes. Either he's going to lose his mind and begin screaming about it being a joke again or he's going to faint.

But he does neither, to my complete surprise. He claps his hands together and speaks to the AI like they're old friends. He observes everything, regarding every inch of material carefully and completely forgetting me in the process. His soft voice mumbles and marvels at the tech.

I sit down at the console and touch the seat beside me, remembering when Joy was there. I'm too afraid to connect to her mind right now, though I see fragments of her legs in my periphery, kicking in the water and the sun.

I hear her voice, murmuring, but I block it out. I feel his touch on my skin—her skin—and it's not beautiful, not the way it feels when she and I touch. Nausea washes over me at the thought of her and him...

"I think—" Thomas stands, a cheek-splitting smirk on his face "—I know what kind of fuel you'll need. We'll need to bring the ship up to the surface tomorrow, but after we fill the tank, so to speak, you can go. It's amazing. You just need detritus..."

I cock an eyebrow. "The guide said that. The ship said that. What does that mean?"

"It means we have to fill it with food garbage. I've never known fuel could be so simple, so sustainable. It's remarkable really. If we could use this kind of technology on Earth—not just solar power, but garbage? That could change everything. That could help not only climate change but..."

"How are we going to bring the ship to the surface?" I interrupt. "How can we do that without drawing unnecessary attention? Your military—"

"Leave it to me. It'll take me a little bit, but I can do it. They won't find a trace, won't even know what to look for. But it has to be done fast." Thomas goes back to talking to the AI, and learning as much as he can. My mind should be on this, on our way to Ocara, a neutral planet away from trackers and Soleil where I can contact my parents, and clear our names. But it's on a Florida beach, in the arms of a beautiful boy.

★ ★ ★

Joy steps out of the bathroom in her pajamas, her hair in a silk bonnet, and a little bit of toothpaste on the cuff of her top. I try not to smile. Everything she does is perfect.

She is perfect, and I've lost her.

We both arrived at the house a little over an hour ago, but we didn't talk. There was no need. There's no need to recap. She knows what I know, and I... I turned the radio in our minds down, not even knowing I could, so I didn't have to feel the happiness she felt with Owen. It took all of my energy, went against my every instinct, but I did it. For me, yes, but for her, too. She needed her privacy, and I never gave it to her before. Not the way she has for me over the years.

I still felt her, though. Which, after years of her being able to pull away from me, and feeling only her absence when she did, is better than nothing.

And now she's standing in front of me, smelling like toothpaste and wearing cookie-printed pajamas and making my stomach flip. And I hate myself because she's clearly interested in someone else who doesn't come with all this baggage. Who hasn't made her life miserable at times. Someone who doesn't carry the weight of the knowledge of her favorite song to sing in the morning as she gets dressed or that time when she wore hand-me-down yellow shoes and kids called her "banana feet."

"Felix," she begins, shaking me from my nostalgia. "About today—"

"You don't owe me an explanation, Joy." I swing my legs onto the bed and lie flat on my back, staring up at the white ceiling. "It's not my place to tell you what to do. This is the first time in…forever that you didn't have to be burdened by our connection and you could make your own choices for once. My… Whatever I was thinking, what I said, it doesn't matter."

"It does matter." She slides onto the bed beside me, propped on her elbow. She gazes down, something unusual swimming in her eyes. I look away because even the sight of her makes me want to say and do things I shouldn't.

"Joy." I run a hand across my forehead. "My feelings… they're complicated and inappropriate and you know this. You've always known this."

"So are mine," she admits, her breath skimming my cheek. "I just… I was afraid." She purses her lips and closes her eyes before continuing. "Nothing happened with Owen."

Now I turn to her, staring up at her pouty perfect lips, and her beautiful perfect face that I know as well as my own. Every freckle, every scar, every eyelash is seared into my brain. She's the first person I see every morning and the last person I see every night. "Why?"

Of course, nothing happened between her and Owen. She's Joy. She's all goodness and propriety. Even if I still felt her happiness, his touch on her waist, the warmth, the merriment…

everything else, nothing else. I can turn the radio down but I can't tune her out completely. Our connection wasn't made for solitude. I wasn't made to be without her. And she wasn't made to break the rules she abides by, which everyone else breaks. Myself included.

"I…" She exhales slowly, and then bolts up to open the window, her back to me. She opens it a crack, letting in a cool salty ocean breeze that dances around us. Silence falls, hanging there limply and sucking the air from my lungs as I wait for my beautiful Joy to tell me her truth. "Because I'm engaged to Maxon."

I swallow the anger rising in my throat. "Is that what you want, Joy?" My voice sounds weak, even to me.

"No, but it's my duty." She turns around, averting her gaze. "I want more."

"Joy," I croak, my heart hammering in my chest. Then why is she going through with this? Why can't she just say no and choose someone else? I'm right here.

"But you aren't right here," she responds to my thoughts. "And we can't ever…you know. Arren told me. My mum told me. The world has been telling me since we were paired. You don't need to worry, I'm betrothed and there's no way out of that now. I owe my youth to Hali. If my world is to ever get better for everyone, we all have to do our best. Part of you may feel something for me, but you're…you've always handled your emotions better."

I laugh at the absurdity of her words. "I've never handled my emotions better. In any possible way. Especially not when it comes to you."

"You've pushed me away. You've been generous with your

love…with everyone else but me. You knew, even then, that we could never… And you…" She leans against the wall beside the window and looks far off, her mind trying to articulate all the things she wants to say.

"Joy." I jump to my feet and cross the distance. "You couldn't be more wrong."

She blinks up at me, her brows threading together. "I'm not wrong. I felt you. If you had feelings for me, you pushed them down and moved on because you knew better. We can't ever be anything more. I have Maxon, and you, you're the heir to the throne."

"No, Joy." My eyes fill and I bite my lip. "Arren. He… ruined everything."

She nods. "He made me get injections so we would have distance and I would feel less…intense." Her voice wobbles, and my eyes widen as I move closer, placing my hands gently on her cheeks. "They told me I couldn't tell you. They made it so I couldn't tell you. And now I missed the injection and I feel everything again. And it's not real, what I'm feeling now. I'm overwhelmed and scared. So are you."

I don't know how to handle all of this information. He didn't just threaten her to keep me in check; he hurt her to keep us apart. What did he do? How much pain was she forced to endure? Why didn't I know?

"I am overwhelmed and scared, too, but I'm not—not about you. It's real. *This* is real." I put my head against hers and I cry. I cry for the years we've spent in fear, keeping secrets, thinking we were protecting each other. The tears are bittersweet and I cherish them, because they're everything I've denied myself for years. The unfairness, the time, the anger. How dare Arren take this away from me.

"Even if it is real—" she pulls away from me, stepping back "—what does it matter? Nothing can happen between us. I'm engaged—"

"Maxon means nothing. He's no one." I shake my head, hating the boy who would have my Joy. "He's not here, he's not me, you don't have to be with him. Right now and forever more, do what you want, Joy. Do you want to draw all of your imaginings and tell stories? Do you want to explore worlds and find your place? Do you—"

"It's not that simple." Her cheeks heat and turn pink. "You've had it so easy in your life. You know nothing of the world outside the one you live in. We have this connection so that you may hear my voice, learn something about what it's like not to be at the top. But you don't use it. The Qadins colonized and destroyed my home. The reason we're poor is because they—your family—kept us that way. My home… Hali needs tradition and it needs us to do what's right so that it may survive, and that's why I have to marry Maxon. Because it's my job as a daughter and a citizen, it's what Indigo wants, and what Ozvios maligns. What do you know about that? Or them? What do you know about duty?"

"You don't believe that. You know Indigo wouldn't want you to give up everything for the sake of traditions some chancellor mandated after The Second Chaos." I step back from her, too. "You think I'm ignorant of all this?"

"I do. Yes." She huffs, her back against the wall. "Because if you knew how the rest of our system worked, you'd be just as angry as I am. Just as focused on proving everyone wrong as I am. Not getting up onstage and running off with fright and then drinking your disappointment away."

"You think I drink because I'm disappointed about not singing up on the stage?" I chuckle, though there's no humor in it. My own face feels hot and my muscles tense. "I drink because I'm disappointed in myself and I feel like I have no purpose outside of music. I drink because I feel powerless. I drink because I can't have the one thing I want."

"And what's that? What do you not have in your pretty privileged life, Felix?" She holds my gaze. For the first time in our lives, we're the closest and the furthest we've ever been.

"How is it that we share minds and yet you can't read mine? How are you so smart and still so frustratingly wrong? You pass judgment when you could be understanding. You call me naive when you could be sharing all the things you know my tutors, my home keep from me." I stalk toward the door.

"You didn't want to know. Because if you knew, how would you look at your royal cousins and your parents, seeing them live in these beautiful gilded estates and palaces while all across the system people struggle just to find food. Just to have clothes. You wanted to have your fun and never take things seriously, because you were told you didn't have to or you shouldn't, and you didn't want to live up to anyone's expectations because you already thought you failed them anyway." She stands there, hands clenching the sides of her pajamas. Her gaze is sharp, her cheeks red, and I've never seen her like this. Never. Her anger washes through my mind, into my limbs, but leaves in my long exhales. She's right.

"You're wrong about one thing, Joy. I always cared about

your expectations of me." I put my hand on the doorknob, but linger. "I may have been ignorant about a million different things, but never about you. Because of you, I know about The Second Chaos. I know about Hali-Monchuri. I know that…" I twist the doorknob and a whoosh of cool air filters in. I close my eyes.

"You are the sweetest, kindest, most caring—the best—person I've ever met, and because of that, through our connection, I know what upsets you. I know what you pray to Indigo for. I know why you cry and why you lie awake some nights, staring at the ceiling, terrified of the future. You may use that injection or whatever to block me out, but during your sleep, you don't. I've seen your dreams. I've danced with you in them. I've kissed you. I've walked the streets of Hali with you, seen the world you live in, prayed with you. I don't talk about it, don't think about it, because I can't change it. I can't make it better—"

Panic flashes in her eyes, but not in her words. "You're the heir to the throne." Her voice loses the edge of anger, and falls softly even if she's still mad with me, at me, because I deserve it. Even if her mind flushes at the thought of me knowing her dreams. We both know they don't mean anything. "After this, after they realize you didn't kill the Qadins, you will have the power to change everything. Everything you thought you knew about not being able to change the world and make a difference will no longer be true. While I'll be a housewife in Hali, you'll be able to make our worlds a better place for everyone."

I step into the hallway, about to sleep on the short couch for the night with the cat. "Right now, I don't—I can't care about making the worlds a better place for everyone, if I can't first make it better for you. Maybe I will have power, but I won't have you."

And with that, I shut the door on her, and the anger that threatens to tear us apart before we can get off this planet and go home where everything is well and truly messed up.

★ ★ ★

Ten Years Ago

JOY

"What are you drawing, honey?" My mum sets the plate of spicy rice down in front of me and my scrap piece of paper covered in red doodles.

"Nothing," I answer, crumbling it up and sliding it into my dress pocket. "Mummy, how come you make the best food?"

Mum cracks a smile, reaching for her fork. "Because my mama taught me how to cook, just like I'm teaching you how to cook. Now tuck in, before it gets cold."

I shovel the hot rice into my mouth, the spices heating the back of my throat. We don't have much but Mum always stretches it out to be just enough. She can use a few ingredients and transform them into a masterpiece. I hope I'll be as good as she is one day.

Ooof, that's hot! Felix's voice cuts into my thoughts with a loud laugh. He's always laughing when he's in my head. *What are we eating?*

The same as every night this week, I say, taking another bite. *Jeruba rice.*

Your food is better than mine. I'm having blue fish from Beyla with the icky gills and slimy eyes again. Mom says it's a dela-a-delasasy.

Delicacy, I correct. *The blue fish is gross, and how come they paint the eyes yellow?*

It's supposed to bring fortune or something. I don't know. The yellow tastes like salt. But I have to eat it. Princess LaTanya is here to join us for dinner again, and this is what she wanted.

"Joy, I have to leave for work soon. You can clean up and take care of the dishes, right, honey?" Mum stands up, having barely finished her food, before leaving our tiny apartment and me alone. But I'm not really alone.

Felix. I cross the short room to plop down on the couch and stare up at the ceiling while sweat slicks to my forehead. *What do you want to do when you grow up? Mum says I have to follow tradition, like she did, and get married. But I want to write books and paint pictures…*

Hmm… Felix stands by the window in his grand family room, light from the Gola suns in his eyes. *I don't really care what I'll do, Joy. Because whatever it is, it'll be with you.*

Oh, shush, I say, rubbing the sweat with the back of my hand. *You have to have a plan like travel the universe or go on adventures or…or… I don't know! See everything. If I were rich like you, that's what I'd do.*

Well, he chews his lip thoughtfully, *why don't we just do it together? And then you can tell stories about all of our adventures?*

You really think we can?

If we want it, we'll do it. He gets that know-it-all look on his face that I hate. *Oh, no, gotta go eat this blue fish. Talk later.*

Bye, I say, taking the crumpled paper from my pocket and smoothing it out. On it, I drew a picture of me and Felix surrounded by tall leafy trees, holding hands and walking toward the sunlight.

My Kindred is my best friend, and how lucky am I that he is mine?

CHAPTER 16
JOY

"THAT FIRST KISS PAINTED THE SKY WITH STARS,
BROUGHT ME TO MARS, AND THEN MADE ME FEEL
DRUNK IN BARS. OH, BABY, DO IT AGAIN AND AGAIN."

—DEJA REESE, "JUST A KISS"

While Felix was with Thomas finding out how to get our
ship out of the water, I spent my time at cheer practice reading about Rashid's mother on the internet and trying not to
think about that holo-lite Felix saw, or the argument we had
last night. Or how we care about each other and that's not
enough.

Or Mum.

Or Arren and Monchuri.

Or my possibly impending death by the Soleil who have
to be close to finding out where were are.

Or our ship being discovered by humans.

So I learned about Rashid's mom, Ayana. There wasn't

much to find but everything I did read made her sound enchanting. She lived my dream; she wrote children's books about the Earth's oceans and Black children having adventures on it. She drew beautiful pictures, most of them inspired by Rashid, I think. He's always there in the background, smiling, laughing, dancing.

I can see the love in her work, the love she had for her family and especially Rashid. The love I'd see in my mother's face as she'd slide a bowl of rice onto the table before me. I can feel the love in her work, and I think… I think that's what Rashid's missing.

Death in Hali-Monchuri is a celebration. Whenever a Halin dies, the street on which they lived is decorated with their blankets and sheets, and in the center, there is a table filled with their most prized possessions. Trinkets representing the life they lived, and the moments that defined it. If their Kindred still lives, they are tasked with giving these possessions to those who will best honor the one who passed on.

We are given the passed one's clothes and allowed to alter them to fit ourselves. We attend their vigil, we eat their favorite foods, we listen to their favorite songs or read their favorite poems. We celebrate this person and we wear their clothes for the rest of our lives. That way we do not forget the fallen. We thank them. Life continues.

This process is different for every single planet in the Monchuri system. And it is much different for humans, as I've seen. But perhaps I can bring a bit of my culture to theirs. If only I can aid in their grieving.

At the break for lunch, Rashid gives me the Wakandan salute before sliding down the wall onto the mat beside Johnny.

He's covered in sweat, but there's something bubbly and positive about his countenance. Like he's doing something that makes him truly happy.

Sarah stalks by, and I try to speak loud enough to get her attention.

"Hey, Sarah," I say with a smile, "would you sit with me? I have a favor to ask you."

Sarah tilts her head as she takes a seat on my other side. Despite her doing flips and twirls and intricate dances for the past hour, she looks far from exhausted. Unlike me. I could barely sleep after arguing with Felix.

"Hey, girl," Sarah says, and I'm reminded again that there's something about her that's genuine and beautiful. I like her. I wish she could come back with me.

"Hey," I chirp. "I was wondering... You've known Rashid for a long time, right?"

"Uh, yeah," she answers, dipping a spoon into her yogurt. "We've been on cheer together for years. We were actually besties once, but like...you know, we went different ways, I guess. Why?"

I politely nod. "I'm trying to do a thing for him, to remember his mom. You probably know Rashid's been lonely...and I want to help."

What I don't say is that I want to help him because we'll be leaving soon and, assuming the Soleil don't catch us here before we get the chance and then kill us (and assuming they drop the charges, and assuming Maxon still wants to marry me), I will go back to being friendless and lonely. I want to have made a positive impact on someone's life. I want Rashid to remember me. I want someone to think fondly of me. I want to repay him for everything he's done for me.

"I didn't know… I mean, I guess I knew, but I didn't know it was so bad. He's been so down. And his dad's been gone for a while. Doesn't check in, nothing." She drums her fingers on the mat. "So what do you want to do?"

★ ★ ★

Sarah skipped the end of practice to drive me around Rocky Apple Key. We bought fruity drinks and listened to Taylor Swift, and she even took me to her favorite bookstore.

"I don't usually take people here, you know? Because, like, don't get me wrong, I love my cheer friends, they're my life… but sometimes I need some me time. And books just do it for me." She smiles shyly, and I return it.

"I used to work in a bookstore back on Hal—Hali Street, in the Northeast. Where I lived," I add, hoping she didn't catch my weird almost-slip. "I love books. My favorites are books for little children. Like those. I want to make those." I point to a display of books surrounded by stuffed animals and toys and funny bags.

"Picture books are adorbs," she agrees. She picks a few up, her face beaming. "I used to read this one to my niece, Abby. She's seven now and has started reading her own little chapter books."

I smile. "What does Abby like to read?"

"Oh, she used to like anything about witches and colorful stuff. The moment she learned to read for herself, she slipped inside a book and wouldn't come out… She's too big to spend time with me now. Anyway, I began cheer because I needed a family, you know?"

"I'm sorry." I sneak a peek at her as she turns the pages, her lips quirking as she scans the pictures. "I only have my mum and I miss her."

"What about your dad?" Sarah puts the book down and looks at me. "Do you still talk to him?"

I shake my head, taking a quick sip of my drink that tastes like…dreams, or something not quite tangible where I'm from.

"Me, either," she says, tossing her hair. "Just trash taking itself out."

"I'm sorry, though."

"Yeah, me, too." Her voice falls softly as she hands me a rainbow-colored book with a little Black boy on the cover. "Ayana did this one. It's even signed." She tilts her head to the side, her blond waves landing on her shoulder. "By the way, I think what you're doing is like, the best. I don't know why we just thought he'd get over it and not need help and care and compassion because he's a boy. Toxic masculinity, ugh." Her eyes gaze off elsewhere. "If my mom passed away, I'd be a mess."

I think of Felix's tears streaming down his beautiful cheeks. And Owen, who's carrying around this burden of his own family, and what it means to have a father who's lost faith in himself. And then I think of Maxon, how he looked at his father after kissing me, with no regard to my feelings, and said I would be acceptable. Did he say that because he wanted his father's approval?

"I know what you mean." I take a few more books by Ayana Williams and then I turn back to Sarah. "I haven't seen any of these books before, but I love them."

"You know, while we wait for the printing place to finish our stuff, I'm gonna give you so many recs. I mean, you probably have seen or read most of these, but like…you need to have them in your life. First, we have to start with Angie Thomas, J. Elle, Dhonielle Clayton, *oh, my God*, Zoraida Cordóva, Justin A. Reynolds *and* Jason Reynolds, Sandhya Menon, Sheena Boekweg, and Rebecca Coffindaffer, and *holy crap*, Holly Black. Your world is about to be blown."

We spend the next hour buying handfuls of books, eating cookies, laughing, and not once is Felix mentioned. It's just us, spending time together, being ourselves, singing Taylor Swift and Deja Reese songs, buying more than anyone would ever need. A few times, little children stop me to ask what book I'm reading, and so I would read them some, watching their eyes round in delight. Sarah would smile my way. She accepts me. She thinks I'm talented and kind, that I have a future that doesn't involve simply supporting a husband. It's so refreshing to have made a friend, one that I hope I can somehow keep.

It's nice to have the distraction from my…everything with Felix. We've never been this upset with each other for this long. We've never argued like this before. I don't regret what I said—I can't, because it was all the truth—but I regret the way I made him feel.

He's my best friend. I need him like he needs me.

I know, he says through our connection.

My heart flips, and I want to respond but I don't. This is a conversation we need to have face-to-face, while we can still have conversations face-to-face. Soon…we'll be apart again and then we'll go our separate ways. We'll think together, see each other from afar, but never close again. Never like this. And all of these feelings will fade. Whether we want them to or not.

I let out a long sigh and scoot into Sarah's car after picking up the prints, and we're all settled when Sarah tosses me a quick look.

"The way you treat Rashid, the way you did this for him, even though you're just some like, distant cousin, it's really cool. You're really cool. You're a really great person."

My cheeks heat again, and I look down. "Thank you, so are you."

At Rashid's house, Sarah parks the car in the garage and we take the bags out, placing them on the ground. The sun is beginning to set, and the air is beginning to cool. I think about my mum and where she is. I think about Felix's parents and where they might be. I think about Arren, and how much I hate him for making me break my connection with Felix. I think about Maru-Monchuri and home and I realize then that Earth feels more like a home than Hali.

Yes, I'm connected to the culture and the people, and our religion, but here…I feel free.

I carry that piece of happiness with me into the house.

Chadwick bellows at us as we hang Ayana's artwork on the walls. Filling the empty bookshelves with her work takes less time than I would have thought. The space is just so bare, missing personality, which Rashid has in droves, and I'd imagine his mother did, too.

We place Ayana's pictures of their family in little spots around the house. Sarah had found some on social media, and had them printed along with everything else. Mostly we just had to place them in frames.

"Will he hate it? What if he wants to forget her? What if seeing her face and her work makes him grieve all over again?" I stare at Sarah, worry prickling the surface of my mind.

She shakes her head, bending to scratch behind Chadwick's ear. The cat purrs loudly like a piece of old machinery. "It's only been three months, Joy. The last time I was here, this place was bursting with color and felt like home."

"What happened?" I wipe the kitchen counter, though it's not dirty. I just need to know if I'm doing the right thing. Loss affects people differently, and I want Rashid to feel comfortable sharing it with me. Before I leave, before I go back.

"Rashid had to sell most of everything to keep them afloat. I knew about it, but I didn't know what to do. I tried to bid on a few things online, but I lost the bids, and I don't know… I felt like I failed him, though he didn't know."

I smile weakly at her as the front door jingles. "You're doing your best." I take a deep breath as Rashid steps inside and lets his backpack drop to the floor. And I wait.

My breath catches in my throat as his gaze wanders to the walls of pictures. Him, a youngling of perhaps five or six, staring up as his mom with awe as she puts a birthday cake on the counter. Him, smiling in his cheer uniform maybe a year ago as she kisses him on his cheek.

Him, laughing at the camera, as his dad hugs them both.

Tears crawl down his cheeks and he bolts toward us, throwing an arm around both me and Sarah. We hold him, letting him sob, rubbing his back, telling him it's okay. Telling him we're here. Telling him she's always here with him, always in his heart.

Sarah's crying, too, and next I know, so am I. Them for their own versions of loss, and me for my mom, and the future. And our ship that still can't take us to temporary safety in Ocara.

And Hali-Monchuri. My poor homeworld devastated by the crash, devastated by The Second Chaos. Struggling already. We all carry such loss with aplomb until we crack. This is us cracking.

Later, Felix finds us having gorged on empanadas and sitting on the pillows, talking about family and the universe. He saw the entire scene through my eyes, felt what I felt— something he must be able to do now without the override injection. We're still angry at each other, and we aren't communicating like we normally do—but he's proud of me. Except about me petting Chadwick, who he believes may be hooking his manipulative cat claws into my mind.

He takes a seat beside me on the floor, but keeps his distance.

"Joy," he whispers as Sarah and Rashid talk about cheerleading and how his mom attended every game. How she would learn the routines and buy them all milkshakes after. "The ship will be ready tomorrow night, if Thomas Gibston is to be believed."

"And then we go to Ocara?"

He nods. "I think… I think—"

The front door crashes open and we all twist around to see a hooded figure standing inside the frame. They have a

Qadin crest on the right side of their chest. But that's about all we can identify on their swatch of black cloth.

Sarah screams. Rashid jumps up, ready to fight, and Felix stands in front of us all, his hands out to keep us behind him.

"You only want me. Take me. Spare them." He says it in English for our humans to understand. "I am the Duke."

Don't you dare! I scream in his head, rocking to my feet. His outstretched arm is unyielding, holding me back. *I will not lose you.*

Your safety is more important. Yours and theirs. His gaze meets mine quickly, and then he walks toward the tall hooded figure gingerly. "Promise you won't hurt them."

"I cannot—" The figure begins, their gloved hands moving up to move their hood back and reveal themselves…when they're suddenly thwacked upside the head. As their body crumples to the floor, we all raise our gazes to an older Black man who looks just like Rashid. Whose face I learned from the pictures I hung on the wall.

His eyes are wide, he's got an oversized beard, and he holds his suitcase firmly.

"I just got home and I heard a…a…a scream," he stutters, staring down at the figure on the floor. The hand by his side shakes, and his body sways a little unsteadily. "I don't… Who is that? Who are all of you? What is going on here? Rashid?"

CHAPTER 17
FELIX

We've tied the intruder to a kitchen stool, and uncovered them to reveal a face I'd seen on holo-vision once or twice, maybe. Which means they've found us. Which means we've endangered not only these humans, but Earth.

Rashid's father—Tony, as we learn—still stands there, holding his suitcase. His gaze wildly flicks to the art on the walls, the pictures Joy placed around their house, to Sarah, who holds Rashid close, and then to Joy and I as we stand over the prone figure.

He swallows, his hand shaking. "Who are you people? Rashid, why are these people in our house?"

"Dad, they're my friends," Rashid answers, springing to action. He tries to pull his father away from us, but the father won't budge.

"Friends don't bring cloaked assailants into our house,

Raz." Tony stands taller, hand on his hip, and his lower lip curls as he regards us both.

"How would you know? You haven't been home in weeks, Dad. You *left* me. They are the ones who came here, who listened to me, who were there for me. Look what they did for us." Rashid waves his arms around at all the pictures Joy hung.

His father's face falls.

The words rush out of Rashid's mouth as if they've been held in too long. "She died three months ago and you left me alone to feed and support myself. I had to sell everything. I couldn't do cheer, SAT prep, and work another job post-pandemic. Mom would've hated that you left me instead of us leaning on each other." A sob wracks Rashid's body as tears stream down his face. "They're my friends. Sarah, Joy, and even Felix." I don't know why he had to say *even* there. "They were here when you weren't."

"I'm sorry," Tony says. "I'm so sorry. I didn't mean to… I don't know where I went. Your mom and I always planned a trip along the West Coast, and I wanted that time to be close to her as I spread her ashes. I'm sorry, Rashid." His father's voice wobbles, and he reaches out for Rashid.

As they embrace, the Monchuran lifts their head, blearily focusing on us.

"Yes…well, while it's very emotionally charged in here, which admittedly I find a bit uncomfortable—" Joy elbows me to keep me on course "—we do have a person tied to a chair using window decor and our only weapon is a dented suitcase. Perhaps it would be best if all of you humans would give us aliens some space?"

"What?" Tony laughs…and then it slowly dawns on him

as the Monchuran tilts their head to the side, exposing a leaking blue cut from the back of their head. Tony takes one look and his eyes roll to the back of his head, and he falls back into Rashid's waiting arms.

I purse my lips. "They just keep passing out whenever something surprises them. Are humans built so differently…?"

"While I'm not a scientist, I do know that humans are comprised of mostly water, and I believe that it makes their bodies more fluid, which in turn leads to nonsense," our captive Monchuran states very clearly. They brandish a smile. "My name is DiOla H'ue. You can call me Di, she or her. I'm the personal guard for Princess LaTanya Qadin and I'm here, right now, to help you get back to your family."

Momentarily, I'm speechless. Thoughtless almost. My family locked up behind bars? The ones who sacrificed themselves so I could run away and clear my name from afar? I would give anything to be back in their presence and off this planet, but I can't. I have to make their sacrifice count, for me, for Joy, for our people and our kingdom.

Joy's hand flaps on her chest as she takes a step toward DiOla. "To the Soleil, who will kill us."

"I don't know what's going on here or why that person has blue blood, or why you called yourselves aliens. Like illegal aliens? Because people can't be illegal." Sarah grabs a pan from the stove and holds it up. "But you won't take them without a fight!"

Di smiles, soundlessly laughing. "You are a very cute human. I've only been on this planet for a day, but I've been fairly unimpressed with humanity till now." She shrugs and all her bindings come off but she makes no effort to stand.

"You want to take me back so what, I can be punished for a crime I didn't commit? So you can torture my Kindred? Why would I go with you?" I stare into her velvety orange eyes, the anger unfurling deep inside of me at all this unfairness and danger and worry about Joy's life more than my own.

"When I say family, I don't mean your adoptive parents." She brushes some of the curtain lint off her jacket and lounges back on the stool, her back hitting the kitchen counter. "I mean the Qadin family. Your mother, Princess LaTanya, sent me before she was captured, and I'm following her orders to get you home. I won't stop till I do. I gave her my word."

I shake my head, thoughts whirling through my mind as I stare at this liar. I cannot be Princess LaTanya's son. She never married. She never even was pregnant. The news would have covered that. But then…the ship did say I had Qadin DNA. No, I can't believe that.

"The Qadins are dead." Joy steps beside me, mashing her skin against mine. "This is a trick."

"It's not." DiOla's gaze flicks to Joy. "Princess LaTanya suspected Arren would revolt when she announced her wedding. She didn't expect him to kill her family, or that he would fake her death as long as he could to get her crown before the kingdom knew." Di's eyes mist, and her lips twist. "She didn't know he would be so ruthless."

My mother, LaTanya. My grandfather, King Jevor… But no, I still can't believe this. "Arren has done things I can't agree with, but he's been loyal. He's even—"

Di laughs, cutting me off, though there's an edge of anger in the gesture. "He even set you up for murder by planting an upload chip with incriminating evidence. He did everything he could to get you to his side, use your status, and have a second path to the crown."

I step farther away, reaching out to Joy as I'm accustomed to, even if we are fighting. "That doesn't make sense."

I have parents. They gave themselves up for me. LaTanya may have showed up in my childhood here and there, but she never treated me like a son. Why would she want me to come home? Why would Arren frame me for murder?

"If LaTanya's alive, then we're safe, right?" I ask, and a strange feeling of relief swims around Joy's stomach for the first time since our birthday.

"No. Arren killed King Jevor and his husband, Duke Midas, and the Queen Mother. He kept LaTanya alive to watch..." Di trails off and no one knows what to ask next. I stand there flummoxed, unsure of what I'm supposed to do with this information.

"How do you know all of this?" The question blurts from my mouth. "Were you there?"

"LaTanya's my Kindred," is the only answer Di needs to give. Her eyes flash while locking onto mine.

"But Johann—" Joy doesn't finish.

"Johann was a paid decoy."

"Arren." That's the one name that falls from my lips with confusion.

Joy's memories of him stream through her mind—the way he made her sign documents, the way he made her scream. All to protect me. To control me. To deny me my Kindred and make her obey him. Like he did to LaTanya.

Suddenly I feel the urge to punch something. Anything.

Anger rushes through my limbs and muscles, tensing me for a fight I can't even have so far from home.

"Arren craves the crown. The moment LaTanya announced her nuptials, he saw it slipping away…" She pauses for a moment. "There's something…off about him. Evil. He wanted LaTanya to marry him, but she refused. He killed her family. She still refused. He killed Johann, thinking he was her Kindred and that she'd be completely broken without him. He kept you close for years, knowing you are LaTanya's child. He plans on using you to sway her hand. Monchuri will never accept someone not having the Qadin name as their ruler."

I scrub my chin with my hand as Joy's fingers lace through mine. Her heart hammers through her body and into mine, and I desperately want to tell her we'll be okay or…more likely for her to tell me we'll be okay. I just want to go back to last night, when we argued and the biggest pain I had was from hurting her. Not this.

Joy's voice quietly pierces through my rambling thoughts. *Do you believe her?*

I don't know, I answer truthfully. I stand taller, trying to regain my posture and my confidence. "What do you want us to do?"

"I want you to save our kingdom." Now Di stands, taking a filled pastry from the counter behind her and touching the edge of her foot against Tony's leg. "You and your Kindred may be our only hope for stopping The Third Chaos."

"You all have a lot of explaining to do." Sarah finally lowers the pan.

"What's The *Third* Chaos?" Rashid's timid voice pulls us from the panic raging through our minds.

"War," Joy and I answer at the same time. "The end of life."

★ ★ ★

The First Chaos was when Indigo created new songs that in turn, created new worlds. But then worlds disappeared and the darkness came to overtake all life, blah-blah-blah, which was God Ozvios. Indigo comprised "A Song of the Universe," where all life came together and defeated Ozvios.

"The First Chaos is basically just a story about a black hole threatening to swallow up whole planets," I sum up. "The Second Chaos was a war of the classes, a revolution. The poor versus the rich. The Second Chaos resulted in the Kindred Program, so that no one was ever truly alone, so that no one felt the need to rebel anymore. They had a voice, and they could use it. Poor and rich connected to understand one another."

Joy clears her throat. "The Second Chaos supposedly gave us unity…"

"And The Third Chaos supposedly will end it." Di exhales slowly, the words seemingly a burden. "A war between worlds that'll spill over. All life-forms will battle and all will lose."

I scoff, shaking my head. "People—specifically those who believe in Indigo and the divinity of the universe—say that if The First Chaos was creation, The Second Chaos is progression…and The Third Chaos must be complete destruction."

"The people of Monchuri believe it. Hali believes it." Joy rubs her temple as a headache begins to pound behind her eyes. The pain of which I feel after years of nothing thanks to the injection, and I really do not enjoy it. But I'd rather feel Joy's pain than her absence.

I try to focus on home. I never imagined the people of Monchuri would fall for such foolishness. But then they fall for anything as long as it doesn't inconvenience their lives. Still, the most pressing question needs to be asked.

They choose not to study the history that led to my people suffering, Joy agrees. *They chose ignorance. They would rather fear The Third Chaos than understand what led to it.*

And so have I, before… I take a deep breath, my shoes squelching on the tiled floor. "What are me and Joy supposed to do?"

Di polishes off the last bite of the pastry before sitting on the stool again. "It's really rather straightforward. You go back to Maru under the pretense of meeting with Arren, you save LaTanya, and then kill Arren." She looks at the pictures on the walls and heaves a sigh.

"No offense, but how are either of these two gonna do that? I've known them for a couple of days, and like… Felix can barely pay attention to anything that doesn't interest him, and Joy was too afraid to kill a mosquito… So…" Rashid gives us both a sad smile while lifting his father onto the couch and putting a pillow under his head. He's probably right. "I legit had to show Felix how to moisturize his own skin and how to open a packet of taco sauce," he continues. "And Joy's form of rebellion is looking at pretty pictures."

"Are you all done?" I glance between them. Joy stays blessedly quiet, her own mind streaming through the possibilities and dangers. "There are several issues with your straightforward plan."

"Oh, definitely. You have one massive issue on this very planet, hunting you at this very minute." Di cocks an eyebrow, waiting for us to ask what. But neither of us will bite. If she wants the glory of sounding smart and informed, it's all hers. We are entirely at her mercy. "Brak Merlbin. The man's driven and filled with rage." She pauses again, eyeing us both. "He has a tracker on him. His every move is broadcasting live on *Monchuri News*. Arren has made your capture entertaining enough to distract people from the rising panic."

I squeeze Joy's hand. "I fail to see how this is our problem. If he's not here and doesn't know where we are, how does it affect us?"

"Because," Di says as Tony groans from the couch, coming to, "he's been ordered by Arren to kill your Kindred and take you back."

No, Joy says. *Felix.*

I can't let anything happen to you, I whisper into her mind at the same time as she whispers, *I will not let anything happen to you.*

"If I die, what would happen to Felix?" She swallows the lump forming in her throat and I wish I could take away the panic, the fear. But I don't know how to until this is all resolved.

"Come now, Arren created that override for your head. I imagine—and he imagines—it's still in place, isn't it? Why else do you think he'd personally give you that injection every year?"

"I didn't take it this year. Didn't get a chance..." Joy says quietly, and Di's eyes flash with the news.

"Well, that's not good." Di stands, rubbing her head from where Rashid's dad hit her. "Is your ship broken?"

"It's fixed," I respond quickly. "We just need fuel."

"Everyone knows you're flying a HAMDI hopper. Don't get me wrong, that's fine, but no way you'll get through the Monchuri blockade and surveillance without a clearance tag. Which Brak Merlbin will have... And I can't give you." She flicks her gaze to Rashid's now-moving father. "Nice swing, old man."

Tony startles up, slowly rising from the couch. "I don't know what you are, and who you are, but I want you out of my house. Now."

Di shrugs, putting her hood back up. "Just as well, it's getting late. I'll find you tomorrow so we can coordinate."

I ignore Tony for the moment. "Where are you staying?"

"An Andarran lives in town, even teaches at the high school you two have been attending. Who do you think let me know you were here?"

"Thomas?" Me and Joy look at each other. "He's human, though."

"I don't know this Thomas, but I know Rae. Pastel hair, wild blue eyes, beautiful smile..." Di trails off dreamily. "I'm quite fond of them, actually."

Neither of us know what to say to that. Who knew Andarrans lived on Earth? Who knew the cheer coach was one? Who knew they were spying on us? And who else is from another world, living in secret on Earth? Far too many questions, and not enough time for answers.

"Brak will find you, soon. You need to leave tomorrow."

And with that Di exits through the door she came and we stand there, silent. Surprised. Speechless. Terrified.

After a few more beats of silence, Tony finds his voice again. "I want you all out now."

"But, Dad," Rashid begins.

"Out." He points at the door. "I appreciate what you did for Rashid, but I don't know you. You've brought danger into our home…and I can't protect him from…whatever the hell you are. I already lost my wife, I won't lose my son." Tony doesn't even look at us when he says it, but at Rashid.

"Dad…" Rashid trails off.

"He's right," Joy says, swallowing down the emotions threatening to overtake her. "We're dangerous. You've already been too kind to us. I know we…we didn't get to know you long enough, but I think of you as one of my best friends, Rashid."

"Joy. I… Joy," Rashid's tone warbles, and he bolts into her arms, hugging her fiercely. I feel the warmth encompass my own body, and the relief swims through her. Relief and sadness. "This isn't goodbye."

She dips her head. "I'm sorry, Mr. Williams. Thank you for letting us stay here."

Tony looks away at his son, and whatever emotion he's feeling I can't quite read. He gives us a few moments to pack our things, and then Sarah offers to drive us somewhere. On the one condition that we *explain whatever the hell we are*. Which we do in the car, despite her many, many questions.

"Is there a hotel, maybe?" Joy ponders from the front seat. "Somewhere we'll be safe and won't endanger anyone else?"

"There are plenty of hotels, but none that'll take two teenagers without ID." Sarah shakes her head, taking a sharp left onto a residential road overrun by palm trees and the sounds of tiny pests.

Joy lets out a heavy exhale. "Where else can we go?"

I suck my teeth, the answer uncomfortable and unpleasant for everyone involved. "Thomas bloody Gibston."

★ ★ ★

MONCHURI MORNING NEWS NOW!

Transcript featuring L'avi Jonu and Nyla Harkibi of _Good Morning Monchuri_, filmed in front of a live studio audience in Maru-Monchuri

LJ: Good morning, Monchuri! The hunt for Duke Hamdi and his traitorous Kindred, Joy Abara, continues on Terra. One of our hunters, DiOla H'ue, is currently untraceable. Her ship is still located in the polar northern hemisphere known as North America. We wonder, sadly, if something has befallen our most esteemed hunter…

NH: That, we don't—can't—know yet. But currently, Brak Merlbin is making moves. He has traveled using stealth abilities from the continent known as "Asia" to another continent known as "Australia," where he has been attacked by very violent creatures and insects.

LJ: Yes, I saw that. Traumatic experiences, I imagine. Terra is as wild as it is dangerous.

NH: You've got that right. Thankfully, Brak is doing fine, if a bit slow in his pursuit after a bite from a…tar-rant-you-la… Am I saying that right?

LJ: Yes, a tarantula, as extraterrestrial wildlife

experts have stated, which have venomous bites to larger creatures, like us. But all Monchuri ships are equipped with state-of-the-art medi-kits. After a quick scan, Brak is back on the hunt, searching for the ship belonging to the Hamdi family line. Though I imagine the Duke has found a way to cut off tracking.

NH: Which brings us to our special guest today. Duke Felix Hamdi is paired with Joy Abara from Hali-Monchuri. While we've been following the Duke for most of his life, there was little interest in knowing about his Kindred…until now. With the hunt ongoing, we thought it was time to know Joy. And who better than her betrothed, Maxon KiBanu *(audience applause as the guest walks onto the stage, waving at cameras)*.

LJ: Maxon, welcome to *Monchuri Morning News*. We are pleased to have you here.

NH: Pleased and excited!

LJ: Yes, excited but desperate for information. So let's get started. How long were you engaged to Joy Abara?

Maxon KiBanu (MK): Hi, thank you for having me. I've never been to Maru, and the capital here on Estrella is gorgeous, the people friendly. I feel at home here… *(the audience cheers)* My own Kindred, Ifueko, once visited on a noble trip and praised our capital planet as being the friendliest, prettiest, and most welcoming world in our system before she died, and I have to agree *(the audience cheers again)*.

LJ: What a good citizen you are! We feel the same way about home, and are happy to have you.

NH: Yes, all true. Now let's talk Joy!

MK: Um…yes, sorry. I met Joy last year at our Temple. We were betrothed that same day, although she wasn't really my type.

NH: Aha, I see. Why not?

MK: Well, because she didn't seem particularly… She was rather poor and her clothes were ill-fitting. I did think there was something amiss with her Kindred pairing. She would sometimes stop talking to me or laugh at jokes I didn't make. I began to see that their connection was not healthy and interfered with her daily life.

LJ: Right, let's see if we have a picture of her here. Ah, there we are (picture displayed in top left corner of holo-screens). I see…

NH: I… (coughs), I can see what you're saying. A plump girl with no discernible beauty.

LJ: On the contrary, I find her beauty almost alluring, exotic. She doesn't look like any woman here on Maru-Monchuri, and that could be why Duke Felix was so easily manipulated by her.

NH: You know what, I didn't think about it like that, L'avi. Good catch. Well, is there anything else you can tell us about Joy, Maxon? Anything you'd like to say to her if she could watch?

MK: (turning to the camera) Joy, I know we hardly knew each other. But… I do hope you'll turn yourself in. Not just for my sake—though my reputation has suffered—but for the sake of our kingdom. I will do whatever I can to make you come home again, and to save Monchuri.

NH: That's exactly what we want to hear!

LJ: And we have the perfect plan for you, Maxon.

MK: I look forward to...serving Monchuri however I can, to see our great system stable and safe for all its citizens.

NH: Isn't this boy darling, everyone? Joy Abara's loss is our gain, and to anyone watching and interested, he's single!

MK: Actually, *(he pauses to laugh)* I'm still very much betrothed. Though we've hit a snag in our upcoming nuptials, I'm not able to break our engagement without her consent and the acceptance of a high-ranking priest *(audience gasps, chatter)*.

LJ: I'm sure there is someone who could help you out of this predicament. You can't be expected to marry a murderess fugitive.

NH: Though can you imagine what a fascinating story that'd make!

CHAPTER 18

JOY

"CARRY THEM ALL. BE STRONG, BE A WOMAN, BE
BLACK. THEY DON'T CARE THAT THE WEIGHT OF
THE WORLD WILL BREAK MY BACK."

—*DEJA REESE, "EXPLODE"*

Owen answers the door, taking in the sight of us with our
bags and my tear-stained face, and invites us inside his dusty
home immediately.

"What happened, are you okay?" He takes the bags from
my hands and sets them down on the floor, his eyes locked
on mine. "Did someone hurt you? Are you cold?"

"Oh, for *Gods'* sakes," Felix mutters before I can answer.
"We're here to speak to your father. If you wouldn't mind
telling him we're here."

The door shuts softly behind us as a whoosh of air comes
from somewhere deep inside the darkened house. The air is

stale, and warm, and some fragrance sticks to my skin that I'd rather not smell.

"Who's that?" Mr. Gibston asks, appearing quite suddenly, his hair frazzled in places, but his eyes bright, voice clear. He squints, head tilted to the side. "What are you doing here?"

He's not drinking. You did this? I ask.

He did it himself. Got his confidence back, I think. Though Felix says it matter-of-factly, there's a twinge of pride in his voice. *That could've been me in the future...if I didn't have you.* Felix stands tall. "Due to circumstances best left unsaid, we need lodging."

"Dad?" Owen turns to his father as he scratches his head. "We can't have students staying here... Isn't that sorta like... against the rules? I mean, Joy would be fine, since she's not really a student, but the other—"

"We aren't *really* students," I begin, swallowing the lump in my throat.

Felix sets his bags on the floor. "We're aliens, and that big structure underneath that tarp in the backyard is our spaceship, which your father is kindly fueling for us. All said, we had a bit of a run-in with a friendly Monchuran bounty hunter and we need a new place to stay, Thomas."

Silence stretches between us as Thomas gets lost in his many thoughts and Owen's eyes widen. He doesn't faint, much to Felix's surprise. Owen's gaze returns to me as he plops down into a seat, running a hand through his golden hair. He's confused and undoubtedly wishes he never expressed his interest in me. I mean, who admits to having a crush on an alien?

Thomas blows out a stream of air. "There's barely room

here, and what if another…bounty whatever comes for you? You're exposing my son to danger."

"We understand. We would never wish to endanger you or any other human." I bow my head.

"We've got a handle on the bounty hunters." Felix tries to gloss over the truth, to everyone's peril. "But if you can't offer housing—which we understand completely—perhaps you can use your ID to help us get a hotel room? We have our own money."

"A hotel?" Thomas narrows his eyes on us. "Two seventeen-year-olds staying in a hotel? That'd draw more attention than you'd want. No." He exhales, his attention reluctantly flitting around the room. "It'd probably be best if you stayed here tonight while I fuel your ship."

"Dad." Owen's voice cracks. "There are…there are aliens? *They're* aliens? What does that even mean? They look like us? How did you… How long have you known?"

"He knew about us before we knew about humans," Felix answers for him, earning him a glare. I elbow him in the side as Owen and his father begin to have the difficult conversation I hope doesn't disturb their relationship. I can only help one family a day at this rate and I'm so tired already.

Thomas puts his hand up to calm his son. "Felix told me yesterday, I—"

"If you wouldn't mind," I intercede. "Would you tell me where the facilities are?"

Thomas tells me they're down the hall on the right, and I leave them all there to talk about aliens and worlds they don't know or understand. I slip into the bathroom, take a seat on the toilet, and put my head between my legs. My breaths come in rasps. Thoughts and scenes slide through my mind's reel. Pain. Suffering. Humanity. My mum. Felix's parents. Owen reaching for me in the water to bring me close, to kiss, and me pulling away gently. *Not you*, I said with a sad smile, *my heart belongs to another*. And here I am in his house, asking for help.

Everything I've touched on this world was never mine to touch and I've made a mess.

I'll never leave you, Joy. Not until death, and I think, even then, we'll be in whatever heaven exists together, Felix says quietly, and just like that, our fight is over. Completely.

I chuckle once, the tears sliding down my cheeks. *I know*.

And then he's gone, informing Thomas about the stars and our sleeping requirements, and I'm left to my despair alone. Which is what I sorta want.

The evening plays out in my mind again. The hopefulness on Rashid's face, the pictures on the wall, the crack of the suitcase on DiOla's head, Rashid's dad…being kicked out. My mum. My home. My world. Felix, the heir. My Kindred, a king.

Brak Merlbin. The name sounds so familiar but I can't quite place it. Maybe I've heard his name in Felix's thoughts or somewhere… I shake my head of the thoughts and grab a piece of paper to dab my eyes. Right, it's not the end. It's not goodbye. I will see Rashid again. I will see Sarah again.

Just because I feel like I've lost something I'm not even sure I wanted—but desperately needed—doesn't mean I have lost them for good. We have so little time left and I can't waste it. No matter if our ship's not ready and a bounty hunter is coming to kill me.

I won't go down without a fight, even if my body and mind

scream at me to stop. To get a handle on the events of the evening before I explode. When I emerge from the facilities with dry eyes and a new attitude, Felix and Thomas are arguing.

"You two can't sleep in the same room. That's…inappropriate," he says, slapping his hand on a table full of papers and books and empty, dirty dishes. I cringe. "I don't know either of you or what you mean about sharing a mind or whatever, but this is not a…a…sex motel. While you're here, you're minors and you'll adapt to our way of life, understand? You are the outsiders."

"Adapt?" I raise my voice while I try to keep the heat from my cheeks. "Felix Hamdi is my Kindred." I put my hand on my hip, all the sorrow pushed to the back of my brain to make room for my furious indignation. "Frankly, you *humans* are children when it comes to understanding such a deep bond. You've never had someone else in your mind, your feelings, your thoughts, your life who is there to listen and feel and think with you. How would you even know?" The anger I've been keeping pent-up finally unleashes. "All I've seen since coming to this world are people who spend too much time burying or hiding their feelings, when embracing them will make your lives so much easier and better."

Thomas's brows rise and Owen's furrow, but neither speak. The room is silent aside from the pounding of my heart.

"I want to love humanity." My voice cracks as the emotions flood through my mind and out of my lips. "Where we're from, I'm treated like a speck of dirt on someone's shoe, easily overlooked or scrubbed away. But you are no different. You are lonely without a Kindred, and you hurt each other. Your news programs show people…" I take a deep breath. "People who look like me, like Felix, who are not pale-skinned or heteronormative…treated without care or respect."

Beje. Felix takes my hand in his. *Don't let this burden your heart. We are not long for this world.*

"You infantilize a culture that has been around longer than your very existence." My tone shifts from rage into disappointment. "You dishonor us, you've dishonored *me* just like everyone else. We don't need to share a room or a bed, but please understand that as outsiders we stick together because it's all *we* know." And who knew I'd lose my temper over a bed, but here I am. Angry. Tired. Resentful. Terrified.

"I'm—we're sorry." Owen doesn't meet my gaze. "He's— we're both trying to make sense of something we could never understand."

"I didn't mean to offend you," Thomas begins. "I know that…it hasn't been easy for you to crash here and be at the mercy of some mess of a teacher. I don't know what awaits you at your home…"

"Death and punishment." Felix kicks at the edge of the ratty rug on the floor. "We left home to avoid those, and we'll go back to face them."

"And they will kill me," I add, almost numbly.

"Then don't go back. Stay here. Be here with us. We can take care of you." Owen rises from his seat, and puts his hands on my arms, staring deep into my eyes. "You can stay. Why go back?"

"You only offer this because you don't understand me. You think I'm a damsel needing saving, that I need to be cared for as if I'm fragile. You like to save people because you feel like you can't save the person who matters the most to you."

I glance between him and his father. "I like you, Owen, as a friend, as a human—you made me feel free and happy. But..."

I know this is hard for you, Joy, but Owen may be right, Felix says quietly. *You could stay and I could go. I have to save them, but you don't. You can live the life you've always wanted.*

There is no life for me without you close. I shake my head. "But...Felix and I are stronger together than apart." I swallow. "Your world hasn't learned that yet, but we have. Kindreds know this in every fiber of their being." Owen's arms drop from me as if he finally understands my heart, and I turn to Felix. "Because I'll never leave Felix. Not until death, and even then," I repeat his words aloud, "we'll be in whatever heaven exists together."

Felix gives me a sad smile, one that holds no guarantees. One that soothes my soul for just a moment. And everything that has been plaguing me since saying goodbye to Rashid falls away as he wraps his arms around me. I let myself cry again, let myself feel and then move on. Because the time we have left is dwindling and I need to be strong to go back. I need to be strong to face the possible end of our story.

★ ★ ★

As Thomas and Owen go about their separate affairs, Thomas to continue the fueling process and Owen to his morning meeting at the school woodworking club, Felix and I stay in bed. We think. We plan. We worry.

"How can we go back, on our own, without help, and save your bio-mother and then...somehow kill Arren?" I prop myself on my elbow and brush a stray hair away from his face. I know there are so many emotions lingering between us, that our argument isn't completely over, but we don't have time for that. He captures my hand in his and brings it to his lips, placing a gentle kiss there. My brain nearly short-circuits at the contact and something warm flips in the pit of my stomach.

"I felt that." Felix smiles as he gazes up at me. "I felt that."

"Don't let it go to your head." I laugh nervously and my elbow shakes, causing me to almost topple over. "No one has ever touched me like that is all. And it's beautiful because I can feel everything."

"I know," he murmurs as sunlight filters in through the grimy window at the end of the room. "It's beautiful to feel everything."

"The override doesn't work anymore, Felix," I admit, though he already knows. He has to. Everything has changed. Who we are has changed. Our bond is stronger, better than before. Our connection is what it was always meant to be. "We are going to die, and we've barely lived."

He laughs quietly, his hand still holding mine against his chest. "I don't know, I've lived a bit in my time."

"I know." I smile down at him. "You've seen worlds and met so many people. For a moment, you almost had everything you wanted."

He stills. "What is it you think I've wanted for so long?"

I don't know why he asks that, as if I don't know. "To play your music, be your own person. Be free from all expectations."

This time he laughs with no humor in it, while his gaze locks on mine. "Oh, Joy. You've read my mind all our lives and still don't know what to make of it." I grimace, and try to pull my hand from his firm grip. "Either I'm a genius with my thoughts, or you've always undervalued yourself."

I roll my eyes. "What does that mean?"

"The only thing I've ever wanted and I was never close to having was you," he says crisply, his voice ringing with confidence. The air leaves my lungs in a gasp. His eyes fixate on my lips and I try to keep myself from shaking.

"I want to kiss you." Nerves thread through his words. "Can I kiss you?"

The answer gets stuck in my throat. I can't tell him an emphatic yes. I can't say anything. I've wanted this longer than I've wanted anything in my entire life. I've wanted this before I knew what wanting him meant.

Still the truth deserves to be said, even if I hate it. "Felix, I'm betrothed. My wedding is tradition. It is my duty. And you're possibly going to be a king—"

He nibbles on his bottom lip and something cracks a little within me. Perhaps my resolve. "If we don't die first."

"So you want to kiss me because this may be the last kiss you have before we die and so nothing matters?"

"Ugh, you are impossible." He groans. "I've been in love with you for most of my life, Joy. And I say most because I didn't know what love meant as a kid, not when it came to you. Once I thought you were my sister. Once I thought you were my best friend. And then... I knew. You were so much more than either of those things. You are everything to me. I dreamed of kissing you—"

I gulp down my nerves. "Dreams don't mean anything, even you said that."

"I lied. Because if they mean something, then you'd know how I felt. And you were pulling away...so I thought you couldn't feel the same—"

"Arren," I mutter. "The override."

"I didn't know. We keep our secrets but I don't want this to be one of them. Not when everything is…uncertain. Do you understand?"

I slowly nod. He loves me. He's in love with me. Why? How? How long? Really? I want to scream and cry and jump on this bed and sing and dance. Felix is in love with me. And despite how it could never be more than this moment, what a beautiful moment this is.

"You're everything I've ever wanted, too."

His nose twitches and he laughs, the sound sending flutters through my entire being. "Your thoughts, Joy."

And then he lifts his head to mine. There's an inch between us and his warm breath tickles my cheeks. With one hand, he clutches the side of my face as if I'm a precious jewel, as if I'm his jewel and he will do everything to keep me shining.

His lips on mine are everything I thought they'd be and I feel the kiss twice. It's all-encompassing and surreal. A groan slips between my teeth as I let him in to explore me, to taste me, and let him be mine for as long as we can. And he, who has kissed a million times, is clumsy. He wants to do too much too fast because it's too good. It's too perfect.

I laugh and he laughs and we keep kissing, finding our rhythm. And I think I'm crying because a tear trickles down my cheek and I laugh again. And his stomach flips just like my own. I feel everything and everything feels right.

"Felix," I whisper.

"Stay here with me, *beje*," he murmurs. "Just for now."

Where once was pleasure is now panic. "I can't— We can't— That's not— I'm not— I don't—"

"I mean to just kiss, Joy." He gives me another quick peck on the lips that feels far too short. "Don't get me wrong," he says hoarsely, "I want that, too. *Gods*, I want that, too. But not now. I don't think my heart could handle it."

"You want that?" My mouth hangs open and I want to kiss him again, slower this time, longer. Forever, forgetting that there are worlds spinning around us, and responsibilities and death and royals. "With me?"

"Are you kidding?" He makes a sound between a gasp and a laugh. "I know you must think I've slept with everyone because I'm...you know, I'm me...but I've never... I've never done that."

I shake my head in disbelief. "But the bras and the boys and the shows..."

He chuckles like a bundle of nerves. "You have no idea. How could you, when you blocked me out with the override? You don't know that every time someone tried to take it to that level with me, I said no. My heart was never in it. It couldn't be. I've fooled around. I'm a pro at fooling around because it's something I can do without needing a connection. But I've never done anything else."

I eye him shyly, my lips twitching, and cheeks heating. "I've never even done that. Or this."

"I know." He leans in again, setting his arm against the headboard to kiss me again. How will I ever get enough of that? His heart drums against my own and I'm startled from the beauty of it when he continues, "I don't need a deep connection to feel attraction and act on it, not like you but I could never be that free, or...vulnerable with someone that's not you." I smile because he knows. "You're my lovely demi-ace girl who needs to feel safe and secure to explore her feelings. I love that about you. I love everything about you. I... I've never wanted anyone else."

My cheeks heat to a higher temperature and I briefly wonder if emotions can make you sick. "I never could want anyone else."

"You and me," he says breathlessly, taking my hand in his as we curl up around each other. "We're forever."

"No, Felix," I interject sadly, crushing my own hope. "We're for right now. If we even manage to make it out of this alive, I will still need to marry Maxon. I will still need—"

A loud knock on the front door has us bolting apart.

This is not a sex motel, Felix says through our connection sheepishly. Though he's hurt. His mind is still processing my denial of the future.

"Should we get it?" But I needn't have asked because the front door opens and we jump out of bed, dart to the door and find Sarah holding up a few bags, glaring at me with a wry smile.

"You may have forgotten about your whole—" her voice drops as she peers around "—bounty-hunter issue. But have no fear, I have an idea. You should lure him here and then take him out."

"Take him out where?" Felix asks, brows furrowed as he stands behind me.

She rolls her eyes. "No, I mean, you know, kill him."

"That's an interesting phrase," Felix answers, while I stand there horrified.

"Kill him?" I shout just as Rashid steps through the door,

holding those frothy pink drinks I like and a bag full of pastries, which I like even more.

"Yes, as that bounty lady said, you need to get him out of the way and get his clearance thing or whatever. And that means we've gotta get him before we get got, you know?"

I shake my head. I do not actually know. "Can't we just turn the tracker back on, or would that hurt the humans? That could alert him to where we are…"

"No," Felix says softly. "The guide said that once you turn it off, you can't turn it back on, remember?"

"Which brings me to my plan about luring him here." Sarah sets her bags on the floor, and opens her phone to begin tapping onto it. "Deja Reese is in town for her concert tomorrow night. So I just posted a video of our cheer team asking her to come on over for a special little concert just for our school, since we're all small and in the middle of nowhere."

"Deja Reese," I shout at the same time Felix asks, "Did it work?"

"She'll be here tonight. And before the show, she said she'd make a video with you that'll go viral. That should get your dude here."

My mouth drops open. That could be the single best night of my life, outside of kissing Felix, or the last night of my life. But at least it would be on my own terms.

"How?" I wonder aloud as Rashid rushes over and locks me in a hug.

Sarah looks up from her phone, and her smile is wide. "I'm just as surprised as you that it worked, but she said yes, right away. Amazing, right?"

"Weird," Rashid says.

"Perfect." Felix puts his head on my shoulder and my stomach flips again.

And then I think about Deja Reese and her songs, her words, her gorgeousness. I have nothing to wear. The bounty hunter is gonna come to kill me. "Oh, my *Indigo*."

★ ★ ★

Two Years Ago

FELIX

My head falls back against the wall and I set the pen beside the holo-screen. The lyrics to my newest song glare back at me from the screen, all perfect and beautiful, just like her, but I can't let her see them. Can't let her know. Can't change this image she's formed of me in her mind.

She's asleep and I should be, too. We're three hours apart, but on both planets, it's bedtime. And we both have too much to do in the morning. She's supposed to go to her domestic-training program, run by the Halin government, and I'm supposed to attend an international leaders summit. Neither of our hearts, mind, or bodies are in it. Although Joy would never admit that to me.

Mom wants me to learn to be a noble befitting my name, a Hamdi who stands tall in front of the cameras and says and does the right things. I should be bringing honor and further prestige to our family, not out of duty—but because I desire it.

But she doesn't know I already do everything out of desire. And it's nothing she wants for me or from me—it's not prestigious, maybe not even honorable. I play my guitar, I strut around like I own the wooden stage beneath my feet when no one's watching, and I compose songs like I breathe air. Music courses through my veins along with my thick blue Monchuri blood. Joy inspires my lyrics. My brain creates the notes. Trouble is, I can't seem to get the words out when I'm up there in front of the lights.

Because I know she's listening along with everyone else and if she listens, then what? Will she know? Will I endanger her life? There's an invisible string between us, and the closer I get to her, the closer I pull her into the fire.

I can't hurt her. I can't see her hurt. I can't feel it. I can't be the source of it.

And so my brain freezes the moment the lyrics come to mind and I drink until I've washed them down. I drink until the truth becomes hidden, even from me, if even just for a little while.

Joy thinks it's stage fright. She even tries to help with the songs that mean nothing, and I let her, hoping she thinks that's all. She's distant. She pulls away more and more recently. It's like she's not here with me in my mind...

What if she's not?

I return to the screen, crossing out the word *adore* for *love*. A stupid rule she decided years ago; to say I adore you and not I love you, because it should be reserved for our future significant others. A laugh escapes my lips, and I toss back a swig of something spicy and hot that I keep under my bed for when I'm feeling low and especially broken.

The lyrics shimmer in front of me like stars I could pluck from the sky. Ugh, I'm so poetic right now.

Don't worry darling, they don't know it's just you and me
This...everything between us was always meant to be
Fate, it's a perfect fantasy
Stolen glances and thoughts between two worlds
How could I ever want someone else, how could I never want
more
When it's you I ~~adore~~ love?

I delete the song with a click of my pen and take another swig, the liquid flowing down the back of my throat, burning the words away. How am I supposed to pretend that all of this is okay?

CHAPTER 19

FELIX

I'm sitting on the ratty couch, pen and paper in hand, going over the plan, when the bedroom door swings open. Joy's radiant face greets mine as she stands in the doorway in her new dress that Sarah bought her earlier. The shimmery silver cloth clings to her curves and brings out the gray in her eyes. Her curls bounce by the sides of her face as she smiles at me.

"Sarah said she'll be back in a bit. She had to go home to change." She bends down to unzip her new snug boots. "She bought this entire outfit for me. Can you believe it? So generous and thoughtful. I would have never picked this for myself. You know I don't know fashion like you two…but these are a bit tight."

Thomas and I fueled the ship with food waste as Joy spent time with Rashid and Sarah. I made sure they had time together. I read her mind, I knew her thoughts—she needs these humans. They care about her and make her feel like she's normal…like she's accepted. They make her feel loved in a way I cannot.

Joy groans when she can't unzip her boot, startling me from my thoughts. I set the notebook aside, grateful Owen's at some sports meeting. I couldn't handle watching him fawn over Joy the way he does. Nor could I handle the inward cringe she feels every time he touches her, though she doesn't exactly know why that happens every single time.

I do, though.

She isn't used to the attention, or the way people look at her and see all of her beauty and intelligence and the way her smile lightens up the whole room. She's not used to people knowing the kindness in her heart and the way she laughs at even the most unfunny jokes. She's a beam of sunlight in a storm. And she's my Kindred.

My writing utensil tumbles to the floor as I cross over the raggedy carpet and fall to my knees. Her back hits the bedroom door, and it shuts, while my hand slips softly up the tight boot.

"Felix." Her voice warbles once as my fingers skim the top of the material and the edge of her dress. She swallows as one hand holds just below her knee and the other unzips the boot slowly, revealing her beautiful bare skin. I lift her leg slightly, and pull the boot from it, my own breath catching.

Her head falls back against the door, her breathing sharp, and I try to restrain myself from doing more. But as I attempt to put her leg back on the floor, I kiss the side of her knee and she gasps. The sound reverberates through me and aches desperately in every muscle and patch of skin.

I do the same to the second boot, as her breath goes shallow and my hands linger on her legs, sliding ever so slowly up her dress. And just when I want to go farther up that smooth, soft body and my brain screams at me to keep going and warmth spreads over the both of us, I stop myself.

"This is not a sex motel, don't you know?" I chuckle, trying to ease the tension. But I doubt there's anything I could say to stop this need buried deep inside of me. Joy looks down, her cheeks a bright pink. We can't do that, not when there's so much at stake and the future's not clear. Not when she still feels like she belongs to Maxon out of duty for Hali.

"You're teasing me," she whispers. "You're…mean. You know we can't. It was a one-kiss thing, Fe—"

"Do you want me to tease you more?" My tone is light, yet the desire settles on my lips and steals air from my lungs. My knee shakes on the hard carpet. "Would that be what you want? I'd give you my world if I could."

She laughs, smoothing down her dress nervously. "Don't ask questions you know the answers to."

I smirk up at her. "When it comes to this, I want to be perfectly aware of your answers."

"We shouldn't." She looks away, embarrassment threading through her gut. "I want you to tease me more."

"Ah, and what would that look like?" I push upward, my body pressing against her as I stand, my lips inches above hers.

"I don't know… Felix," she mumbles. She leans forward, and I kiss her like I've been wanting to since the first time. Our bodies are closer than they've ever been, and every place we touch burns. Her hands sink beneath my shirt and rove over my chest. I push her back against the door, lost in her and overwhelming my senses.

Everything she feels. Every desire. Every yearning and glimpse of what she wants stream through my mind. And she has to know that I want her to have everything. She has to know that my body was made for hers.

"Joy," I croak, my own hands unsure of where they want to go first. Everywhere, I think. My fingers skim over her thighs and then the doorbell rings and Joy jumps away, eyes wide.

"Great," I say through the sudden lumps in my throat.

She giggles, catching her breath and looking me over, before pulling the parlor door open. Rashid stands there, hands on his hips. His face is grim, severe. And we're reminded of our parents. Monchuri. Arren. Birth mother princess. Murder. We have no time for flirting and teasing and...

"Hey." His gaze darts between us and his brows lift. "Our alien cheer coach is on the way so whatever you two were doing that has you all—" he swings his hands around at us "—you better wrap it up now."

Joy smiles, though her heart's not in it, taking a seat on the edge of the chair. "Nothing was going on. He helped me with the boots. They're too tight."

"Yeah, I've used that line before." He walks inside, setting his bag on the ripped chair.

"No, you haven't." I shake my head, letting my breath stabilize and pushing that sudden lust as far down as I can. I quickly take a seat on the couch, and put a pillow over my lap to give myself space.

"No, I haven't, but I want to." Rashid runs a hand on his neck. "I was wondering when you two would...you know. Finally kiss."

"You knew?" Joy blurts, her eyes finding mine briefly.

"Anyone who has ever spent time with you two knows, sweetie. It's written all over his lovelorn face." Rashid smirks my way and I fight the urge to give him the middle finger, a thing I learned from the cheerleaders, which means stop talking, I think.

"It's only temporary," Joy says at the same time I admit, "We've waited forever."

And that's when the peace of the evening is ruined, and the mood alters further.

DiOla enters in her Monchuri guard fatigues, followed by Sarah, who's preoccupied by her phone, and the Andarran teacher, Miss Rae. DiOla scans the room like a true soldier, while the teacher bounds over to Joy, lifting her into a hug.

"Look at you in that dress! What a bright future you have." Their pink hair tosses to the side dramatically, and they remind me of every Andarran I've met with their vibrant personalities, colorful eyes, overdramatic nature, and predilection for emotional expression. How did I ever imagine they were human?

I rub a hand down my chin, wiping Joy's kiss away to distract myself from the need. "Do you see the future?"

Miss Rae's icy gaze flicks to mine. "Not all Andarrans have been kissed by destiny. We don't all serve some higher purpose." Their words are edged with a slight anger, and I find myself flinching away from it.

"I apologize for my offense," I state plainly, though it is a fair question and the answer would've been really helpful.

Rae huffs, letting their hands drop from Joy. "The only glimpses of the future I've seen have nothing to do with you two. I see a girl far away, an Ilori, a purple hat—I think?—fragments of some song I may have heard somewhere, and war. The Ilori are dangerous and someday soon…" They trail off.

"Oh," Joy says, her voice slipping into my mind. *Never ask an Andarran about the future. It'll freak you out.*

You're right about that. "So nothing about Monchuri," I say, laughing slightly. "Or Earth."

"I don't know." Miss Rae scrunches up their lips. "There are other Andarrans here who might."

"So some aliens can see the future? Good to know." Rashid sways a bit on his feet and I swear, if he faints again… "Can you do anything else?"

"Andarrans are empaths," Miss Rae says cheerfully. "I can tell that you're uncomfortable with the idea of aliens who can see the future, but it's something you've seen before?"

"X-Men." Rashid shrugs.

"And I can tell DiOla is worried…probably about the bounty hunter coming…and these two—" Miss Rae points at Joy and me "—are feeling very amorous yet conflicted."

Joy coughs and I chuckle, earning a glare from DiOla.

"Well, I mean…have you seen her?" I glance at Joy and back. "That's my Kindred. I'm the luckiest man in the universe."

"Love, the kind that develops over a lifetime." Miss Rae lets out a theatrical sigh. "Andarrans love love. I think we're all a bit jealous of the Kindred Program. And you two… I think you would've been together even if you weren't paired. There's that spark, you know?"

A spark that can never be a flame, Joy corrects. *Not if we want to save our kingdom. Your parents. Your bio-mother. We are trapped in these roles. Arren made sure of that.*

There's no response I can muster that could change what she said. We are trapped. The moment we leave here. And leave here, we must, if we don't want The Third Chaos.

Miss Rae prattles on about love and we fade into our thoughts.

You think we would be together if we weren't paired? If everything were different? Joy asks, dropping onto the couch beside me.

I laugh through our connection. *I think I would have fallen in love with you the moment I saw you, Joy Mirari Abara. You're the other half of my heart, the other half of my soul.*

She smiles as the creeping pinkness that colors her cheeks reaches her eyes. *Who knew Felix Hinada Hamdi could say such beautiful things without a joke or wink attached?*

Don't tell anyone. Wouldn't want to sully my reputation.

She frowns suddenly, her thoughts turning dark. Patches of my parents stream through her mind, the Soleil, the destruction on Hali…and then me. Questions float around. She's wondering what would happen if we die? What would happen if we live? Would I tell the world about her and our love? What will happen with Maxon? With Arren?

Shhh, I say with forced confidence. *We will stop The Third Chaos. We're going to live, Joy, and we're going to love. Nothing else matters.*

Joy nods, though the thoughts linger until Thomas appears in the back door, carrying his *handy-dandy tool kit*—his words, not mine. He doesn't bother coming in, but looks straight at me as if I'm the only person in the room while everyone turns toward him.

"Come see this." And with that, he disappears through the back door.

I reach for Joy's hand, letting her fingers thread through mine and soothe my rising panic. We walk through the door, our eyes flitting to the ship as it stands on the soggy ground in all its glory, blocking out the stars peeking through twilight. Joy strips her socks off quickly before we walk barefooted toward our way home, the others following us.

Thomas hits the panel, allowing the hatch to open. The lights greet us from within, shining bright like new. Rashid gasps behind us but manages to stand upright—I think he's finally grasping the reality of us. DiOla steps inside, commenting to Thomas about the ship while he stands there, tall, sober, and proud. I think we may have given him something he felt he needed to be whole again.

As everyone filters inside to look around and marvel at Thomas's good work, Joy and I stand there on our patch of soft dirt, staring at our salvation and our destruction.

"It's ready," I tell her, squeezing her hand tight, the words leaving my mouth without emotion. "We can go home."

"Humans say home is where the heart is." She glances at me, her lips parted in a frown. "Monchuri is just a place…" *Where I'll die*, she doesn't say, but it courses through her mind before she can stop it.

"We have to get it to the school." DiOla stomps down the ramp, holding some fancy gadgetry, distracting me from Joy's hopelessness. "Are you ready for tonight?"

★ ★ ★

DiOla takes a few moments, in between bossing everyone around, to regale us with stories about our homeland and Princess LaTanya. She sits on the faded threadbare carpet, her eyes far off as we eat the last bites of lo mein.

"I have the best LaTanya story." She sets her chopsticks aside and her voice rises theatrically. "She loves to cook and bake. She often would feed anyone around her, so much so that the kitchen staff were given three days off a week. And this one time—" she stops to laugh "—the XiGran King An-Yeck ZumBuden came for a royal visit. He ignored LaTanya, refusing to acknowledge her as not only his equal, but royal. He called her '*that* woman.' I guess he thought King Qadin would never die and leave the throne to her." DiOla shakes her head. "So LaTanya snuck into one of the meetings and presented him with a lavish cake decorated like the XiGran royal crest. It was stunning. Everyone was impressed. Pictures were taken before LaTanya offered him a slice. When she cut into it, an avalanche of red paper hearts tumbled out of the center. The King took one and read it aloud. It said... Well, it said the Monchuri equivalent of the English *fuck you*."

Joy laughs and Sarah's mouth drops open. "Yasss Queen."

"Soon after, Yecki was smitten with her. Sent her flowers, cakes, candies, jewels. And I think she liked him, too..." DiOla trails off.

"I never heard that story," I say through a smile. "I didn't—I don't know anything about her. I don't know her as anyone but the princess who stops by and is interested in my schoolwork. She never tried—"

"Shame." DiOla brushes crumbs off her lap as she glances up at me quickly. "She knows absolutely everything about you. So do I, as her Kindred."

"How do you know she's not dead?" Rashid asks suddenly, surprising us all.

"Because I do." DiOla tosses him a quick look that brims

with all sorts of emotions. "We're too close, she and I. If she died, so would I."

"Wait a minute, if one of you dies, the other does, too?" Sarah's eyes widen as Owen pauses, his fork to the container.

"If he dies, you die?" He stares at Joy, brows raised. "Is that why you wouldn't stay without him?"

Joy gives him a frown. "Some go on to live their lives without their Kindred. The ones that can't live without each other don't."

Owen's shoulders sink and he turns away, picking up his food again. That wasn't the answer he wanted.

But the only answer I could give, Joy finishes. And I imagine kissing her again, this time slower, this time surrounded by stars and privacy without worries of death or bounty hunters or imprisoned parents or war.

Just us and the stars and music.

Sarah lets out a long exhale while putting her container of rice on the table. "So, what's the plan for tonight? We've got two hours before Deja Reese shows and we lure this bounty hunter here."

"Are you sure you can't just call him?" Rashid scrubs his chin. "That would make all of this easier."

"He wouldn't believe me if I did." DiOla shakes her head as Rae puts their head on her shoulder. "We're competing. Make a video; I'll ping it to my friends at *Monchuri News*. That'll get him here. If everything goes to plan, you two will be jetting off this planet by the end of the night."

I ask it of Di, but I'm staring at Joy because this is it. This is the end of our freedom. This is going to work, and we'll be back home, back in our separate worlds. "How long will it take?"

"In our ships? With an actual destination in mind? An hour. We have to get ready. Now."

CHAPTER 20

JOY

"TAKE A DRINK, JUMP AROUND. LIFT YOUR SPIRIT,
SINK BACK DOWN. IT'S A PARTY, AND WE'RE
GONNA LIGHT IT UP. DO IT RIGHT, THERE'S NEVER
ENOUGH."

—DEJA REESE, "A LITTLE PARTY AIN'T HURT NO ONE"

We're in the only unlocked classroom—Thomas's—while we get ready for the concert. Sarah's friend Mikayla brought over makeup, snacks, and decorations for the gym, and Miss Rae is making it fit for a human goddess, they say.

Sarah is teaching me how to do a cat-eye liner in a mini-mirror while Mikayla drinks something strong-smelling—alcohol, I think. Felix hasn't touched any since we've been here. The thought that he's healthier here, happier with me… it means the world.

Sarah laughs as I squint my eye after poking myself. I smile at her pink dress that matches her lipstick. Everyone's dressed up and laughing and talking about music and life.

My Kindred winks at me as he sits atop a desk like a model of casual perfection. The brightness of his white shirt causes his brown skin to shimmer and his eyes to nearly glow. He's wearing an outfit that he would never have worn back home. When I say as much through our connection, he answers aloud for all to hear.

"Men are expected to be *masculine* here, whatever that means. As if wearing well-fitting pants and blouses that bring out the color in your eyes isn't *masculine*." Felix picks at the thread of his pink shorts.

"To be fair, no one calls men's shirts blouses, and you're still wearing the shit out of those shorts." Rashid smirks and then his cheeks redden when he glances over at Johnny.

Johnny (whose last name is Tamihana, Sarah informs me) sits there in all of his adorable (a word Rashid taught me) glory with his ruffled jet-black hair, fashionable glasses, plaid button-down and skinny jeans. He waves his arms around while talking to a bored Mikayla about some book he finished yesterday that gave him *all the feels*.

"You have to read it; it's atmospheric and luscious and it's…" He trails off as she begins checking her phone, shamelessly zoning him out. "You know what, it's like Taylor Swift's cottagecore period."

She puts her phone down and looks up at him through her fake eyelashes. "You should have led with that." She smacks his arm. "Is it on online? Let me buy it right now."

Johnny gives Rashid a big goofy grin and I try to look away as they lock gazes, even though it tells me one thing's for certain: Johnny likes Rashid, too. Suddenly I feel like I'm intruding by being in their vicinity. That they have a special spark and all of us could ruin it by our proximity.

How are we going to get these two humans to kiss already? Felix wonders, his hand splayed on the desk as he looks out the window, watching cars pull into the parking lot and teens pile out of them.

I have a plan.

He cocks an eyebrow. *Of course, you do. Humans seem to be your favorite project.*

I smile. *Before them, you were.*

And now I'm not?

I look at his silhouette by the window, the way he shines against the darkness. *With the override between us, you pulling away and me, me pulling away from you… I just wanted you to be happy, to live your best life. But now we're here—*

Together, he adds.

You don't seem so…

Broken, he finishes. I look into his eyes and even from across the room, I find so many emotions swimming within them. *I'm not broken anymore, Joy. I'm learning how to be a whole person. Meeting you, coming here…talking to Thomas Gibston…it taught me to value what I have and to fight for it.*

I shake my head as Sarah shimmies off to check on the gymnasium. *You were never broken. You were just a bit lost.*

And you found me. He lets out a long exhale.

Well, actually, I chuckle, *you found me, if you recall.*

He laughs, too, the movement shaking his body. *Your dress torn in bits, running from the Soleil. You took my breath away. And when you looked up at me, I knew.*

I huff, shaking my head. *That we'd go on a dangerous adven-*

ture to some weird planet in the middle of nowhere and make friends with humans? And then we'd have to go back home and save your princess mother so that the diabolical Arren doesn't take the crown?

He stands, humor gone, and then he stalks over to me. When he speaks, it's not into my mind, but aloud, for everyone to hear. "No, that somehow, in some way, you would let me kiss you. All I wanted was one kiss, just to have had it, propriety be damned."

My heart races and I nibble my lower lip. "Oh, was that all you wanted?"

This time he leans closer to me, the rest of the world falling away and it's just us. Our bodies close and our minds connected. "I want everything."

And then he kisses me softly, a whisper of a kiss, as we lack privacy and he knows I don't love the attention—or making anyone uncomfortable with our display of affection, but enough that I can stop thinking, stop analyzing, and feel it all. The way he wants me, the way he loves me. The way I make him feel and the way he makes me feel.

We don't know the future, and the present is slowly slipping away from us, but right now—we have this.

★ ★ ★

There are humans everywhere. At least a hundred of them, all clad in showy, cute outfits and face paint. Some wearing shirts of different artists than Deja Reese. Ones that read The Starry Eyed and have a rainbow rose surrounded by silver glitter.

Sarah stands next to me, her eyes wide at the small black stage Rae somehow found and erected at the end of the packed gym. There are guards clad in black with white letters stating

Security standing around the stage. There are drums—these I've seen before in Felix's mind—and large black things and lights... It's a new room.

I point to The Starry Eyed shirt hanging on someone squeezed in next to her. "Is that a band?" I shout over the cacophony of voices and shouts and people and my thoughts.

"I enjoy their music as much as you enjoy Deja Reese's," Felix says beside my ear. "I've listened to their first three albums since we've been here. I find their sound inspiring."

Sarah leans into me, her brows knit together. "They are the biggest band on Earth. Bit weird for me, but like...really good. You'll see. They're opening for Deja on tour. They call it 'The Last Concert At The End Of The World.'" She smiles at Felix as his hand creeps up my back and then someone bumps her shoulder and she starts a conversation elsewhere.

Felix and I sink into our connection, sharing thoughts and replaying kisses and singing songs and it settles my nerves because all of this is a lead-up to the end of our time on Earth. Whether we live or die. Whether I live or die. I wonder if Brak Merlbin brought Arren's device to sever our connection. I wonder if he'll kill me fast or slow to torture Felix. I wonder, and he wonders, and neither of us have answers.

A guard maneuvers through the crowd and stops before us, pulling us from our many terrifying thoughts. "Deja would like to see you both...backstage. Come with me."

He doesn't say it like an invitation but a command, but I can hardly complain.

We follow him through the set of double doors to the hallway leading to the locker rooms. Guards stand outside the door, not even glancing our way, as our escort holds up a finger and disappears inside. We're left standing there, looking at the chairs lined up against the walls, holding all sorts of strange instruments.

Felix stares longingly an electric guitar until the door opens again and we're ushered forward.

We slip into Deja's room and the guard closes it, giving us a look of absolute confusion in the process. Our hands intertwined, we turn to who we assume is Deja Reese.

But there's no one in sight. Before we can call out and ask, a person struts from around a corner. They're tall, with sequined red pants, hair the same shade of electric blue as the guitar, and a cape that flaps in the wind like Mr. Gibston's fictional superhero.

The person stops and smiles. "Oh, you're so adorable… I knew it would be worth coming here just to see you cutie pies."

The caped stranger sits on the gray bench between the blue cupboards—lockers, I think Rashid calls them—which contrasts with their colorful presence.

With a sigh, still watching us, they speak. "Kindreds. Our kind are so jealous of you. It's unfair, really. When Rae convinced me and Deja to come here after watching that little video your friend made, we couldn't say no. I've never seen a Kindred pair in all my life, but seeing you now, I feel for you. It's so romantic."

Felix coughs and I splutter. How? What? Who? Their kind?

Andarran, he says through our connection. *How many Andarrans are just hanging around Earth?*

I had no idea they'd all look so pretty. I never knew Andarrans could be like this. Like Rae. So human and yet not.

Before he can answer, they cut in, eyes narrowed. "Stop using your Kindred thing," they pout while offering a slight laugh. They run a hand down their sparkly cape before addressing us again. "I'm Allister. My pronouns are he/him, and I'm the lead singer of The Starry Eyed. And you are… I've seen glimpses of you but never your names."

"Uh…" Felix begins as I say, "Um. Felix and Joy?"

Allister claps his gloved hands. "Of course. The cutest names for the cutest couple."

"We aren't," I interject but don't finish. We aren't, no matter how much I want us to be. I swallow down the pity and get on task.

But then she walks in.

Deja Reese. The Deja Reese. All body and beauty. Her skin is dark like mine, and her thick purple braids are piled high on her head, her legs clad in gray sweatpants, similar to Rashid's, and her body in a Beyoncé T-shirt. Her bright brown eyes lock with mine, and my breath flees my lungs as she takes a seat beside Allister. She holds a light blue box in her hands but doesn't open it.

My tongue's tied. I want to know her. Ask her how she got into this life. Into this profession. How she found her voice and confidence.

"Normally, before I get onstage, I warm up all energized and ready. But tonight, I'm feeling like chilling with my boy Allister and eating macarons. Besides, tomorrow's the big night, and tonight's all about you two. You feel me?"

I don't know what feeling her means, but I think I could, I want to.

"Right." I gulp. "Um… First of all, I'm such a fan of yours

and I can't believe you're this pretty in person and your voice is incredible and you make me want to be more...everything. How do you do that, by the way? You just get onstage and then you're just yourself and full of energy and confidence and I don't—"

Felix coughs again, trying to get me back on track, and Allister laughs. "I ask her that all the time. I just turned eighteen and I tried doing her routine. I made it through fifteen minutes."

"Twelve," Deja corrects with a chuckle.

"You're eighteen?" Felix tilts his head to the side, surprised. Allister looks older; there's something in his eyes that sparkles with knowledge and weariness.

"Don't be fooled by the makeup. Humans tend to freak out if you stop aging." Allister shrugs, slouching farther down in his chair. "And no, I'm actually seventeen. Time is measured faster here than back home. It'll be many more years till I'm eighteen." He sighs theatrically.

Our eyes swivel between Deja's nonchalance and Allister's smirk.

"Deja already knows. She's one of my mentors. You can only hide you're an alien for so long, you know?"

"Awww, baby. I'm just happy you trusted me." Deja taps his arm. "Take a seat," she orders Felix. She waves me over. "You and me gotta talk real quick. I won't keep you long." I nervously sidle up to her, away from Felix and Allister, wondering what she might say. "You've got something about you. You're a beautiful soul, has anyone ever told you that?"

My cheeks heat, and I nod as I peer around at Felix. "People have always told me my skin's too dark, my body is too big, my laugh is too loud, never that I'm a beautiful soul."

"Oh, sugar, people have been telling me the same thing all my life. But you know what you gotta do, right?" The corner of her lips twitch and I find myself staring at her gorgeous face. I can't imagine people telling her in any world that she's too much of anything. She's unique, one of a kind, brave, confident, everything I want to be. Even the sight of her, the sound of her voice, inspires me.

"No," I finally answer. "I have no idea."

"You say fuck everyone, and do you, boo." She smiles again. "Trust that you deserve love not just from that boy who is head over heels in love with you over there, but from yourself. You gotta look in the mirror every morning and tell yourself you're not too much, you're enough. You feel me?"

I wrinkle my nose, my heart racing.

"Girl, don't make me say it again." She lifts my chin with her fingers. "You deserve love. You are precious and don't you forget it. Now, let's join the others. I can see you got a lot going on."

And though I walk back to Felix and Allister, my head is still in that conversation. Still with Deja. I will remember this moment for the rest of my life.

Deja sits beside Allister. "So why are you two here? Nothing else would've dragged me outta Key West like two lovestruck aliens needing my help." She opens the blue box on the bench and holds it out to us as we scoot in beside her on the bench. "Eat something. You look stressed."

Felix and I sit, and I take a yellow macaron, which is…

delightful. Light, citrusy, crunchy, soft, perfection. I might even moan aloud as the flavor explodes across my tongue.

"We need you to help us make a viral video that'll lure a bodyguard to Florida so we can kill him and steal his clearance pass right now——" Felix begins, but I cut him off, elbowing him in the ribs. "Or just, you know, incapacitate him, because murder is wrong."

"Right." I pat his knee with my hand although I know he's lying. "We also need to start a campaign in our system that'll possibly endear Felix's people to us, make them think we didn't kill the royal family, which also happens to be his family, because he was adopted but the——"

"The Princess is my birth mother and being held captive in the palace by a——"

I interrupt. "An incredibly cruel——"

"Arren." Felix shakes his head. "Anyway, we have to save her, and not die, because if I die, Joy dies, and if Joy dies, Arren may have found a way to spare my life but there's no point if Joy's not with me."

I exhale loudly before continuing. "And Felix is next in line for the throne. Which means he'll be king, one day, of our really unfair system, and maybe he can change everything. For the first time in his life, he'll be able to think beyond the box he set himself inside."

"And Joy will obviously be my queen, one day, and will possibly help me fix everything if she so desires, but doesn't have to, but it would be really good because she's better at people than I am." He takes my hand and brings it to his lips to place a tiny kiss upon my knuckles. "So…yeah. That's about it."

My brain flashes a myriad of colors. Queen? But I can't. Maxon. Home. We couldn't. No. What's he talking about? But why do I want to believe this is possible, too? We aren't— we can't.

Allister and Deja stare at us, their faces blank as they take in all of the information. Silence falls and Felix keeps squeezing my hand as if everything's gonna be okay and this is all normal and he didn't just declare that he wants me to be his queen.

"That's a lot to unpack," Allister says, eyes wide. "And there's not enough time for us."

"You want me to make a video with you?" Deja's eyes narrow as she purses her lips together, though the question hardly registers in my overwhelmed brain. "Because, baby, I can make a video."

CHAPTER 21
FELIX

Once the words come out of my mouth, I don't regret them. I wish I had spoken them sooner. I can't let Joy go. I won't. No matter that we're leaving Deja and Allister to coordinate sending the video out, and we're supposed to go back to the gymnasium to watch their performance, stay on track with our plan—I can't let this go yet.

If I'm the heir, then I can change everything, she said that. I'm not sure where I'd start, I'd have to learn, but I can. I will. I will change Hali and the unjust system it operates under. I will listen and make our worlds better for everyone. I will change Joy's fate. No one deserves her, but I'll try.

We can't, Felix. Arren will kill us. LaTanya. That's not how anything works. And I'm betrothed to another. I cannot break this commitment, no matter how much I want to. I took those vows in a church in Hali.

Just wait… My gaze darts around as my mind whirs. We

can't go home like this. With her thinking this is impossible. I need Joy more than I could need anything or anyone else. My eyes land on the electric blue guitar placed on the chair leaning against the wall. Right, well. If ever there was a time…

I drop Joy's hand and bolt to the guitar. I pick it up and hang it around my shoulder, my fingers finding the strings even though I've no pick to help me. Doesn't matter.

Once I begin strumming, I get her attention. Some rose-tatted musician stumbles into the hallway—probably the one whose guitar currently resides in my hands—but they make no attempt to stop me. There's a playful smile tugging on their face as I begin to sing as loudly as I can.

"Don't worry, darling, they don't know it's just you and me. Everything between us was always meant to be." Joy's eyes light up as my voice rings out strongly like she's never heard it before. *"Fate, it's a perfect fantasy, stolen glances and thoughts between two worlds. How could I ever want someone else, how could I never want more. When it's you I love and adore?"*

The musician in the doorway sighs, hand over their heart.

"I've got your name in my heart, darling. I've got your mind in mine, dearest… You're not just my Kindred, I'll always hold you… nearest." I make that last line up because I never finished the song and it's ridiculous, but Joy smiles, her eyes brimming with tears. *"I was meant to love you, Joy. You're my girl and I'm your boy."* It's not beautiful but it makes her giggle. Two others from the band, maybe, sway to my basic music, and I find myself missing the stage because I could've made this so much better…

Yet, the way she looks at me, nothing really could.

"Don't tell me we can't. That this can't happen, Joy."

"Don't ask this of me." She swipes a tear from her cheek.

"Let's watch the show and enjoy the last few moments that we can before…"

Before it all falls apart.

★ ★ ★

On the stage, there are four musicians in bright colors. One wears a stiff tuxedo with a rainbow blouse, one has rose tattoos covering their bare chest and arms as they dance around, another is in a neon pink ball gown, and Allister has changed from his glittery cape to a feathery purple one to match Deja's hair. His dark blue hair swings around.

"Good evening, Rocky Apple Key!" Allister says and the crowd goes wild with cheering and screaming and hopping around. Joy and I exchange a glance. "We're The Starry Eyed!" More applause and cheers ring out and Joy fights the urge to cover her ears. I smile.

All concerts are like this, no matter the world. They're energetic and fun. You'll see.

I nod, although I'm still nauseated with the worries of waiting for my inevitable doom. I'm used to being on the stage, not below it. I'm used to having no expectations, not having to save our world from The Third Chaos.

"Tonight, we were going to share a song from our upcoming album *The Sound of Stars*, but we'd rather like to sing a special ditty for a guest in the audience tonight, if you don't mind. It's called 'The Girl Who Would Be Queen'…and I wrote it about a girl who will be queen of a kingdom far, far away, who needs to stand up for what she believes in, to be bold, be brave, be herself. This is a song about joy and luck, good and bad, chaos and help, because we will need it. Let's go!"

Allister's voice is mesmerizing, and the crowd's silent and the music sways through my core while Joy takes my hand.

It's like they're singing to you, I say through our connection.

What? She shakes her head, watching them strut around on the stage as the crowd stares up in reverence. *No*—

I shift on my feet, my voice confident. *You are the girl who would be queen.*

But, Felix—

Before I can listen to her detail all the reasons we can't, though I know in my heart and my mind that she wants to, The Starry Eyed wrap up the song and the lights blink out onstage. A hush falls. Beams of light flicker above us like lasers piercing through my big overwhelming thoughts. And a voice, angelic and melodic, whispers on the air and I get bumps on my arms.

Deja Reese stands behind a white screen, her beautiful plus-size silhouette posing provocatively.

Joy inhales sharply beside me, her eyes as wide as saucers. She's mesmerized.

When Deja saunters forward in a gold leotard body suit in tall high heels, with a golden crown on her head, Joy's mind whirs with thoughts.

I wish I could move with her confidence.

I wish I could hold myself high and be strong like her.

I wish I was as beautiful as her.

You are, I say, as my gaze follows Deja and her voice rips through the crowd. She is power and determination, a talented force of nature. She's everything I'm not up there. She's what I want to be. Seeing her so brave, head held high, I realize that I don't just want that presence onstage, but in life. I want to use my voice to make change and be strong. Do the right thing. Joy taught me that. These humans have taught me that. Deja may inspire Joy for their shared attributes, but Deja inspires me, too. To get over my fears and change the world.

For a while, as we wait for Brak, who is surely coming, we allow ourselves to be transported by her voice, her dancing, her movement and emotions, her trauma and words, her many outfit and scenery changes. We don't think. We feel. We let the music wash over us and through us. And as her voice belts out, "'We were in love before we knew what love meant,'" I turn to Joy.

It's only us again and the world has melted away. My lips touch hers and I breathe her in, everywhere tingling with the rightness of us together. Everything is how it's meant to be, at least for the moment.

What will the future be like with us together? If we live through this, will she deny Maxon and choose me? Choose the throne? But I push that thought aside, that fear of the future, and focus on Joy. On the moments we can control.

As the crowd calls out for an encore, Allister shimmies onto the stage and joins Deja at the microphone.

Deja gives us all a big smile. "This very little song we wrote backstage goes out to all the lovers who are too shy to take their crushes to the next level."

Allister leans in beside Deja. "Especially two beautiful boys, Rashid and Johnny."

And then they both sing. "'I look left, you look right, I smile your way but you walk away... Baby, these missed chances are awkward dances, you and me are destiny, at least for a little while. Maybe more… And I want so much more. One of us has to take the lead. Will it be Johnny or Rashid?'"

Joy's plan. She must've told them as we worked on the video. She's amazing.

Rashid and Johnny turn to each other, beaming, and I have to fight my own cheesy smile. I'm becoming a fan of love and relationships, because of Joy. Because I had a taste of it and I want more, not just for me, but for everyone. If love makes us better, then we need far more love in the universe.

And I'm thinking this embarrassingly ridiculous thought when Allister's voice cuts through the packed gymnasium. "Felix, where are you? Get on up here and play with us. Sing us something you love."

My mouth drops open and Joy smiles at me as she pushes me forward. And people cheer my name and my feet walk me up that stage and a guitar is handed to me. And when I open my mouth… I find words.

A love song for my Kindred. Well, a love song I didn't write by an artist Joy listened to on Earth in between Deja's albums. It's catchy and beautiful, Joy loves it. I love it. And Allister and Deja join in. So do the audience.

I don't vomit. I don't run offstage. My voice harmonizes and the lyrics leave my lips like they're meant to. And Joy's thoughts are of pride and happiness. The song finishes and we take a bow and I never felt better in my life until… I see a Monchuran in the crowd. In Soleil garb. Staring up at me while he stalks closer to Joy. Brak Merlbin.

I lean over the microphone, my heart pounding. "Now can I direct everyone to the football field? There'll be music and dancing. Please join us."

The crowd cheers and pushes against Brak, getting him off the path of Joy.

Run, I tell her. And then I dart off the stage, the guitar still strapped to my shoulder.

★ ★ ★

Three Months Ago

JOY

I stand in the hall of the Temple, smoothing down the white dress I stitched together from scraps of sheets. It's not beautiful, not like one of those dresses seen in the windows of shops I can't afford to walk into, but it's simple enough to look like it could have been bought somewhere. Simple is always in style—at least that's what we poor people say.

A hunched-over priest stalks by me, tapping the base of my spine quickly to get me to stand straighter. I adjust myself and plaster a fake smile on my face. There are many religions in Monchuri, all of them accepted, just as the people who do not practice.

I believe in the Gods, in Indigo and Ozvios and the countless others because I love the idea that the universe was created through music, just like Felix. Music is universal. If people cannot hear it, they can feel it. They can see it. They can dream it.

Our heartbeats make music.

But after The Second Chaos, the Qadins installed a ruler who used our Halin religion about acceptance and love, and twisted it to value duty above all. The Qadins knew our religion was precious, and they used it to prevent us from ever rising up again. I feel beholden to the duty aspect, though I don't imagine Indigo would ever impose that on their people. Yet, I can't stop believing, either. It is the one thing that is mine. Even if, on Hali—and only on Hali, it is run by and in favor of men.

Maxon should be here any moment for our chaperoned meeting. A meeting where I'm supposed to impress him with my obedience and good nature, as he's wealthy and I'm not, while managing to leave him wanting more.

A meeting I'd rather skip, not that I would. My fate revolves around keeping Maxon KiBanu happy enough to marry me and put a roof over my head. I'll be expected to support him and give him children, perferably a male heir to his fortune. I'm supposed to be happy that he accepted me, that my life will be stable, like Mum's always wanted, so that I won't have to live like we've had to over the years.

I'm not. But that doesn't stop me from keeping the barrier between Felix and me in place. I don't need his pity or snark in this moment.

After another few minutes, the doors are pushed open, their creaky squeals causing me to cringe. Maxon struts inside shadowed by two beautiful people holding large black metal cases. His eyes lock on mine as he approaches, a small smirk marring his pretty face as he takes me in from my simple dress to my threadbare shoes.

"Well," he says to the person on his left, who wears a silver jumpsuit, their thinly braided hair sitting in a perfect pile atop their head, with silver lips, light brown skin, and yellow eyes that sharpen on my flabby arms, "do you think we can make her look like someone who looks good splashed on holo-vision?"

The person on his right, in the same ensemble—only in gold, with a short pixie cut of curls—whispers something I cannot hear that elicits chuckles from the other two.

Maxon stops before me, his head tilting to the side as if he's trying to imagine someone else, someone better instead of me. "There's something you need to know about me, my betrothed."

My smile falters only slightly. I'll have my lifetime to learn all about him, why start right now?

"If you weren't the Kindred to Duke Hamdi, I would have never chosen you. You're too round, too tall for a girl, and far too poor with those clothes. But—" he cocks an eyebrow and nods to his assistants "—I can make you presentable, as-suming you can lose some weight on your own, yes?"

Somehow, I manage to find my voice after shifting on the warped wood beneath my feet. "What do I need to be pre-sentable for, Sir KiBanu? University lectures?" He will be, after all, a mathematician. They don't tend to live out in the public eye. I hope he'll be so busy teaching that he won't be home. Is that a bad hope to have so early on?

He treats me to a full-fledged grin, one that lights up his eyes and changes his entire demeanor. The room seems brighter, as if the sun could live inside this man's being. He's beautiful, and he knows it.

"Let's say an opportunity is coming my way to not only use my brilliant mind, but my incomparable countenance for the greater good." When I give him a puzzled expression, he rolls his eyes. "I've been offered a chance to appear on television as a mathematical game-show presenter. It'll combine my love of math and my showmanship. I've been told it'd be a hit for the upper echelons of Maru society. This is good for Hali, for us. The more they treat us as peers, the better it will be for our home. They will accept us into society; we can reclaim our sciences and wealth. We must put our planet first."

I try to keep the disinterest from my voice, though I'm sure I fail. "I thought you were going to be a professor?"

"That's what my parents want. That's what we're told is the highest profession I can achieve in life here. We're Black. Our skin's dark and our home is backward compared to the rest of Monchuri." The light dulls in his eyes, and his assistants chitter behind him. "But I was meant for so much more than a stuffy classroom teaching riffraff that couldn't get into better universities on Maru."

He pauses, his voice falling as he steps closer to me. "Like you, my Kindred pairing was a mistake. I was paired with another little girl from Hali. We were the best of friends. I loved her. We spoke about becoming more, being more. Living beyond the limit someone else set for us." He looks away suddenly, his voice uncharacteristically forlorn. "She died when we were twelve. She didn't get to have a voice. She didn't get anything, not even a funeral. We were too young to be fully bonded, so her death scarred me, but I'm fine." He shakes his head of the thought like he can slough off the trauma of loss. "Unlike my Kindred, your connection will actually help us. Your Duke will keep us in the news, once we move to Maru that is, and we can ask the Duke to come to my shows… That is how you'll be useful to me. That is how you'll be useful to Hali. That is how you'll keep me happy. Understood?"

I nod once, even though it kills me inside. I resent that I have to use my head and not my heart. Nausea sweeps through my stomach and I try to ignore it and put a smile on my decent face. This is hopeless.

"Now, these two will try to determine how many ways you could look better, and how you can do that with your... paltry resources." He claps his hands and then stalks away, leaving me standing there, staring at two glittery assistants whose gazes rove over me with critique and distaste.

"First, you will go on a strict diet," the silver one says in a thick accent. "No more cakes." They poke my stomach. "More salad and fruit—if you can afford it."

"Your hair is too big," the gold one murmurs, more to themselves than to me. "And before the wedding, we will lighten your skin."

I shake my head vehemently, my voice strong and angry as I call out to him. "Maxon—I mean, Sir KiBanu, is all of this really necessary?"

He turns by the doorway. "I cannot love when I am consumed by ambition that'll be better for our people. I will never be a man who sings to you or dances for you. Do this, and I will keep you and your mother from destitution. I will save Hali-Monchuri."

★ ★ ★

MONCHURI MORNING NEWS NOW!

Transcript featuring L'avi Jonu and Nyla Harkibi of *Good Morning Monchuri*, filmed in front of a live studio audience in Maru-Monchuri

LJ: We're interrupting your programming to deliver shocking breaking news.

NH: A video from Terra featuring Duke Felix Hamdi and his Kindred, Joy Abara, pinged through our networks shortly ago. We didn't have a chance to review it.

LJ: But before our producers can—they're signaling us right now. They don't want us to show you this video, but it was addressed to us specifically, begging us. I watched the Duke grow up on screen, I watched him—

NH: Let's play the video while we have the time. We'll try to keep this on air as long as we can.

video appears on holo-screens across the system displaying the two fugitives, Felix Hamdi in a colorful top and Joy Abara in a silver frock. Both stare at the camera as two unknown figures stand behind them.

Duke Hamdi (DH): Hello, Monchuri, this is Felix Hamdi and my Kindred, Joy Abara. We're coming to you from Rocky Apple Key, Florida, on Terra Earth. As of now, you believe Joy and I conspired against our government and—

Joy Abara (JA): Murdered the Qadin family. We did no such thing. From the very beginning, we've been set up to take the fall by Arren—

DH: Arren Sai, Royal Advisor. He has not only engineered the attacks on our royal family—my family— he has kidnapped Princess LaTanya. She's alive. He wants war. He wants The Third Chaos.

JA: And he wants to rule.

DH: Please help us. Please—

```
*video cuts out*
```

LJ: No, I will not stand down. No, you will not arrest me. I work for the free press. I will not continue spreading misinformation, I will— *(screams)*.

NH: Stop that! You've hurt her. You've… L'avi! She's my Kindred. She's my wife, my life—how dare you!

```
*broadcast ends, and a new one begins outside of
the Royal Palace on Estrella*
```

★ ★ ★

Hello, this is Arren Sai, Royal Advisor to the Qadin throne. Please do not fall prey to this false information. The Duke and his Kindred are very much guilty of royal conspiracy, and it is my job as your…temporary steward, to assure you that no one in this government or this system is interested in war or The Third Chaos. We are only interested in justice. Please disregard any of the events that have transpired in the last few moments. Both news anchors will be penalized for their role in undermining our current leadership. Thank you.

CHAPTER 22

JOY

"THESE TEETH LEAVE BIG WOUNDS BABY, AND I'M
GONNA BITE AS MANY TIMES UNTIL I GET WHAT'S
MINE."

—*DEJA REESE, "TIME FOR A FIGHT"*

I run onto the football field where we had the astronomy lesson. My heart's pounding. Brak Merlbin is here.

He's coming for me.

He's coming to kill me.

The plan worked and yet… I'm unsure if I'm ready to leave. This is it. Our last night on Earth and we can't keep putting this off anymore.

And then I run right into one of the band members, standing still as a statue. The tuxedoed one with long black hair and an easy smile. "Hello, Joy. I'm Rupert. So lovely to meet you."

I smile as I turn, searching the field full of gathering people for a Monchuran. My tight boots sink into the damp field and I try to calm my racing heart. "Hi, Rupert. I just have to—"

"You know, in a few human years, Earth is going to need you Monchurans. If you'd be so inclined as to return." Rupert doesn't seem to register my jumpiness or terror. "Otherwise, it could be a disaster, which would make me most distraught."

"Rupert!" Another band member covered in rose tattoos appears beside him, elbowing him in his tuxedoed chest. "You can't tell them that. What would Allister say? Also hi, I'm Cecil. You're Joy, right? Queen?"

Before I can answer, the last band member, in a pink ball gown, lifts her hem and stalks over to us, scowling at Cecil. "I'm Whisper. And Allister's busy, so tell her whatever you want, but you—" she stares cautiously at me "—better not tell anyone we told you the future or anything. We could get in trouble, you know." And with that, she slinks away, her ball gown billowing in a nonexistent Florida breeze as if she commands the wind.

"Well, I have to run—" I start, until an arm wraps around my shoulder, and the air dries up in my lungs. Brak Merlbin is out there, and he means to kill me.

★ ★ ★

I'm tracking him, Joy. He's not even close to you. Felix's voice pierces through my thoughts as Rashid suddenly places his hand in mine. I let out a small gasp. *Stay there.*

Felix, be safe. Please—

I've got this, beje.

"We invited mayhem to Rocky Apple Key," Rashid says briefly as I try to coolly survey the crowd, watching for Brak.

Watching for Felix. Concern thrums through the pit of my stomach. If anything happens to him...

"Only to find the mayhem lived within us all along?" Sarah suddenly appears by our sides, her eyes flashing as a bunch of humans without shirts dance near a makeshift table with loud speakers blasting some mediocre pop music.

Sarah belts out *"Wooo,"* raising her arms up in the air, and people repeat the sound back, the cacophony hurting my ears a bit, if I'm honest.

"I told you I had a plan for tonight. I got music, I got beer, and I got the hottest boys in the Keys. Now it's up to us to find this asshole and root him out before he hurts you. I'll keep making my rounds and if I see someone who looks beautiful but also doesn't fit in, I guess I'll find you." She winks and gives a small smile to Mikayla across the field. "Tell Felix to stay safe. Deja's security guards are everywhere, no one's alone out here. But if anything happens to you guys..."

Rashid's eyes are wide, scanning the crowds covering the field. "How did they all get here so fast?"

"The internet," Johnny stalks up to him, smiling because he doesn't know how much danger there is lurking in this field, ready to end my life.

The hunter won't kill humans, I tell myself. He's being broadcast live on holo-vision, that would look bad. Besides, why would he? I have to believe the humans—my friends— are safe, and that the crowd will help us lure him toward our ship on the far end of the football field's parking lot, where DiOla will knock him out. We just need to shepherd him through the dancing and music. We can do this.

More people push past us as Rashid and Johnny stand there,

holding hands. Rashid has to yell a bit over the next wave of screams. "We'll look around for someone unusual. But this is bigger than I thought it'd be."

Johnny's brows scrunch. "Who are we looking for?"

We decided not to tell more people about our grand plan or that we're from a different galaxy. We've already freaked out enough people.

"Just someone who looks off. C'mon." And with that, they walk up farther into the fray and disappear into the mesh of people.

I know somewhere on this field, Thomas Gibston and DiOla are watching the skies for a flicker of a ship. DiOla plans on stealing the clearance pass, while we do…something with Brak. I can't imagine killing someone else. Or even hurting him, really. I don't know how we'll manage tonight.

Don't think about that. Right now, I'm tracking him. He's getting closer to our ship, to Di. We're going to be fine. Felix is on the other end of the field. Away from me.

I adore you, Felix, I tell him through the fear, the hopelessness. Through the long glances around me. Through the knowledge that somehow, I won't come out of this.

I love you, Joy. My stomach flips and I feel delightfully warm all over, as if his words unlocked something in my heart and sent heat to every place the cold had ever touched me in my life. And before I can say those words back, the memory of our first kiss plays through his mind and into mine. The way he leaned into me and kissed me softly, his lips not desperate to be felt but to feel me. I breathed him in, our noses mingled, and I gasped as he drew me closer, his arms around my thick waist. The memory stops, leaving me standing there, wishing for more. *We're going to have a million more kisses, Joy. I promise you.*

I hope so. You're...very adept at kissing, I add a little levity though my heart is pounding against my chest, threatening to burst free at any moment.

I'm adept at a great many things. Like fashion, obviously, music, without a doubt, lopsided grins that set your heart aflutter... There's humor in his voice, though we're both terrified, both unsure. *And kissing you. Specifically you. And I have ideas of what I'd like to become adept at next.*

Such a flirt, I say through broken breaths. *Let's get this over with. We still have a ship to fly, a princess mom to rescue, a kingdom to save, and parents to free.*

This doesn't feel real.

He's right. None of this is how we thought we'd celebrate our seventeenth birthday or how we'd finally find our way to each other. But here we are. And if we want to succeed, the only way is with a clear head.

I'm the bait, Felix. He may be leading you astray to get to me.

Joy. Panic threads through his tone as he steps through dancers drinking alcohol in red cups and their easy happiness. *Be careful. You are the world to me.*

As you are to me, Kindred.

We fall into a silence as we walk around the field, on different sides of the milieu. My boots, which once looked so pretty and perfect for the concert, now pinch even more and are streaked with dirt. My feet are sore, my mind is a maze of emotions and worries, and there are too many people. Too many people everywhere, laughing, dancing, having their fun and not caring about the world they're living in because they don't know The Third Chaos could happen and everywhere in this universe could be engulfed in war.

I slip through the throngs of dancers, my gaze flicking through their faces, looking for Brak Merlbin. Felix has him in sight, but what if he's wrong? Now, all I can go on are eyes that seem intent on my murder.

Monchuri tech on a wrist prepared to deliver a killing blow, which they'll broadcast on holo-vision.

And my mum will see it and know her only child, her daughter, died for being connected to a royal. She'll know I was innocent, but that it didn't matter. Maybe she'll somehow be able to move on with her life and...

That's when I see it.

I see him.

I stop in my tracks to stare.

Maxon. Maxon KiBanu. My betrothed. Standing there in the crowd. His lips curled in distaste as Floridians dance around him, shaking their asses and screaming with their friends, drinking alcohol, and chanting about chugging, which I assume is some sort of initiation game?

Maxon finds me there, his expression shifting from disgust to something wholly different. Not happiness—no, he never was truly happy in my presence and this is no different. But there's excitement in his gaze.

My feet stay frozen in place. My hands cling to my sides. My brain's barely working.

Brak is walking off the field, leading me somewhere. Stay safe. Felix's thoughts flit to mine and I can't respond. Maxon Ki-Banu is here. Why is he here? Oh, *Gods*, what has he done? What is he planning?

He moves across the space between us fluidly, his eyes locked on mine. And then, when he's just inches away from me, his velvet brown skin attracting a bevy of different humans intent on staring at his otherworldly beauty, he smiles.

"I wasn't sure I'd see you again," he says in Monchuran, the words shooting up red flags in my brain that I need to switch my language, that it's been a few days and I forgot how rigid we must sound, how detailed and proper. How hard we have to try just to appear that we belong.

Still, my response lingers on my tongue and refuses to leave. No matter how my thoughts whir past in a stream of consciousness.

The corners of his lips twist in superiority. He always did love appearing above his station. More Maru than Hali.

"Dance with me?" He extends his hand but I ignore it.

The questions that lie frozen in my throat finally thaw enough to break free in a fast and furious flurry. "What are you doing here? Are you part of the team to take us back? How did you get here? Why...just why? Am I being recorded?"

His hand still hangs in the air, waiting for me to take it. "Dance with me and I can answer your questions, my betrothed—unless you forgot your promise to me?"

Every inch of my body is screaming no, that this is a trap, and Felix's mind feels miles away. Busy. Preoccupied. Focused. All the things I should be. But I'm not. Because I still feel duty bound to accept Maxon's advances with propriety. Something he knows.

And I know, I know none of this will matter. If we somehow survive this and Felix eventually becomes King... But part of me still thinks he'll cast me aside. Advisors will tell him no. Monchuri won't allow some nobody Kindred from poverty to become Queen. Deja Reese's words flicker through my mind: "You deserve love. You are precious and don't you forget it." They haven't sunk in. Maybe they never will.

I take Maxon's hand and he yanks me into him, my chest flattening against his. The scent of his honey perfume overwhelms my senses enough that I almost forget that I'm on high alert. Almost. His hand is slick with perspiration and his bright Monchuri clothes look like a costume. Not that anyone notices.

He smiles down at me and tugs me even closer before whispering in my ear. "You're in quite a bad situation, wife."

"Don't call me that," I growl by his ear. "Tell me why you're here. Tell me what you want."

"I traveled the universe for you, and this is how you talk to me?" His smile twists into something ugly and dangerous. "Your little stunt nearly ruined my family name. But then something wondrous happened."

"They promised you a fortune to take me in?" My monotone question merely earns me a wink.

"You think too small." He chuckles mirthlessly. "You're too Hali-Monchuri for your own good. No, Joy Abara who comes from nothing and will always be nothing without me, I found fame." I try to pull away from him as people stream by, oblivious to my despair. "I'm offering you a choice."

My head falls back so that I can glare up at him. "A choice."

He stares at my lips as if he can't decide whether to kiss them or squeeze them shut. "A choice. Come with me. Marry me. We've already vowed to do so in a year, why wait longer?

We can have our own reality holo-show about us evading the Soleil. About our love despite your misdeeds. We could see the world and make a name for ourselves. You owe me this."

"I— That's ridiculous." I shake my head, and extract myself from him. Anger threading through my tone. "I don't owe you anything. I'm in love with Felix."

He scoffs, lip curling. "People like us don't get to fall in love with royals. We don't get chances to leave Hali, we have to make them ourselves. With me, you'll live. You can change our home by having a voice with your Kindred. If you try for more, they will kill you, Joy. Stop being ignorant."

"I'd rather die than go with you." I'm about to turn away from him, to connect with Felix and end this thing, when Maxon grabs my arm and sticks something sharp into my skin. I yelp, and struggle against his hold on me. As the world begins to blur at the edges and my legs wobble, Maxon holds me in his arms, his mouth inches from my ear.

"I gave you a choice. You chose wrong."

CHAPTER 23
FELIX

I'm trailing behind the mysterious figure, who may be Brak Merlbin or just a strange human in cosplay, when my vision becomes hazy. I stop to lean against the flimsy metal railing of the school bleachers at the other side of the field to catch my bearings. Part of my mind isn't functioning. It's silent. It's gone.

Joy, I scream through our connection. *Joy! Where are you? Joy?*

When an answer doesn't come, I panic, my breaths short and my body swaying involuntarily. I think back to what she was feeling... I was so focused on finding Brak, stopping him from finding her, killing her, that I wasn't paying attention. I didn't see what she saw. I didn't stop to feel what she felt.

Now I do. I range through the moments. She was surprised. She was scared. She was angry. Someone spoke to her, though I can't access who. And now she's... Something's wrong. Seriously wrong. I'm about to turn around, to find her, when Brak Merlbin emerges from the shadows, his face grim, yellow eyes peering into mine. His hand clutches a stunner by his side. He led me here exactly as he wanted.

"I came to kill the peasant and lo, I caught the Duke." His voice is deep, gruff, and edged with rage. His teeth gleam in the moonlight as he gingerly steps closer, leveling the stunner at my chest. Though the party rages across the field, the silence between us is deafening. He's shorter than I thought, and he's built like a tank, all muscle on his small limbs. "How would you like to do this?"

I clutch the side of my head that's pounding with the absence of Joy. "I'd like to *not* do this. In fact, could you come back later? We had a whole plan on how to deal with you and this isn't how it was supposed to happen."

Brak lowers the stunner, his lips twitching. "My apologies. I do hate to disrupt plans."

I try to stand straighter, try to stamp the panic deep down inside of myself. Where's Joy? "I didn't kill the Qadins."

"I don't care," he says, his tone shifting. "I don't care about whatever justice Arren has in store for you. None of that is my business."

My brows furrow, a knot forming in my stomach. "Then why are you here?"

"I came for your Kindred." He shrugs rigidly, though there's an anger in his eyes that make them dark and fiery.

Why? For what reason would Arren's lapdog come here for Joy? I bite the inside of my mouth, fury threatening to consume me. He will not harm my Joy. How dare he act as if I'd let him.

"Well, as you can see, she's not here. You should probably just leave. Ta-ta." I wave goodbye, stepping back as if this could actually work. As if he'll just walk away and make all of this so much easier.

"You have no idea who or what you're dealing with, Duke." He sucks his teeth, the sound grating on my nerves. "Joy Abara is the daughter of my wife's Kindred. Joy's mother is the reason I haven't seen my family, why my own children refuse to call me Father. Why my wife would never love me the way I needed. Now I'm in the position to take something from her, to make her feel the loss I've felt."

"That's fascinating." I search through the connection to any flicker of life from Joy. Anything at all. But it's eerily quiet. I take another step back, flexing my legs, my response a bit flippant. "Not really any of our faults, though, is it? You know how it is with Kindreds. Where there's a spark can come a fire."

"Danio is *my* wife!" he snarls, his finger on the stunner. He's a hurt man with nothing more to lose, who can't take the blame for his own failings. I can use that.

I smirk as my heart thunders against my chest. "You're one of those 'good' guys, right? The kind of guy who thinks he owns someone else because he wants to."

He aims the stunner, his hand shaking, and pulls the trigger. I dart around. The blast hits the railing beside me, leaving a small smoking hole in the metal. He aims again and I bolt toward him. The blast hits my shoulder but I'm too amped up, too panicked to stop myself and feel it. I knock him on the ground, the impact scrambling my thoughts briefly as I slide the sleeping tab into his neck like Joy asked me to do.

Killing is wrong and all that. And she's right, I'm more a lover than a fighter, but I don't mind a fight. Not when my mind is so suddenly quiet.

His legs twist around my center, nearly cutting off my breath as he reaches for the stunner again.

I gasp for air, my hands angling for purchase. "Who Danio loves has nothing to do with you. She has moved on, and so should you. Stop blaming Joy and her mom for something out of their control." His grip loosens and he kicks me off him.

I land on my back, my head screaming on the warm concrete. Before I can get my bearings, he's up and walking toward me, stunner in hand. Lips curled.

"You're not ugly. You can find someone else. You're not even old, either. And you obviously work out."

"Shut your ferking mouth!" He rushes toward me, and I kick my feet out, tripping him to the ground in a violent rage. He rolls over, striking at me, but swinging too wildly to connect. I bring my arms around his shoulder and his neck and put the pressure on him. He struggles against me, caught off guard. No one expects me to actually have any fighting skills, but I needed them to get through my fear that I couldn't protect Joy from Arren and the royals. It was the only way to feel like there was something I could control.

"The problem with men like you is that you think your masculinity entitles you to love and power. You spend so much time pretending not to feel that when you do, you lose control." As his short limbs flap around in an attempt to get away from me, his elbows poke into my ribs. His energy ebbs and he's finally succumbing to the sleep tab. I bring my mouth close to his ear. "The only reason you'll live is because my Kindred is a better person than you or even me."

And with that, I dump him to the side of me. His body is ramrod still, but his eyes follow me as I stand over him, smiling. I'm not sure how long the tab works, or how fast it works, but I have to hope it lasts a while.

"I was just the diversion, stud. Thanks for the clearance pass." I wink, and begin to walk away in a hurry. Joy's gone and something's very wrong. I don't have any more time for this.

I blearily tear across the field, back toward Sarah and Rashid, who don't know that Joy is missing. I see a brief blinding flash and stop, twisting around as light flickers in the distance.

Humans dance and grind and laugh and carry on carelessly as my world shatters and a ship, set on mirror mode, stands at the edge of the field. But I see it, because I know what it looks like. And it looks like a teeny self-piloting pod. Not a ship I expected to see here.

My thoughts flit to Joy and then to the ship. She's in there. She has to be. That's the only explanation for her absence in my mind. Someone took her. Someone who apparently can't fly all that well.

The ship wobbles and even Rashid runs up behind me. "Is that a...?"

"They've got Joy," is all I can say, the words leaving my mouth in a flurry. "We need to—"

And then the sky lights up and the ground shakes as an explosion rips through the night. Fire erupts in the distance and the crowd cheers, thinking it's all part of a show, while my stomach turns. The ship wasn't driving poorly. It was aiming. Aiming at another.

Taking out another mode of transportation. Taking out another ship. Taking out Brak Merlbin's ship, to be precise. Maybe the pilot was another Soleil working for Arren. Maybe they thought that ship was mine. Maybe they hate Brak, which makes sense.

And then it aims again. I bolt forward as if I can stop it. As if I have a chance. Then another explosion rips through the sky farther away.

At Thomas's house. At Thomas's backyard.

Our ship.

They hit our ship.

I collapse onto my knees and scream.

* * *

I'm in the grass, staring at the smoldering fire that was once Brak's ship and now burns like all my dreams and desires. Hating them, hating myself. There's no way forward.

We did all of this for nothing. Thomas bloody Gibston. Earth. Deja Reese. The Starry Eyed. We came all this way and lost.

I've lost. I've lost everything. My parents. My home. My bio-mother. My ship. My Kindred.

DiOla wipes a smudge of soot from her face, shaking her head at me as she blocks my view. "I got the pass, but... Doesn't seem to matter now." She lifts her pants leg, revealing a bloody blue calf. "Hurts worse than it looks." She sniffs, leaning on Miss Rae. "What are you going to do?"

My answer's immediate, if a bit impractical. "I have to get Joy back."

"Mhm. But how?" DiOla cocks an eyebrow. "I can't get you to my ship up north, and I'm in no condition to travel. LaTanya trusted me to set you on the path, but I'm to remain behind and prepare for...the Ilori threat."

I'm listening but it doesn't matter. None of it does. Joy's up there, and I need her. I can't do this or anything else without her. I can't function without her words and thoughts and feelings in my mind. She's my other half, my better half, my dream girl, the only person I understand and love without conditions. The only person who loves me without conditions. "I need a ship."

"I get it, kid." Di rubs a streaky blue hand through her hair. "I wish I could help you. I really do, but there are bigger things at play than you can imagine."

I think I have an idea of the importance—Brak hinted as much—but I can't think of that now. Joy's up there and I'm down here.

Rashid's hand plops down on my shoulder. He must've left Johnny and the party behind and joined me where there's only fire and destruction and absence. "We'll get her back."

"How?" I nearly sob. I'm stuck here. "Everything we did. Everything we learned and became. It's over. Someone else will come here to claim me. Joy..." I can't finish the thought. Can't imagine what'll become of her.

"You can take my ship," Miss Rae offers, and I whip my head around. "I mean, it's Andarran and a bit old, but it should get you to where you need to go."

For a moment, I'm speechless. "You have a ship?"

"Well, how else would I have gotten here?" Miss Rae's

brows rise like I'm a fool. "Come on, hop in the truck and we'll get on over to my house. It's in my shed."

I rise slowly from my knees and can barely think straight. "Thank you."

"I'm coming." Rashid shoulders past me to follow behind Miss Rae. "Joy saved me, and I want to be there to save her."

"I'm not one to miss a party, especially one like this, but I'm going." Sarah maneuvers around DiOla, coming into view. When did she get here? "You'll need us to get Joy back and save your whole world or whatever. Besides, this has been a seriously boring summer, and imagine if we go to space? Like who would even believe us? I could use it on my college application."

"No." I shake my head. "You could die. You're just humans. I couldn't live with myself if anything happened to you."

Sarah's brows furrow and her hands rest on her hips. "If it was any of us, Joy would do the same. We're coming. We decide our own fate. Besides, it's not like we'll be gone long. You've been here like three days. It's the weekend. We can be back by Monday."

I throw my hands up. "Look, if you come, time moves different. I don't know when—"

"Felix, we're coming." Rashid huffs. "You need all the help you can get. We can contact our parents, and Miss Rae will be here. We're going to help you and Joy. Mostly Joy because you are literally the worst." He smiles, and I find myself returning the gesture.

"What about your dad, and Johnny? You just found each other. Don't you want—"

"It took us months to admit our feelings; it would take way longer for either of us to move on now. And I already gave Johnny a kiss to remember me for like the two days we're gone. My dad won't notice I've left."

I stand there, momentarily perplexed. "Well."

DiOla nods her head slowly, pain crossing her features in the process. "I'll take care of Brak and the human parents before I leave. Go save Joy and our kingdom."

Just the mention of her name sends another spike of panic through my gut. Joy. My Joy. I have to get her back. My head swivels back to the two humans waiting for me to say yes. "If any of you die, Joy will kill me."

"Make sure we don't die, then." Rashid rolls his eyes.

"This is a terrible idea, you all know that, right?"

No one answers, but DiOla groans as Miss Rae takes the keys to their truck from their pocket, displacing DiOla.

Rae steps close to me, their mouth near my ear. "Chaos will come. It's inevitable, Felix Hamdi, future King. But love, and friendship…these soften the blows. The humans are safer with you up there, than down here. You'll understand soon." And then they switch subjects, cutting off my many questions. "Do not be afraid to rely on others as you have with Joy. Be open, and be prepared to make difficult choices."

"Do you know what'll happen?" I ask wearily, knowing they said they can't see the future.

Miss Rae only gives me a sad smile. "No one truly knows what's to come. Change is just as inevitable as chaos. I believe in you, and I know I'll see you again."

With that, they help Di away from the fire, away from the field where humans have no idea what's going on, toward the parking lot. We follow after them, through the darkness and the quiet, toward the cars and trucks where a few humans mill around, doing who knows what.

Including Thomas and Owen, standing near Miss Rae's truck. I'm surprised to see them here, surprised they came to see us off.

"I'm sorry about your backyard and the explosion. I hope your house is—"

Thomas throws up his hand. "Bit of debris is all. The metal alone could get me back into NASA."

"Well, if that doesn't work, I left a few gifts from home inside the bedroom," I say. "You'll get your job back by exposing us."

"Our world's not ready for the truth of you… Besides, I have a life to live and a family to take care of." Thomas looks over at Owen and smiles before returning his attention to me. "I'm sorry for the…for everything." There's so much left unsaid between us and I hope, somehow, that I've changed his life as much as he has mine. His was the path I could've gone down if I let the world—the universe—break me. Loneliness and anger and depression and feeling powerless could've ended him, but I want to believe that he is on the other side of it for now. That he now knows he was right, and he finds that confidence to go on. "Good luck up there."

Owen angrily swipes at a tear that slides down his cheek. "If anything happens to her—"

I nod, wishing Joy were here to be annoyed that this guy cares too much about her, even after she broke his heart a little. But she's not here. She's far away. How did I manage to live with her across worlds before? "I'll do my best."

After a moment of silence between us, I scoot into the back seat beside Sarah in the truck.

This could be the single worst idea I've ever had, but I'll do anything, brave anything for Joy. Just as she would for me. For these humans. For anyone.

The truck pulls away and Thomas grimly waves. I hold my head in my hands. *Joy, please wake up.*

PART III
CHAOS KINGDOM

CHAPTER 24
FELIX

The Andarran ship has three seats and a compartment full of stunners should we run into trouble. We buckle in as the hatch closes and my seatmates shake beside me. I wish I could say something calming or even helpful, but I can't. My Kindred was the one who knew the right thing to do. And I'm not calm, either; I'm stricken with panic that I may never see her again.

"Begin launch sequence with reflective stealth," I order the Andarran console. I miss my sexy AI, and the way Joy hated her.

"Launch sequence commencing," the system says in a singsong voice. "Autopilot malfunction. Manual operation required."

"Right," I say, looking for the thrusters. "So how do I pilot this thing?"

"I am not a 'thing,' I am a ship," the system corrects, and I shake my head. Of course, this ship would be super intelligent and annoying. "You may pilot me by using your intellect."

"She's got an attitude." Rashid laughs, though his face is pale and pinched.

"What does 'using your intellect' mean?" Sarah swallows, breathing heavy. "Was that a burn? Did you just get burned by a computer system?"

"Mmm," is all I can say. I need to use my intellect. There are no thrusters. Nothing for me to hold, nothing for me to control. The console is a flat shimmery slab. There are no numbers or buttons or anything I've seen before.

I place my hand on the slab and it lights up in an amalgam of colors, finally settling on a greenish orange.

"Welcome, Monchuran. DNA: Qadin, Felix. Your emotions read: fearful and anxious. Is this correct?"

"Uh, yes?" I answer, earning a nervous laugh from Rashid. Sarah's dreadfully silent, the first I've ever seen her like that.

"Okay. Using these emotions, is it safe to assume you would like us to follow the ship near Earth's moon?"

"Yes? How did you know that?" I nearly jump out of my seat, but the belt tightens in place. Can this console read my mind? How did it do that?

"You can research how this Andarran craft operates using the detailed guide in the compartment labeled Guide on the lower left quadrant of this craft. Please sit back as I take us closer to the ship ahead. If you feel nauseous, please feel free to ingest calming digestives located in the compartment labeled Weak Sensibilities."

"This ship is wild," Rashid rasps behind me.

"I'm totally going to use this experience on a college

essay—no way I'll get rejected with this." Sarah's eyes are shut and her hands cling to the edge of her seat for dear life.

"I will play some calming music so that your emotions are less intense. Would that be acceptable?"

"Yes," Sarah shouts in response. "Please."

A strange electric-style song with a haunting melody comes on and before I can complain about it—because, of course, I would complain about it—the ship spurs forward fast, and my breathing settles on its own.

Calm washes over me and I suddenly just feel so…peaceful. My body slouches in the seat and though I know I'm afraid, and worried about Joy, I just think of her smile. Her eyes. Her curly hair. I know I miss her, but this seat is so comfortable…and the humans are kind and wonderful.

The console transitions to a light blue color.

Rashid's voice slurs behind me. "I can't believe I'm in an alien ship, leaving the only world I've ever known, flying off into a universe of other planets I've never even heard of. I've been waiting for this my entire life. It's just like *Star Wars*."

"It's not like that nerdfest," Sarah says through a haze of sleepiness. "It's like *Guardians of the Galaxy*. And I'm Gamora—fashionable, hot, and determined."

"Then I'm Rocket," Rashid responds, with a lazy smile. "Very raccoon-like."

I happily ignore their human nonsense and point to the glimmer of light circling close to Earth's Moon. "There's the ship." The voice that leaves my mouth sounds drunk on happiness or something.

Rashid exhales. "I wish Joy were here. I'd tell her that everything's gonna be okay. That we love her like…like we're her Kindred, too." A smile tugs on his lips as the ship swerves, following that tiny glimmer of light that must hold my Joy. *Our* Joy.

I twist in my seat to look over at him. "She loves you. I love you, too."

"We all love each other." Rashid speaks to Joy as if she's there, holding his hand. "All the stars are closer, Joy."

★ ★ ★

The Inkara Royal Palace of Maru

For Immediate Release

The Duke and His Kindred Have Been Located

Steward Arren Sai denied the rumor spread on *Monchuri Morning News* by Duke Hamdi and his Kindred, Joy Abara, that Princess LaTanya is alive, but has instead offered that there still may be hope for the Qadin family line.

Duke Hamdi, the heir apparent, may have not known the royal family was assassinated by his Kindred. Steward Sai has released documents detailing how Joy Abara was able to close her Kindred connection with the Duke. Using these moments of absolute privacy, she contacted XiGran assassins. The proof Steward Sai found suggesting the Duke's involvement, an upload passed to the Duke on Outpost 32 a day prior to the assassinations, has been discredited.

The Duke is innocent. His power-seeking Kindred is to blame. Proof is forthcoming. Steward Sai will travel out of the system to collect the Duke and elevate him to the throne, while his Kindred will be brought to justice for the loss of our beloved Qadin family.

The Royal Palace would like to thank you for your patience.

CHAPTER 25

JOY

"THE TRAP WAS SET BEFORE I EVEN KNOW THERE
WAS DANGER, BABY, AND NOW ALL I CAN DO IS SHAKE
MYSELF FREE. I WANTED SO BADLY TO BE YOUR GIRL,
BUT THANK GOD IT WASN'T MEANT TO BE."

—DEJA REESE, "I FOUND ME"

When I awake, I'm strapped into a chair across from a ship's dashboard. I groggily turn my head to catch Maxon staring at a guide, brows furrowed.

Felix, I say through my connection. *Felix, I'm alive. I'm awake. Maxon took me.*

My beje, he sighs through my mind. His voice is very calm, and slightly drunk? *Oh, you're okay. How are you doing? Where are you going? Everyone says hello and we love you.*

Maxon has me. "Maxon." My throat is dry and scratchy, and my voice warbles, all full of unease—which I certainly am.

He ignores me as if I don't exist. How could I have ever thought life with him would have been bearable?

"You can still turn around. You don't have to do this," I plead, but he doesn't care. He only stares at his guide. Nothing I can say will change his mind. I know that. He was never one to listen to others, especially those he deems beneath him. I try a different tactic. "Where are you taking me?"

He finally peers over at me, his modern, if a bit small, ship moving at a glacial speed. "I bet your Kindred would love to know, right? Did he tell you he's grounded on Terra yet?" He chuckles to himself, an ugly smirk stretching his cheeks. "I blasted the two ships in the region before we left. In a way, I did him a favor. If he's smart, they won't find him and he'll live, which means you'll live. I did tell you I'd find a way for you to be useful to me and to our world." He laughs again before resuming his research of the guide. "I'm taking you to XiGra. If I can just figure out this navigation system."

Are you grounded? I ask, my heart racing as I try to break the straps around me to no avail. *Did he destroy our ship?*

There's a patch of silence followed by, *Yes...*

Maxon shouts suddenly, flicking some buttons and levers on the dash. There's a warning sign flashing on the dock, drowning everything in an angry red light.

The AI cuts in, "Warning, close proximity! Warning, close proximity to another aircraft identified as Andarran. Warning, close proximity! Collision likely. Warning." The voice almost makes me miss our sexy AI. This one's got zero personality.

"Andarran? What are they doing out here?" Maxon curses, taking the thrusters in his hands aggressively.

I try to adjust myself in the seat, but I'm locked in too tight. I gasp at air as our ship tilts to the side. *Felix, are you in the Andarran ship?*

His answer comes slowly. *We're rescuing you.*

I stare out at the universe beyond the dash window and the warning signs. The Milky Way, as the humans call it. All vibrant and underdeveloped planets that won't be ready for advanced life for another few millennia at least. *He's got weapons aboard. Don't get close.*

Despite this, his voice is calm, casual even. *Everything's fine, Joy. Even better than fine. I brought the humans with me. And we love each other.*

I close my eyes and travel to where he is. We hadn't needed to on Earth, but now… He lets me in and I drift through the ship, through space, to Felix sitting slightly ahead of Rashid and Sarah. They all look dazed. Happy but not at all with it.

My eyes threaten to bulge out of my head. *It's too dangerous.*

Rashid and Sarah say hi. Rashid's having the time of his life right now. He loves space, did you know? He's just like someone he calls Hans Solo. Or Chewbaccus. Or I think he said a yeti?

Felix! I nearly scream through our connection. *They're humans! And you barely tolerate anyone but me. They could die out here!*

They love you and want to be there for you… Can you tell Maxon to please stop driving so erratically? It's upsetting my stomach. He seems a bit off, but I can't contemplate that right now.

XiGra, is all I can say before the thrusters hit full throttle and we do a quick space jump through the sky and universe, our ship rattling around us. I try to connect to Felix again but I can't. Our connection must've been broken the moment we jumped.

Felix? I try again and again but it's of no use. I don't think the tech works when we're in between worlds and space.

Maxon lets a long exhale loose as his body shakes with momentum. My own's probably doing the same, but I'm so restricted in this seat that I can barely move of my own volition. I'm so worried about Felix, Rashid, and Sarah. Why are they with him?

"We lost them." Maxon coasts through the GoLu system, vacation destinations comprised of artificial planets that have the most beautiful luxurious hotels and simulation machines that cost a fortune. That's where the upper-middle class visit. I doubt anyone from Hali-Monchuri has ever been there.

"One day, our people will be welcome there, you'll see, Joy. Because of us." Maxon says it to me, but it seems like he's saying it more to himself.

We pass by the "island worlds" into the darkness between galaxies, past black holes and dead space, and to the hyperspace bridge we'll need to get to XiGra. Colors light up the sky before us, different colors leading to different destinations like jet streams only far faster. We don't need permission to cross. We just need coordinates.

"I can't find XiGra in this book," Maxon mutters aloud to himself. He's apparently a genius but doesn't know that all he has to do is bring up the star map, select the planet, and the coordinates will download into the system like a directive.

I smirk, the anger starting to leak to the surface of my voice for the first time with Maxon. I've always been so obedient, worried about displeasing him, but it can't matter anymore. I may not have experience flying, but Felix does, and he's read a ton of books on it. Which means I know how to fly, too. "You haven't flown much, huh?"

He stops to give me a withering stare, as if he wants to

slap me across the face for witnessing his cluelessness about something so basic.

"I could still bring you to Arren and watch you die. Be a hero to the crown. Who knows, showing that kind of loyalty might be good for Hali."

I shake my head, trying in vain not to struggle against my restraints. "But then you wouldn't be famous the way you want… Heroes are forgotten, stars shine bright for years and years. You need me."

His nostrils flare, but he doesn't deny it. "Shut up."

I laugh, though I know this isn't who I am… Anger, snarkiness, and being someone worthy of capture is so outside my comfort zone. Even now, my first inclination is to politely assist; he is my betrothed and superior back home. But stalling is all I can do before we land on XiGra and whatever is meant to happen there happens.

Maybe they conned him, too. Maybe they want to kill me or torture me for knowledge of the kingdom I don't actually possess. Maybe they'll use me to lure Felix there and then ransom us to Arren. Maxon may be smart, but he's naive about politics and evil people doing evil things. He has no idea what he's gotten himself into in the name of bright lights and a chance at celebrity.

"Oh." He brings his hands up to the map, touching the screen. "Right. You just touch the destination."

The screen lights up. "Destination selected: XiGra Prime. Specific location?"

"The…" Maxon shuffles through some papers while biting his bottom lip. "The Royal ZumBuden Summer Palace, please?"

"Destination finalized and will be reached within three hours," the AI says as if bored. "Please enjoy your journey."

And with that, the ship slides onto the yellow bridge and we're about to thrust into hyperspace. I have precious moments to try to connect to Felix. Hoping, somehow, he'll hear me.

The Summer Palace, I say, unsure if he heard me.

I'm coming, he says calmly, and relief washes over me. *Though that's the one place I've been banned.*

★ ★ ★

XiGra Prime is the first and biggest of the five planets in the XiGra system. It's known for a glittery man-made ring around the planet that collects stardust. Stardust is their biggest export; everyone buys it from them. It's why they're so rich…and ruthless.

While some Monchurans choose to worship Gods like Indigo and Ozvios, the Ilori choose only to worship Ozvios—believing themselves already gods of creation—and the XiGrans don't believe in any of those stories. Sure, they believe in life and destruction, but more so in good decisions and bad decisions. Good leadership and even better business. Their King, AnYeck ZumBuden, called King Yecki by mostly everyone, is a veritable grump. Worse, Felix apparently broke the west wing of his palace after throwing an epic party that got way too out of hand. I mean, who even decides to bring a herd of "trained" Calefs to a palace party?

All in all, none of this can be good for us. On a planet neither of us will be particularly welcome, ruled by a king who's not a fan of my Kindred, and we're currently fugitives, accused of killing the royal family who ruled a kingdom just an outpost away. And now what? Maxon's gonna deliver me there and begin filming a reality show?

This is…this is bad.

The ship startles as we hit the peak and I'm thrown back into my own body, back to Maxon. A moving picture of the XiGran palace fills the screen before me. A voice suddenly speaks through the comms.

"Sir KiBanu, we see two signs of life aboard. Did you obtain the Kindred?" The tone is calm, even, but despite their best efforts, they sound excited. Why do they want me so bad?

"I have Joy Abara, yes," he nearly stutters. "What do I do now?"

There's chatter in the background before a thick voice comes through, their heavy accent twisting the Monchuri language into something flat, their tone bringing bumps to the surface of my skin. "Bring her to me."

The line cuts out and I turn to Maxon, hoping he'll reconsider, that he'll have heard the authority and danger in that voice and decided that whatever they offered wasn't worth it. But he doesn't. He smiles.

"That was the King Yecki himself, can you believe it?" The ship's display changes to a moving screen saver of XiGra Prime. The pan shot is of a ship cruising over the capital, through the pale pink clouds and violet sky, down into the sun-sparkled city where rays of light bounce off fountains of silver water and translucent buildings. The XiGrans, with their various hues of multicolored skin and multicolored hair, look at the drone as it drops down for a more personal touch. Maxon smiles at the screen, shifting in his seat. "This will be the start of something new for us both and for our world. Can you feel it?"

I feel it, too, only I'm not foolish enough to think any of this will be good. This is a trap, a political one, and I'm not sure there will be a way out.

CHAPTER 26
FELIX

I try not to sigh loudly and give the humans the impression that I find them annoying, which I absolutely do. The system has stopped manipulating our emotions, but now the humans are panicking.

Sarah started shaking the moment we stopped at the hyperspace bridge and colors they've probably never seen unfurled before us. Our Andarran vessel piloted itself to XiGra Prime, and yet we've been on this ship too long for my crewmates to suddenly realize we're in space and everything they knew wasn't enough to prepare them for this moment.

Sarah looks a little green as she curls up in a ball, rocking herself back and forth in comfort, I guess?

Rashid's eyes are unfocused, terror pulling them wide. "I don't understand."

"I did tell you it's not like your fictitious stories." I pat him on the shoulder as if that'd help. What would Joy do? "This is the universe. It's full of color and worlds you couldn't imagine, inhabited mostly by beings that breathe oxygen like you, though maybe a bit less polluted than what you're used to. It's vast and beautiful, and I will be here with you, with both of you, to show you the way."

I will take care of them, Joy, I say, though she's not on the other side of the connection. I know what she'd say, though. She'd look me in the eyes and tell me to be gentle. That humans aren't prepared for the vastness of the universe, and that they trust me. She trusts me.

I imagine her running her fingers along my jaw. Her smile, her longing, her kisses. My heart aching to hold her, be near her. How could we ever go back to the way things were?

Rashid's gaze meets mine. Tears dribble down his cheeks, and Sarah stops rocking momentarily. "Are we going to die out here, Felix?"

"No." I shake my head, pressing my fingers deeper into his skin, hoping that this invokes confidence and calm. "Believe me, Joy and I will tear this universe apart for all of you, which is why we need to go. I don't know how long we have…" As Sarah sits up and a bit more color comes to Rashid's face, I put a little more pressure on. "Right now, Joy is on XiGra. She doesn't know what the King has planned, and I'd like to be there when she finds out—" What would Joy say if she were here? How would she make this situation better? The words come to me, even if they aren't as beautiful as hers. "I know you're afraid; so am I. I can't promise you that all of this won't get overwhelming or that there will not be a moment when you wish you were home. But we are here for you."

Rashid gulps. "We can do this."

"It's what Joy would do," Sarah agrees.

The AI cuts in, "Where would you like to go on XiGra Prime?"

"Eh…" I can't say the palace. I mean, I'm a wanted fugitive, the King loathes me, we definitely don't have the clearance to get in, and worse, I'm carrying two humans aboard. Who even knows how the XiGrans will react to that? "Somewhere near the palace?"

The Andarran AI doesn't waste time. "The XiGran Royal Museum is located two kilometers from the Royal Palace. Acceptable?"

"Yes," I state quickly. As we enter the bridge, the ship's controls lock. We inch along on the path without me needing to put my hand on the screen.

"I thought autopilot wasn't working?" Rashid's eyebrows rise into his forehead.

"It's technology. The bridge and hyperspace are like self-operating highways. Manual piloting isn't allowed, otherwise we could collide with other ships, or drive inconsistently." I rub a hand through my somewhat greasy hair.

"Does this thing go any faster, or—" Sarah begins before they both fall back into their seats and we bolt down the yellow bridge. The pressure causes tears to stream down their eyes, and their hands clutch at the seating, trying to hold on for dear life. Meanwhile, I scoot forward and put on Deja Reese's album.

I'm coming for you, Joy. But this time, I can only say it into my own mind.

★ ★ ★

Three Years Ago

FELIX

The light of the three distant suns of Gola bounce off every surface on the city below. Even the people are attired in the light; their white linen tunics, matching slacks and headscarves glitter so bright I have to shield my eyes. I'm supposed to be going over my recent upload on interstellar conflict, but how can I when the world outside beckons me? Who cares about some system called XiGra when there's so much beauty to be seen? And why does this King Yecki care so much about me? Doesn't he have his own system to care about?

Joy, I say for the millionth time today. *What are you doing? Where are you? Entertain me.*

I expect her to ignore me—she has been doing that a lot as of late—but she sighs dramatically through our connection, annoyed with me for the millionth time today. She appears beside me at the window, staring out at Estrella with me.

Her usually pleasant voice sounds sharp and nervous for once. *I'm not here to entertain you, Felix. I have my first interview for the bookstore today. Mum lost her job and we have no food.*

Money. It's always about money. I've offered her my weekly allowance since we were children, since the first time she wanted a toy I had and she told me her mother couldn't afford it. She refuses every single time, even though my allowance could pay at least twice their rent with spare change. She's too proud, too stubborn, and I'm sure she believes that if she accepted, my parents would find out and think that she's been using me. Just the idea of them thinking (more) poorly of her causes her to panic.

How can they let you work if you're only fourteen? That's child labor. Isn't that illegal?

She breathes heavily. *We are allowed to work at twelve years, as long as it's not considered hard labor. The bookstore is not hard. I'll only be putting books away and it'll give me a chance to read new stories. The pay is good and it's not too far. I can walk there alone.*

I know it's selfish, but I can't help myself from asking it nonetheless. *Will we still be able to talk during the day? Will you still answer me and be with me?*

She regards me, something uncertain swimming in her eyes. I can't read her, though. She's been so distant these past months. Her fingers touch her own window back home. *I'm always with you, Felix. This will never change.*

That's not really an answer to my question, though. I'm about to say as much before she cuts me off.

One day you will marry, you will have noble children, and someone who will love you. You will crave the quiet and separation from me. You should prepare yourself for this…inevitability. I am only your Kindred. Nothing more. We're connected but apart.

I know she can't believe this, I know this is something her mother has told her many times so that we never cross the line of propriety. And yet, the words sting. *I will never tire of your voice, never wish for our connection to diminish. You are everything to me.*

Her face softens. *What will you do without me, Felix?*

I'd be lost without you, Joy, so let's hope we never find out. I wish I could hug her, feel her warmth, have her presence linger with mine. *We will be together forever, and there is no one I'd rather have as my Kindred.*

CHAPTER 27
JOY

"BREATHE THROUGH THE FEAR, BABY, IF THE CLOUDS
COME CRASHING DOWN AND THE STARS FALL BEFORE
YOUR EYES, KNOW THAT I'LL BE THERE IN THE END,
WAITING FOR YOU HIGH UP IN THE SKIES."

—*DEJA REESE, "GOODBYE"*

Hyperspace takes forever but it's beautiful.

I would love to take it all in, take mental pictures of it so I could draw it in children's stories, but I can't focus on anything but my own situation.

I'm locked into my seat and my legs are numb.

Maxon nodded off while I watched different images of XiGra Prime on the screen, including facts about King Yecki. So far, I've learned that he has been king since he was sixteen years old following the death of his mother, he has never married, he has revolutionized the XiGran economy by providing jobs in the stardust industry, and his reign is fairly socialist. Seven out of ten XiGrans are happy with his leadership and agree he is not a dictator, which in a universe filled with them is a good thing.

Although I'd like to be free from my bindings so I can somehow mill about this tiny ship and use the sole wash closet, I can admit that watching XiGra is a lot prettier than watching Maxon sleep. Or peering out the side window, which is just blurry darkness dotted with other systems and planets, some inhabited, most not.

I try to connect to Felix, but the signal's silent. Dead. A feeling of unease spreads through my stomach. With the override, I could give him space and silence, take my own space and silence when needed. But with hyperspace disconnecting us, it not being a choice I could make, I suddenly understand why Felix was so uncomfortable and frustrated. We need each other. I need Felix.

When we lurch off the bridge, the real XiGra fills our screen. It's all blue and pink with patches of green, yellow, and purple. It's not nearly as vibrant or bright as the pictures would have you believe, but it's clean and orderly, rich without flaunting it like Maru-Monchuri, with their golden fountains and imported poisonous water.

Maxon startles awake as we drop onto the airway lane, the current taking control of the ship. The XiGrans stare and point at our foreignness. Some even smile. A little child with light blue skin and black curls waves at me, and I'd return the gesture if my arms weren't strapped to the seat.

Maxon leans back, gazing at the new world unfurling before us. He's eerily silent. And I wish he still had a Kindred, one who didn't die when he was too young to bond. If he had her, he wouldn't do what he's doing. He'd be a better person.

I stare out the windows as ships pass by us, self-piloting, as their inhabitants watch holo-screens and chat amongst themselves.

"We can still turn back. You could bring me to Felix, you could—"

"Stop." Maxon rubs the sleep from his face, shaking his head. "The XiGran King had this ship sent to me after I taped the *Monchuri News* interview. He wrote me an entire letter, telling me I'm a star shining bright, and if my own system couldn't see it, he'd set a show up for me over here. The one condition was that I bring you here. There's nothing you can say to change my mind. We are bringing Hali-Monchuri to the universe, and no one can deny us our place anymore. This is bigger than you."

I swallow the anger rising in my throat. There's no use talking to him. No use trying to make him see reason. He always wanted fame—for himself and for our world—and now he believes all of that is within his grasp. We both want to make Hali better, but he has to see this way won't work.

After another few moments coasting in silence, our ship slips onto a private underground tunnel. Lights flash and scans scour our ship's interior as we pass soundlessly along the track. When the ship stops, the hatch pops open from the outside.

Maxon turns quickly in his seat as two armed guards, both obscured in black tech, approach.

"I was personally invited by King ZumBuden." He throws his hands up as one levels something akin to a stunner at him. Maxon's brow beads with sweat and his eyes flick around the ship. "I'm not armed. I mean no harm!"

The other unlatches me, sheathing their weapon in the

process. Well, at least they don't think I'm a threat. They help me to my feet, their support gentle.

"Are you able to walk, or do you require assistance?" Their voice is mechanical. Despite this, I don't believe they're an AI bot, something I've only ever heard of in Maru-Monchuri. There's something very lifelike about their movements.

I take a step forward, just as my knees lock up. A gasp involuntarily leaves my lips and I stumble forward only for the guard to catch me in their strong arms. A whiff of chemical solution hits my nostrils and I cough.

Their mechanical voice is quiet in my ear. "You are safe."

Felix, I whisper, but there's no response in my brain. *Felix, please tell me you're on your way. Please.* I know he can't hear me. I know that he's still in hyperspace. There's no way he could have gotten here yet. I'm wishful-thinking.

My legs shake when the guard sets me down on the hangar ground. There's a tightness in my throat, I try not to panic. I'm on XiGra. In the personal palace of King Yecki. I could die here. Or worse.

We're greeted by a large group, two of which hold scanners that rove over our bodies, even though the guards know we're unarmed. But I guess royals can never be too safe.

We're led down a series of ornate and intricate hallways. The decor is rich, if a bit repetitive, and I have no idea where I truly am. If it weren't for the guard's arm beneath mine, I don't think I would have managed this much exercise so soon after being locked into a chair for so many hours.

At the end of one hall, we're forced on our knees on dark purple stone, me far more gently than Maxon, before an empty golden throne. A large window sits behind it, dark blue water speckling it. Rain. It never rains on Hali-Monchuri, and yet water is real here just as it was back on Earth. I marvel at the way it slides down the windowpane until the view is replaced by the King.

The King from Felix's memories.

He stares down at us, but never once attempts to sit on his throne. His black robes are embossed with shimmering maroon thread. It's otherworldly, and as I scan over his deep brown skin, and wavy black-brown hair that's cropped at his ears, I'm surprised by the familiarity it strikes within me, and how young he looks.

When he deigns to let us hear his royal voice, I notice its deep timbre. "I assume the flight was bearable, and must apologize for your poor treatment, Miss Abara." He nods to a guard, and I'm gently pulled to standing before a poufy chair is rushed under my legs. I plop onto it, letting out a whoosh of air.

"Oh, yes, Mr. KiBanu. Thank you." He barely glances Maxon's way as he demotes him from sir to mister.

Maxon stiffens. "You're welcome, Your Majesty. Thank you for this opportunity. I have so many—"

King Yecki holds up a hand. "You are dismissed. You and your father may take your payment and go." He waves a guard over to drag him away, but Maxon leaps to his feet.

"Wait a minute. You said you'd grant me a show. You said—" he whines so unattractively I try not to crack a smile, even if I end up dead in a few minutes. Even if I have no idea what's going on. Even if I'm shocked the King would not uphold his end of the bargain. "I trekked across the universe for her! All for my planet."

"Yes." King Yecki furrows his brows, taking a step down, a step forward, causing panic to turn in my stomach. I'm either going to be sick or I'm starving. I wish I had those chocolate-covered raisins. But I guess they're melted among the rubble of the HAMDI hopper. "I told you what would motivate you the best, so you'd bring me the Kindred. I don't actually care about you. You were disloyal, you betrayed and kidnapped your own betrothed. I'm aware it's a moral conundrum for me since I told you to, but I don't surround myself with such... unsavory characters. I'm sure you understand."

"But Hali—"

"I assure you, I do still have your world's best interests at heart." The King looks at me as he replies. He nods again to the guards, and Maxon is led away, screaming and name-calling and pleading. King Yecki doesn't bat an eye. Instead, he takes a seat on the bottommost step to look closely into my eyes.

A myriad of emotions flood through me and I can't decide which one to focus on first. Maxon wanted more for our home, but he went about it all the wrong ways. Whereas I... I want what's best for my home, but I may not have the chance to do it. I may not even leave this room alive.

My life is in King Yecki's hands. I take a deep breath and try to hold my head high.

He stretches his legs, his violet eyes piercing mine. "Now, tell me, Joy, is your Kindred on his way?" When I don't answer, his hands reach out and clasp the ends of the chair. "Do you know why you were paired to the Hamdi boy? Your people considered you nothing and no one, voiceless, but I don't. I want to hear you. I can sever the connection. I can give you everything if you wish it."

Deja Reese's words filter through my mind. *You're not too much, you're enough… You are precious and don't you forget it.*

"I was never nothing or no one." My words tumble out strong and confidently, even if I feel neither. "I am Joy Abara. I have a voice, you don't need to give me one, and I won't use it to hurt my Kindred. You only surround yourself with loyal people and I am one…to Felix. I love him."

The moment the words leave my lips, I know it's true, and I've admitted it right here to the world. Not just because Maxon's gone. Not just because I've loved Felix my entire life, but because he loves me, too. My heart pitter-patters and I feel lighter than I've ever felt before in years.

I am enough for Felix Hamdi. I am precious to Felix Hamdi. He is enough for me. He is precious to me. I could be a queen. And then I'd be able to do what Maxon wanted for Hali, without duplicity, without forcing someone into unhappiness.

We sit there in silence, and I expect something. Pain. Anything. Instead, he leans back, his body strewn across the steps. When I squirm a bit in my seat, my fingers shaking while grasping my knees, he gifts me a smile and claps.

"Well, aren't you a delight!" He laughs, causing the nearby guards to flinch. "I knew I chose well. I told LaTanya that he needed to pair with someone from a strong mother, someone who would raise the Kindred to be thoughtful, brave, and moral. Your father was useless and wouldn't have added much to your upbringing. I asked him who he would rather be, a father or a rich man. I always ask new fathers this question.

It's a bit of fun—weeds out the ones I don't want to work with. Most say they'd like to be both. The very best ones always choose being a father. Yours took the money without a glance back."

"What? Why would you do that?" I blurt, my breath lodged in my throat. His gaze is distant as my eyes fill with tears and I turn away, willing myself not to cry as the rest of what he said sinks in. No one wants to find out their dad never wanted them, but finding out that he chose money over me? Danio was right—he never deserved my mom. But Deja was wrong—maybe I was never going to be enough from the beginning for him.

My own thoughts whisper in the back of my brain for a change, telling me I was enough for Rashid, for Sarah, and always for Felix. Along with Mum, I'm full and surrounded by love. Still, I imagine how much it hurt her. I imagine what it would have been like to have had a father who wanted me.

"Why do *you* care?" The question's whispered between us as I swallow down the tears and sit straighter, though my heart hurts.

"Because you were my first choice of a Kindred for the Duke, and I didn't want you brought up by someone who didn't deserve you."

I don't understand, though. Why would a king from another world be interested in who got paired with Felix? La-Tanya is his mother, that's true…but…?

King Yecki continues on, like he's telling a juicy story that happens to be my life, "Your mother washed her hands and stood tall. She rebuffed any money we offered. And look at the young woman you've become." He claps again and then stands abruptly, offering me a hand. When I refuse, he shakes his head. "Now, now. There's no reason for tears and anger. He wasn't worthy of being called a parent. Come."

I don't take his hand but I stand, trying to keep the shakiness from my legs. I follow him up the stairs to the window. Through it, I see XiGra Prime. It's stunning. It's nothing like home. It's nothing like Florida. It's another world, another people. It's blue and modern with silver speedways and colorful people, all drizzled with rain. The palace is gorgeous. It's gold and deep red, ornate but not ostentatious. People walk through the watery garden beyond with parasols, laughing in their understated yet tasteful clothing. They look happy. Not alone on some foreign world.

None of my friends are here. My mom's not here. My life isn't here. Felix isn't here. Looking out over the city and royal gardens won't make any of this better.

It won't stop me missing the life I found away from home.

"Do you really love him?" he asks, his voice soft as he watches the ships zip past in the distance.

"Yes." My answer comes quickly, ringing with truth. Loving Felix was the easiest part of my life, allowing myself to love him has been the most difficult. But I can't go back now. I won't. Even if it means it kills me in the end.

Silence spans between us and I don't know what's going to happen next. "Arren is on his way here for you and Felix Hamdi. I offered you both in exchange for LaTanya."

I stop breathing, and place my hand against the cool glass. I'm going to die. That's what's going unsaid. Arren is going to use me, torture me, do whatever he can to get Felix to take that throne…

King Yecki breathes deeply, turning to me. "I had to meet you, to know your mind and your heart."

I swipe another tear that slides down my cheek. "Why?"

"To know you and your Kindred are worth protecting and elevating to the throne." He places a hand on my shoulder. "I've watched Felix Hamdi his entire life. He had very few aspirations, felt lost, afraid, hopelessly in love with you. He destroyed part of my palace. Which I found rather reckless." He inhales and exhales deeply. "But with you... I think he's different. You make him strong and brave. You are his anchor."

"I'm not." I hold his gaze. "Felix dreams big. He has always been brave, always strong, and he doesn't need me to be his anchor. He's not going to float away. He's solid. He'll be good for Monchuri. He never imagined he'd need to be, but he'll step up because he has to. He'll step up because now he knows he can. And because he knows what I know."

King Yecki pins me with a gaze. "And what is it you know?"

"That our worlds are unfair. No place is perfect, but we need to take care of each other and use compassion and not oppression. We need to give more than we take, help more than sit idle. It's time for change."

The King turns toward a ship bearing the Qadin emblem as it descends from the sky. He gasps when the ship shoots at his guards, and then barks into his comms to let them through, let them pass. Let them think they've won.

His entire demeanor changes. Arren is here and he won't be diplomatic. The King has invited a viper into his nest and now he's in danger like I am.

His voice is strong, though he looks almost lost in thought. "Do you trust me, Joy Abara?"

I nod, though I'm not sure. I've only just met him, and now I know he sent my father away and conspired with La-Tanya to have me paired with Felix. And he brought Arren here to trade for her life and that plan was skewed from the beginning. "Yes."

"Good," he says, beckoning his guards over. "This may hurt."

CHAPTER 28
FELIX

Joy, I'm coming, I say through our connection for the millionth time, only to not get a response. I know she's here, but for some reason we're being blocked from each other. This doesn't bode well.

The moment we entered the atmosphere, we were picked up at the museum and escorted to the Royal Palace, told that King Yecki was expecting us. Since then, though, we've been walking these translucent tech walls with teal flooring—which are excessively boring—for twenty minutes. They're stalling us, taking us the long way.

And still, there's no Joy in my head.

Nor any eye-catching art. It's like they put all of the dull pieces on display here, while keeping the true beauties inside the throne room for the King's private perusal. At any rate, the humans seem to be rather taken with it.

I sidle up to one of our escorts, a guard in teal and black, with vibrant red hair. "I've been to the palace before. Where are you taking us?"

"Sir, I'm under the orders of the King," is all they answer.

"Look at the display!" Rashid's eyes are so wide they might fall out of his head. He almost touches it when a holo-AI appears, brandishing a smile and speaking in XiGran. Rashid steps back, only for the holo to follow, asking him if he'd like to switch languages or which exhibits he'd most like to see. It's ancient tech, which would explain why no one bothers with the west wing of the palace. Maybe I should throw another party so that they may remodel here, too. I feel like we might have been the first guests to traverse these halls in ages.

As Rashid tries to escape the holo, Sarah gazes at the bowl of pea-sized upload capsules.

"Don't eat the capsules." I rush over and pull her away from it. "I don't know if it'll be too much information for you. Your weak human brain could explode."

"What do you mean?" Sarah's hands shake by her sides as she jumps back from the upload dish.

"They're uploads...you know...like how you download information?" This is like talking to a group of children, which I wouldn't mind if we didn't have so many other pressing issues. "Well, imagine there are info uploads, and instead of sticking them into a computer, you can swallow them. And the info is like powder intelligence that disintegrates on your tongue, seeps into your system and then appears in your brain. That's an upload. I doubt your human brains could handle it."

"Please keep up," one of our escorts says, their black garb swishing as they stalk farther down the hall.

I pull Rashid and Sarah along, following like a dutiful

guest, even if the last time I was here, they treated me like royalty.

At the end of another hallway, this one adorned with the royal portraits I'd seen once in the east wing, I know we'll round the corner to where there will be two armed guards standing before a heavy metal door. I've been there before. It leads to the private hallways and the throne room. It'll lead to Joy. I just know it. I take a deep breath and exhale with relief.

Yet, as our escorts turn before us, there's a split second when a quick *bang* pierces the air and they tumble onto the carpeted floor. I'm in front of Rashid and Sarah when I notice the tip of one of a Soleil's shoe, and throw my hands out, stopping the humans.

We're in danger.

I push the humans back and out of view into a coral cove with low light shining on a sculpture of some old king. The escorts lay unconscious or dead in front of us. Footsteps thrum down the hall. "We need to take out the guards before they come to us."

Rashid's voice is louder than intended. "You want to *kill* them?"

I roll my eyes, whispering harshly. "No, I mean take them out to a restaurant, ply them with alcoholic beverages, and then we can share stories about our childhoods while we eat melted chocolate desserts. And then when they—"

"Great sarcasm, but can we get to the part where we save Joy and don't end up dead?" Sarah heaves a sigh and bumps her shoulder into mine.

I want to mumble some obscenities, but I don't because

she's right. I swear to all the Gods in the universe, when all of this is over, I will take a break from humanity.

"Should we use these things I found in the ship?" Rashid holds up two silver stunners, aiming them at me. Where did he find those? "What do they do? Flash bombs?"

"Those are poison dispensers like in one of those old heist movies." Sarah reaches out and takes one.

I gingerly grab the other stunner from Rashid. "These are base stunners. You aim and, if they aren't modified, they send electrical charges through the body. Which is why neither of you will handle them."

Rashid looks put out. "I've played video games before."

"Raz and I used to play *Mario Kart* and RPGs." Sarah's brow rises. "Yeah, I know what RPGs are."

"We're your best bet is what I'm saying." Rashid holds out his hand, giving me a confident smile and I'm just about to give it back when Sarah peeks her head out the hallway, aims, and hits both guards in two quick shots.

Their bodies crash to the floor and we all stare at her.

"You were taking way too long. Come on." She struts out, stunner in hand leaving us to follow her.

Rashid and I share a look. "That was some Princess Leia shit right there."

I push him out of the cove behind our apparent marks-woman. Well, at least one human is coming in handy. When they aren't turning my brain to puddles.

Felix, Joy whispers through my mind finally. *Arren. Here. Blocking. King. Don't—*

Joy, I screech back. *Arren's here? What do you mean? Where?* But again there's no answer.

I quicken my pace, not telling the humans what's happening. They don't need the pressure. As it is, my heart hammers in my chest. Arren's here. In this palace. On this world. He locked up my parents. He kidnapped my birth mother. He may be with Joy, who he also wanted dead. He wants me dead. He wants a kingdom and he will stop at nothing for it. And as I can see it right now, he may have infiltrated King Yecki's palace.

We're walking into a trap, but as I pass the fallen guards spread out on the floor, an idea forms.

"Let's grab their gear. I have a plan."

★ ★ ★

Already my plan is failing. Sarah and I have changed into the guards' armored clothing—which I can confirm is extremely hot, although the face mask is breathable, and in other circumstances would make a cool concert ensemble—while Rashid has commandeered a holo-screen.

He doesn't know how to use it, and can't offer any surveillance help. I thought he was a genius, but it seems he's just a lovestruck cheerleader with some computer skills.

"This is Tony Stark–level tech," he mutters. "Nah, more like Shuri."

"Who cares," Sarah hisses. "We have to keep moving."

I motion my fingers in front of the holo-screen, and the images move from translucent in front of our eyes to full-colored and onto the blank wall before us.

"That helps," Rashid admits. "Basically, you don't need language to use it, but movements…like in *Black Panther*."

I take the holo-screen from him and speak into it. "Holo-AI, switch to human English."

"Scanning," the AI states robotically. A little swirl appears on the screen and wall. That could take a while.

"Sarah and I have to find Joy." My feet shift anxiously on the fabric flooring. "If I know anything, she's in the throne room. And we need to communicate with you. AI, create two radio frequency lines."

"The AI is still scanning, you have to wait—" Rashid begins until the AI asks us to press our fingers to the screen. "How can it perform so many tasks at once?"

I try not to roll my eyes. It's not his fault he doesn't understand technology, I mean he comes from a tiny underdeveloped planet that's already on the brink of extinction. But it's not really my place to say that and I don't need to break his poor fragile heart.

"Because we're better than you."

Rashid huffs. "You mean your tech is."

"Sure." I put my hand on the screen, and my fingerprints are scanned once before a testing sound rings in my ears.

"Connected," the AI says. "Next scan."

Sarah does the same, and then she clutches her head when the test happens. "Oh, my God. Holy shit. I can hear the computer."

I sigh. "Now, Rashid, speak into the holo."

"Testing, one, two. Testing…"

"What the hell?" Sarah's eyes widen. "I heard you in my head!"

"It's like we're all Kindred now," Rashid says with an uncertain, panicky smile.

As if I needed that reminder that my Kindred is here and

unsafe. And waiting for me. And Arren could be doing who knows what to her. She needs me. I need her.

"Scan complete," the AI says in perfect English.

"Show us a layout of the palace and the occupants, please." Rashid stares at the wall as it transforms into a map, complete with warm bodies. "Right, go save Joy. I'll clear the way for you."

Sarah and I jog off together, stunners in hand.

CHAPTER 29
JOY

*"YOU CAN KILL ME ALL YOU WANT, BUT YOU AIN'T
NEVER GONNA GET MY CROWN."*
—DEJA REESE, "QUEEN SHIT"

King Yecki gave me a tiny chip to put behind my ear that'll
cut off the Kindred connection. I'd just gotten adjusted to
it when Arren broke through the walls and seized the King.
Yecki expected this, planned for this, it would seem. He's
strapped to a chair, watching me. There are guards all around
us, Arren's Soleil in the throne room, and Yecki's guards behind the doors.

I have no idea what's going on, only that I'm expected to
play along. Only that there'd be pain, and he was right.

Arren's hand collides with my face and I slump onto the
hard stone floor. "Where is your Kindred?" He stalks toward my crumpled body, anger marring his once-placid face.
"Bring him to me!"

"I won't," I repeat for the fifth time. It's not just that I won't, either; it's that I can't. Yecki's chip tweaks the Kindred reception, making it impossible to trace—should Arren try. I just have to hold out until… Arren gives up or King Yecki decides it's not worth it anymore.

I have to hope Felix won't know the pain I'm in. If he did, he'd rush here and try to save me, which is exactly what Arren wants. What Arren is counting on. And I can't do that.

I want to save Monchuri, but I want to save my Kindred.

Joy… Felix's voice crackles in my brain and I realize the chip must've come loose. I know he's here, but I hope my warning kept him away. He and our human friends have to be safe and as far away as they can be.

Arren's feet stop beside my face, and I look up into his vibrant red eyes that I always thought were gold. His yellow robes are rich against his white skin. His blond hair shows signs of black roots. His skin ripples and undulates and when he notices me observing, he kicks me to the side.

I wince, but the pain is brief. My mind is elsewhere. Arren is different, and my brain can't seem to connect just how or why yet. All those years of meeting, him using tech no one has ever heard of, manipulating the Qadins, killing them, trying to win LaTanya… What if it's more than power to Arren? What if he's seeking something else and he's losing control? I never once saw him as anything but confident and unflappable. Either I'm hallucinating or he's changing into something wholly else.

"War is here. Your royals are dead. Your government is a mess. Only I can save it." He paces behind me, his voice growing louder, angrier. "Your Kindred must anoint me King of

Monchuri to be safe. LaTanya won't. Only he remains. I've cleared his name, kept his family safe. He must do this. For me and for them."

I stay put on the cold floor as I hug my body close to me. He can hurt me, he can threaten me, but he won't break me. And he won't harm my Kindred.

If he steals the kingdom, so be it.

He stands over me, yanking the collar of my silver dress in his hands. He pulls me up, crushing my neck in the process. I choke, and the corners of my sight blacken at the edges. He stares down, and those red eyes shift to a hazy purple. Suddenly, his entire form shifts briefly to a strange translucence before returning to normal. His voice is deep now, anger punctuating every word precisely. He's not...he's not normal. He's not right. My eyes could be playing tricks on me, or...

"Hand over your Kindred or you both will die."

The doors open and Arren unceremoniously drops me back onto the stone. I gasp for air, my legs shake, and my brain's flashing red warning signs that I may pass out. Still, I manage to look at the guards who enter. They quickly assemble beside the others, and bow to Arren.

King Yecki looks down silently as a sword presses to his neck in warning.

A muffled mechanical voice comes from one. "There's been a breach in the...west quadrant corridor. Two guards were left unconscious."

"Hamdi is here." Arren smiles something evil. "If he shows, I'll give you LaTanya." This he says to King Yecki. "She's hardly herself. Her useless Kindred died and she can't function. Monchurans..." When Yecki's brows furrow, a question lingers in the air. An unspoken question that silences the room. Arren knows the mistake he made the moment he made it, and tries to backtrack. "I don't have a Kindred. My parents were smart to not let anyone tinker with my mind."

But that can't be true. *Every* Monchuran has a Kindred, or the system fails. You can do whatever's possible to sever, block, interrupt the connection, but everyone must have a Kindred. The Second Chaos dictated that, made that into law.

No one is exempt. No one can escape its grasp.

Arren's lying. And if he's not, he's not Monchuran. If he's not Monchuran, what is he?

He lets out a long sigh, his lips twisting at the edges. His gaze flicks to his own golden-clad Soleil. "Search the palace, find him."

"You have seized my palace, held me captive as you've harmed a young girl. Did you come for a war or did you think this would pass?" Green blood drips down the side of Yecki's face, but his voice remains strong. Adamant. "I want to see LaTanya."

"Naturally," Arren proffers. He taps a few buttons on his holo-watch, and a holo-screen widens in front of us. In the picture, LaTanya sits in a soiled white sheath of a dress. Her once-beautiful coils sit ratty and disheveled on her shoulders. Her hands are bound behind her back, not that she seems to care. Her eyes stare at something far off. She doesn't move. Doesn't fight. Doesn't speak.

"As you can see, she's a shell of herself, but she's yours the moment we have her son. I assure you, we don't want war. We simply cannot trust you to give us the Duke and his Kindred. This is just business."

Yecki's voice pierces the air, sending chills down my spine. "What have you done?"

"We didn't know how…emotional it would be for her to lose her Kindred. We've gone easier on her. We tried compassion." He shrugs. "I'd had so many plans for us, and now she's a broken doll."

And then something—someone screams from behind us and lunges at Arren, knocking him to the floor. There's a tussle as the guard pommels Arren into the stone over and over and over again. Until Arren's body goes slack, and a spirit breaks free. No, not a spirit.

A person.

Arren stands above the body, his body. He looks the same, only not quite solid. A thick violet haze sticks to his form, pulsing like a heartbeat. For some reason, he's even scarier now than before.

"An Ilori," King Yecki calls out, understanding flooding his expression. "The Ilori Colonies are so far away from us, never in my life did I think they'd blend with us…"

Guards filter through the doors, swooping in around Yecki to protect him as planned. But not us.

"Worlds will fall," Arren states, his voice crisp and different than before, deeper, wiser even. He stares at the guard who separated him from his body. "Do you know what you've done?"

The guard tears the gold mask from their face, revealing a face I know as well as my own. Felix's eyes meet mine before roving over the cut lips, the gash in my forehead, the twist of my body. His gaze catches on the little chip that severs our connection beside my ear. He swoops down upon me, removing the chip, and my brain floods with emotions and pain.

And love, so, so much love.

Felix stands tall in front of me, protecting me, as his chin juts upward to hold Arren's gaze. "I've exposed you for what you really are."

"You've brought destruction to Monchuri. The Ilori have already taken Ocara. The Juxto warlords have pledged allegiance. And an army of Ilori are on their way to your precious little Earth. Your kind fear a Third Chaos; as if it is an inevitably brought on by poor morals and carelessness, without realizing Indigo is dead, Ozvios returns, and there is money to be made. We don't want to destroy life, we want to control it." He grits his teeth. "Anyone who dares to stand against us, will fall."

I throw a hand over my mouth. Earth. Humans. *No*.

Felix is about to say something when the holo-screen flashes out from Arren's watch. The image of LaTanya, the way she suffers, is gone from view but not from his mind. Arren took his mother, his father, killed the royals, kept La-Tanya locked up and tortured. And he hurt me.

Felix's face contorts in rage, pure unfettered rage, which means he's going to do something he's never done before. Fight, even if the chance of losing is too high. Because if not now, when?

Be careful, I speak through the drumming of our hearts. *I love you*.

He jumps to his feet and dashes back to Arren's form, unsure of how to even hurt the being who stands there with a smug smile playing on his face. Soleil run forward, but another black-clad guard holds up a stunner shakily, shouting in English to stop. I scramble up and push through the pain to stand between them. My dress is torn in places and blood weeps down my face from the gash. But I can't stop.

Sarah takes off her mask and swallows. Her hand still shakes, and her eyes widen when the Soleil pull their own gold pistols from their holsters.

It all happens so fast. Too fast. I scream for them to stop, that she's an innocent, that she's a human, that she doesn't understand what she's doing.

"Hands up!" they yell in Ilori, their voices gruff and uncaring. They didn't come for her—her life means nothing to them. Sarah continues holding a stunner, not knowing what they've said, not knowing they hold serious weapons that could end her life, and before I can translate, before I can defuse this misunderstanding, they fire.

Sarah bellows my name as I throw myself in front of her. The laser hits my stomach like a bolt of fire. My body loses balance and I fall, involuntarily crumbling onto the stone. Felix gasps somewhere behind me and stumbles, his own body giving out.

His head lands opposite mine, and we're too far away to grasp each other. My blue blood spreads between us. My breaths come fast, and my vision blurs. I can't move my legs. I slowly blink as the world stands still. *Sarah. No.*

Felix crawls toward me, his eyes nearly closed. His hand threads with my own. *She will be fine. She will be.*

Are we dying? The pain steals the breaths from my lungs, leaves unsaid words on my tongue. A XiGran guard steps between Sarah and the Soleil, and whatever he says gets them to lower their weapons. They exchange yells and someone shouts for a medic but it'll be too late. Too late for us.

Sarah screams something to me, but it's lost in the silence of our world where it's just me and Felix. Arren points at someone or something, his mouth dropping angrily. King Yecki raises a glittery obsidian sword that pulses with electricity and swings it at Arren's neck and I watch it in slow motion. It slices through the violet sheen of his body and penetrates his skin.

I look away.

I stop caring.

What does it matter anymore? We can't save or change the world. The choice has been taken from us. So has the future. All the things I wanted to do, the places I wanted to see, and the stories I wanted to tell. The kisses I wanted to share...

I don't want to die, I tell Felix. Our hands mingle together, though the grip loosens. It's cold. And my eyesight wavers. *I know we're supposed to be brave but I want to live with you and make art and love and help people. I don't want to die, Felix.* A sob breaks through the shock washing over our connection. And his own agony and anger of a future denied wrenches a long sigh through him.

Joy. His body acts as if it's been hit, too. As if he's bleeding inside and beyond repair. His brain tells him it is, that our bodies are one and our pain is shared and that if it's real, it's real. We live together. We die together. That is the curse and the gift of Kindred who fall in love.

He's dying. *Because* of me.

I want to say I'm sorry, that if there were anything else I could've done, I would have. But I can't. Sarah came here for me, for us, and I couldn't let her die. I couldn't.

Don't, he says quietly. *I would have done the same. I don't regret anything. Being close to you, kissing you, touching you, Joy…it was worth a million lifetimes.*

My breaths become raspy as blood dribbles from my lips. *I'm sorry, Felix.*

I'm sorry… We don't have more… He pauses as the pain reverberates through us. Our hearts slow …*time.*

I remember our last kiss and our first kiss. Memories upon memories. A short life filled with sweet moments we were blessed to share. I can't regret it, either. I could never regret him.

A movie flickers through his mind and into mine of a dream. Of me dancing in a dress sewn from the stars and space, and him asking if I want him.

I love you… he whispers.

Our hearts slowly stop and the worlds and galaxies and moons begin to spin on without us.

★ ★ ★

Eleven Years Ago

JOY

Felix plays with his toy as he sits in the palace hall and the suns shine down from the grand windowpanes above. I sit on the hot apartment floor, playing with a pencil.

My belly is full from Mum's rice, and my heart is full as I look at my best friend.

His hair stands straight up and all over the place as if it hasn't seen a brush in weeks. There's ice cream smeared across his chubby left cheek and he pushes his holo-truck on the polished wooden floor. I take my pencil, which is doubling as a superhero figurine, and pretend she's shooting her powers on his truck, mimicking the sound of a big crash.

"Villains aren't allowed here!" I shout. "I shall save the silver city from your badness!"

Felix groans. "I am not a villain! You're a villain." And then he takes his own figurine, the fanciest doll I've ever seen, and he pretends to fight mine.

Our dolls are worlds apart, but we imagine they clash together and we exhaust ourselves until we fall down in a puddle of giggles. His hand reaches out for mine and mine to his, and though they can't touch, we act like they do.

"You're my best friend." I look over at him. The sunlight catches in his twinkling eyes and his own smile must resemble my own.

"Well, you're not my best friend." He bunches his lips together, crinkling his nose. A lie. He's a very poor liar. But still, the thought tugs at my heart a little bit.

"I'm not?"

"No, you're my Kindred. And that's better than a best friend. You know why?" He gets to his feet and holds his hand out to me. I can't take his hand to stand up, but I stand up just the same.

"Why?" I respond, standing before him as rays from the sun filter through his hair, showing patches of brown through the black.

His face beams. "Because we're going to know each other forever. If you die, I die. If you live, I live. We're going to be forever, Joy."

"Forever," I repeat. "That's a long time, Felix."

"Dad says forever only seems like a lot when you're young, but when you're older, it won't be enough." Felix says it all matter-of-factly, nodding his head in agreement.

"I can't imagine forever not being enough." I shrug, looking down at the toys strewn around our feet. "We're almost seven and life's a really long thing."

"I don't know. When I'm not playing with you, I think time moves really, really slow. But when you're here, it's fast. And it's less boring. And lonely. I think maybe forever won't be enough for me with you, Joy. I'll always want more." He laughs, and his nose crinkles again.

He leans closer and pretends to kiss me on my cheek. His face turns a rosy shade of pink and then he runs away, nearly slipping on the holo-truck in the process. I touch my cheek and wonder why he would do that. Mum does that, but that's because she loves me. Felix must love me, too.

I'm his Kindred and we're going to be together forever.

CHAPTER 30
FELIX

I gasp for air and propel myself upward, finding my legs locked down. My eyesight is blurry and my chest is sore but whole again. I have no idea where I am, but my hands grasp for her.

"Joy," I yell aloud through the haze of uncertainty and pain and panic. *Where are you?* There isn't a response.

"Slow down, there." Rashid bends over me, his gaze roving over my unmarred body. "You Monchurans are so dramatic." He flashes me a smile, and brushes the hair from my face while cocking an eyebrow. "We're on—or in?—Maru-Monchuri. In your house, so I was told. And dude, you're super rich."

The suns of Gola shine through the windows around me at different angles. I'm on my bed. In my home. And Joy's not here.

"Estrella is like Wakanda. All sunny and pretty and techy. I love it here."

I nod and try to move, but my unwounded body won't cooperate.

Sarah steps into view, carrying a glass of Calef juice. She's unharmed, smiling. "So you died for a bit and then you were saved and then we were all loaded into a transport ship-thingy and brought to your homeworld. Weird, huh?"

I grimace before I shout for Joy again. If I died, so did she. What if she didn't wake up? What if Yecki found a way for me to live without her? No, there is no life for me without Joy.

Sarah elbows Rashid out of the way.

"Joy's asleep. Look." I follow her line of sight to find Joy strapped to a hovering med-table on the other side of my room. She's hooked up to machines and medics whisper around her, though they don't seem stressed. Her chest rises and falls and her clothes have been replaced with a clean white fluffy robe of sorts. A medi-visor floats above her head, scanning and repairing. She's okay.

We're okay.

I nearly collapse with relief. How are we okay? "Humans," I rasp. "If the Soleil didn't almost kill us, all of you will. You could have told me that Joy was alive from the beginning."

Sarah rolls her eyes, smooshing onto the edge of my bed. "Sorry. I mean, I thought you'd know she wasn't dead because you'd be dead? Like didn't you say the stronger the connection, the stronger the whole pain-thing?"

"Yecki had his doctors perform extraordinary measures to save both your lives. Apparently, you both are very important to the future of the universe." Rashid pokes me in the chest. "I think his exact words were, 'Joy will lead us into the future.' Which I guess means you're necessary, too." He winks and I stifle a laugh, not wanting to stretch my aching muscles.

And then the whole scene plays out in my head again—Arren, an Ilori, Joy stunned, war, the sword... "Is Arren dead?"

"Yeah, Yecki chopped his head off with a cool-ass sword. Looking like something made out of vibranium from *Black Panther* or...the Darksaber from *The Mandalorian*." Rashid steps back. "We're supposed to get your parents when you woke up."

"They're alive?" I nearly cry, nearly sound like a whiny child. "I need to see them." I'm still a teenager, I still need their love and comfort and approval.

But when Rashid and Sarah leave and the door opens again, it's not my parents. It's King Yecki and Princess LaTanya. Holding hands. She's not a broken doll. She nods at me, while wearing a long black dress of mourning and a crown upon her head.

She and Yecki slip onto opposite sides of the bed, taking my hands in theirs. Which is weird, to say the least. Why would Yecki care about me? Why is he even here? I swear, if this is about his palace again...

"When we gave you up, we never imagined how hard it would be," LaTanya says, batting away a sudden tear before it can slide down her cheek. "I've always watched you—"

"We both have," Yecki interjects, and I stare at him in confusion. His laughter is deep enough to rattle the bed. "Surely, you can see the resemblance, yes?"

I stare up at his face...and I realize then that I've seen pieces of it in the mirror. The same dark skin, the same wavy hair, the long eyelashes. Only I have LaTanya's mouth, her eyes.

"You're my biological father?" I nearly stutter.

"Yes. LaTanya and I had a rocky relationship, always on and off, but we kept it a secret all our lives. We kept it a secret for you." King Yecki sighs. "A child with claims to two thrones would have drawn danger from every reach of the universe. We always suspected the Ilori would come, and with you as the heir, we couldn't take the chance that there'd only be one person to control two kingdoms."

"It was the hardest decision I've ever made. To give you up, and to stop seeing Yecki." LaTanya's hands fidget by her sides. "But it was Yecki's idea for safety, just as it was with pairing you with Joy."

I don't know what to say, how to take all of that in. I have a million questions, especially one about why he paired me with Joy, but… I think I already know. So I ask the one question that matters.

"What now?"

Yecki holds my gaze. "LaTanya's leaving Monchuri and coming to XiGra with me. You can imagine the painful memories that linger in this palace after Arren…" he trails off, and I don't need him to finish the sentence.

"We will be here to coronate you, and we will always be here to guide you. You will not be taking over Monchuri alone." LaTanya rises, and Yecki follows.

Yecki meets LaTanya at the foot of the bed, and locks arms with her. "You know that Kindred of yours—she's going to make a perfect Queen. And she believes in you."

Before they leave, I call out to her. "Arren thought he broke you. I almost believed he had."

LaTanya pauses and twists around to look at me. "I imagined what it would be like to lose DiOla, channeled all the pain from losing my fathers and my grandmother, of losing you, my son—and I used that to let him think I could not be reached anymore." Her voice cracks. "DiOla is safe for now. My family, though, is gone. Except you. You and Yecki and Joy, you're all I have. I will never lose you again—I will do everything I can to earn you and your love. I will never replace your parents, but I want to be a part of your life, if you'll let me. You don't have to answer now."

And with that, they leave me there. I sit with all my feelings and thoughts alone. Until my mother and father arrive, safe. Healthy. Whole. Annoyed that I didn't manage to contact them, though my mom is very pleased I'll have no choice but to go into politics now. Though I doubt she'll love the politician or the decisions I'll make. Meanwhile, my father regales me with the very dramatic story of him defending Mom from the Soleil—who were actually Ilori spies, while Mom gives me a to-do list that makes my head spin. When I keep glancing over at Joy, they excuse themselves.

Eventually, I push to my feet and cross the room to sit beside Joy. I place my hands over our hearts and pray to Indigo for us. I remember our earliest memories, our favorite jokes, the way she'd smile at me when I'd help her pick out her clothes, or the way she'd chastise me for not applying myself. I think of that application to the Grand Academy she wanted me to fill out.

I did fill it out. Just as I filled out an application for her, too—no one could tell me I couldn't when I'm about to be-come a king. I'll go for music, her for art. She never had the chance to figure out what she truly wanted to do, but maybe she'll be able to find out. Maybe I'll help her find out.

As I'm picturing the storybooks she'll make, praying for her to be okay, she startles awake. It takes all the power in me not to cry.

She grasps for something, someone, and tries to wait for her eyes to recalibrate.

I'm here. I'm here, over here. I put my hand in hers.

Oh, thank the Gods, she says. "Sarah? Rashid? Are you safe? Are you hurt? Have you eaten?"

There's a collective screech as the humans burst into the room as they swarm around her and I slouch into the seat. They must've been waiting, watching the monitors. I let them capture her attention, and comfort them as I still hold her hand.

For the first time in a long time, I'm not selfish in her pres-ence. I don't push them out of the way to hold her and kiss her and apologize and promise her all the moons and stars in the universe, because I want her to be happy and safe and to remember that I'm here and I love her with every part of my body, soul, mind, and molecules.

After too much attention, she gives me a small smile that lights up the entire room more than the suns of Gola. Disbe-lief flits through her mind and I laugh.

We don't need the connection to know each other's minds. We're lucky to be alive. We're lucky to have each other. And there will be plenty of time for kisses and hugs. But for now, we can just be.

Well, until the coronation, I guess, and then everyone'll expect something from me.

From us, she corrects. *We are in this together, Felix. We love each other. We are Kindred.*

★ ★ ★

MONCHURI MORNING NEWS NOW!

Transcript featuring L'avi Jonu and Nyla Harkibi of *Good Morning Monchuri*, filmed in front of a live studio audience in Maru-Monchuri

LJ: Welcome back, Monchuri! Let's get right to business. It's been a few days since our unlawful arrest and the continued downfall, now salvation of Monchuri.

NH: But! But we are here today, free, and with joyous, momentous news.

LJ: Yes, you're absolutely right. Momentous, indeed. The palace was in shambles yesterday when Arren's head was raised on a pike outside the gilded fences, and the Ilori masquerading as the Soleil fell. The XiGrans and Monchuri armies defeated them, with—thankfully—few casualties. The infiltration of the Ilori seemed to have only been limited to the Soleil and Arren. However, we are asking for anyone with information to please contact authorities.

NH: But that is a job for the new King. Yes, the new King! *(audience cheers)* King Felix Hamdi Qadin, the once-wrongfully accused Duke, has reunited with his adoptive parents, and has officially been given the title from his birth mother, Princess LaTanya. She has stepped down and out of the public eye as she recovers from the loss of her family.

LJ: We wish her the best in her mourning. Now, though, the more pressing matter is The Third Chaos, and I don't want our audience and viewers to panic. The Third Chaos has always been something we've collectively feared and avoided. Even speaking about it has been met with criticism.

NH: Until now.

LJ: Yes, until now. The Third Chaos is a reality we must face. But maybe it's not what we've always feared. We've watched for the past century as the Ilori Empire expanded and then colonized planets that were not our own. We made our jokes, we thought that since it didn't happen to us, it didn't concern us. But we were wrong.

NH: We were very wrong. An Ilori named Arren stole a Monchuran body and entered the Qadin government. He was the ear to our King, and manipulated his way into exacerbating the division between classes.

LJ: And, we believe, we now understand why. The Ilori are on another campaign of expansion across the universe. With Arren ruling, he would have kept our homeland from opposing the Ilori. He would have primed our system for colonization. And the Ilori, those immortal beings made from power and stardust, are slowly depleting their own resources.

NH: The Ilori survive by consuming life energy. They *needed* the Kindred system.

LJ: And that's why, we believe, Arren was here. What matters now is that we tell you the truth henceforth. We're sorry that we've ever helped spread disinformation for our government. And it's time to admit, that as of tomorrow, Monchuri will go to war. A necessary war.

NH: During Duke Hamdi's exile, he was stranded on Terra. Home to humans. And that home is now threatened by the Ilori.

LJ: We also know that neutral allies, like Andarra, have decided to take a stand with us. While plans are yet to be made, tonight we will focus on the unification of our kingdom.

NH: The royal ball, calling all potential allies to Estrella! Have you got your dress, L'avi?

LJ: You know I do. And I personally can't wait to talk to Joy Abara again, who is an extraordinary, gorgeous young woman.

NH: I can't wait to see her dress, and see how King Felix dotes on her—

LJ: And the humans! Two humans temporarily reside in the Royal Palace! I can't wait to see how our cultures differ and how they find Monchuri.

NH: I'm really looking forward to the possibility of a big announcement…

LJ: Oh, I have no doubt there'll be one.

CHAPTER 31
JOY

"I SAID, BABY, WE AREN'T IN LOVE, WE ARE LOVE, AND LOVE IS A FORCE TO BE RECKONED WITH. SUIT UP, SUGAR, 'CAUSE THE BATTLE'S ABOUT TO BEGIN."

—*DEJA REESE, "LOVE WAR"*

Deja Reese's voice plays softly through Sarah's cell phone as I smooth my hands down the sides of my midnight blue dress, and fiddle with the pin locking an errant curl down on the right side of my head. My gaze flashes to the wall-length mirror as Mum smiles while passing by, her arm interlocked with Danio's. They smell like flowers. I've never seen her happier.

"If you keep playing with it, it'll come undone." Felix's mom, Marivia, stands behind me, covered in gold. For the first time today, she's not looking at me with disdain. "What is this music and why is your hair so very difficult—"

"Pfft, it's Joy's favorite singer," Sarah interrupts, stepping closer in her own bright pink gown that's so very human it takes my breath away. "And her hair is only difficult on this planet, 'cause on Earth she could find a hairdresser on any corner." Sarah asked to stay a few days for the betrothal and the coronation, but part of me—and Felix—worry that Earth is in serious trouble. That the Ilori will invade any moment. And we won't know what to do. How they'll cope. If they should even go back yet.

Marivia huffs and saunters off, maids following her. She's a difficult woman, but I think I'm growing on her.

I touch the tip of my finger to Sarah's chin. "Maybe you should call DiOla and Miss Rae. Check on Earth and your mom."

She nods, her face lighting up again, and she snatches her phone from the dresser. "Yeah, you're right. Thank God, you guys have super-duper chargers up here in space, and weirdly good reception." She turns the music off, and I already miss Deja's voice. "Did Rashid tell you he spoke to his dad and that he sounds better than he's been in a long time? He started therapy. Speaking of therapy, I bet my mom is freaking out. I'll have to show her my dress and all of the…" She leaves the room, taking all the excitement, music, and Earth-ness with her.

I'm left standing there alone with my thoughts. I swallow the panic climbing up my throat as I think about the changes throughout the universe, about Earth and destruction. The Ilori are The Third Chaos, threatening everything we hold dear. And it's up to us to stop them.

I'm scared, too, Felix whispers through my mind. I close my eyes and see him standing in front of a table of councillors, who are arguing and yelling. The one in charge, it would seem, is a newly appointed general from Hali-Monchuri. Miya Kinata is brash, strong, sturdy, and sensible. Her light brown skin stands stark against her white robes, and her painted purple lips pull into a tight smile as the men before her cower.

Felix respects her and so do I. She's new to the role, but we both believe we have to actually give people a voice in Monchuri, not just through the Kindred Program but in the government. In politics. In everything.

She nods at Felix as she continues to talk about military strategy, and why we must abolish classism within Monchuri if we plan to unite under one system and one banner.

Felix stands and shimmies through a back door and into a tiny hallway used by servants and maids and all of the people who live within the palace walls.

They don't need me in there.

I purse my lips, watching him slide against the tiny gap and into the hallway. *I can't believe you're already shirking your duties and it's been one day.*

He stifles a laugh and I find myself returning my attention to the mirror in front of me as I pinch the silver stars embedded into the fabric of my dress.

As he cuts across the palace on his way to me, Rashid walks by. "Hurry up or you'll miss the party. Don't tell Joy, but we were able to get all of Deja's collected works by hacking iClouds from home. It's awesome. I'm a genius. Wait till we play it on the dance floor. Oh! And I got them to serve milkshakes." He beams and so do I, he's the best. He's wearing an extremely beautiful tan suit that makes his brown skin shimmer, made specifically for him by the royal tailor. He looks more himself than I've ever seen him. And he looks happy.

Less alone. I know he misses Earth, Johnny, cheerleading, Chadwick, *Black Panther*, and his dad, but we'll take him back soon—we hope. "And okay—they're not actually milkshakes since you don't have milk here. But you know what I mean. Although it would've been cool if they had blue milk…"

Felix only laughs. "I have no idea what you're talking about."

"One day, on Earth, I will make you watch those movies, Your *Highness*." And with that, he keeps on walking down the hall like he owns the place. I'm going to miss him terribly.

That thought flees my mind as Felix opens the door to my suite and shuts it firmly behind him. He stops, turns around, and locks it, too. I swallow slowly before he rushes toward me. A few excruciating milliseconds pass till we're in each other's arms. And everything feels right again.

We haven't been physically alone since Earth. Everything since then has been disastrous or filled with family reunions, calming our poor human friends, or making plans. And I sorely wanted his perfect lips on mine.

He lowers his head, and kisses me softly, breathing me in and staring into my eyes as if he can see the stars in them. His fingers skim my neck and jaw, so gentle as if I might break. I push him back and smother him with quick pecks until I explore his mouth.

It'll never be enough. Forever is not enough.

When we finally pull apart, after how many minutes have passed, we're flushed and hot and not at all prepared for the night that lies ahead of us. His head rests on mine. We breathe in each other and exhale everything else.

"How do you think they'll handle the news?"

I smile up at him. "Which news? The one where you tell them that you'll be transitioning the monarchy into a republic with you serving as just a figurehead after the war? Or the one where we tell them we're going to art school? Or—"

Or, he laughs. *The most important news. The news that I'll ask you to marry me in front of all our allies and the cameras, and you'll say yes.*

"Oh, that news." I bring my hand up and admire the sparkly pearl gifted from King Yecki. I smile. "You'll make a nobody from Hali-Monchuri, a girl with her head in the clouds and pictures in her head, a queen. Are you sure you want to? My vows to Maxon were just dissolved this morning."

"Joy Abara." Felix caresses my cheeks with his thumbs. "If you ever say anything like that again, I will ban chocolate-covered raisins in the entire kingdom."

I laugh and nibble my lip. "Is that the best you've got?"

"Punishing you is punishing myself, and you know how spoiled I am." He kisses the tip of my nose. "You are the very best person in this world, and worlds beyond. Monchuri will be lucky to have a queen like you." His breath tickles my face and warms my cheeks. "I am lucky, every day, to have a Kindred like you."

"So that means you're going to give me a gorgeous, incredibly expensive, one-of-a-kind ship so I can explore the universe one day? Preferably one with a sexy AI?" I cock an eyebrow and smirk, watching his eyes narrow on the action.

"You've already got a gorgeous, incredibly expensive, one-of-a-kind, extremely good-looking Kindred. And lest you forget, you already own my heart, body, soul, and mind. Is that not enough?" He laughs, drawing closer as his thumb trails along my chin. "Everything I am is yours."

"And you're mine." I kiss him softly as my hand slides down into his. There's a rightness that washes over me as our fingers intertwine like our minds. "I adore you, Felix."

"I love you, Joy," he says, cracking another one of those life-altering smiles that make my legs jelly and my heart race. "Now let's go. We've got a war to wage, a kingdom to run and make better, and an engagement to announce."

I chuckle as the realization that everything's about to change flutters in my stomach. But I push that aside, because change is necessary. Change, for us, is good.

We stride down the halls, our heads held high, no longer having to defy the rules that kept us apart for so long, no longer caring about everyone and their opinions and their ideas about propriety.

We are Kindreds. We are unstoppable. We are inevitable.

We are love, and love is a force to be reckoned with.

Now it's time for the universe to know it.

★ ★ ★ ★ ★

ACKNOWLEDGMENTS

CAN YOU BELIEVE I GET TO WRITE THESE AGAIN?
I'm completely awed and honored to write another book, especially with Inkyard Press, especially because I adore getting to tell sci-fi stories—which is so lovely since that's the genre that made me fall in love with reading! I'm just so grateful. So here goes.

THANK YOU to:

The reader holding this book. Thank you for taking a chance on me and my stories. I hope you'll stick with me. I've got more to share with you!

My mom, who is in some heavenly realm shaking her head and going, "They let her write another book?" I hope I made you proud. I miss you.

My dad, for always making me laugh, especially about that ghost in your kitchen who swatted that fork from your hand. Thanks for sharing your goofiness with me (and passing it down to me).

Natalie Lakosil, who is the best advocate, puts up with my very tired ramblings, and helps me get my quirky stories out in the world! Thank you for working with me and believing in me.

My incredible editors, Natashya Wilson, Melissa Frain, and Stephanie Cohen. It's been such a privilege working with all three of you, and I'm beyond thankful for all your notes, feedback, and laughter at my very strange naming "m"istakes. It's been a pleasure.

The Inkyard Press team: Bess Braswell, Linette Kim, Brittany Mitchell, Laura Gianino, and Connolly Bottum. Thank you so, so much for helping me make this book a reality and your continued support. And a huge thank-you to cover artist Aleea Rae for bringing Joy and Felix to stunning starry life, and cover designer Gigi Lau who has given me the most gorgeous covers! They mean the world to me.

Tracy Badua, we've worked together for over five years. You've been with me in the margins, helping me, showing me the way, and making sure I was telling the best story possible. I wouldn't be here without you, and I'm so incredibly proud of you and your books. You are a star.

Rae Somer, thank you for everything, always. You understand me, you're kind to me, and you listen to me even when I'm a mess of emotions and thoughts.

Sheena Boekweg, you are a stunning human being, and I'm so lucky to have you in my life.

My AWESOME sci-fi group: Rebecca Coffindaffer (who helped me make this book a book), Andrea Tang, Lora Beth Johnson, Meg Long, and Claire Winn. You all are AWESOME.

Kendell Penington, Jessica James, J. Elle: I cannot thank

you enough for your support, for letting me whine, for sharing your talent, time, and friendship. I couldn't have done any of this without you.

Tamara Mataya. I'm still inhaling art and exhaling words because of you.

Tori Bovalino, Adiba Jaigirdar, Faridah Àbíké-Íyímídé, Jesse Sutanto, Ayana Gray, Zoraida Córdova, Bethany C. Morrow, and the Inkyard Squad (Mara Rutherford, Laura Taylor Namey, and Eric Smith). Thank you for absolutely everything.

My sisterpants™, Nicole Redd-McIntosh. You light up the world with your creations. I'll always be awed and inspired by you. And I'll always want your cookbook recommendations!

Adrienne, Amani, Amya, and Christopher, Jr. I can't wait to see what the future holds for you. I'm so glad to call you my family.

RAPID ROUND. Saundra Mitchell, the Hirt Familie, Carmen of Tomes & Textiles, Nora Shalaway Carpenter, Rocky Callen, Rosiee Thor, Lili (USOM), Alexa Donne, Cassandra Newbould, Beth Revis, Mike Lasagna, Hannah Capin, Jordan Ifueko, Nandi Taylor, Anika Wegner, Jamie Pacton, Darrah Stranahan, Tiffany Jackson, Dhonielle Clayton, Write or Die Podcast, Aisha Akeju, and Erin O'Neill Jones for the most beautiful art. My library homes: Brooklyn Public Library, West Warwick Public Library, and Milford Town Library. Black Panther, Chadwick Boseman, and "All the Stars" by Kendrick Lamar feat. SZA. Still living rent free in my head.

Christoph, thank you for giving me the time and space to keep trying to make my mark in this industry. Many thanks for those months where all I wanted to eat was pizza. Still do. I love you.

Liv. You are going to move mountains. I love how many dreams you have and how you always dream so BIG. I love how you're so outspoken, smart, and bold. I love you.

To all the librarians, media specialists, teachers, booksellers, book bloggers, vloggers, bookstagrammers, and the online book community. You are superstars, and so much of this community relies on you. Thank you for everything you do.

To the teens who found this book while meandering through the bookstore or skimming the library shelves and decided to give it a chance, I wrote this for you.